THE S

A novel

Grant Patterson

2033

Eureka

Detroit Bio-Frontiers
Detroit, Michigan
November 9, 2033

As usual, Dennis Rosso was the first to turn the lights on. He kicked the snow off of his boots and changed into his loafers as the lights flickered on, section by section.

This was, after all, *his* lab. So, it figured that he should be first in, last out, all the time. This was a tiring routine to say the least. It would, perhaps, had been easier, if he had a staff of lazy Americans working for him. But his people were almost all H-1B Indians, who would deliberately race him to the lab (Arjan lived across the street from him and must've had his driveway set up with a beam), and then pronounce they needed to finish "one more thing, sir" while he leaned, exhausted, over a lab bench at 10:30 PM.

Cocksuckers.

This was why, well, at least partially why, Dennis Rosso was divorced. The death of a child didn't help. He stopped in front of the mirror in the changeroom and wiped away a tear. *Poor little Ronnie. Ten fingers, ten toes. No brain.*

The mirror told Dennis Rosso nothing he wanted or needed to know. You are past the age where you, as a specimen, have anything intrinsic to appeal to the female of the species. Your sexuality is inextricably bound up with the price of your stock options. He was egg-headed, near-sighted, stoop-shouldered, and weak-chinned. Only his brain had potential. And, up until now, that potential was strictly unrecognized.

He put on his lab coat and walked onto the Experiment Floor. A checkerboard pattern of lab tables, fridges and freezers, workstations, and cleaning sinks greeted him. His area was the closest on the left.

"Mary! Mary, goddamnit!" There was no response. His facilities manager, who was the one person who was supposed to beat him to the lab, was not there yet. As usual. *Lazy Americans.*

Dennis peered through his thick glasses at his lab table. Under the bright lights of the fume hood, a pink slab of...no. No, it could not be. Those cells were dead. Sterilized.

Slowly, hearing his heart hammering in his ears, he walked over to his lab table. The pink thing, on closer inspection, was a glistening, apparently healthy, piece of pig muscle. Grown well past the microscopic size it had been in its petri dish last night, to the point where it was the size of a passable sausage.

It was pig muscle with the right genetic sequence suppressed. He could see it in his head, like he imagined Mozart must've seen music.

That genetic sequence could only be one thing. The kill switch.

The thing that makes mammals die. Last night, bleary-eyed, working only because there was nothing to go home to, and because he wanted to beat that rat Arjan home from the lab, he had done something extraordinary.

Dennis Rosso had killed the kill switch.

Dennis Rosso had made a miracle.

Dennis Rosso had really, really, fucked things up. Death had just been minding its own business.

And now, he had murdered it.

2117

The stale miracle

Seattle, North America
Lake Union

Dennis Rosso, if you could call him that now, would be unrecognizable to anyone who had known him from his days at Detroit Bio. In fact, he would be unrecognizable to anyone save a handful of people on another planet, almost all of whom were dead.

He was now tall. Everyone was tall.

He was now muscular and fit. Everyone was muscular and fit.

He was now of strong jaw and sharp eye. Everyone was...well, you get the picture. He was now also Henrik Kassabian, if anyone was asking.

Nobody tended to ask. The two things that Dennis Rosso and Henrik Kassabian had shared in life were a wealth which put them beyond almost any possible scrutiny, and a dearth of relatives to come asking for said wealth.

All that mattered to anyone he interacted with now was his DNA, which identified him as a "Normie," and his credit statement, which identified him as someone who could make real trouble for anyone, from Traffic Cop to Senator, who pried too much in his affairs.

"Rich People," were, as in the past, subject to rather different treatment than other people. Even though all "Normies" were guaranteed a Basic Income, hence eliminating the unfortunate scourge of "Poor People," this did not mean everyone was equal.

Not everyone, like Henrik Kassabian, could afford a reserved first-class cabin on the SS Olympic, now fitting out in Jovian orbit for the twenty-year trip to Epsilon Eridani, for instance. "Rich People" could, though.

But you only got the benefits of Basic Income and Guaranteed Infinity Health Care ™ if you were a "Normie." That was not a matter of fate, talent, or inventiveness. It was a matter of ruthless policy. Normies had been altered, at birth or later, to live forever, having Dennis Rosso's Deactivator ™ implanted in their cells. Now, only the most grievous accidents or intentional trauma could kill them. What always had to come with the Deactivator was the Sterilizer ™, a kill-switch for the reproductive organs, reversible only by the state.

Henrik Kassabian had designed that one. Sometimes, people sought him out with questions. Dennis Rosso had learned credible sounding answers. When he faltered, he blamed it on the booze. He was due for a new liver next year, he remembered.

It was not, strictly speaking, mandatory to be a Normie. But you couldn't live in the cities, the arcologies, or the colonies if you weren't. *Officially.* Hence, the Uncontrolled ™ roamed the UV-ravaged scrub between the cities or eked out a precarious existence on Mars. They could have babies, yes. But they also died. In numbers some people thought were a bit funny.

Unofficially, of course, like the illegal migrants from Latin America before them, the striving Uncontrolled, existing without the benefit of Basic Income or free health care, kept the dishes washed and the flowers pruned. Everybody else, as before, was too lazy, and robots were still too clunky and stupid to wait tables or arrange flowers.

Entire cultures had refused to go with the project. There were, technically, Muslim Normies and Orthodox Jewish Normies, and Catholic Normies. But to the true adherents of these faiths, the thought of modern normality made them want to puke. So, they lived according to the old ways, and died in droves.

Sometimes, their children were sold to people as rich as Henrik Kassabian. But Dennis Rosso didn't know anything about that.

In fact, Dennis Rosso knew very little about anything. Anything modern, that is. He no longer practiced the science that had once been his obsession. He no longer knew about politics, current affairs, or culture. He barely knew how to dress himself in a socially presentable manner.

This was the regrettable result of spending the better part of six decades in a cave dug into the walls of the Hellas Basin on Mars. On the plus side, he did have a front row seat as Merlin Duplessis' magnificent Hellas Sea took shape. In later years, you could even swim in it, if you'd had enough vodka.

On the lakefront, the crowds passed. Walking, cycling, rollerblading, hovering. Many more than there would've been on a Monday one-hundred years ago. Most people didn't have jobs. They "self-actualized," which more often than not meant hours a day spent in virtual reality sex games or watching moronic holos on Holocast. This was one main reason Dennis did not care to mingle. People were so very dull these days.

Every once in a while, he caught a glimpse of a child. The crowds would part, and people would stare. They were so rare in the cities, allowed only to replace the unfortunate carnage of fate. Hover car motors cut out. Reactors exploded. Airlocks failed. Maniacs went on killing sprees with plasma lances. It happened, and thus, a little angel took the dead person's place. The state subsidized everything, from diapers to college. So few kids were required that it was a minimal drain on the bulging treasury.

A tow-headed girl, wide-eyed, walked past his perch on the patio, her hand firmly in mommy's, as Dennis watched. *I hope you have someone to play with. I guess that's my fault.* He frowned to himself as the girl disappeared into the crowd. He faulted the empty glass for the random thought and held up his glass for another pint.

Lucy walked over. She was young-looking (she could've been a hundred) with black curls, wide hips, and dark brown eyes. In the past, his good looks and money would've been quite the entrée with Lucy. But now, Dennis reflected ruefully, everyone was hot. And lots of people were rich, too. Perhaps there was charm?

"Mr Kassabian, you sure must like those IPAs. It's a good thing liver is a renewable resource now. You want another?"

He laughed at her insouciance. She had a slightly raspy voice that also made him mental. "I'll say. You only live once."

"Not anymore." She took his empty. "Busy here today."

"Nice weather in Seattle. As rare as rain on Mars."

"So they say. I wish I knew." Her eyes took on a wistful look. Lake Union glittered in the sunlight. Dennis was unsure which was comelier.

He patted her hand, the gesture of an old man. Which, he reminded himself, he was. "I'll have to take you there one day. Lake Hellas puts this muddy old pond to shame."

"I might take you up on that one day." She turned to leave.

"Lucy?"

"Yes, Mr Kassabian?"

"Why do you work here? You and the others could do nothing and get paid anyway."

She shrugged. "I like people. And we get a bonus to our income for actually doing something. That way we can get ahead, save for things we want. Like a trip to Mars. Excuse me."

"Hmm." Dennis shrugged to himself. There was so much he didn't know. Like he was an alien.

Sixty years on Mars, Rosso? You ARE an alien!

He tapped the table and brought up a holopaper. The Seattle Revolution was a nest of Marxist claptrap, but the wire stories were reliable enough.

Wire stories? We're on our way to the stars, and we still call them "wire stories?" How quaint.

His eye caught a small story on A5.

DISEASE CONTROL REPORTS 25% INCREASE IN SUICIDES FOR LAST QUARTER

The Disease Control Council has reported in its Morbidity and Mortality report for the last quarter a 25% increase in suicidal attempts and successes in the last quarter of 2116.

The report lists no suspected causative factors, but notes the increased mortality was largely among men (73%) and those older than 80 years (77%). Dr Craig Feng, the Director of Mortality Research and Prevention, stated that the figures were a concern, but that in-depth research would only be undertaken if a long-term trend surfaced. He refused to speculate on the causative factors.

Emily Bree
Atlanta

Dennis flicked off the paper and watched the people at the lakeside again. He had turned off the kill switch. Now, were people growing tired of life all on their own? Was his miracle going stale?

After all, he hadn't exactly brought mankind good news, had he? Far from it, in fact. Seventy years of upheaval, war, and genocide was more like it. Now, there was peace, but at what price?

From the looks of the paper, some people were voting with their DNA. They were checking out. Lucy set another pint in front of him. Lost in thought, he forgot to flirt. She drifted off.

Dennis sat and stared at the people by the lakeside, until their shadows grew long, and his beer grew warm.

2035

A staggering discovery with far-reaching effects for the future of humanity

Stockholm, Sweden
City Hall

Dennis looked out at the grandees listening to his acceptance speech, all clad in ridiculous, archaic, 19th century dress. He straightened his stiff bow tie.

"Ahem. On behalf of myself and my colleagues, Dr Rafjani and Dr Bains, allow me to accept this year's Nobel Prize in Chemistry."

There was a spontaneous round of applause, forcing him to pause. Arjan Rafjani watched him from the side, smirking. He'd made sure his name went on the award too, even though he'd mainly played Devil's Advocate. Satwant and he had done most of the actual goddamned work.

In the audience, watching him intently, chins on fists: Kevin and Derek, his business partners. Clearly worried about what he was going to say, but they couldn't say he hadn't warned them. He sure as hell had. And he'd already been paid out.

He didn't owe them anything anymore. He had enough money for "Go fuck yourself" to be his permanent default answer to any question, criticism, or inquiry. *So here goes nothing...*

"Many have said words to the effect of those by the *New York Times'* science editor about our discovery, that it is, and I quote; 'A staggering discovery with far reaching effects for the future of humanity.' I agree, it is. After two years of secrecy and debate, we can finally call it what it is: The Key to Immortality."

Another round of applause followed. Dennis guessed half the audience had already gotten the treatments, in secret. Everyone just looked *too damned good.* "But, as with all scientific breakthroughs, there will be a downside. One that could destroy the very civilization we seek to cure of the scourge of death. I am speaking of course, of the scourge of inequality!"

There was a ripple of decidedly less enthusiastic applause. Kevin and Derek stared daggers at him. *Fuck you. You're hedge fund managers. I'm the hero.* "Right now, a treatment of Everlife ™ goes for 500,000 $ US. That makes immortality the toy of only the very rich. That reality will not long be lost on the toiling masses, ladies and gentlemen. They will only be more inspired to turn on us, not only for our wealth, but now too, for having defeated death, with our wealth! We are staring into the abyss, until we decide to make this miracle available for everyone, and until we consider every implication and stumbling block arising from it. What about overpopulation? What about space colonization? What about wealth distribution? Ladies and Gentlemen, this is not a drug! This is a revolution!"

He had held the prize aloft in that exact moment, just as the rocks started coming in the windows, just before the police started ushering the guests to their escape routes. Dennis saw the picture in the next day's *Times of London.*

After that, things got blurry. Hands grabbed at him. He was half-dragged, half-pushed to the rear of the building, where phalanxes of riot police guarded a fleet of unmarked vans against surging crowds of black-clad protestors. Firebombs exploded on the edge of the police lines.

"You'll be okay! Keep going!" He looked to the source of the voice, and saw a tall, athletic blonde with short hair and piercing green eyes, her hands clamped around his elbow and pudgy waist. She wore a windbreaker with "Polis" written on it.

Dennis let her and her colleague push him into the back of an electric van. With a hum, the van came to life, and followed a procession of police cars to safety. On the edges of the column, cops shoved and clubbed rioters relentlessly, while their opponents swung iron bars and 2X4s. He saw a cop tumble from a strike, helmet knocked off, and fall beneath a kicking and punching mob.

The blonde was almost on top of him. She smelled amazing, even while sweating profusely. She excused herself and settled in beside him. "I'm Anita." She offered a long hand. He kissed it decorously.

"Enjoying my party?" He smiled sardonically at her. Anita frowned, but did not look away. After all, he was hideous to look at, but he was a Nobel Laureate now, wasn't he? Dennis looked up to see the rest of the van, all clad in ridiculous coats and tails and Victorian evening gowns, staring back at him. He began to laugh helplessly.

"What's so funny, Doctor?" Anita looked at him with concern. He noticed a mole on her cheek, subtle, beautiful. *What a silly thing to notice, in the middle of a riot.* A brick dented the windshield, and they swerved. Impulsively, he opened a window partway. "Don't do that!" Anita scolded.

Dennis Rosso, Nobel Laureate, shouted out to the cops and the rioters. "Goodnight Stockholm! There will be no encores!"

2117

A world without hotdogs

Seattle
Wallingford

Dennis came awake, thinking of Anita.

He sprawled in his massive bed, alone, as always, feeling every second of his 127 years. It seemed to him sometimes that, simply from personal experience, not any sort of scientific investigation, that the body's cells *knew*.

They knew, despite his having murdered death, how old they were and where they had come from. Perhaps the increase in suicides was a natural pushback from nature? A predestined return to the original intended path of life?

He scoffed to himself, determined to put yesterday's article out of his mind. *Fate.* What rubbish. His cells were young! His body was young, and fit! He couldn't remember the name, but hadn't a 20th century comedienne once said she couldn't act in pornography, since most of her was under 18? That was him!

Dennis guessed the time was noon…ish. Never too late to get started. He hit the floor of his bedroom with a thud and started vigorous calisthenics.

Ten minutes later, he'd decided that there was no fucking point, as he always did. Why bother? With Dennis Rosso's secret access Swiss accounts, and Henrik Kassabian's more public funds, he could afford new bodies from here to eternity. Why strain oneself taking care of them? Instead, he nursed a Pike Place and stared from his deck to the view below.

The Wallingford Arcology #5 was a giant, sloping pyramid looking out over the lakes and inlets of Seattle. It was well over eighty stories tall, but Dennis had taken one of the lower penthouses, cut into the slope of the giant structure. Otherwise, your ten-million-dollar view got eaten by clouds. He'd grown up in Seattle, and this awareness had saved him a few bucks and a lot of frustration. As it was, he was only twenty stories up, close enough to spy on individuals on the endless leisure circuit below.

Yes, it was voyeuristic. But hadn't he earned the right to see what his people were doing with the miracle he'd granted them?

Jesus. He was sounding like Duplessis now! He made a sour face and sipped at his coffee. Starbucks. The one constant, besides the rain, of Seattle life. Not even wars and revolution could alter that.

His mind drifted back to the news story on suicides. Why was this bothering him so much?

Perhaps, asshole, because you have nothing with which to occupy that prize-winning brain of yours anymore.

In the years following his Nobel Prize, he'd finally taken his own treatment, plus a lot of other modifications he'd been wanting, convinced Anita to leave the Stockholm Police, and the two of them had gone into hiding.

It was exciting, at first. They had the money to go anywhere and do whatever they wanted. The problem, though, was that the possible world was getting smaller. The widening gap between rich and poor now extended to the living and the dead. So, each year, there were fewer places they could visit.

Dennis Rosso, AKA "Timothy Vance," then took refuge in a boyhood pleasure.

Hotdogs. Dennis loved hotdogs, of all varieties, from dirty water franks to hipster mutants like Japadogs and Pukas. He began to prowl the US and Canada, seeking out the best varieties, and posting his critiques on his blog, "The Dog Slog."

Anita, in the manner of women everywhere, merely rolled her eyes. She loved Seattle and saw no reason to travel to Cleveland for a new variation on the Chilli Dog. They became used to living apart, happily.

Then, the world collapsed utterly, and it became as impossible to travel to Cleveland as it was to travel to Tonga. The Practical Socialist Party emerged from the upheaval of revolution, for which, in Seattle, they had a front-row seat, promising to tax the living shit out of the rich.

Then, came Merlin Duplessis and his big, phallic spaceships. Mars was the only logical escape.

There were no hotdogs on Mars. No real ones, anyways. And so, Timothy Vance and his wildly popular blog died a premature death.

But the thought of blogging, of doing what they used to call "crowdsourcing" an answer to the question in his mind, still nagged at him. When he'd returned from Mars after the *Götterdämmerung* of Duplessis, he faced the sober realization that the consumption of slaughtered animal flesh on earth had been outlawed in 2110. No more hotdogs. Oh sure, they had the cloned, lab-grown variety. "Tastes exactly the same!" They said.

But it wasn't the same. You could tell. No more hotdogs.

Perhaps it was time for Timothy Vance to return? Perhaps, this time, with a more important job to do?

Dennis sat down at his workstation. Outside, a retro seaplane buzzed over Puget Sound. He brought up an old template for his blog. "The Dog Slog" would no longer do. How about, "Timothy Vance, the Quest for Truth?" *Hokey.*

Well, why not? People were really just perpetual children these days, never having to grow up or accomplish anything. Why wouldn't they go for hokey?

He activated an old hologram of Timothy Vance, the way he'd looked in 2040, and began to dictate his introduction. As he did so, he heard the old, familiar voice, the one he'd taken to Mars and lived with for sixty years, in his ears. It was deeper, more confident, more…reliable than the reedy tenor of Henrik Kassabian he lived with today.

Timothy Vance was his favourite "him." And since it was widely rumoured anyway that Timothy Vance and Dennis Rosso were the same person, why not take advantage of the ambiguity to bolster the message? After all, hadn't he seen the graffiti downtown just the other day:

ROSSO LIVES

Remembering to switch on his location scrambler, he began his challenge to his new audience:

"This is Timothy Vance. Some of you may remember me from my championing of the tubular meat arts in the last century. Then, some shit went down, friends. But I survived. And I am back on the blue marble to ask a question. Not about where to get the best hotdog, since we all know that's futile, but another, more serious question:

In an age of everlasting life, in an age of practical immortality, why are more and more of us killing ourselves? Are we, having tasted so much life, growing tired of it? Or is something in our cells driving us to rebuild our kill switch? Does nature want us to die?"

A phantom thought of bratwursts, dripping juice onto their buns, superimposed with the slab of pink flesh on his lab bench, that morning in Detroit. Dennis grasped for insight but he lost the thread.

As he lost one thread though, he picked up another. "84 years ago, humanity discovered a miracle. Has that miracle gone stale? Ladies and gentlemen, welcome to Timothy Vance: The Stale Miracle? Please, share your thoughts and stories. Let's start the conversation."

He switched off the holocast and sat in his wingback for a long time. Eventually, he realized he was crying, for some reason he could not fathom. Was he the father to a stillborn child?

Dennis shed his clothes, walked out onto his deck, and jumped in his swimming pool.

2038

Man, with a vision

Q-Space Dynamics
Mercury, Nevada

Out in the desert north of Las Vegas, where the mushroom clouds once bloomed, they went to meet a prophet.

As Dennis Rosso had changed the ground rules of biology, so had Merlin Duplessis changed the ground rules of space exploration. Running out of options in an increasingly chaotic world, Dennis and Anita decided to exercise their only option remaining. They decided to emigrate.

Now, they stood in an air-conditioned showroom in front of the only man who could make that happen. The Q-Space plant was so enormous from the air as to be almost non-descript. Only the low, mildly radioactive hills to the north hemmed it in. Much of it was underground, powered by Duplessis' new, patented Tokamak reactors. The chopper pilot who had ferried them from McCarran Airport had tried to do the place justice with a few low turns, but he'd failed.

"You only really get a sense of it from the inside." He'd sighed, before touching down.

But first, Duplessis, like any master showman, had to stage-manage the experience. First, he kept them waiting. As Dennis frowned and checked his watch repeatedly, Anita laughed. "What?"

"Are you suddenly forgetting how often you do that? Keep people waiting? He's just as important as you, you know. You might be the two most important people on earth, next to Rosario Sanchez."

Dennis shrugged ruefully. Rosario Sanchez, the 30-something leader of the Practical Socialist Party, was one of the reasons he was here. Her campaign promises of 90% tax on men like him were the most important motivator, the anarchist claptrap of police and prison abolition not far behind. He hated her, as he knew Duplessis did too.

Dennis looked around. Two security guards waited unobtrusively on either side of a door they knew Duplessis was sure to emerge from. Display cases showed off the various stages of Q-Space development, from disposable rockets, to partially reusable shuttles servicing the ISS, to the massive Starshot III rockets, one of which the CEO had just returned from Mars on last month.

In the centre of the room, a recurring hologram reel of The Triumph. Duplessis himself, stepping onto Arcadia Planitia, planting the flag of earth 100 million miles away. Hard to believe it had only been six months ago.

Now, with two dozen men and women directing an army of robots in building the first planetary colony left behind, the boss was back to sell the dream. Rich people, prominent people like Dennis were part of the dream.

He emerged suddenly from a side door, catching them both by surprise. "Pretty cool, eh?" He was American by birth and temperament, but Canadian by speech. "Wait till you see the real thing." He was short, but dynamic, bearded, wild-haired, and healthy. Like a cross between Brad Pitt and Johnny Depp, Dennis thought. He smelled like weed.

Duplessis' hand shot out. "Merl Duplessis. You don't much look like Dennis Rosso."

"That's the idea."

"Life is getting hard here for men like us, isn't it?" A robot vacuum cleaner passed between them, unobtrusively. Duplessis casually kicked it away.

"Men like who?"

"Men of ideas. On Mars, there will be no censors."

Dennis looked over at Anita, who nodded subtly. "Show me the goods, Merl."

The chopper pilot had been right. The scale of Q-Space was impossible to grasp from the air. Once inside the factory, it took the mind sometime to accommodate the images presented: Endless rows of Starshot III fuselages marched slowly on mobile jigs, tended to by a smattering of humans. Other lines manufactured cargo drones, booster rockets, tankers, and shuttlecraft.

"Well?"

"My...my God." Was all Dennis could stammer. "You're going to colonize the solar system."

Duplessis drove a golf-cart down the aisles at old lady speed. "It's not like I didn't tell anyone I wanted to. You see, Dennis, I fully intend to. I not only mean to colonize Mars, but to harness the resources of the solar system to create a new America, a vital, striving republic out of the bones of the old world. But we don't have much time. Before your invention, I was proceeding at a more leisurely pace. But now, your miracle has upset the applecart, Dennis. The Bolsheviks are making their move, and soon men of capital and industry like us will be forced to flee. My inventions make this possible. Yours make it possible to wait until we can reclaim what is ours."

"I don't know." Anita proclaimed petulantly while some loafing workers waved at Duplessis, who waved back. "I like some of Rosario's ideas."

Duplessis stared at Anita until Dennis stepped in. "She's Swedish."

"That's too bad. Look, here's the Starshot III-X. Luxury version. The III-P hold 50 passengers, but the X only 22. Much nicer way to spend three months, don't you think?"

"Is there a shower?" Anita quizzed him.

"Private, in each cabin." Duplessis grinned smugly. "Come on, Dennis. I need more than just hydroponic farmers and egghead engineers. I need people ready to remake Man, Mark One."

Dennis looked up at the giant, bulbous, silver ship and rubbed his neck. "I think I've done enough damage for one century."

"What if I threw the resources of the colony behind you? Gave you whatever you needed to make the miracle everyone's miracle?"

Anita breathed in his ear. "Do it."

He put out a hand to Duplessis, who put a scotch glass in it. "Where do I sign?"

2117

Litany of tears

Wallingford Arcology
Seattle

When he checked his workstation the next morning, Dennis almost fell off his chair.

YOU HAVE 215 NEW MESSAGES

After a restorative and very fortified coffee, he began to plow through the messages. It was pounding rain outside, so there was precious little else to do.

Dennis suspected many, if not all of the messages were from cranks, and they were certainly well represented.

I WAS PROGRAMMED BY ALIENS TO JUMP AND KEEP AT IT TILL I GOT IT WRITE.

BILL S, ALASKA

THE ANAL PROBE LEFT BY THE VISITORS HAS CAUSED UNBEARABLE PAIN. EVEN HOME SURGERY HAS NOT HAD THE DESIRED EFFECTS.

KIM Q, TEXAS

Why the continual obsession with anal probing?

Soon, though, there was more serious material to grapple with.

I AM WORLD-CLASS CHEF AND RESTRAUTEUR. SINCE RECEIVING A LIVER IMPLANT IN 2106, I HAVE BEEN FIGHTING SUICIDAL IDEATION. LAST MONTH, I STEPPED ONTO A LEDGE BEFORE I REALIZED WHAT I WAS DOING. I AM AFRAID I AM SO DETERMINED TO DO IT, THAT MY BODY WILL BYPASS MY RATIONAL MIND.

LANE B, SAN FRANCISCO

I AM FORMER FOSTER CHILD WHO BECAME A NORMIE IN 2109. SINCE I STARTED A DOCTOR-ORDERED DIET OF CLONED PROTEIN, I HAVE STRUGGLED WITH SUICIDAL THOUGHTS. I DREAM OF BREAKING AWAY AND RETURNING TO MY REAL FAMILY IN THE FLYOVER. IF I CAN'T DO THAT, I WANT TO KILL MYSELF.

LARINDA P, CHICAGO

I AM 97 YEARS OLD, AND I FIRST TOOK THE TREATMENT IN 2045. SINCE THEN, I HAVE HAD NINE DIFFERENT TREATMENTS AND GRAFTS. AFTER MY SEVENTH TREATMENT, I BEGAN TO NOTICE THOUGHTS OF SELF-HARM. I DON'T KNOW WHY, I AM VERY HAPPY, AND I HAVE EVERYTHING TO LIVE FOR. BUT EVERY TIME I STAND NEXT TO A LOVELY VANTAGE, MY MIND PRODS ME TO "JUMP."

NEIL S, MIAMI

Dennis was certain there was a common thread, but he couldn't quite see it. Then almost at the end of the messages, another note caught his eye.

I AM AN ADVANCED LIFE SUPPORT PARAMEDIC IN SUBURBAN ATLANTA. IF YOU ARE PUZZLED BY THIS PHENOMENA, I MAY BE ABLE TO HELP. I'VE BEEN STUDYING IT SINCE 2107. CALL ME.

LATOYA S, GEORGIA

He paused before responding. Was the miracle's father really ready to admit to it had not merely gone stale, but actively toxic?

But then again, what scientist ever achieved progress by turning from the truth? Had he ever really expected that immortality would come with no downside? Had the last eight decades taught him nothing?

Welcome back to Earth, Dennis Rosso. He composed a suitably professional message, careful to explain the unlikely alliance between Timothy Vance and Henrik Kassabian, only of one of whom he still looked like, and hit "send." Then, he spoke into the empty room. "Train to Atlanta. Friday."

"Flights may be cheaper." The autosec responded with saccharin sincerity.

"Train, please." He'd spent enough time on Merlin Duplessis' contraptions for one lifetime.

"Amtube to Atlanta from Seattle Free Station leaving 10:50 AM, arriving 4:30 PM at MLK Central."

"Charge it to my account."

"Charged."

Determined to forget his legacy for now, he ordered up an old movie and a pizza and let his mind drift off.

2040

Ss john carter

Kourou
French Guiana

Dennis and Anita held hands in the ungodly humid night, swatting at unrelenting bugs. They would never have been in this isolated, overgrown patch of South America, but for the apparition on the launch pad, two kilometres away.

The Starshot-III SS John Carter stood over 320 metres high, resting on its booster rocket, bathed in the obligatory floodlights, cryogenic vapours drifting from its base and joints.

"There." Anita pointed at a red speck on the horizon. "There it is, Dennis. Our new home."

Mars blinked weakly at them, as if beckoning them to step into the void. For a man who'd always been uncomfortable on airplanes, tomorrow's journey was a definite leap of faith. Not to mention the 100 million dollars he'd already invested in Duplessis' colony, now growing by leaps and bounds, if the reports were to be believed.

"We've gotta get there first." Dennis replied glumly.

"Have a little faith." Anita wrapped an arm around his waist. "I left everything for you. I did it first."

"I know." He nodded. "And I'm glad. But you know this may be a one-way trip."

"I know. But we can't stay here, Dennis. We've left it too long, as it is. The world is coming apart."

"So much for Rosario." The leader of the Practical Socialist Party, now in power across North America, was proving to be every bit as strident and intolerant as her black-suited disciples who'd held society hostage for two years now.

"Another politician, like the rest."

"And Duplessis?"

She kissed him on the neck. "He is one you have been smart enough to get close to. Let's hope that is enough. Maybe when we return, people will have learned one Swedish word."

"Ah. Lagom, right?"

"Yes. If only there was a Lagom Party."

As near as he could understand it, "Lagom" meant, "Just enough, not great, not bad." Anita would watch the riots from their ever-shifting homes and mutter it under her breath.

But Dennis knew that North Americans were not creatures of Lagom, not even the Canadians. They wanted it all. And what's more, they wanted the other guy to get fucked too.

Would that really change on Mars?

A woman's soft voice sounded over the PA system. "Passengers on tomorrow's flight, curfew is in fifteen minutes. Be rested for your great adventure."

"Are you ready?" He nudged her. "No more Swiss chocolate, no more caviar. Nothing but hydroponic veggies and tofu cakes."

"We could both use it. Mars awaits, John Carter."

Dennis Rosso smiled back at his wife. "You would look good in one of those bikinis."

The Next Morning

The pre-flight ritual was one of those spacefaring touches that Merlin Duplessis, a lifelong space nerd, was addicted to. First, the embarkation crew awakened you at a ridiculously impractical hour. Then, you feasted on steak and eggs, guaranteed to sit in your guts like a rock, and sat around for five hours while everyone got suited.

Dennis had hovered over the last piece of steak on his fork, certain it would be the last beef he ever tasted.

They were fitted into their survival suits, designed to keep them alive should the cabin depressurize on ascent, and then they chatted nervously with the suit technicians and each other before the buses arrived to take them to the pad.

Now, when they stepped out of the air-conditioned building onto the sweltering tarmac, the humidity greeted them like their home planet's last kiss. They rode in silence to the pad, the crew having proceeded them hours before.

Dennis knew none of his fellow passengers, knowing only that they were rich. Some of them had been out here for two weeks, training and practising. Anita had wanted to come, too, but Dennis had begged off. Securing his funds in Switzerland was more important. He had no intention of returning to Earth a pauper.

In a situation like this, every mundane step was a "last," nervously commented on and chuckled over by the soon-to-be extraterrestrial immigrants. The couple ahead of them on the gantry lineup were rich ranchers from Texas named Jerry and Patricia. They were, Dennis thought, exactly what you'd expect.

For some reason, Anita was quite taken with them.

Jerry was a large and florid man with what seemed like too many perfect teeth, and a penchant for stating the truly obvious. He was not fat, merely big-boned, yet he seemed to bulge out of his pressure suit. "Last time standing on two legs in one gee."

Patricia was tiny and hyperactive. She also seemed to have too many teeth. "Last time you'll see a bird in the wild." She pointed out a multi-coloured creature with a tremendous beak that hovered by the rocket, examining them curiously, to Anita's delight.

"Are we making a mistake, Dennis?" She whispered in his ear.

"We are playing the best hand we have from the bottom of a shitty deck." He whispered back.

"I think I get your metaphor." She pointed at a biplane buzzing overhead. It towed a banner that read, *Good Luck SS John Carter*.

"Last time you'll see a biplane flying!" Patricia trilled.

"I wish I could have one more steak, you know, for the road." Jerry moaned.

Dennis nodded. "Gotta agree with you on that one, Jerry."

Two Hours Later
T-Minus Five Minutes

There was no denying it now. Mars was no longer a philosophical question, a late-night, blue-sky, too many rum and cokes parlour game. It was imminent.

Too imminent for some. They would've been in orbit already were it not for one man, who changed his vote at the last minute. He was a little Asian man, seemingly stoic, who began to moan quietly as they closed the hatch and would not stop.

The Chief Steward exited the launch compartment and put a

stop to the countdown, returning with a doctor. The doctor could not make any headway with the man, whom Dennis understood was an applications billionaire.

All that money couldn't buy him the nerve to go up. Whatever problems he was facing, he wouldn't find the solution on Mars. The doctor and two of the closeout crew bundled the man and his luggage off of the *John Carter.*

The countdown resumed. They were seated in two rows across the breadth of the ship, having entered through an absurdly thick wall from the gantry. The room was pristine white, with no windows, only two massive screens taking up the front bulkhead. A little hatch marked *Crew Access Only* lay in front of them, with another, identical one, behind.

They carried no belongings, reclining in ergonomic launch chairs, listening, if they wanted, to the music of their choice through their suit headphones. Other jacks provided air, water, and, if necessary, urine relief.

It was all oddly relaxing, Dennis felt. At one point, like a *Right Stuff* astronaut of old, he almost drifted off to sleep. He listened, suddenly fascinated in the details of the journey, to the chatter between the crew and the controllers.

"Carter from Flight."

"Go."

"How's that engine four tank pressure?"

"Nominal, flight. We just had a normal vent sequence."

"Rog, keep an eye on it."

The cool banter of professionals was what Dennis needed to hear right now. He had given them his money, and now he'd signed over his life. At this point, short of embarrassing himself like the Asian man, there was no way out.

Strangely, the knowledge that he was inside a huge water tank reassured him. The launch deck was a triple-purpose room, displaying the talent for using all available space that aerospace engineers excelled in. Once they were in the interplanetary coast, the crew would break down the chairs and store them in the floor. The deck then became a zero-gee exercise facility, unless the solar activity alarm sounded. In that case, the passengers and crew would herd inside the deck again, to be protected from dangerous radioactivity by the massive tank of drinking water around them.

Nothing, it seemed, was left to chance on the gleaming, silver, inescapably phallic *John Carter*.

Jerry turned to him with a hand outstretched. "Good luck, neighbour."

Surprisingly touched, he took the massive mitt and shook it. "You too, Jerry. Hey, last handshake on Earth."

"Ha ha ha, right!"

Anita squeezed his thigh. The sensation caused him to wonder about zero-gee sex. "I love you, Dennis."

"I love you too, Anita." He doubled checked his comm settings to make sure he wasn't proclaiming everlasting devotion to the cabin boy. "The start of a new life."

"A new life." Her eyes teared up. "I can't wipe them. Isn't that crazy?"

"Not half as crazy as this." Over the intercom, the chatter picked up, as they entered the final phase of the countdown. On the monitors, venting gas was replaced by spraying water as the pad prepared for the fiery ordeal to follow.

"T-minus ten, nine, eight, seven, ignition sequence start."

"Fuel pumps nominal."

"Five, four, three…"

"Clock is running, all power internal mod one."

"Two, one, zero, liftoff, we have liftoff at nine thirty-seven AM."

The monitors flared over white, then resolved their contrast as *John Carter* rose steadily and then briskly on its booster. Underneath them, a steady, firm, but not uncomfortable push between their shoulder blades was the only sensation of movement at first, followed by jerks and bumps as the computer steered them clear of the tower.

"Tower clear."

Soon, the launchpad was invisible beneath them, the 21 passengers and ten crew breathing a collective sigh of relief as they floated against their restraints.

Mars beckoned.

2117

Excess mortality

Atlanta
Martin Luther King Hyperail Central

The pneumatic tubes that sent maglev trains across North America at speeds that would've been the province of aircraft decades before had once fascinated Dennis, when he'd returned to Earth.

Now, he slept through the journeys, as he did much else. Was he feeling old and tired? Biologically, he was not old, so how could he be tired?

Add that to the stack of questions on this journey. He stirred slowly as the train slid quietly into the station, dominated by a giant full-figure of MLK expounding his vision on the steps of the Lincoln Memorial.

A memorial now destroyed, like much of the rest of the Capitol, by people who thought they knew better. Hate, as it turned out, was a better seller. The 2043 destruction of the Washington Mall, an act of either White Supremacists or Antifa, depending on who had the megaphone at the time, was something he'd missed. He'd seen the MarsNet special report at the time, and he and Anita had congratulated themselves on their foresight, for getting out when the getting was good.

That was when life, though hard, was still good, and hopeful, and clean on Mars. How reversed would things seem a few decades later. Dennis looked up at the brooding bronze face of King and thought of the little Asian man from *John Carter.* If he had lived through the upheavals of the middle-21st century, would he have thanked his lucky stars he didn't go to Mars?

Could you escape the fire, anywhere? Even with eternal life, were we all doomed to burn?

That was, in part, what he was here to find out. He heard Latoya before he saw her, which was good, because she was tiny.

"Hey, Doctor! Over here!"

She was a small, shapely, grinning, dark-skinned woman. She embraced him sooner than he would've usually felt appropriate, but in this case, he would make an exception. "I'm Henrik. We spoke by holo? I'd love to hear about your work."

Latoya became suddenly emotional. "I prayed to Jesus you would come. I've been carrying this burden all on my own for too long now." She wiped a tear away with a nail he would've believed impractical for a paramedic.

"I'm at the Station Inn. Let me get checked in and you can show me what you have."

"One thousand, four hundred and fifty-five cases."

"Pardon me?"

"That's just since I started paying attention. In 2110 things really started taking off."

There was something about that year that made him pause. But his brain, miracle or no, was not what it had been. His doctor had suggested cosmic ray damage on Mars. Genetic therapy had helped a bit. "Wait in the restaurant for me. I'll be a half-hour, tops."

Latoya looked around as the crowd from the arriving train thinned out. "Um, have you been to Atlanta before, Doctor?"

"Not since the last century. And stop calling me Doctor. It's Henrik."

"Well, Henrik, I don't know how to say this, but since the trouble a few decades back, white people need to be careful here. You're only 10% of the population here, you know."

Dennis sighed. "I know." He'd seen the lurid crime stories on the holo, heard breathless tales of brutality from the recovered dead, and the lamentations of the loved ones of the unrecoverable. "I'm carrying."

A weighty Glock U92 sat on his belt, an unfamiliar weight since the last days on Mars, his cross-national permit courtesy of friends in the New Democratic Party. It fired depleted uranium rounds, usually with lethal effect, even in recipients of the miracle.

"Now I feel better." Her nails touched his arm. "Shall I order us some wine?"

"Anything you like." He smiled at her, feeling a dangerous stirring. "How will we get any work done?"

Latoya's face clouded over. "After you see my files, Henrik, you're gonna need another bottle."

Station Inn
Le Soul Restaurant

The restaurant was, from the looks of it, a typical mash-up attempt to feed all tastes, with a phony southern flavour. Local kitsch dotted the walls, much of it from the 19th and 20th Centuries. There was precious little said about the agonies of the last one.

NFL teams played on the walls. The southern obsession with football was one of the few survivors of the last century's upheavals. Racial mixture was not. Almost all the faces in the dining room were black. He felt the stares as he walked to meet Latoya. When he sat down in the booth with her, he could hear the murmurs.

She looked up from her personal screen, blurred in privacy mode, and brightened. "The wine's good! You like Pinot Noir?"

He smiled. "I love it. I went decades without it."

"Tried to quit? Why? They'll just grow you a new liver."

"It wasn't that. I was on Mars."

"I know. I looked you up."

"I looked you up, too. Paramedic of the year, 2106 and 2109. Impressive. It's a tough job."

She smiled bashfully. He decided that he liked her dimples. "That was just for Metro Atlanta. But yes, it's tough. I got into it after I got divorced. I needed some purpose. I was sick of being a trophy wife."

"Bet you were a good one." The wine was already hitting him. *Calm down.*

"Oh, stop it, Henrik." But her face did not say *stop it.* "I was surprised by how many problems there were, still, in a world full of people who can't die. We seem to look for them, don't we?"

"You're telling me. One minute we discover eternal life, the next minute it's riots, wars, and plagues."

"But I guess you missed most of that, didn't you?"

"Yes, I did." Henrik Kassabian and Dennis Rosso showed very similar timelines, emigrating to Mars in the same decade. It made keeping stories straight easier. "But we paid for it later."

"How long have you been back?"

"Since thirteen. A lot has changed."

"It sure has. Like no meat, for instance." She held up the menu. "Makes being a vegetarian easier."

"You don't like the substitutes?"

"No. I'm a 'Tastes like it died screaming' kind of girl."

He laughed and poured more Pinot for them both. "Speaking of death…"

She moved closer to him and shifted her screen so he could watch. Dennis caught the eye of a waiter staring daggers at them. "I never noticed a thing before 2110. Maybe it was there, and I just didn't see it. But I doubt it. I think it started then. Look."

FORD, MARCELLUS
B/M
AGED 102
SUICIDE
RISK FACTORS: MULTIPLE IMPLANTS, TRANSPLANTS, GENE THERAPY
2110/08/13

BLASEY, FIONA
B/F
AGED 122
SUICIDE
RISK FACTORS: MULTIPLE IMPLANTS, TRANSPLANTS, GENE THERAPY
2110/09/02

CONSTANT, PAUL
W/M
AGED 47
SUICIDE
RISK FACTORS: APPETITE CONSTRAINTS, PANCREATIC REGULATION

2110/10/14

ABDULLAHI, SYED
O/M
AGED 56
SUICIDE
RISK FACTORS: APPETITE CONSTRAINTS, PANCREATIC REGULATION, STOMACH REDUCTION
2110/10/22

OWENS, LEFONTAINE
B/M
AGED 57
SUICIDE
RISK FACTORS: APPETITE CONSTRAINTS
2110/10/29

CORLLS, LESHAWNA
B/F
AGED 140
SUICIDE
RISK FACTORS: MULTIPLE IMPLANTS, GENTETIC THERAPY, CRIMSON FOAM SURVIVOR
2110/11/06

And so on. For 237 pages. In one city.

"Survived the Crimson Foam, practically immortal, and she kills herself? Why the hell would she do that?"

"That's been my question for seven years now."

"You mentioned that something like 70% of the victims were men. You think is a causative, or correlative factor?"

"73% was in the Disease Control report. But you know what it is in the under 80 group?"

"No."

"82%. Among the over eighty group it's more like 56%."

"So, there's two distinct risk-factors: being male, and being over 80."

"I still think the male thing is a red herring." She shook her head and took a sip of wine. "My God that is good. I hope you can afford it, because I sure as hell can't."

"Don't worry about it. If it's a red herring, then why is it so strong?"

"I'm no epidemiologist. Maybe I've been taking some online courses…but still, no. But I think the question for both groups are not genetics per se, but more behavior. What do men do more than women, and what do over eighty types do more than us young ones?"

"Young ones? Speak for yourself."

"I know, I read you bio. If you looked me up, you'd know I was born in 2060. So, according to these numbers, I won't be taking the final dive anytime soon."

The waiter took their orders with a surly restraint. Dennis was starting to feel tempted to ask if there was a problem. But he knew that was just the gun making him feel tough. Both of them ordered vegetarian.

It came to Dennis then. "Meat."

"Excuse me?"

"Men like meat more than women."

"Maybe. Maybe they're eating the lab grown variety more…"

"And what else is grown in labs, Latoya?"

"Replacement organs. Jesus…and all it took was a visit to a restaurant. If only I could get some post-mortems…"

"Which you can't do, because there's nothing left, right?"

"Usually, no. Swan dives into solid concrete from high enough up, tissues get jellified. Hell, even if Dennis Rosso was still alive, he couldn't bring that back."

Dennis smiled ironically. It was something he'd worked on on Mars, how to keep the miracle alive in victims of decompression accidents. But there was still no way. "Electrocution?"

"The good old third rail, yes. Explosion, incineration, vats of acid, extreme radiation fields. Hell, I even found some 'consultants,' snooping around."

"Consultants?" Dennis raised an eyebrow. "Suicide consultants?"

"Yeah, it's a thing. They can't legally do it themselves, though if you ask me there's a lot who'll cross that line for the right price. They can, here anyway, tell you how to do it, suggest a place, even facilitate your check-out."

"So, these people aren't doing it spur of the moment." He thought for a moment. "This takes time. Planning, rational thought."

"Yes. The only ones who can tell us about that are the ones who failed. I can introduce you to a couple of those, too."

"I smell a road trip, Latoya."

They clinked glasses. The glaring spectators ignored them now, focused back on their football. "And here I thought my fortune cookie was full of shit. Why the hell not, Henrik? I've got some time off. Let's solve a mystery."

2040

Interplanetary cruise

3.5 Million Kilometres from Earth
T-Plus 73 Hours

Anita stared at the tray in front of her. Dennis "sat," one might say, his feet hooked into Velcro straps, across from her. Beside them, a vista they had quickly gotten blasé about: the unfettered spray of stars that would be their home for the next eleven weeks.

"Eat, honey. It's been three days on nothing but saltines and water."

"Mmmm." Anita had puked like a hero for the first two days. The vomiting might have stopped, but she was still mightily uncertain about any form of solid food.

Half of the rest of the dining room's occupants shared her plight. The rest, like Dennis, were mercifully left untouched by Space Adaptation Syndrome. Well, 'untouched' was a bit of a stretch, considering that he'd spent all of his trip of a lifetime so far cleaning up puke and ministering to a 40-year-old baby.

Finally, she took a mouthful. "Well?"

"Mmmm. I might have another. Next week."

"Do I have to play airplane and hangar?"

That, at least, resulted in a smile. "Not in public you don't."

But he already had a spoonful of chicken a la king on his spoon and was steering it towards her mouth. "Here comes the airplane. Vroom!"

She acquiesced, collapsing in laughter. "Okay, okay!"

Jerry and Patricia entered the dining room, still pale and wan. Dennis beckoned them over, glad for their company now that most of their fellow passengers had been revealed as cold Emiratis and secretive Chinese. Jerry helped Patricia secure herself at the table, then anchored his own feet.

"Hungry, kids?" Dennis waved a spoon at them. "Chicken a la King, and it's not half bad. Still missing that steak, Dennis?"

"Ugh."

The intercom crackled to life. "Ladies, gentlemen, and non-binaries, this is Captain Leuprecht speaking." He had the typical voice of calm command passengers had come to expect over a century, whether on their way to Cincinnati or Mars. "We've reached our final cruising speed, and we're about to shut down our booster pack for the coast phase. You may notice that objects you let loose hover in place, rather than float to the aft of the ship. Other than that, there won't be much difference. Stand by for SECO in 3…2…1…SECO!"

"Wow." Jerry held up a water beaker, which station-kept perfectly until Dennis gave it a spin. "Hot damn."

Outside the window, droplets of frozen hydrogen coalesced and floated past the big picture window. "It's lovely, isn't it?" Patricia trilled. Dennis noticed that her breasts did not move in zero-gee and calculated some expensive augmentation had been acquired.

The dining steward floated up to them. He was a sleek young Hispanic doing a waiter's job, one he'd probably had to get a Master's degree at least for. "Excuse me Mr and Mrs Cornell, Mr and Mrs Rosso, it is now Happy Hour. Is anyone interested in a…"

"Vodka martini, dry, with three olives." Dennis didn't let him finish.

To his surprise, Anita held up her hand. While he wasn't looking, she'd finished her dinner. "What the hell. Mars isn't for the faint of heart. Make that two."

Jerry and Patricia held up their hands, too.

And so, they went from playing games of "lasts" on Earth to playing games of "firsts" in space.

First Drunk in Space. It was much nicer than all the other ways of getting sick.

Two Weeks Later

Though the *John Carter* had looked large on the launch pad, once you had to spend every day there, it quickly began to feel small. It was only forty metres end-to-end, and about twenty metres wide, in terms of habitable space that the passengers could access.

One-by-one, they did get invited to the flight deck. It was essentially an enlarged airliner cockpit, with large windows, and stand-up sleeping bags on the walls where the crew were stored until needed, like CDs in a rack, Dennis thought. It made him appreciate his own quarters, which until then he'd found spartan.

Captain Leuprecht was superficially charming, though a hint of impatience simmered beneath. He had the dark looks and full-moustache of a Mexican bandido, packed into a wiry, compact frame. He put up with Anita's determined quizzing for a while before seeing them out. She'd finally found her space legs and was her old energetic self.

"Have you been to Mars before, Captain?"

"Well, as you see on my biography, yes. I captained the first voyage with Mr Duplessis."

"So, this is your second trip?"

"Yes. The whole thing, round-trip, tends to take nine months, so it's not something you do more than once every three or so years if you want to have a family life. Which I am lucky not to have."

Dennis caught himself before snickering at that last report. Like the astronauts of old, Leuprecht was a confirmed poon hound, making full use of the little Asian man's spare cabin with the Chief Steward, and one of the guests, Mrs Cairns, a widowed heiress with a twenty-year-old body.

"What is Mars like, Captain?"

"Like a hazy, red-tinted, desert dream. Now, if you'll excuse me, I have a mid-course correction burn to prepare for."

"Everything alright?"

"Of course! Simply routine spaceflight!"

As he disappeared back into the flight deck, they floated in the hatch and looked at each other. "I'm horny." She said, finally.

"Me too. But how do we…"

She touched his thigh. "I watched a video. It's easy."

Their cabin was small, practical, and multi-purpose. The sleep station folded away during the day to make room for two chairs and a small table. The shower stall could fit only one. Anita snatched a handful of wet wipes from the lavatory.

"We'll be needing these in thirty seconds."

"If that." He agreed.

They stripped down and squared off. Anita's tits floated strangely in the zero-gee, like a strange combination of voluminous and perky. Dennis felt his erection rising at the mere sight of it. Soon, they were grappling like space-aged Ninjas.

There was much bouncing off the walls and grunting. Every attempt at exerting thrust was met with counter-thrust. Finally, he found himself in her, a tiny blue and white marble over her left shoulder, as he performed the ritual of the ages.

"It's…it's beautiful!" He moaned.

"Oh God, yes!"

They spent the next half-hour mopping up.

And the next six weeks replicating the experience. Anita and Dennis had become zero-gee sex addicts.

Halfway to Mars

After six weeks, there was nothing left on board to explore. Even the taciturn Emiratis and Chinese had become garrulous, seeking other people's cabins to explore, something, anything to do besides watch the mandatory Q-Space training vids, do their mandatory two hours a day exercises, or lose themselves in the endless media library. Duplessis had offered his passengers twenty Marsbucks for every song, movie, picture, or book they could not find. So far, nobody had claimed.

Dennis stared out the bedroom window, drifting in his sleep station, listening to Bach, unwilling to move. Anita was at breakfast. He was not hungry. There was nothing to see. Space out here, in the blinding light of the distant Sun's aurora, was featureless.

What would it be today? Movies? He'd watched every James Bond film ever made now, all the catalogue of Ridley Scott and

James Cameron, and now he was on to Roman Polanski. Reading? Once, he'd thought of *War and Peace* as a slog he'd never have time for, but he'd completed it yesterday after a mere four days. *Bloody depressing.*

Of course, there was always work. Since perfecting the miracle, Dennis had not gone near a lab bench, but Duplessis had made it clear that his services would be called upon in the new colony. He resolved to bring himself up to speed on the last five years in his field.

The miracle was completed, but not perfected. People still died too easily from accidents, transmissible diseases, and violence. Aging still crept into some systems, though more slowly and hesitantly than before.

Perhaps, in the quiet and solitude of Mars, his passion for science would be reborn. *Perhaps.*

Suddenly, an insistent alarm jolted him from his reverie. Lightbars on the seams of the walls lit up in eerie red light, and a notice screen over the door flashed a deadly warning.

SOLAR FLARE IMMINENT-LETHAL RADIOACTIVITY-SEEK SHELTER NOW

"Solar flare imminent! Solar flare imminent! Lethal rad levels in 56 seconds! Proceed to shelter now! Solar flare imminent! Emergency!"

Unthinking, he propelled himself to the hatch, clad only in boxer briefs, and shot out into the corridor, being almost steamrolled by a giant Emirati. The man had a massive beard and spoke no English. He reached back for Dennis and pulled him along as he deftly made his way down the corridor. Relieved, he caught a glimpse of Anita, who was being ushered into the storm shelter by a steward.

The entire population of the ship was flowing towards the

shelter, in which they'd launched into orbit six weeks before. The last of the stewards pushed Dennis into the shelter, looked around for stragglers, and dogged the hatch behind them.

"Solar flare imminent. Lethal radioactivity outside shelter in five seconds! Stand clear of hatch!"

"Pick a side, folks! Either side of the red line! The centre aisle is no-go!" The Chief Steward, an imposing Amazon of a woman, bellowed at them while her staff deployed nets to keep the passengers in the area of best protection. Dennis caught Anita's eye on the other side of the netting. They exchanged an ironic smile.

"Solar flare arrival. Radiation outside lethal. Do not exit."

"Oh God! Patricia! Where are you?" Beside him, Jerry was losing his mind, striving to rip away the netting. Dennis joined the big Emirati and Captain Leuprecht in restraining him.

"We can't let you go or you'll kill us all! Sophie, get me some tranks!" The Captain struggled to get one of Jerry's thick arms free.

A needle slid into Jerry's arm. "Captain?" The ship's medic, Lawson, was a mousy woman with a sardonic sense of humour. "Have you seen Steward Gonsalves?"

"Jesus Christ." The Chief Steward cursed. She opened a panel on the bulkhead and started flipping between interior monitors. Lawson flipped a chair out of the wall and helped Dennis and the Emirati secure Jerry's bulk.

"Look." Lawson pointed to a monitor.

"Goddamnit!" Leuprecht cursed. In Jerry and Patricia's cabin, Gonsalves, the quiet cabin boy who'd served them dinner so many times tore at his clothing and frantically gestured at the camera. Patricia floated in the background, unconscious. Vomit floated around in the background. "He wouldn't leave her behind. He wouldn't...fuck it!" The Captain pounded on the bulkhead, comforted by the Chief Steward. The passengers watched in stunned silence.

Dennis turned to the Emirati. "You saved my life. I know you don't understand...how do you say...is it, *shakar?*"
The Emirati dabbed at Jerry's head with a wet wipe. "Yes, okay. You are welcomed."

Dennis turned to see Anita crying. He looked over at Lawson. "Please turn that off."

Lawson nodded and slid the panels closed. The inhabitants of the *SS John Carter* floated in silence, millions of kilometres from home, now minus two of their own.

2117

People to see

North American Disease Control Council
Atlanta

There were certain advantages to being Henrik Kassabian. One was the ability to book interviews with men like Craig Feng with practically no notice.

The cab was waved through the guardhouse with a cursory look. The self-driving car accelerated, following a beacon. Neither it, nor its passengers, had any real idea where they were going.

"This is so strange." Latoya breathed. "Where are all the buildings?"

"Underground." Dennis answered. "In the Upheaval, the mobs burned down the old CDC buildings. They even let out the Smallpox. Not that anyone noticed, what with Red Foam and all that." He sounded like an expert. But he'd watched it all from a hundred million kilometres away, in safety and comfort.

Outside the windows, the grounds looked like gently rolling farm fields. Only the occasional heavily guarded entrance or antenna farm belied the reality. "My momma told me. She was trying to get out of the city, to the mountains, then. She was the only one of her family who made it." She wiped away a tear with a long nail. "Sorry."

"Don't be."

"We're here, folks. That'll be 29.50." The car chirped at them.

Dennis touched the PayPad with his fingertip and keyed in the amount. "Have a return on standby, please."

"Understood."

They stepped out to find themselves facing an unguarded door. The heavy construction and half-buried look reminded Dennis of the early hab modules in Hellas. Which reminded him of the night before.

After seeing Latoya off, he'd stayed up half the night reading her reports, an endless litany of tears. He drank good Beaujolais and tried to forget about death, but Anita and Patricia, the poor steward Gonsalves, they all visited him in the night.

So, he returned to the joyless list, looking for connections, some substantiation for their theories the night before. Dennis felt committed now, in a way he hadn't since he'd first landed in Hellas all those years ago.

If he were older, if it were still possible to be older, in any meaningful sense, Dennis suspected he would feel a culmination. One last mission to make sense of his legacy as the father of the miracle. One last chance to set things right.

But he'd killed that, hadn't he? He'd killed that with the kill switch, that snowy day in Detroit. So now, over a life of millennia, possibly eons, was there any possibility of culmination?

Or would a man live a million lives, as he almost had...one decade, a food critic, the next, a scientist, then, a rebel...now?

A slit in the door slid open. Narrow eyes stared out. "Dr Kassabian?"

"Yes. And Ms Summers. To see Dr Feng." They both held up

their hands for the expected scan. There was nothing. Instead, a heavily armed security guard stepped out of the bunker.

"Never mind." The mesomorphic flat-topped man blinked. "We've already had a good look." He smiled at them with steel teeth. "Come with me."

Swallowing their doubts, they followed the massive machine/man into the labyrinth of corridors, arriving quickly at a small office with its door open. An Asian man in a white coat hunched over a holo display.

"Doctor Feng? Your 9:30 is here." The mesomorph's voice went up an octave. Dennis wondered if he really were a cyborg, optimized for a combination of menace and PR. Stranger things were about these days. Convicts, now looking at *really* serving hundred-year sentences for their crimes, were choosing to volunteer for some far-out experimental programs. Ironically, the same laws which forbade withholding the miracle from them; also forbade commuting their sentences.

Feng squinted at them through thick glasses. *Why would anyone forego myopia treatments now?* "Hey, hey, welcome to the DCC. Sorry about the security routine, but last time..."

"Yes, we know." Dennis offered his hand. "Dr Henrik Kassabian. This is my associate, Ms Summers."

Feng shook Latoya's hand, but kept his eyes on Dennis. "Wow, Dr Kassabian, inventor of the Inhibitor, wow. You were gone for so long on Mars, nobody knew what happened to you!"

If you only knew, Feng. "I am sure you're very busy here. We don't want to take up too much of your time."

Feng looked at his watch. Internal readouts inside most people made this an anachronistic gesture, but perhaps that also explained the glasses. Feng was a "Waybacker," a hopeless nostalgic for a world with death and wristwatches.

"I'm afraid I have a meeting with my South American colleagues at ten, so I can only give you twenty solid minutes. What can we do for you, Doctor? Please, sit."

They sat in ergonomic chairs, which, like all ergonomic chairs, nobody knew how to set up properly. "It's about your last Morbidity and Mortality Quarterly Report." Dennis said, matter-of-factly.

Feng's face froze. "Oh, what do you want to know, Doctor? I shouldn't think a few anomalous suicides should trouble a man of your stature." He blithely ignored Latoya.

"Is that what they are? Anomalous? My colleague has information to the contrary. Latoya?"

Latoya opened her laptop and put it on Feng's desk. He pursed his lips, but, intimidated by the Great Kassabian, said nothing. "I have the records of all the suicides I've attended as an ALS Paramedic in the Atlanta area since 2110. In that year, I noticed what appeared to be an increase in non-recoverable self-terminations, and I began to keep track. I found that there appeared to be two main risk groups: males, and persons aged over-eighty."

Feng waved a hand dismissively. "Yes, our report publicly stated the same thing, for an overall increase of 25%. There's no mystery here." His tone had changed from deferential to sniffy.

"Who's implying a mystery?" Dennis leaned forward. "I was merely wondering if you could shed any light on this trend, that's all?"

"Trend? Who said it was a trend? It could be exactly as I said: Anomalous."

"As far back as 2110?" Latoya was incredulous. "I'm not an epidemiologist, but…"

Now, Latoya had Feng's attention. "No, that's right, you are not! If your employer became aware that you were keeping unauthorized patient records…"

Latoya blanched and shut the laptop. Dennis intervened. "Then I would have to go public with my concerns as a Nobel Laureate. That rather than investigating a troubling new trend, the health authorities were conspiring to silence those sounding the alarm. Heavens, what bad press. Perhaps we could find out how the new design keeps out rioters, eh, Dr Feng?"

It was Feng's turn to blanch. "Now, listen, Dr Kassabian, that is not my intention. I apologize for any inferred threat. I can see you are well-intentioned. Believe me, sincerely, if I thought there was a need for your expertise, I would be calling you for help. If I thought there was a need to investigate clonal food, organ re-supply, any bio-medical industry, I would appoint you to head the commission, or recommend the President do so. Sincerely. I mean, you're the most influential biochemist of our times, save of course The Triumvirate."

The Triumvirate. Dennis suppressed a twitching eyelid. How he hated this term. The attempt to spread credit amongst Rafjani and Bains for *his* miracle. He recovered and thought of a way to take advantage of Feng's discomfiture. "Of course, I believe you, Dr. Feng. But I was wondering if, as a show of good faith, you might assist my private enquiries into this matter. Reporting directly to you, of course."

Feng swallowed. He appeared to realize that he'd backed himself into a corner. He looked at his watch again. "I regret that I have only five minutes left…"

"Oh, this won't take long. That's what subordinates are for. Consider us your subordinates. All we need is a letter of authorization, signed by you, to conduct inquiries in this matter on your behalf."

"I suppose, I…"

"And." Latoya added.

"And?"

She smiled sweetly at him. "A copy of your files on the subject. Let's say, as far back as 2110."

"But…"

Dennis moved his chair closer to Feng. "Have you ever been to Stockholm, to the Nobel Ceremony?"

"No." Feng shook his head. "I imagine it is marvellous."

"'Marvellous?' Yes, indeed, that's a good word for it. A fitting reward for two men who had collaborated to wipe the resurgent scourge of death from the face of the earth yet again! Don't you think?"

Feng brightened. "Yes. Yes, I do think."

One Hour Later

They were leaving in a cab with a signed letter of authority from Dr Craig Feng, and two data disks' worth of inquiries and reports on excess mortality since 2110. Latoya hastened to plug one into her laptop. Dennis stopped her.

"No." He whispered. "If those discs aren't full of spyware, then I'm Dennis Rosso." It was a line he liked to use often. "We'll buy another one just for reading the files."

"Right. Where to now?" They cleared the gates and drove along a tree-lined boulevard to the highway, the car's interior dappled by shade and sunlight in alternation.

"Well, how about JC Bryson Foods? They're headquartered here, right? I mean, did you see you he reacted when I brought up clonal food?"

Latoya shook her head. "But that's just it, Henrik. You didn't bring it up. And you didn't bring up organ re-supply, either."

"So, clonal food and organ re-supply it is, then."

"He knows something, Henrik. He knows, and it's killing him."

He nodded in silence and stared out the window into the bright sunshine.

2040

Burial at sea

Halfway to Mars

They were not allowed out of the solar flare shelter until the crew had cleaned up the mess and secured the bodies. Then, with Dennis still in his underwear, they floated back to their cabins somberly. He imagined he could smell crackling neurons and vomity death, and mentioned this to Anita, who scoffed.

"Don't make it worse. Let's get drunk."

So they did, en masse, even the big Emirati joining in, to the scowls of his countrymen. He appeared not to care. Across the dining room, Dennis could see two Chinese, husband and wife, crying unrestrainedly.

He was learning a lot about his fellow humans, out here among the stars. The Emiratis were not heartless, and the Chinese were not robots, either.

He wanted to comfort Jerry, out here the closest thing he had to a male friend, but it was impossible. Captain Leuprecht had relinquished his cabin and now Dr Lawson had him sedated and secured there.

Everyone drank until they could feel nothing, then retired to their cabins. Dennis nodded at the Emirati, who surprised him by giving him an effusive hug. Soon, only Leuprecht remained at the bar. Dennis sent Anita on alone and drifted up beside him. "What are you having?"

"Hmm? Oh, nothing fancy, just a Glenlivet. I'm afraid I don't know much about scotch. I was saving it for planetfall." He squeezed the plastic bulb and sucked back a few drops. "Not my usual drink of choice. In honor of my dad, you see."

"Was he a spaceman?"

"No, he built the rockets. He worked on the Space Shuttle, then went to work for Q-Space when I was in the Air Force. He lived to see me make it to orbit at least." Leuprecht raised his bulb to an invisible presence. Dennis reached behind the bar and filled a bulb to the brim with Bordeaux.

"I'm good for it." Dennis raised his bulb.

Leuprecht chuckled. "With the amount of money you've pumped into this program, I should be buying."

"To Gonsalves! And Patricia!" Dennis raised his bulb again, and Leuprecht clinked against it.

"He was a good kid…a real smart guy. He was gonna be on the flight deck one day. He spent every spare minute he could there, learning. That's the good thing about Q-Space. The way Merlin thinks, he'd rather have a guy like that, who's learned it all the Q-Space way, than a guy like me, who needs re-programming." Leuprecht shrugged.

"He knows?"

"Yeah, I just got his reply. Never heard him swear that much. Q-Space has never lost a passenger before. The stock price is gonna take a hit."

Dennis sipped at his wine. "Space is inherently dangerous. We all knew that, before we got on this thing, and now we're all damn sure. This is no game. Surely, he's not blaming you?"

"Yes, he is, and don't call me 'Shirley.'" They both chuckled at the ancient joke. "Anyway, it doesn't matter. This is my last trip. No matter what I do, or try to do, I'll always be the first Q-Space Captain to lose a passenger. I won't be going back."

Dennis shook his head. "Waste of a good spaceman, if you ask me. You're going to fly back as a passenger?"

Leuprecht paused. "I'm not going back at all, Dennis. The whole reason I jumped ship from NASA to Q-Space was Mars. I want to be a Martian, just like you. I've convinced Merlin to let me work as an Engineer in Hellas Community. Paula and I are getting married, and we're never going back. Once I land this sucker next month, I'm never flying in space again."

Dennis had an idea why Duplessis was being so accommodating. Leuprecht on Earth could be summoned to testify. On Mars, there was no way. But he kept that to himself. He raised his bulb again. "Well, then Mars or Bust!"

Leuprecht smiled ironically and drank. "Mars or Bust."

The Next Day

Despite the fact that Q-Space had never lost a passenger before in space, there was, like anything in spaceflight, a checklist for that.

The entire ship's company of the *John Carter* and their guests floated in a narrow corridor. The small coffin of Patricia Cornell sat inside the trash airlock already. Jerry read the Episcopalian Rites in a monotone. He seemed to have shrunk five centimetres from the events of the previous day.

Above the hatchway, where it usually read:

CAUTION: TRASH AIRLOCK

ZERO ATMOSPHERE

Someone had thoughtfully placed a sticker over top:

FAREWELL AND GODSPEED

PATRICIA AND JUAN ESTEBAN

Dennis had spent much of the day commiserating with Jerry. Stunned by tranquilizers and burdened with grief, the big Texan now had the affect of a small, slow child.

"Dennis?" Jerry had asked him as Dennis fit him into a dark suit with a matching bolo tie. Outside, a pale red dot in the window announced their destination, growing larger each day.

"Yes, Jerry."

"Isn't there something you can do? You know, like with her cells? You're the guy who killed death, ain't ya?"

"No, Jerry, I'm sorry. Radiation like that damages human cells so badly...there's nothing left to reprogram."

"I feel so bad...so damn low, Dennis. I let her sleep in, with them damned pills she takes. Oh God."

Now, Anita held Jerry's hand as the First Mate and soon-to-be-Captain, Daniloff, launched the tiny coffin into space. Dr Lawson took Jerry back to his room as the airlock was reset, and the larger coffin containing Gonsavles was put inside.

As they stood in the corridor, the inner door open, Dennis imagined he could feel the ungodly cold of space. Captain Leuprecht read Psalm 23 in Spanish over his protégé's body as it passed through the second-to-last door it would ever use.

Another push of a button, and another human consigned to orbiting the Sun for eternity.

But that was not their fate, at least not now. In the distance, a pale pink dot beckoned.

2117

Exit through the gift shop

JC Bryson Foods, Inc.
Smyrna, Georgia

After a hurried lunch, Dennis and Latoya had put their new-found clout to good use.

"After all," Dennis had observed, "how long before he changes his mind?"

They had fuelled themselves, picked up Latoya's Q-Coupe, another of Duplessis' technological tentacles, and stopped in a fabricator to have a new laptop synthesized. Now, Dennis drove as Latoya scrolled through the DCC records.

JC Bryson foods had taken over the entire southern part of Smyrna, in the north-west suburbs of Atlanta. It was a megafactory, a thoroughly modern enterprise into which nothing but sacksful of nutrients, small shipments of cell culture, and a handful of workers entered each day.

What exited was tons of manufactured, cloned, and designed food.

Dennis had lived next to a slaughterhouse for a few months when he was going to college. He remembered the clanging trucks full of wide-eyed animals, surely in some suspicion of their fate, pulling into the plant at all hours. He remembered the smells. He remembered the blood being hosed out of the slaughtering floor. He could see it from his fourth-floor window.

As much as he missed the irreplaceable taste and texture of meat; real, live, meat…he knew he would never regret its elimination. The months he spent next to that charnel house were surely little better than living next to Auschwitz. We were better off as a species, doing things this way. *Certainly.*

And yet, the doubt gnawed. *Were we? What new horrors awaited them, in there?*

They arrived at another gatehouse. The guard was another convict/cyborg. "Yes?" He hissed at them. The eyes were narrow and unforgiving.

"Dr Kassabian and Ms Summers for Mr Lontraine."

"Yes sir." The guard hissed again. "First left. You take the tour, then Mr Lontraine will meet you at the gift shop."

Gift shop? They have a gift shop? He stifled an urge to laugh out loud. He looked at Latoya, who shrugged. "Okay."

The guard handed them two badges with *Tour Visitor* stamped on them, and crude close-up photos of themselves from a gate camera. "I can't believe they have a gift shop." Latoya announced.

"Yes, I mean, what do they sell? "Junior's first Cloning Kit?"

"I Got Replicated at JC Bryson" t-shirts? Latoya twittered.

"You know, I used to live next to a real slaughterhouse, back in the day."

"How was it?" Latoya made a face.

"Offal."

"Oh Gawd!"

They parked in the visitor stalls and joined a throng of people who clearly had nothing better to do today, in the tour line-up. A cheery guide named D'Antrey kept them moving through nutrient tanks, sampling robots, and wash stations. Finally, they caught the smell of muscle and sinew in their noses and rounded a corner.

In six vast, open vats, jiggling masses of pink tissue wobbled and shook. Extruders at the bottom shat evenly-sized bits of the ungodly substance onto conveyor belts, where robots sliced and diced the bits into smaller bits with lasers.

"Goggles on, folks." D'Antrey intoned seriously. "Those are pretty powerful lasers up there."

They obeyed and followed their guide until they were standing abreast of the giant tanks, looking down inside. Dennis stared at the wobbling, flabby goo. He thought back to that snowy day in Detroit. The muscle growing out of his petri dish was much firmer, but of course this was not what people would want. People wanted fat. Fat is flavor.

"I did this." He muttered.

"Pardon?" Latoya whispered.

"Er, a...gross."

"You got that right."

"And now, here's the part y'all have been looking forward to! Let's exit through the gift shop and hit the Barbeque!" D'Antrey let loose a whoop of phoney excitement.

"Oh Christ. I never thought I'd say this but thank God we've got an interview." Latoya wiped her brow.

Lontraine met them at the bottom of the stairs to the gift shop. He was a wide-shouldered and imposing black man of solidity. They shook his massive hands. "Welcome to JC Bryson. You can always hit the gift shop later. For now, come with me, please."

They entered an obviously private elevator, Lontraine signalling his security man to take the next one. "I take up a lot of room." He chuckled.

Dennis showed him the letter. "Here is the letter I mentioned on the holo."

Lontraine waved it away. "I know, I know. I called Craig." *Craig?* "So, there's a slight uptick in suicides, and you think my burgers might be behind it? Please, whatever it is you're gonna do, can you wait until *after* the Fourth of July?"

They arrived at their stop, which opened right into a private office. "Membership has it's privileges, an ad in my time used to say."

"I remember it well." Dennis looked around the spacious setting. Outside the picture window was not a view of the Georgian hills, but of the Martian ones. The road to Schiaparelli, if he had to guess. "You're a fan of Mars?"

"A former resident, Doctor, don't you remember me?" An alarm began to sound in Dennis's head. "I moved out there in 2086 to set up a pilot plant for Bryson. Stayed ten years. We met several times. Come now, I can't be that hard to remember."

"I…am sorry, Mr Lontraine. I hope you will understand that I have blocked a lot of that time out of my mind." He was aware that Latoya was starting to look at him funny and he was beginning to feel faint.

"Ah well, I'm sorry. Sorry to bring it up. The last years there were hard, I am sure. Now it's all UN bureaucrats and half-crazy rebels there. More fun when Merlin was in charge, am I right?"

He steadied himself against the urge to pass out. "Sure was."

Lontraine sat on the edge of his desk and beckoned them to sit in two superbly comfortable chairs. "Now, Craig said you had some concerns about excess suicides? Not sure what my products would have to do with that…hell, unless you run out of our burgers or brats, that is!" He tittered away at his own joke, and Latoya joined in.

Rattled, he tried to steer the ship closer to shore. "We're hardly suggesting causation. But we do have a remit to examine any and all facilities specializing in cloning mammalian cells. Like this one, like organ re-supply banks, etc."

Lontraine stared back coldly. "A remit, which, if I understand correctly, you specifically demanded, Dr Kassabian."

Latoya must've sensed he was going to pieces, and intervened. "So what? We've identified some possibly correlations, and we're investigating them. The only people who could possibly object would be the ones with something to hide. Now, from the looks of that spotless factory floor down there, that couldn't possibly be you, could it, Mr Lontraine?"

Lontraine's cold stare dissolved in laughter. Dennis made up his mind right there and then that he hated the man. *Fucking head games.* "Whoo-ee! If there is one thing I have learned in 90 years on two planets, it is never to mess with a smart, powerful black woman."

"Momma taught you well." Latoya raised an eyebrow.

"Uh-huh. That wasn't Momma. That was painful experience. Okay, Doctor, go on, ask me anything. Anything at all."

There was only one question he could think of. "Is there some reason you treat your clonal meat cultures with the miracle? I mean, just to grow them, it's not necessary. And they'll hardly last forever."

Lontraine shrugged and folded his hands in his lap. "You've

seen the size of those vats, right? We produce two million tons of clonal meat every year. 8% of total North American production, in this one facility, right here. We use the miracle because it only stops growing when it hits the lasers. Not before."

"You're sure about that?"

"Do you see anyone walking around with three heads, Doctor? 'Course not! You know what really simple, cheap substance kills the miracle, in direct application?"

Dennis nodded. "Salt. You salt the meat."

"Of course! You sure that's it, Dr Kassabian? Can I ask you just one?"

Latoya sat up to intervene, and Dennis held her back. "Sure. Whatever you want."

"Remember how you used to name all your dogs 'Nobel Warrior?' Like 'Nobel Warrior, 1, 2, and 3?"

He did remember that peculiar trait of Kassabian's, right down to his favourite breed, the Jack Russell Terrier. "Yes, I do." A little, *fuck you* to his scientific rival. Cute.

"Now that Nobel Warrior, she was number 3, I think. Two different colored eyes, I remember. How did she die? 'Cause she was real old, remember?"

"I got her the miracle. Asked Rosso to do it just for her. She died in the Civil War, when the rebels blew up the Hellas Tokamaks."

"Hell of a shame. Hell of a shame. That was one smart dog. Ain't too many people smart as that dog. No sir."

Twenty Minutes Later

As Latoya and Dennis exited the guardhouse, Lontraine made a call, watching them through his now transparent picture window.

"No, he ain't. You know how I know? Because I asked when his dog died. And he don't know. You believe that shit? What kind of man doesn't know when his dog died? How do I know? How do I know?"

A Jack Russell Terrier with two different colored eyes entered the room and sat at Lontraine's feet.

"How do I know? 'Cause he told me it's dead, and here it is, sitting on my fucking shoes. If that was really Kassabian out there, this dog would've gone nuts. Not a peep. That's how I know. And what's more, he never even mentioned what that dog brought back with him. Remember? Whoever he is, he is not Henrik Kassabian. You understand me?"

Lontraine listened to the man on the other end of the line and smiled contentedly. "I know, right? Guy walks in here, looking like Kassabian for damn sure, then forgets that the secret to all of this was smuggled in from Mars in his dog's ass. This guy, whoever he is, is no professional. Don't you worry. I need to make a call now."

Lontraine watched his guests leave, weaving their way through the clonal vats, relishing the irony of millions of picky eaters feasting on the literal product of a dog's ass.

2041

Planetfall

Three Days from Landing

With the conviviality of the early days of the journey killed, the passengers of the *John Carter* largely stayed in their cabins, leaving only to exercise and eat.

That morning, knowing the braking burn to slow them for their landing was coming, Dennis and Anita stayed in bed late. They watched from their window as the flow of particles and objects shifted, the ship tilted, and a growing pressure shifted their weight towards the nose of the craft.

But what they had stayed in for was Mars itself. Together, they gasped in awe as the Red Planet was fully revealed for the first time, now, the size of a basketball at arm's length, the shield volcanoes of Tharsis standing tall above the clouds, the engorged northern icecap reflecting a blinding light.

Together, they shared silent tears. "Never in my wildest dreams did I think I would see this. I thought my life was over." He confessed.

She kissed him gently. "You made this possible for us both. Mars. I can't believe it."

There would be times in the years to come that he would curse the place; it's isolation, it's choking red dust, the insanity of the people, the foibles of its rulers. But those times were far in the future. For now, Mars was an oasis in space, one of only three worlds of man, a place where, soon, his feet would rest on the ground again.

Already, the lights of the Northern Settlement in Acidalia glinted faintly. Hellas could not be seen yet, but their destination was already a town of 500 people. Dennis was desperately keen to see it. Was it like the brochures? Was it a place of hidden savagery?

Which one would he prefer?

He took Anita's lead, and soon they were making love under the unblinking eye of the God of War.

Two Days from Landing

Late that night, with the ship still braking, he left Anita dozing under Mars and half-floated, half-pulled his way to the bar.

He found a handful of the hardcore drinkers there, and Captain Leuprecht.

Leuprecht was upending the last of a martini when Dennis pulled in beside him and hooked into the footholds. "Captain. Last orders?"

Leuprecht smiled at him. "Twenty-four hours from bottle to throttle." He looked at his watch, the sort of ornate thing favoured by pilots. "This here says I've got another hour."

"Well, then how about I join you?" He signalled the bartender, a slip of an Asian girl, for two more martinis. "Are you okay?"

Leuprecht popped an olive out of the end of his bulb, watched it spin for a minute, then pounced on it like a hungry trout. "I am now."

Dennis took his martini and nodded slowly.

Leuprecht caught his doubt. "Don't worry. It's my last chance to land on a planet. I'm looking forward to it."

"Then why don't you stay?"

Suddenly, the Captain lowered his voice. "You don't understand Merlin Duplessis. He blames me for what happened, and if I ever put myself in his back pocket again, he'd crush me without a second thought. With all the shit that's going on back on Earth, Mars is the safest place for me. In the end, Merlin will destroy himself, and things will change."

Dennis shook his head, confused. "If you hate him so much, then why did you fly with him?"

Leuprecht shrugged. "Only game in town, man. Who else was doing what he was? I guess I'm like one of those German generals. 'I like all the making Germany great again shit, just not the other stuff.' In the end, it's always a package deal."

"Aren't you worried he'll find an easy way to dispose of you on Mars? Big planet, no cops."

"Why would he? I'll just be a middle-grade engineer with no private comms access, toiling away like a good little drone. Pioneering a new world. Raising a family on Mars. No threat to him."

"Even if you're in his back pocket?"

"Pockets are a little roomier in $1/3^{rd}$ gee."

Dennis chuckled and polished off his martini. "If you say so."

Leuprecht finished his and pushed away from the bar. "Better get some rest and polish up on my descent procedures. See you on the surface."

"Okay." Dennis waved a hand, absently, and took out a dog-eared copy of *The Martian Chronicles,* one he'd had since he was a kid.

Leuprecht noticed it. "I loved that book as a kid. Say, Dennis, Juan always sat in a jump seat up front. Nobody's claimed it yet. Considering everything you've done for this colony, not to mention making us all immortal, would you like to watch the landing over my shoulder?"

What would Anita say? She would say, yes. "Yes. I would."

"I'll see you this time tomorrow for pre-planetfall briefing. Meet me in Paula's office, I'll bring you up."

"Hey, thanks…uh…"

"Josh. My name is Josh."

"See you tomorrow, Josh."

Dennis moved to a table with a better view of Mars, ordered another martini, and took out Bradbury's novel. As the world of the novel hung tantalizingly close, he read the almost century-old words of the tale of men against a harsh and mysterious planet.

We earth men have a talent for ruining big, beautiful things.

He meditated on that one for a long while, as Hellas spun past him slowly, and he sipped at his martini.

Landing Day

Dennis floated up against the restraints as the long braking burn finally ended. In front of him, the two flight engineers worked their checklists and adjusted switch settings. In front of them, Leuprecht and his First Officer worked in silence, their glass cockpit displays bathing the cockpit in eerie blue light.

Dennis' jump seat was bolted to the bulkhead, on the left of the entrance hatch. One of the other stewards, the Asian girl from the bar, sat opposite him, engrossed in the spectacle. Another future starship captain, perhaps?

Suddenly, his stomach pitched forward. Mars filled the cockpit windows dramatically, now dominating the view.

"Pitch over! T-minus five. Arm descent thrusters."

"Armed. Give me an altitude reading." Leuprecht was tense, speaking through gritted teeth. Dennis hoped he was really as cool as he tried to maintain.

"Twenty-four-five. Descending. Three minutes to drogue deploy. Twenty-three. Down one-five."

"Right."

As the two pilots called out to each other tersely, the engineers worked silently, monitoring the critical balance of the spaceship turned glider, as it lifted its wings against the heat of re-entry. A pale pink glow filled the cabin. Dennis remembered the *Columbia* disaster of his youth and closed his eyes for a minute. Surely, that would not be their fate.

His stomach fluttered upward again, and now red surface filled the entirety of their windows. The angle of attack drifted downward, and the heating phase mercifully ended. But now, for Dennis, a new terror. They appeared to be headed straight for the middle of Hellas Basin, at a 100-degree angle. He closed his eyes again.

"Drogue deploy in three, two, one…"

The thrusters' continuous pinging was silenced. And then, a great force pulled him back against the bulkhead. Over the engineers' shoulders, he spied an aft-looking screen, a bright white parachute cover flying backwards at speed before plummeting to the desert below, followed by a massive, red-and-white canopy billowing out behind.

His stomach swam figure-eights. He looked over at the Asian

girl, saw her going green, and touched the vomit bags sticking out of his breast pocket. With effort, he swallowed his bile, focusing his eyes on the center of Hellas basin.

With another jolt, the chute was gone, shooting back into the winds and tumbling as it disappeared. Now, it began to look like a spaceship landing, the kind he had always imagined.

Leuprecht was in full control now, events having slowed to a speed manageable by human decision. "Final approach, I have the beacon."

"You're level at three-zero. Approaching datum point."

Now, all they could see on all sides was the walls of the great basin. Stacks and layers of geologic time, punched through by the great bolide, rose above and past them. It would've been claustrophobic, but Dennis understood how massive the Hellas Basin was. Leuprecht could've flown aerobatics with room to spare.

Fuel was the only concern now. Leuprecht had *John Carter* flying as smoothly as an express elevator. "Six percent remaining, one-five, take her down."

"Nothing to it. Stand by for landing."

One of the engineers made an announcement. "Passengers and crew, brace for landing." Dennis wondered what Anita was feeling.

"Ten, nine, eight, seven, six, five, four, three, two, one…contact light! Shutdown!"

They fell the last few meters with a thud. Then, silence. Outside the windows, nothing but pink dust was visible in every direction.

"Ladies and gentlemen, welcome to Mars." Even through the thick walls of the storm shelter, Dennis could hear the applause.

The dust fell away, gradually. They could only see the pink sky through the rendezvous windows on the cabin ceiling. Ahead, and around, the multi-layered walls of the Hellas Basin surrounded them. A cluster of habitation modules, linked to their landing pad by a raised, sinuous tunnel, were the first evidence of human habitation.

They rested on a broad landing pad, and as the engineers safed the switch settings and the pad's ventilation units cleared the dust, a long gantry reached out towards them. Rugged little vehicles approached them from all sides.

Just like an airport. Only gradually did it dawn on Dennis that he was feeling the unfamiliar pull of gravity again. Only this was a thin, weak imitation of that on Earth, and he still felt his movements to be languid and slow.

Leuprecht unhooked from his chair and stood suddenly, removing his helmet. "Whoa." He quickly braced himself against the console. "Never ready for that."

"Captain." One of engineers, a compact, scarily fit woman with a serious butch cut, called him over to her monitor. "Feed from the access gantry."

"Oh." Leuprecht sagged a moment, then stood up straight. Dennis could see three men in uniform, apparently armed, bracing themselves as the gantry rattled towards *John Carter*. "I suppose that's my reception committee."

"For what?" Dennis was indignant. "He promised you! Let me go down there with you, I can intercede. He owes me!"

Leuprecht rested a trembling hand on Dennis' shoulder. "No. This is my row to hoe, Dennis. I'll call you if I need a really good lawyer. Okay?"

"You'd better."

Leuprecht turned to the engineer. "You come down with me to open the hatch and equalize the pressures, Brenda. Tony, organize the deplaning. Make sure the passengers don't see whatever happens, okay?"

The First Officer stood tentatively. "You gonna be okay, Cap?"

"Of course, I will. I'm on Mars." With that, Leuprecht straitened his suit and descended to the lower deck. A minute later, thuds and thunks announced the arrival of the gangway. Dennis watched in silence as Leuprecht exited the ship and spoke to the armed men. Momentarily, they led him away.

The other engineer, a tall blonde with laugh lines and dark brows, sighed. "It's Mars, all right." She whispered back to Dennis. "And Mars is no democracy. Don't forget that, Dr Rosso."

Dennis watched as the last of the landing dust settled. They were on Mars.

But it was no brave new world. That much, was already apparent.

2117

Inhibitors and facilitators

Station Inn
Atlanta

Dennis had spent a nearly-sleepless night fighting off nightmares of giant, tumorous clonal meat blobs, complete with screaming women and stampeding crowds.

It was either that, or Leuprecht, emerging from his exile, a hollowed-out shell; Kassabian and his bitter end; or Anita…Anita.

Finally, he'd surrendered at 3AM, swallowing a Sonambulol with a Shiraz chaser. Maybe that was why the increase in suicides, he reflected. Long lives left too many memories. Too much mental flotsam bobbing to the surface. Before he fell asleep, he'd dictated a note.

Morning was announced with the lifting of the opaque shades on the windows, revealing Atlanta from 30 stories up. Compared to the views he got at home, or the ones he'd had in Hellas, it was nothing.

Hellas. Dennis stood in front of the window, naked, thinking of Hellas, Hellas and that fucking little dog. *Ah.*

Lontraine had seemed so damned interested in that little dog. A worrying sign in someone who'd actually lived on pre-revolution Mars. All his buggered luck had led him there. But had he let anything slip? He needed to concentrate, and the after-effects of the Sonambulol were not helping.

"Doctor Kassabian, good morning. Would you like your usual?"

The suitebot greeted him in the manner he preferred. Not cult-like cheeriness, but resigned, professional servitude. Like he imagined an old, tired dog would.

"Yes, suite. Java roast, dark, two crème, two brown sugar. And a *pain raisin,* if you please."

Old, tired dog. Fuck!

He'd forgotten about Nobel Warrior 3. Nobel Warrior 3 was *not* the last of his line. That distinction belonged to Nobel Warrior 5. How could he have forgotten? The entire colony had laughed when Kassabian had sent Lontraine, then a junior JC Bryan Executive on his way home from a ten-year-tour of Mars, back to Earth with Nobel Warrior 3 in stasis.

That fucking well was Nobel Warrior 3, back in that meat plant, sniffing his Oxfords. And Lontraine knew it. He texted Latoya.

Road trip time. Bring a suitcase and pick me up at the hotel at 11.

Why so soon

I'll explain on the way. This suite makes a great cup of joe, but it also has ears.

10-4

The dispenser produced his coffee and pastry, and he stood before the view of Atlanta's towers and parks, enjoying it all with a prodigious erection.

He never did get aroused by the simple things. Imminent death and a road trip would have to do.

North of Tallahassee

Florida Unincorporated Zone

They had left civilization behind on the other side of the Georgia/Florida state border. Two bored State Troopers manned an armoured car at a barricade. Two more vehicles waited in a nearby stand of woods.

"Whatcha all goin' south for, ma'am?" The trooper was freckled and red-haired, looking to Dennis like he was all of twenty. Of course, thanks to Dennis, he could've been a hundred. He carried a rifle that looked like it could kill people in at least five different ways, depending on the switch setting.

It was already noon, and a sweltering vapor rose from the woods and shallow ponds.

"We're medical researchers with a letter from the DCC." Latoya slowly reached into her briefcase and withdrew Feng's note. "Here it is."

The Trooper sleepily scanned the document. "Some kind of disease outbreak we oughta know about?"

"Suicide." Dennis interjected. "There was a story on the news not too long ago."

"Well." The Trooper looked towards Florida and chewed a piece of gum in consideration. "That is where them 'Facilitators' live. But they's all in some pretty bad areas, y'all follow? Hope you's armed."

Dennis handed over his permit. "Here is my authorization."

"You know how to handle it? Ain't no good if you don't know how to handle it." Dennis noticed blast scars on his armour. Despite the looks, the kid had probably seen ten years' worth of action down here.

"I'm a combat veteran, yes." Dennis had never described himself as such to anyone. But it was certainly a true statement.

"Then I don't need to hold you up. Be back before dark, okay?"

"Thank you, Trooper." Latoya waved as they drove away. She looked back at Dennis. "Combat veteran, eh? You got the license plates, an all?" She laughed, a high-pitched twitter.

He smiled at her. "Not sure I'd qualify. But yes, the last year on Mars was…well, it was pretty damned bad. I killed people to survive, Latoya. So, I do know how to use the gun."

"I don't mean to make fun." They passed roadside shacks advertising all manner of vices. Illegal drugs. Illegal guns. Illegal sex. "Why Florida, I wonder?"

"A comedian back in my time described Florida as, 'Hot, flat, and dumb.' I guess they couldn't adapt."

"Yeah, I suppose. All the white folks who got driven out of Atlanta in the riots wound up here. Then the war and the Red Foam added more." They passed a knot of angry looking, barefoot kids in a weedy field. "Defensive screens please." Latoya's command energized the vehicle's force barriers, just as rocks and old glass bottles flew in their direction. "Georgia vehicles are not popular here."

"Hopefully it's not far." Dennis looked back. The kids had poured onto the road and were now shaking fists and dragging tree branches and logs into the thruway.

"It's okay. Gandalf has a crew here."

"Gandalf?"

Latoya laughed. "He thinks he's a wizard. A wizard of death."

"Sounds pleasant."

"Actually, if you didn't know his business, you would think so. Very well read, if not formally educated. Soft spoken, so's you've got to ask him to speak up all the time. And well-mannered, like southern gentlemen used to be."

"Oh."

"People here have to make money any way they can. Almost all of them are Uncontrolled, so there's no legal way for them to work up north. Those that do get the miracle, a lot of the treatments are bad. They use the same stuff that JC Bryson does, not for human consumption, you know?"

Latoya's monologue got him thinking about JC Bryson again. "Tumors."

"Pardon me, Henrik?"

"Tumors. That's basically what JC Bryson is growing. Without inhibitors, the cells in their clonal meat are giant, out of control tumours, their growth killed only with salt. It took us two years how to learn to inhibit that kind of relentless cell growth, you know. We couldn't publish, wouldn't publish, until we had that down pat. The moment we did, we find out that Arjan has built his own fucking lab in India, double-crossing Satwant and I, who'd been working 24/7 on the inhibitors."

Latoya was staring at him. "Henrik? I didn't know you worked with Dennis Rosso so soon."

Jesus. You fucking idiot. "Part of the 'Untold Story of Henrik Kassabian.' Coming soon to your holo. We were a small, incestuous bunch."

"I guess." She slowed the car. A gravel turnoff lead to a house surrounded by overgrown elms. A small sign next to the turnoff read:

LIFE COUNSELLING. PALMISTRY. SPECIAL NEEDS.
H: 850-667-55664

"Special needs, eh?"

"Yeah, this is it." They drove down the gravel drive and

pulled up in front of the house. It was an ancient, antebellum affair, shambolic and grand. A massively pregnant skinny girl emerged from inside.

"You all here to see the Wizard?"

Dennis stepped out of the car. "The Wonderful Wizard of Oz."

"Ha ha." She wiped her nose. Dennis tried hard to supress his white trash prejudices, but the pregnant girl in the halter top with the runny nose was not helping.

Latoya stepped in. "We have an appointment with Gandalf."

"Oh yeah, you're the doctor lady. Um, can I ask you something?"

"What's that, sweetie?"

"There ain't no good doctors down here. Would you check out my baby and me, see if things is all right? I done lost my last one, is all."

Dennis stared. It was like going back a century and a half, maybe further. *And I have lived on Mars.* "Sure, honey." Latoya answered. She retrieved a paramedic bag from the back of her car. "What's your name?"

"Marigold." The girl looked back into the house. "The Wizard will see you now."

They walked up the steps slowly together. "This is so fucking weird. These people would've fit right in at Woodstock." Dennis whispered.

"Where?"

The house was gloomy, lit by a few faint bulbs powered by windmill, and a hundred tea lights. Indian music played in the background. The Wizard, a tall, thin man, sat at the other end of a long dining room table. He wore, true to his chosen name, a thin black robe with a hood that concealed his face.

"Welcome Latoya." His voice was surprisingly deep. "Still studying my troubled flock?"

"Yes, Gandalf. And now I have interested a Nobel Laureate."

"Oh, really?" He stood and walked towards them. "You are?"

"Dr Henrik Kassabian." He watched Latoya out of the corner of his eye as he introduced himself. No expression.

Gandalf took down his hood. The man was shaved bald, his narrow skull and thin eyes giving him a piercing expression. He offered his long, thin hand, and Dennis shook it. "What an honour. I suppose you have already deduced that we don't accept the miracle in these parts, nor the sterilizer."

"I can see that. Freedom of choice."

"Not quite. The people in the north do not really believe that. But anyway, how can I help?"

"We're still researching excess mortality. Our working theory is, it may be related to the miracle."

Now, Latoya was looking at him. "Remember how last time, I asked you to make up some case notes, on the people who come to you for aid?"

Gandalf lifted a finger. "One moment." He walked over to an ancient rollup desk, slid open the cover, and retrieved a file folder. He handed it to Latoya. "Thirty-five cases since you last came to see me. I've documented them all. What's more, I've obtained the agreement of one of my Facilitators up north. A man named Virgil. He'll show you how it's done. I believe he has a case at 4PM today. If you hurry, you may be able to witness it."

Dennis shook his head, his mouth suddenly dry. "Witness what?"

Gandalf gave him an unnerving smile. "Why, a suicide, of course."

2041

Pioneers

Mars
Hellas Base

Dennis took his first steps onto the surface of Mars ten minutes after he witnessed the arrest of Captain Leuprecht. When he did, there was someone waiting for him, too. Anita was behind him on the gangway, escorting a barely functioning Jerry.

A diminutive brown man in a sharp black suit, his bald head shining in the lights, barged through the arriving passengers to meet Dennis. "Dr Rosso? I am Prithpal Deo, the Q-Space Manager of Operations for Hellas Base. Mr Duplessis was certain you would have questions. Why don't we meet right now and get them answered, yes?"

Dennis stared at him, emotionally and physically exhausted. "I need food and drink, a shower, and a bed I can actually lie down in. Then, we can talk."

Anita grabbed his arm. A group of medics had Jerry on a gantry and were taking him away. "Dennis, what about Captain Leuprecht? There's all kinds of rumours flying around back there."

Deo smiled tightly with a row of perfect teeth. "There are always rumours, Mrs Rosso. But I can assure you, Captain Leuprecht has merely been taken in for questioning as regards the events during the voyage. An extra day of rest will not change this situation. I assure you he will not be harmed."

Anita nodded, a tight expression on her face. "That's good to hear."

"Please, which way to our quarters?" The sudden burden of three months of travel was crushing him down. Or maybe it was the gravity?

"This way, please." Deo led them to an elevator. A large, imposing aid who looked like a sumo wrestler followed at a distance. "Arthur, that will be fine. Please ensure Mr Cornell is looked after." The aid retreated and waited as they boarded the elevator. "Level two, please."

Everything was spotless and white. It reminded him of a TV show he'd watched as a child. Duplessis, a fanatic about science fiction, had consciously aped the designs of the future from the fantasies of the past.

The elevator was soundless, as were nearly all of Duplessis' creations. It deposited them on a quiet, spotless floor with narrow corridors and numbered doors. To their right, a picture window of thick glass allowed them to look up at the bulk of *John Carter*, seemingly big again after three months of claustrophobia.

Deo watched with them as little vehicles darted around the giant spaceship, and space-suited men hooked up umbilicals and opened doors under a salmon sky. "The future is finally here."

"Hmm?" Dennis was so tired, he leaned against the glass, even as he couldn't take his eyes from the scene.

"The future, Dr Rosso. Didn't you wonder, growing up, what had happened to the future? I remember how slowly space travel progressed. How we got sick and died from the same things, year after year. How our cars belched fumes, like our grandfathers' cars had. And then, suddenly, the future arrived.

Thanks to men like you, and men like Merlin Duplessis."

"Thanks. We're on Mars. It still seems funny to say it…"

Deo smiled for the first time. "And so it will be for weeks, maybe months. I have been here a year, and I still have to pinch myself. Come, let me show you your quarters."

They followed Deo a short way down the narrow hallway to a room marked *223*. "This is your new home. Please rest, and I assure you a conference call with Mr Duplessis at your earliest convenience. Once again, welcome to Mars." He gave a slight bow and retreated down the hall.

Anita had already opened the door with a thumbprint scan. "Wow."

Another thick and wide window looked out on Hellas Base, a place of flat, buried domes, snaking tunnels, and transparent greenhouses. Four and six-wheeled vehicles hurried along roads of hard-packed dust, occasionally emerging from or entering into a massive garage underneath their window. There was no sound. In the distance, the great rim of the basin rose towards the sky in one direction, disappearing beyond the horizon in the others. Lights in the basin wall suggested work on Duplessis' great new city, soon to be the capital of a terraformed Mars.

"Look at this." Anita rolled back the covers on a compact, but serviceable queen bed. Then she fiddled with a remote that substituted a variety of views for their real surroundings. Deep space, country meadow, coral reef…

Dennis put a steadying hand on the bed and crawled under the covers. "Don't you want to see the bathroom?" She called.

But he was already facedown and snoring hard.

The Next Day

Dennis awoke with an awful taste in his mouth. He looked at the clock embedded in the headboard. It displayed Universal Earth Time and date, and Mars time and date:
UET 41/01/16 05:34:22
LST 46/7/402 197.7

Dennis rubbed his head. He was beginning to regret missing so much of Duplessis' boot camp. Maybe he'd actually know what time it was. He did know that Mars had a 25-hour day, so hopefully that shouldn't be so disorienting. The year was more than twice as long, he knew that too. But telling time? What the hell did 197.7 mean? Was this *Star Trek*?

He stepped out of bed uncertainly. The gravity came again as a surprise, and if it weren't for the low ceilings, he'd have been tempted to jump on the bed. The picture window was opacified, so he tried a voice command. "Room, open blinds." The black screen disappeared, leaving him staring directly at a low, rising sun. Or was it a setting one?

The sun, over Mars. All of the men and machines, none of whose pace appeared to have slackened, were now cast in long shadows. Dennis looked at the scene in satisfaction, then padded to the bathroom.

He enjoyed a seemingly endless piss, for the first time in months, not having his dick plugged into a hose. The golden stream arced lazily into the bowl of the toilet but was difficult to correct quickly if your aim was off. *Good to know.*

Once he'd finished, he stepped into the tiny shower cabinet, guarded by high, translucent walls, no doubt due to the gravity. To his dismay, he noted the warning under the shower head:

> DUE TO SUPPLY LIMITS, MAXIMUM
> SHOWER TIME IS FIVE MINUTES
> LET'S MAKE MARS GREEN!

Q-SPACE HELLAS BASE

It was glorious, nevertheless. "Room, Vivaldi please. *The Four Seasons.*"

Despite the events of the previous day, which he was determined not to forget, Dennis was entranced by his new surroundings. How could one not be? He had accomplished a boyhood dream, and he hadn't even put on a spacesuit and gone outside yet!

But part of him knew very well; this was Duplessis' game. Impress and seduce. His money and his talent had secured him a special place. He was certain few of the other colonists lived like this.

A thirty-second warning let him rinse off in the nick of time. He stepped out of the bathroom, towelling off, to find a closet full of identical pant/shirt/shoe combos. *Great. I'm going to spend the rest of my life dressed like a Gerry Anderson character.*

Resigned, and hungry, he dressed, and set out to find Anita.

Dennis quickly determined the boundaries of his own assigned world. Schematics on every info screen in the corridors were there to help the lost. He saw some of his fellow passengers in the corridors and exchanged waves.
Nobody seemed particularly glad to see each other. Maybe three months was enough.

"The Mound" or Primary Combined Complex 3, was four stories above, and two stories underground. It was linked to the rest of the complex by tunnels, whose node was in Sub-Level One. Above-Level Four housed administration, dining, and social facilities, as well as the landing control center.

Above-Levels Three and Two were First-Class residential and Family residential units. Above-Level One was 3D printing and Pool/Fitness, as well as Operations and Maintenance Offices, and Surface Airlocks One and Two. Sub-Level One, in addition to housing the transport tunnels, was home to the Surface Transport Garage, and Storage Cubes One and Two.

Sub-Level Two housed Storage Cubes Three and Four, as well as Waste Treatment, Recycling, and Water Facilities.

A quick walk around The Mound revealed picture windows on every axis. At the opposite end of the launch/landing pads, which from the signage Dennis deduced was "South," a window revealed a steadily rising sun (his guess was right), as well as four clusters of low shelters in the distance, with a single, shared tunnel linking them to The Mound. On the "West" side, two massive shapes topped with heat shimmers occupied the far horizon, the rim of Hellas too far away to be seen.

Those giant shapes had to be the Tokamaks, Duplessis' fusion reactors, the engine of growth on a planet too far from the sun and too windblown to rely on solar.

Putting it together in his head, Dennis visualized a drone's-eye-view of Hellas Base:

In the Center: The Mound, the other two massive Combined Complexes.

In the North: The launch and landing facilities, spacecraft storage.

In the West: The Tokamaks, and Waste Handling 1 and 2.

In the South: Basic Habitation Complexes 1-4, and Greenhouse 3.

In the West: Basic Habitation Complexes 5-6, Greenhouses 1 and 2, and the road to Rim Project Sub-Base.

He was sure there was much he did not yet understand, but that could wait until after something more urgent had been addressed.

Breakfast.

**Above-Level Four
Dining Room 6**

Dennis found his breakfast, and Anita, in the dining room. He walked over to find her talking with Jerry over coffee, in low tones. "Hi partner." He put a hand on Jerry's big shoulder. "Nice to see you."

Jerry smiled at him, some light back in his eyes, a huge change from the Jerry of the last month. "It's nice to see you, too, Dennis. I tell you, this place sure is something. I could get used to it around here."

Anita stood. "Let me get you something, honey. Be warned… the bacon is…challenging."

Dennis sat. "That's okay. I don't recall seeing any pigs being brought on board."

"Man, one more thing I'm gonna miss." Jerry smiled. "Coffee's not half bad though."

"I'll be the judge of that, Jerry. I'm from Seattle."

"Okay then." The big man seemed fragile still but headed in the right direction. "I got a notice today from the Manager, that Deo fellow? He says he wants me out there with a team, looking for water, as soon as I feel up to it. Guess it's a match for my previous experience."

"You sure you ready?"

Jerry waved a hand. "Ah hell, I checked myself out of hospital and into my room last night, Dennis. I come up here and had a long look at the stars. The stars from Mars, Dennis. Including one bright blue one. Yessir, that's the one. I came all this way for a reason, sir, and I am sure Patricia wouldn't want me a crying and a moping, no sir. Time to get back to work."

Anita arrived with his breakfast. A bowl of porridge, an apple, which looked half the size of a regular apple, and three strips of...something. He tentatively picked up one of the strips and tasted it. "Jesus! On what planet is that supposed to be bacon?"

Jerry chuckled. "Not this one, anyway. We're all gonna have to adjust."

Dennis nodded. "You got that right." He sipped his coffee. "Not bad."

Anita laughed. "Finally, I may be able to teach you what *Lagom* is all about." Her face changed to a serious one, and her voice got quiet. "What about Captain Leuprecht?" She looked around to emphasize her point. *Be careful.*

Dennis nodded slowly. "I'll talk to Deo and set up a meeting with Duplessis."

"Some meeting. Twenty-minute time lag each way?"

"Are you suggesting I wait?"

"No." She shrugged. "It can't wait. It can't wait at all."

Out on the landing pad, a massive tow vehicle began to slowly move the *John Carter* into a gigantic hangar, to prepare it for its next voyage. Without Captain Leuprecht.

2117

This phony eternity

US-319 (Restricted)
Northbound

They passed long, flat, shimmering lakes surrounded by crumbling levees, burned out houses, rusted cars. The afternoon was getting hot, and only a few of the denizens of this borderland were out in the shadeless sun.

They were stopped, twice, but luckily there was still a military presence here, and the presentation of Feng's magic letter smoothed things over.

"Why on earth is the Army down here?" Latoya asked, as they pulled away from a checkpoint manned by bored conscripts in threadbare uniforms, most likely former Uncontrolled paying off their transition to Normie status with a five-year stint.

"It's still part of the country. If we weren't here, maybe the Brazilians or the Argentines would move in. Maybe even the Russians. Anyway, we harvest these people. All those kids back there, wearing our uniforms? All on a hitch to pay off their miracle. Nobody who is already immortal wants to join the army anymore."

"Are we back in Georgia?"

"Haven't seen any Staties yet. Vehicle, map." A holo screen shimmered in front of Dennis. "No, another twenty minutes."

"Can't come fast enough. This place gives me the creeps."

Dennis chuckled. "Then stop doing the limit. There's no traffic cops down here." Dennis paused as a thought occurred to him. "If Virgil's on your list, why did we have to come down here to meet him? I mean, isn't that a bit risky, not to mention… inefficient?"

Latoya nodded. "What Virgil does may not be technically illegal, but people like him are usually into lots of things that are. They often change their contact info five or ten times a year. If you're serious about meeting them, you've got to commit to a road trip to the swamps. In California, on the other hand, you can practically find them in the directory."

"Bad people, doing bad things. And a sweet Southern girl like you. Quite a mix."

Latoya smiled bashfully. "My mother would be so angry." The little electric hummed and accelerated. Up ahead, a log rolled out of a stand of trees and into the road.

"Watch out! Swerve left!"

"Oh my God!" Latoya threw the wheel over, and suddenly they were on a frightening incline, a sodden morass below them, only a crumbling shoulder holding them to the road. Dennis braced himself against the door, ludicrously trying to shift his weight to keep them from toppling over. Latoya gave the car a burst of power, just enough to give the tires some scrabbling purchase on the gravel, and they mounted the bank just as the engine cut out. "Oh no, Henrik!"

Dennis reached into his waistband for the Glock. With no power, the defensive shields would not activate. "It's just rebooting. Look."

On the displays, a maddening orange palm said *Please Wait. Restart in Progress.*

The log was well behind them, but the people who'd pushed it onto the road were not. A dozen men and women, with dull clothing and bright hair, were running full tilt for them. The first shots sounded. The mirror next to Dennis exploded as he took a knee on the pavement and aimed the Glock.

"Come on baby, come on!" Latoya watched the display, her nails tapping the glass.

Dennis spotted a string bean figure with bright orange hair, carrying a shotgun in his right hand, and some sort of skull-topped standard in his left. *The leader.* Another round punched through the windshield between them. Latoya ducked.

"Please, Jesus, please."

The red dot from his laser sight showed right over the leader's sternum. The leader looked down, then locked eyes with Dennis.

Dennis fired, and a hole the size of a baseball appeared in the leader. He toppled. A woman behind him didn't pause, grabbing the shotgun and the standard with a grim determination.

Dennis opened her head with a second shot, and she toppled over the leader's body. That was, apparently, the total supply of leaders for this group. The rest of the mob began to run in the other direction. Dennis sat back in the car. The console lights were now green. "Go."

Latoya took a deep breath and peeled back onto the highway. Behind them, Army drones were chasing the group back into the woods.

"Oh my. I've had some excitement as a paramedic, but that takes it all."

"Breathe, Latoya. You did great." Dennis topped up the Glock with a fresh magazine. "Look, Troopers. We're safe." Three sleek grey hovercars were parked around a chicane of barriers.

She rested a long hand on his thigh. His body began to respond in the only possible manner. Suddenly, she turned red and pulled the hand away. "Sorry."

He put his hand on her thigh and left it there. "I'm not apologizing."

Thomasville, Georgia
The Interlude Motel

They say danger is an aphrodisiac. Dennis had never seen anything to repudiate this statement, and now, wordlessly, they acted on their instincts.

The room was nothing fancy, clearly a place for "interludes," but at least the area seemed more comfortably mixed than Atlanta had been. No hostile stares or threatening glares.

They stripped each other with uncontained passion, then showered together in a lingering, sensual ritual. Dennis' ardour needed no artificial assistance, propelled by Latoya's solid curvaceousness and the sheen of her skin.

Their lovemaking was reckless and without grace, punctuated with brief bursts of laughter. It was exactly what they both needed. She trembled to the touch when he took her, as did he, the aftermath of their adrenaline surge fueling them both. Better judgement overcome now; they crossed a line they would not have they would not have the day before.

Their "interlude" concluded; they resumed their travels.

Buford Power Complex
Lake Lanier

The old dam that had created Lake Lanier, a lush oasis of parkland just north of the city, was dwarfed by Tokamaks now, the new means of powering the world.

They pulled into a scenic overlook and admired the view. At the far end of the long lake, arcologies rose into the clouds. Down here, flocks of waterfowl settled in the waters, overlooked by spreading deciduous trees. Dennis breathed deeply. The greenspace and the Tokamaks were a curious juxtaposition for him, one reminding him what he'd missed about earth, the other taking him back, decisively, to Duplessis' Mars.

"Lovely, isn't it." Latoya slipped her hand into his. He didn't mind, being with a woman was natural and right; although he still doubted that he was capable of love after Anita.

Perhaps the worst aspect of immortality: all of pretences to "eternal" this and "forever" that would be tested in the end. Maybe there was no such thing. Maybe he should just let go.

A tall black man called to them from across the parking lot. "Y'all is late! Another five minutes and we go without you!"

Dennis walked over to him slowly. "Sorry about that. You must be Virgil." He extended a hand.

Virgil sucked on a row of gold teeth and ignored the hand. A white couple stood behind him under a gazebo, checking the straps on hoverpacks fastened to their backs. "Yeah, that's me. Gandalf send you?"

"Yeah."

"Whatchu wanna know anyhow?"

"What do you do, exactly?"

Virgil looked over him. "Hey, Latoya, this chump witchu?"

"This chump has a Nobel Prize, Virgil. He's trying to help me find out why everyone's killing themselves lately."

Virgil shrugged. "Don' know nothing 'bout that." Though his manner was more 'last-century pimp' than most's, Virgil dressed like a middle-class technocrat. The gold teeth were the only conceit of a gangster. "I just take the money."

"So, these people pay you?" Dennis indicated the couple. They had completed their preparations, and now made out, heedless of their audience. Virgil looked back at them.

"Aw, now that's nice. Nah, Professor, that's the beauty of it. Yeah, I used to take money, but it ain't cheap. Now, my new business model is pay-per-view."

"Say again?"

"Those jetpacks, they ain't cheap, amirite? These people ain't got the money for them, and my services besides. But who does? Holoscene, that's who! I set the kids up with everything, plus I negotiate access with the power company. Holoscene already has cameras set up on the grounds, and reporters to cover all this shit. See?"

A woman reporter and a holocam man were already interviewing the couple. "They're not gonna…"

Virgil sucked his teeth again. "Nah, they know better."

"Is this legal?"

"Um, well, kind of overlooked, you see. Ain't nobody supposed to be so unhappy anymore, what with the miracle and all. So, I just kind of prefer to avoid…uh…controversy, yeah."

"And the power company knows?" Latoya was incredulous.

"Why do you think it's just us on a nice day like today? They knew you was coming. The amount they get from Holoscene is like, one day of power bills for Atlanta, man. These holos make cash, know what I'm sayin?"

"Nobody says anything?" Dennis shared Latoya's open-mouthed response. "I mean, it's all over the place…"

Virgil sighed, as if he were explaining things to two slow children. "Wait till you see. Ain't nothing left. *Nothing.* Besides, suicide ain't even illegal! Yeah, I get some bullshit sometimes, especially from tax motherfuckers, but nobody push too hard, ya' understand?"

"How come I haven't heard of this?" Dennis persisted.

"'Cause you so square you make a coffin look cool. Besides, I only been doing it two months now. Most people still think it's fake. Okay, they done. Showtime." The reporter and her holo man retreated, and Virgil led them down the hill to his clients.

They were a bright-looking couple with hope written on their faces. They greeted Dennis and Latoya like it was a wedding reception. "Hi there!" The man wore a nervous grin. He was sunburned, under a lion's mane of blond hair. "I'm Dave Phillips. This is my wife, Tammy!"

She was thin, with piercing blue eyes and perfect teeth. "Hi there. Thanks for being here for our special moment." They performed a ghastly ritual of handshaking.

Dennis looked them over. They were both dressed in thin white jumpsuits. The hoverpacks were late models, light weight and compact. He noticed with distaste that they bore corporate advertising.

"I see you have sponsors."

"Oh yes, we could never have afforded this on our own. Google, Coca-Cola, and Holoscene have helped us achieve our dream."

"Which is?"

"To find true eternal life, not man's hollow version, in the bosom of Jesus Christ Our Lord and Savior." Tammy smiled warmly.

A sudden gust of warm wind came up, as if God himself was accenting the message. Dennis absorbed it in silence. *Man's hollow version.*

"But doesn't God abhor suicide?" Latoya pressed.

"In a world without natural death, how else to achieve eternal peace?" Dave challenged her. "The so-called 'miracle' is a one-way street. After we have violated God's plan for us, we must wait for an unlikely accident or act of violence. Most of those result only in suffering, then unholy rebirth. We are tired of being withheld from receiving God's reward."

"One-hundred years for me on the earth, one-hundred-three for Dave. We have seen everything we wanted to see, done everything we wanted to do. Our children have moved to the Colonies. We will never have grandchildren. Frankly, we're tired." Now, Dennis could see the sadness in Tammy's eyes.

"What if there's nothing?"

Dave was dogmatic. "There's something, you bet!"

Tammy was more pragmatic. "Then at least Google paid for it, not us. Would you pray with us?"

Dennis stammered. "Okay."

They formed a ring while Virgil, of all people, led them in the Lord's Prayer. Dennis' head was swimming. Only Latoya's grip on his hand kept him from fleeing. At the conclusion of the prayer, Dave looked up, jaw set firmly against the azure blue sky. "It's time."

Dennis and Latoya held hands and walked back to the gentle knoll at the edge of the parking lot. There they sat and awaited the Phillips' date with eternity. *Real eternity.*

Birds sang in the distance. Ducks splashed. All of creation, going through the eternal rituals of life and death. All except man. *All because of you, Dennis Rosso.* Latoya looked at him, concerned. "Are you okay, Henrik? What are you feeling?"

Henrik, Henrik. He was sick to death of carrying that man's name around. So desperately, he wanted to tell her. "I don't know. When this is over…I…I want…"

"What?" But Virgil returned and sat next to them. He carried a little control unit with a camera attached.

"Liftoff time. I can take over if I need to, but they usually do okay. Here we go."

First Dave, then Tammy took off, a straight vertical ride that appeared to thrill them both. Then, they did lazy figure-eights over the lake before heading back for the Tokamaks. Suddenly, the air was split with a thunderous alarm.

"What the hell was that?" Latoya was startled.

"Plasma gas venting. Thirty seconds. Look." Virgil pointed at the Tokamaks, where an electric blue ring had formed, one-third of the way up the venting stacks. "That ring is a level 2 force field. Gets rid of anything left over from the encounter."

"Like what?" Dennis' imagination was taking ghastly leaps.

"Don't know. There's never anything." He whispered into his mike. "Get over those stacks now. It's time. God bless you." He winked cynically at Latoya, who frowned in response.

The two flying Christians positioned themselves dutifully over the exhaust stack of the nearest Tokamak. Another deep tone sounded.

"Five seconds." Virgil explained. He raised his camera and zoomed in.

"Oh God, they're holding hands." Latoya embraced him. Dennis remembered, a snapshot from his childhood, two office workers plummeting from the World Trade Center on 9/11... holding hands.

There was a sudden rush of incandescent, pastel light. The two Christians were framed in outline for a second. Then, they were gone. The plume was still burning ferociously when Dennis and Latoya walked away.

2041

No democracy

Hellas Base
Mars

Dennis Rosso had noticed long ago that it was the habit of the rich and powerful to make others wait. In this, Merlin Duplessis had few equals. As did his wealth and power.

He knew he needed to be careful. On Earth, Duplessis might be powerful; here, he was virtually omnipotent. So, he'd kept his powder dry and his mouth shut as Deo put him off with one excuse after another. Two weeks had passed.

God knew what was happening to Leuprecht. He'd reassured Anita, whose sense of Swedish social justice was outraged by the case, that the good captain was unlikely to be hung upside down in a red-soiled dungeon somewhere. He was likely, Dennis had argued, to be suffering from the same torture as your husband:

Boredom. For not only had Duplessis kept him waiting on his hearing and failed to keep his promises to allocate VIP bandwidth to his calls home to Earth, but he had committed a far more egregious crime, in Dennis' eyes at least:

He had failed to give him anything to do. Dennis had taken advantage of VIP access to roam the facility far and wide. He'd visited his spotlessly clean and magnificently outfitted laboratory just down the hall from Deo's office. Twice as big as his workspace in Detroit, a major accomplishment on a planet where space was at a premium.

"Too bad they couldn't have given us a bigger room." Anita had observed sourly.

The problem was, everything was under plastic wrap. His supplies, which he was informed were here, were in freezers. His staff? He had no idea who they were.

So, he contented himself with sticking his nose in where it didn't belong. When Deo would send him a tut-tutting message about this, he would always respond the same way:

"Don't want me snooping? I'm a scientist. Give me a project."

Deo always let it pass, and soon stopped objecting. Dennis explored the proletarian abodes beyond the Mound, the cramped, stifling, smelly accommodation of the surface workers, greenhouse farmers, cleaners, and cafeteria workers who made the place run.

He showed Anita some holo, and she stopped complaining about the size of her room. "I guess that's not very *Lagom*, is it?" But the people who lived there, they were the real attraction for Dennis, and soon he was bringing along Anita on his expeditions.

There was no remoteness or stuffiness there. There couldn't be. People lived cheek-to-jowl, either on the promise of a homestead in the terraformed Mars of the future, or on a five or ten-year contract with the promise of riches on return to Earth.

The people were grimy, yes. They could only shower twice a week, unlike he and Anita. When he asked, he was startled to discover how many of them had not received the miracle yet. How could they afford it? It was one enticement that Duplessis had offered, one he suspected he would be asked to produce.

Why not? These people deserved eternal life every bit as much as any stuffed-shirt yacht owner back on Earth. These were the real pioneers, the ones drinking piss-flavoured water instead of single malt, the ones sleeping six to a room in tiny bunkbeds, with a communal sex room at the end of the pod, available only by reservation. The food was bland and repetitive, the entertainment being the only thing that closely approximated life on the Mound. Amazingly, after working ten-hour shifts on the surface or in the basement levels, many of these people were taking correspondence courses to better themselves.

There was a Horatio Alger aspect to it all that appealed to Dennis. So much so, that Anita had cautioned him drily: "Don't get too fond of it here. That Terry is quite a hunk, and I've seen Luz making eyes at you. We can switch bunks, just say the word."

"Slut."

"There's no word for that in Swedish. There is a merit badge, though."

But it was Terry who had given him his best idea yet for passing the time. Terry was a massive Canadian who drove heavy tractors, spending ten hours a day, six days a week in a little pressurized compartment. His wife Luz was a tiny Filipina. She joked about how she was getting far more than most internet brides expected in terms of culture shock.

"Calgary is crazy, ok, but Mars? Omigod, my mum still does not believe me!"

Terry had suggested a new pastime for them. "You been outside yet?"

"No. I didn't know who to ask."

"It's no secret or anything. My buddy Phil runs a class through the Rec department. Four hours in the classroom, then three trips outside. Last one is a blast. It's at night, eh?"

"Wow." He thought of Jerry's description of the Earth at night from Level Four, and knew they had to invite the big Texan.

And that was how he'd gotten here. Main Airlock One, nine of them arrayed around Phil, a taciturn Australian, and his assistant Trinh, a compact Vietnamese with a Sydney accent. The inner door was closed already, and now, only a thin wall stood between them and the perilously low pressure and temperature of Mars.

Dennis and Anita formed a protective detail for Jerry, holding hands with the big man.

They needn't have bothered. Jerry Cornell had undergone a sea change on Mars. "This is gonna be neat. Woo-ee!"

Phil laughed. "You bet, Jerry. It's fun every time I do it. Just remember the safety tips from class. Stay tethered to your mates, hit the alarm on your left wrist if things go to shit, and remember how to switch over to your backup O2 if your main is compromised. Any suit alarms or other anomalies, gift me a holler. Easy enough, ya reckon?"

"Yes!" They replied in unison.

Phil nodded to Trinh, who yanked a striped handle. Amber strobes went into overdrive as the air sucked out of the lock.

"Warning, warning! Fatal low pressure and temperature imminent! If not suited, hit emergency repress now!"

"Shutup." Trinh yelled good-naturedly. "Mars, here we come!"

"Oh boy! I really feel like a spaceman now!" Jerry tightened his grip on both their hands until they winced.

Tentatively, in the blowing red dust from the sudden opening of the airlock, they stepped into a new world. Some of these people had been on Mars for months, one of them for two years, before venturing outside.

They emerged into what could best be described as a little park. Hard-packed red dirt and flat stones covered an area the size of a football field, fenced off or shielded by the Mound on one side, Complex 2 on the other. Here, there was no chance they could be run over by tractors or get seriously lost. Phil had called it "The Playground."

But it was still on Mars. *They were walking on Mars.*

As if stealing his thoughts, Trinh yelled, high-pitched and joyous. "We're walking on Mars! Woo-ee!"

Some of the tethered walkers were already trying high jumps in the low-gee, landing in clouds of dust. "That looks like fun!" Anita shouted. Together, they launched, but Jerry pulled them back to Mars with a dusty red thud.

"Whoops!"

Phil brought them back down for a moment. He pointed to a plinth, surrounded by buried pot lights. "Might I interrupt the fun for a moment? Let us pay our respects to those who have perished in the founding and growing of this precious piece of civilization, so far from our home. Let us be silent a minute." He bowed his helmeted head, and the others followed suit.

As the tractors roared by on the roads outside, Dennis read the rapidly eroding etching on the plinth. He counted 24 names.

Death. Death still lived here. He may have conquered it for a few, the few with money and safe lives, but here there was so much to be done. He looked up, seeing a rare summer cirrus cloud passing overhead in the sonic winds.

Never had he felt more distant from Earth, and yet never had he felt so close to other people. There were so few of them, less than a thousand on a whole world. They had to be a family.

"Okay! Sad time is over, let's play!" Trinh got them moving again.

One hundred million miles from home, they played as children again, until their parents made them go inside.

Office of the Base Manager

After three weeks, he finally got his sit-down with Duplessis.

Given the distance, it could not be a real conversation. That would have to wait, until Duplessis arrived on an inspection tour in six months. Two days before, Deo had him record a series of questions for Duplessis, then to ensure nothing was being omitted, made him watch as he hit the transmit button.

"Just curious, how much does that cost?"

"Our Earthside phone bill averages a million three every month." Deo had smiled. "That's why you get an hour a month as VIPs."

"How much do the proles get?"

Deo had winced at the non-PC term. "We prefer 'Regular Staff.' They get fifteen minutes."

"Holy shit."

"They can save up for longer messages. Many of them prefer to spend an hour at Christmas, etc. We allow for this."

Mighty white of you.

Now, Deo watched him as he drank his proffered Scotch and watched out the Manager's panoramic windows. The *SS Mark Watney* was being mounted on a mobile launch gantry, in preparation for a take-off in two days' time.

"Amazing, isn't it? I still have to pinch myself sometimes." Deo was now beside him. "Ten years ago, I was running a battery plant in Bengal. Now, I am here." He sniffed at his scotch. "A large percentage of my personal effects was given over to this, I'm afraid."

"Not enough of mine was, I'm afraid. Any idea when we'll open a Duty Free?"

Deo chuckled mildly. "Not as crazy a question as you might think. Once the new Starshot-IV freighters come online, and our balance of payments sheet starts looking better, we'll begin importing more luxury goods."

"What goes back now?"

"Mainly samples for researchers on Earth, machinery that can't be fixed here, but is too expensive to throw away, and personnel. But there's been some exciting rare earth metals finds in the basin lately. If that pans out, expect to be drinking more scotch soon. After all, like everyone here, you're a shareholder."

"More scotch...don't know how I feel about that."

"Scotch is better than the rotgut they make over there." Deo waved his hand dismissively at the prole accommodations. "Greenhouse workers smuggle it in. You should hear the police channel on a Friday night. By the way, Anita reports for training next week."

Dennis swallowed. It was what she wanted. She'd been missing police work terribly. But on Mars? A chime sounded at Deo's desk. He hurried over. "Incoming message."

They sat in front of a huge viewer. Duplessis materialized in front of them, blips of static blurring his image regularly. He sat on a *tatami* mat in front of a small waterfall. The man's face was one of bliss and relaxation.

Or so it appeared. Dennis already knew he was dealing with a master of the head fuck.

"*Konichiwa* from Japan, gentlemen. Dr Rosso, Dr Deo. I hope you are well. I just received that status report on the *Watney* launch, and it all looks good, Prithpal. I'm sure they can speed that engine refit up on the *John Carter*, though. Q-Space can't afford hangar queens. Tell Vaughn to get his ass in gear."

Deo nodded. It was a strange scenario, Dennis thought. Given decades of video communication on Earth, it was natural to assume you were in a two-way communication, and to want to respond. But the message wouldn't get there for more than twenty minutes.

"Now, Dr Rosso, in answer to your queries." Dennis sat up straight, another retrograde gesture. "I've sent you a full synopsis of the evidence against Captain Leuprecht, which I trust you will share with his defense team in total confidence. While it's too detailed and technical to go into in this forum, the evidence from *John Carter's* onboard systems and the witnesses present suggest that standard protocols for a high-risk radiation environment were not followed. Hence, the charges against him. He had a weather forecast, if you will, predicting solar activity for the 48- hour period encompassing the accident. He chose to ignore it, Doctor. That's gross negligence. We have procedures in place that have, up until now, kept all 2400 people Q-Space have transported to and from Mars, alive and well. They should have been followed."

That's right. You keep them alive, then kill them on Mars, where there's no independent media to ask questions. Dennis shifted in his chair, careful not to let his feelings show. Duplessis probably knew anyway. New technology allowed minute analysis of body language and facial expression.

"With regard to your request to supply counsel, please do. If you're paying for it, I have no objections. But the representation must be strictly long-range. The case will proceed no later than next month. As for verifying the conditions Captain

Leuprecht is being held in, you can do that for yourself! A suborbital shuttle makes the monthly run in three days. There's a spot held for you. Don't worry, you only stay two nights and return. Quite a fascinating place, the North Pole. Never been there myself. I'm jealous!" Duplessis rubbed his hands together like a kid on Christmas. Dennis couldn't help but smile. He reminded himself not to make an enemy until the facts were in.

"Last but not least, Doctor Rosso. I take it you've already seen your magnificently appointed lab, outfitted to your specifications? Merry Christmas. Within two weeks, the *SS Nathaniel York* will arrive, and ten of the passengers will be working for you. You'll have lots of time to mess around on your own, but part of our deal is the extension of the miracle, as we discussed on several occasions back home. Included with the documents on Captain Leuprecht will be your detailed remit. It's time to get back to work."

When it was over, Dennis stared at the screen, his suspicions and prejudices confirmed.

Duplessis was a dictator. A benevolent one, perhaps. But Mars was not, perhaps could not, be a democracy. That would have worried him more.

Except that what he was sure was to come on Earth worried him more.

2117

That fucking dog

Atlanta
Station Inn

They had returned from Buford Dam Park in silence. What do you say after watching two happy, healthy, optimistic people with eternal life end those lives in front of you?

The only thing that registered with Dennis on the trip back were the holoboards. Virtual billboards that popped up with 3D messages on sensing nearby traffic, they dotted the route back to Atlanta.

Dennis had always ignored advertising, being impervious to it even as a child. He never wanted the toys and the sugary cereals pushed by TV. Only chemistry sets and science books. But now, for the first time, hoping to learn something about this culture he had so greatly shaken, he watched and absorbed.

Gone were the concerns of the pre-miracle days. Health, it was assumed, was taken care of, so vitamins, prescription medicines, diet foods…all had disappeared from the popular discourse. In their place were the monstrous constructions of high-calorie, unrestrained cooking:

ALL THE CHEESE. ALL THE CREAM. ALL THE TIME.

THREE PATTIES, EXTRA FRIES. IT WON'T KILL YOU!

JUST SAY "EXTRA" FOR FREE EXTRAS. LARGE PIZZA WITH

THREE TOPPINGS ONLY 19.95!

ADD AN EXTRA SCOOP AND SAUCE FOR ONLY 50 CENTS! FRIDAYS ONLY!

It was all presented in glossy, pornographic detail. Speaking of pornography, with organized religion having declined in influence, and precious few children to taint, explicit advertising for adult urges was accepted. Lurid sex acts and full-frontal nudity threatened to cause car accidents all the way to the city limits.

Few children meant more disposable income for toys and travel. New cars were advertised with naked models slung over their hoods, causing Dennis to titter once.

"What?" Latoya had asked.

"Are they suggesting you run over nudists in the new Mercedes?"

"Apparently it makes them happy. Look at that smile."

It was the only laugh they got on the way back, and once they returned to the room, they were glum again. Latoya showered, poured Dennis a scotch, then pointedly stood in front of him, her bathrobe open.

He chose her first. After, they shared the scotch in silence. Sibelius played in the background, music he always associated with Mars. Finally, she could take no more silence and Scandinavian darkness.

"You're not Henrik Kassabian, are you?" She touched him gently to prove her intent was not hostile. "I deserve to know who you really are. That's what you wanted to tell me back there, isn't it?"

After a while: "Yes." Dennis sighed. "I am not Henrik Kassabian. I am his sometime collaborator and more often rival,

Dennis Rosso. I am the creator of the miracle."

Latoya stared at him, her mouth agape. "But...but why?"

"That is a long story. In order to understand it, you'd have to understand what Mars was like in those last days. But it's all true. Remember when Lontraine asked me about Kassabian's dog, back at JC Bryan?"

"Yeah. Brave Fighter 2 or something..."

"Nobel Warrior 3, yes. I fucked up the answer, Latoya. That dog, the ugly one sitting on Lontraine's shoes, that dog was Nobel Warrior 3. Kassabian had it put in stasis because it had some incurable disease, he wanted me to treat, and I wouldn't. He wanted me to give the dog the miracle."

"Dogs everywhere get the miracle now."

"But back then, we were on a planet with limited resources, recovering from years of isolation after the Red Foam and the war. I refused to make people wait in line so his ugly fucking dog could get the miracle, Latoya. So, he got Lontraine to take it back to Earth with him, where I'm assuming, they gave it the miracle. The dog I saw die on Mars was a later clone, 5 or something."

"How can you be so sure?"

"Because there was something wrong with just that one. Different colored eyes. And it was the one Kassabian loved the most."

"And after that, he hated you."

"Yes. All over a fucking dog." He didn't have the heart to tell about Larissa yet.

"So, you think Lontraine knows you're not Kassabian. What can he do about it?"

Dennis stared into his scotch. "There's a hell of a lot of people who would love to get their hands on Dennis Rosso. I fucked up the world, you know? At one time, after the war, there was a warrant out for my arrest. Duplessis protected me."

"The Madman of Mars?"

"He wasn't always mad. He used to be…inspiring. He inspired some of my best work. But Mars was cut off for decades. A big man on a small planet, with absolute power…well, you understand, right?"

"What did you feel today, Doctor?"

"Dennis!" he caressed the length of her body, coming back as always to her breasts.

"It's just maybe I feel we need to be reintroduced, that's all." She cinched her bathrobe tight. "I wonder what you felt when those people killed themselves today. Two people who looked happy but were missing something. They called the miracle false. How does that make you feel?"

"Religious fanatics, Latoya. You heard that shit they said."

"Yes, but you made a miracle. And that wasn't enough for them."

Dennis went to sleep with that last statement in his mind. And it kept waking him up.

The Next Morning
Braves Grill

Unable to sleep, Dennis had risen at 6:45, left Latoya in bed, and went to the ground floor in search of waffles.

He was so determined that he did not see the Asian man rise from his seat in the lobby and follow him.

He was just pouring himself a coffee when the man slid into the opposite side of the booth. "Dr Kassabian, I presume?"

Dr Craig Feng was holding a single sheet of paper, wearing a plastic smile and an expensive, shiny blue suit. "Nice entrée, Feng. To what do I owe the pleasure?"

Feng slid the sheet of paper across the table at him. "You do know that most of our facility was destroyed in the Red Foam riots in 2045. Some of our facilities did survive, however. Parts of the BSL-4 lab, for instance, were too solidly built to destroy. As were the security archives. Anyone ever granted a pass to work at our facility, or it's CDC predecessor, had a signature kept on file. Later, DNA as well. Curiously, while your DNA matches Dr Kassabian's, your signature does not."

"Decades change people, Feng. That signature is 77 years old. And why would my DNA match, if I wasn't Kassabian?"

"Oh please, remember who you are talking to, Doctor! Don't think I have not heard of the 'Masking Project' experiments carried out during the Martian War. Martian agents were able to pose as others using a surface layer of impostor DNA. Caused the UN a tremendous amount of havoc."

"That was my enemy's project. You're saying I used my enemy's project to pose as myself?"

Feng smiled thinly. "There was one notable figure who was also attached to that project. The father of the miracle himself. Dr Dennis Rosso."

"Who is dead."

"Ostensibly. The only witness being one Henrik Kassabian. Convenient."

"Is this about that fucking dog?"

"Bahahaha...the eternal Nobel Warrior 3. Yes, Mr Lontraine did rather feel you had your pooches misplaced. Curious that you not feel any emotional attachment for a dog you spent millions to keep alive. Curious."

"Also curious that the nation's top disease fighter is on the speed dial of a sludge merchant like Lontraine. Shared interests?"

Feng poured himself a coffee. "How I wish we could verify your statements electronically."

"How I wish I could look at how many zeroes there are in your Swiss bank accounts."

Feng reddened. "Now look here, whoever you are…"

"Doctor Kassabian, Nobel Laureate, until proven otherwise. Very substantial donor to the New Democratic Party, and a man trying to do nothing more offensive than investigate an unexplained spike in suicides. Which very much causes me to wonder at your approach."

The waitress arrived with Dennis' waffles, which Feng took as his cue to leave. "Don't think we won't be watching. We will." He looked down at Dennis' plate. "That looks delicious. Maybe a hot dog for lunch, Mr Vance?"

Dennis watched him leave, pursued by two of the mesomorphic guards they'd seen at DCC the other day. He knew about that stupid podcast, and that stupid dog.

Thank Christ Dennis Rosso had never set foot in the CDC. But Feng already knew enough to make things hard. Maybe he should just head for his starship and forget about it.

Maybe if he hadn't seen the Phillips' flight into eternity, he could do that. But he couldn't now.

He was Dennis Rosso. He was responsible. And he needed to know what had happened to his miracle.

2041

North polar shot

Mars
Above the North Pole

The ballistic transport *Eagle 7* was a snug little contraption with 4 rows of 4 seats. Today, only two other seats were occupied, by a couple of bureaucrats who paid him no heed. Dennis looked out the window as his stomach began to fall.

Below him was an endless expanse of white. In Northern winter, the polar cap was an impressive sight. He could only imagine what it would be like from the ground.

The last few days had been filled with reading, first the Leuprecht case file, then the remit for Rosso Labs Mars, the direction that would shape his future. As Leuprecht's case was the more immediate concern, he resisted the urge to read ahead, and plunged into the Captain's file.

Anita of course, could not resist. She said her police training was boring anyway. "Mainly they're telling us how not to blow ourselves out into the vacuum. Anyway, your remit is to make people indestructible. Not too much to ask."

The transport levelled off, and Dennis' stomach settled down. "Prepare for landing." The pilot announced without frippery or ceremony.

Phoenix Base

They landed in a swirl of icy powder in the darkness. A large, bus-like contraption with wheels the size of cars backed up to the transport, then extended a rickety-looking tunnel to the hatch. "Secure your suits." The sole steward called out.

They clambered onto the bus via the tunnel, which felt more like a suspension bridge than anything back at Hellas. Once the tunnel had reattached itself to the vehicle, they began a bumpy ride across the snowy dunes.

Dennis marveled at the topography outside. An alien land of sculpted white domes, frosted with pink dust, it extended in all directions evenly. "How close are we to the pole?" He asked the steward.

"Couple of degrees." He responded with gay English disinterest.

They entered a vast chamber cut into the ice, passing through a double set of airlock doors. Then, the door opened with a hiss, and one by one, they stepped onto the Martian permafrost. It had the look, and feel, of a slightly pink concrete.

"This way." The steward waved a hand, a tote bag over his own shoulder. They passed a group of technicians huddled around a tractor.

"Anybody got any booze?" A bearded man asked plaintively. Dennis rooted in his bag, produced a priceless flask of McCallan, and handed it to the man.

"Cheers." He kept going, despite a massive pat on the back from the now elated ogre. They entered another set of airlocks, then stepped into another overheated, stinking warren of pods and passageways.

"Guests! Hilton Hotel North Pole, right here." The steward indicated a pod with an open door and six empty, hurriedly made bunks. "You can drop your stuff here. There's no theft at Phoenix Base. Up here, it's trial by airlock. Yes?"

Dennis gripped his folders. "Which way to the detention block?"

"Ah, you're that bloke. Follow me. Rest of you, meeting is in two hours. There's no food on right now, might as well get some sleep."

He followed the steward away from the grumbling bureaucrats. The pilots had already claimed the bottom bunks. They passed rows of glaring, hard men in grimy coveralls, sleeping fitfully in over lit pods or clamouring in the hallway. The steward flitted amongst them like a ballet dancer.

Even out here, Dennis pondered, flight stewards were gay. "You know, I saw that, Professor."

"Saw what?"

"You giving that Sasquatch back there free booze. Not allowed up here, you know. One hundred people, almost all men, half of them on some sort of sentence or other, and exactly three cops. It's a dry base."

"Sorry."

"Just watch yourself when they get wild. When I was talking about trial by airlock, I was only half-joking."

Dennis wondered again about the names on the plinth. How did they all get there?

"Detention block. Up the stairs, to the right. Pardon me, I'm off to get some kip."

"Thanks." Dennis struggled up the narrow metal stairwell and found himself in a small corridor. Four cells occupied most of the space. An office at the far end with a sign that said "Security" occupied the rest. A thick-browed man with a dark moustache glared at him through a window.

The second cell to the left was occupied by Josh Leuprecht. He sat stiffly at a desk in front of a generous picture window. Outside, the Martian dust and ice danced in the dusky light of the brief winter day, stacking up on the windowsills like a frosting. Leuprecht sensed his presence and looked up from the legal pad he'd been scribbling on. He waved absently.

The thick-browed cop confronted him. He was a barrel-chested man with greasy, too long hair, whose name tag read "Shalikashvilli."

"You here for the Captain? Good, good, we like the Captain. I am Ohan, this piece of shit posting is my paradise! My reward!"

Dennis shook the man's meaty hand. "Reward? For what?"

"I saved the President of Georgia's life."

"And this is how they reward you?"

"He was supposed to be dead. Oh well. I am first Georgian on Mars. My mother is very proud. I bet you want to talk to the Captain, yes? Hey, aren't you…"

"The guy who made the miracle, yes."

"Hey, that's great! Back home, I could never afford this in a million years, but here, the man himself promises me I get it soon. Ah, the things I could do with eternal life!"

Dennis smiled. "As soon as I get back to Hellas, I'm going to work."

"Good, good! Okay, I let you in." The cell door slid open. There was no pretense of security. Where would a man run to, anyway? Dennis stepped inside, and the door closed again behind him. "Thanks for coming, Doctor."

"Of all the crazy places to meet."

"I know. But isn't it beautiful? They've even let Paula and I go out for a couple of EVAs. Ohan is the best."

"Where would you run to, anyway?"

"Nowhere, Dennis. This is where I want to be." He motioned to the only other chair in the room. "Have a seat. I see you've gotten Duplessis' version of the truth."

Dennis sat, and opened the file. "It's pretty thorough, Josh. The damning part is the one where your solar activity early warning was a 32% probability of a fatal flare. Yet you chose to maintain a normal watch, instead of the recommended 2/3rds. Why?"

Leuprecht nodded and turned his gaze back to the window. "Did you discover the miracle by following the book, Dennis?"

"Ah, not exactly." He recalled shouting matches with Mr Plebesly, the play-it-safe CEO.

"You don't become a shit hot military, and then corporate pilot that way, either. Two-thirds watch means two-thirds speed. Not typically what Q-Space wants. Boeing is about to start flying this route. My instructions from Duplessis were to ensure that it took them five years to touch any of our flight times."

"Do you have that in writing?"

"Of course not. Duplessis isn't stupid. I am. I trusted him, and when the bribes flowed my way, I was happy to shut my eyes and gulp them down. What's in that package, there?"

He could've lied, but he didn't. He knew Leuprecht would prove his point. "My remit. For Rosso Labs Mars."

"Ah. That's a good bribe."

"I'll be doing good work."

"I know you will, Dennis. You're a good man. You can make Mars a better place. That's why I'm not fighting it."

"Why? Regardless of the evidence, I've got you Raymond Criss on retainer. The best aerospace attorney in the business. Hell, he saved that cosmonaut last year, the one who crashed on the Moon, drunk out of his fucking tree…" The look on Leuprecht's face stopped Dennis short.

"No. Save your money. I appreciate it, I really do. But I will take my lumps. Five years here as an Engineer 3. I get to stay with Paula. Then, we both move back to Hellas. No more flying. I can handle that. Tell everybody back there I'm okay. And tell Jerry…" He began to sob. "Tell Jerry I'm so sorry. I let him down."

Dennis walked back to his cabin with those sobs in his ears.

Guest Pod 23-A

Dennis lay on the middle bunk. He had no window, so he had to imagine the sights outside from the scraping sounds of blown rock and icy dust against the pod's outer hull.

He could not sleep. He could only imagine a man of the sky and stars, a man like Leuprecht, stuck in this colon for five years. But hadn't he done what he could?

The bureaucrats were up, and arguing, possibly in Portuguese. Then, the hatch opened, and they left behind quiet. "Thank fooking 'ell." The co-pilot exhaled. "Fucking twats."

Cautiously, Dennis rolled out of his bunk. "They're gone?"

The steward swung his feet down from the bunk above Dennis' and landed with grace in the low-gee. "Bloody marvellous. Now we can have a drink!" He went to the intercom and dialled on the handset. "Ohan! Come on down for a piss-up. Bring some of that Georgian jet fuel, mate!"

Soon, they were swapping shots of his one remaining bottle of scotch, Ohan's formidable *Chatcha,* and the crew's collection of pilfered assortments from varied interplanetary and intercontinental routes. "Dry base, my ass!" Dennis knocked glasses with Ohan, who laughed heartily.

"Just don't want you getting raped by the heavy machine boys." The steward, whose name was Lionel, clucked.

"Yeah, that's 'is job!" The co-pilot chortled.

The pilot, a steely-eyed Kiwi straight from Central Casting, brought things back to Mars. "How's Josh? What's he looking at?"

Dennis looked around. All of them looked back, Ohan included, hopefully. "He's going to fall on his sword. I offered to pay for Raymond Criss…"

"Best in the business, he is." The co-pilot nodded.

"But he's content to work here for five years, and then settle in Hellas. I think he just wants to be a Martian."

"Fuck." The Kiwi spat. "All Josh ever did was what Duplessis wanted him to. Mark my words, Professor, you watch your ass around him."

Dennis turned to Ohan, who poured him more fiery *Chatcha*. "Ohan, promise me you'll look after him."

"Josh and Paula will be like my brother and sister. You know I am good at saving the lives." He winked. "Even when I am not supposed to."

They toasted, then drank until they heard Portuguese voices in the hallway.

The Next Day

Dennis had no idea what time it was. His hangover did not help. He awoke, having the cabin to himself, and gulped water from a bottle he'd thoughtfully stored in his catchall next to the alarm clock.

After a month on Mars, he was falling victim to a syndrome he was calling "Rolling Mars."

The 25-hour Martian day was practically impossible to follow, so humans retained their earthbound time, while the clock progressed an hour a day.

Soon, what had been night was now day. But this had certain advantages. One was that all shifts were rotating shifts, and nobody was shortchanged. 1500 hours two weeks ago was daytime, now, it was night.

Not that it mattered at the Pole. This being Northern Hemisphere winter, it was dark almost all day.

They lived the life of permanent shift workers. It was easier than figuring out what a fucking "sol" was anyway. A drilling tone announced a call. Dennis pressed the respond button.

"Did I wake you?" It was Leuprecht.

"No, but can you kill me?"

"In enough trouble for that already. Listen, I hear you missed a night EVA back home. Ohan offered to take us out tonight, and he's got one more suit and tether. Night EVA at the North Pole, you in?"

Suddenly, his headache diminished. "Yes. Yes, let's do it."

"Set your alarm for 1300. Then come down to dinner. We suit up at 1430."

"Okay."

The North Pole
Mars

Leuprecht drove the massive tractor the last five hundred meters to the pole. Then he stopped it with a shudder of gears. Outside, starlight glittered off the polar cap, giving the impression of deep, irredeemable cold. "Minus 130 Celsius folks! Brrr!"

"My God, look at that!" Dennis stood in front of the airlock window while Ohan roughly adjusted his suit fixtures. "The stars!"

Paula smiled at him through her suit visor. "You ain't seen nothing yet!"

Soon, they had dropped in slow motion, one-by-one, down a long ladder to the crunchy, textured surface. Dennis found his childhood sense of snow wonder reignited, and he went off bounding across the gentle hillocks, Ohan struggling to catch up.

Then the four of them came to a lonely staff in the middle of the blackness, a red beacon affixed to its top. "This is it." Leuprecht announced.

"Wow." Dennis' talent for higher language seemed to have deserted him. He bounded up to the pole in silence. A scattering of rough boot prints declared he was hardly the first visitor.

Now, he was alone with Leuprecht. "You understand why I'm willing to stay. Here, now, with this woman? I can ignore all the rest, if I still have this. Out here, there's no bullshit, and nobody is worth more than anyone else. The only things that matter are a functioning suit, and a full tank of O2. Kind of reduces life to its basics, doesn't it?"

Dennis looked up past the beacon. The stars of the Northern Hemisphere surrounded them in a chaotic, jostling show. "You forget how many there are."

"Not here you don't. Go back to Hellas. Go back to work. We're expecting miracles up here." He surprised Dennis with a sudden hug. "Promise me you won't worry about this, will you? I have my reasons."

"So does he. That's what worries me, Josh. I don't know how to read him."

"Keep making him look good, and you'll never need to worry. That was my mistake." Leuprecht looked up at the stars. "And it was a mistake, Dennis. I'm not an innocent man."

"You're not a guilty one, either. Thank you for sharing this."

"You're welcome. Mars has a golden age coming. I can feel it."

They loitered under the stars until the alarms sounded in their earpieces, telling them to go home.

2117

Survivors

Atlanta

After Feng's sinister visit, Dennis was itching to leave Atlanta, reasoning that he could just as easily find all the evidence he needed in the much friendlier territory of Cascadia.

But Latoya insisted. There was one more person he needed to meet.

They came to the place, a long-term care facility on a leafy street, and parked in the lot. Latoya touched his arm. "Ronald contacted me during his recovery. He retained the services of a facilitator. Just not a man as accomplished as Virgil, that's all."

"Who lives here? There is no elderly anymore."

"Not among the Normies, no. But there are defective births, those chosen to live for one reason or another."

"There wouldn't be, if people did proper bloody screening. I mean, they won a lottery. You'd think they'd…"

"Some of these babies were born on Mars, Dennis. Where sterility is not a pre-condition for immortality."

"Oh." Duplessis had developed a distasteful policy in his last years in power, sending back the defectives and their parents if they refused euthanasia, arguing that Mars could not afford long-term care of the non-viable. The radiation environment of Mars was not the best place to produce a healthy baby.

"The rest…the majority, they're the survivors. People like Ronald. They spent all their money on a facilitator, and when it didn't work, the state penalizes them by refusing to pay more than a pittance to rebuild them."

"I…I didn't know that."

"The miracle is a one-way-ticket, Dennis. It has to be. Our society is built on it's promises. Not it's failure."

He followed her inside, hearing his heart hammer in his veins. They checked in with an orderly, and were immediately confronted with a sea of staring, open-mouthed faces.

"Which exit did Ronald choose?" he whispered to her.

"Be strong, Dennis. Acid."

"Oh Christ."

He was in a private room, seated in a wheelchair, facing a window bathed in sunshine. When he turned, Dennis stared into milky, sightless eyes, set in a face of flowing lava. Ronald's entire upper body was a sculpture born of nightmare.

"I heard you. Hi there. You must be Dennis. Thanks for coming." Ronald had that off-putting friendliness commonplace to so many of the severely disabled. Demonstrating his ability to smile while you sulked over a hangnail.

Dennis shook a shrunken hand. "Hi, Ronald."

"Tell him how it went down, Ronald." Latoya prompted him.

Ronald laughed, a strange, pipe-rattling sound through seared vocal cords. "Brother said he was an expert. That he worked at an industrial etching plant. Full access, he said. He doped me up real nice and started lowering me into the vat. Then, his boss walks in, starts yelling, 'The fuck is this!" He drops me, upside down. Even through the drugs, I could feel my skin sizzling. My eyes went white, then red, then black. I hoped it would be over soon. But the boss and his crew fished me out, and then Latoya showed up."

Latoya walked into the hall, wiping away tears.

"And so, it's been four years of hell, brother."

"I...I'm sorry."

"What for? You didn't do nothing."

"No, you're wrong there. I'm Dennis Rosso. I invented the miracle."

Ronald bobbed his head for a second, absorbing the message his shrunken ears had just retained. "Bet you thought you was helping people, am I right?"

"Yes, I did."

"So, it ain't your fault."

"But...why can't they help you? They should help you."

"They come here and film holos. They want to use us as examples. 'Don't throw your miracle away on a shady fac! Know the facts about suicide!'"

"And yet, they let people film death holos on public land."

Ronald nodded again. "Uh huh. Latoya told me about that. That is some fucked up shit."

"Can I ask you a personal question, Ronald?"

"I ain't got nothing better to do."

"Why didn't you want my miracle anymore? Why did you want to die?"

Ronald was quiet for a moment. A breeze blew in from the garden outside, a smell of lilacs and lavender. Dennis wondered absently how he could've lived so long without open windows and garden breezes.

"I was a young man, still am. Only thirty when I got the miracle. I wasn't tired of life, no sir. I had a good job, a beautiful wife, we was on the lottery for a baby, you know?" He paused, the story, the memories, too difficult. "I been to the Moon, you know? I could do things like that."

"Then why in God's name did you lower yourself into a pit of acid, Ronald?"

"I kept having these dreams. Once in a while at first, then... all the time. Every fucking night. Like there was all this life in me that was fighting to get out. I'd see it in my dreams, like red bodies, babies trying to be born, crawling over white ones. Soon, I couldn't sleep no more. I couldn't work, couldn't think...nothing."

A thought occurred to Dennis. His visit to JC Bryan. "Do you eat meat, Ronald?"

"Yeah. I love meat. I can't eat it no more, on account of my stomach."

"Do you still get the nightmares?"

"Not no more."

He excused himself from Ronald and found Latoya in the hall. "Get out your notebook. We're going to interview every survivor we can lay our hands on. And we're going to ask them two questions."

"Which are?"

"Do you eat meat? Or, have you received cloned tissue, organs, or bone?"

"And then?"

"Ask them about their nightmares."

"Is that all?"

"No. Think about how you want your name to appear on your Nobel Prize."

Latoya smiled at him and went to work. He went out to the parking lot and called his personal banker. "Jurgen? Yes, this is Dennis. You heard right, Dennis. Rumours of my death have been greatly exaggerated. Keep that under your confidentiality cloak, will you? Now listen. Open account 23944156 to Latoya Summers of Atlanta, Georgia. No, the other Georgia. Why?"

Dennis paused a moment and looked back at the home. A place full of broken promises. Promises he could help keep. "Keeping promises. Righting wrongs. Good enough?"

Martin Luther King Station

They barely made it to their seats, settling in just before the train started moving. Dennis looked around, still alert for interference from Feng and his cronies. He was still frankly surprised there had been no sign of it.

"Relax, Dennis. They're probably glad to be rid of you. Why would they mess that up with a gunfight in a public place? Besides, they know you wouldn't stay dead anyway." She smiled and patted his thigh. "Ronald's a real downer, isn't he?"

They train was slowly chugging out of the suburbs now. Clean, happy, well-fed people, living far into the future with the miracle. *His people.* Ads for "Body Upshifts" and "Dura-Spines" catering to their endless desires to be better. While in the next state over, a girl in ragged jeans went without pre-natal care.

If there was one thing consistent between the America of Dennis Rosso's birth and the America of today, it was inequality. All that the revolutionaries of the 2040s had done was make that misery a little more color-blind. But it was still there.

"Ronald's life is about to change. I left those folks back there a little gift." He told Latoya about his impulsive gesture.

She shook her head in disbelief. "All this concern about tails and goons…and then you announce to the Swiss banking system that you're alive and well, and back on Earth? Jesus, Dennis, I never believed it when my momma told me how stupid smart men could be." She folded her arms and stared out the window.

"It's a Swiss bank. Confidentiality is the name of the game."

"Everyone's tongue can be bought. Or at least rented. And since it seems they've got a pretty good idea you aren't Henrik, you've just made it easier for them."

Dennis sat back in his chair and considered his peril. So far, there was lots of innuendo and insinuation, but no real action.

Or had there been? So far, they had both accepted the ambush in Tallahassee as just…well…Florida. But couldn't that have been a very low-risk option for ridding Feng and Lontraine of their pesky inquiries? Who was investigating murders in Florida these days?

The thought unsettled him. More so now that the train had picked up speed, and now accelerated into the deep tunnels that crisscrossed the lawless center of America.

Only a few hundred meters above, anything could be bought. A holo played in front of each passenger, advertising speed, location, and bearing. A surface view would've been fascinating, but modern America did not advertise its excised parts.

Dennis was lulled to sleep by the smooth acceleration, and soon slept the deep sleep of the comfortable and invulnerable.

2041-2045

Golden years (1)

Mars

When he returned to Hellas Base smelling of Georgian rocket fuel and sweat, Dennis Rosso disappeared into the scientific journals for the better part of a year. When the *Nathaniel York* arrived, with ten, no doubt competent, but certainly loyal to Duplessis, staff on board, he left Larissa Bolderova, the hand-picked lab manager, to sort them out.

It bothered him that Duplessis had picked his staff. That should've been his job. And yet, looking through the CVs of his new people, he couldn't spot a single damned thing he didn't like. Duplessis had read his mind. If you considered all the myriad weird shit Q-Space was into, it was not exactly a stretch to suggest it.

Besides, hadn't he been too "busy" to pay attention? Whose fault was that?

Looking at Bolderova, a compact little Belarussian with sparkling eyes and bee-stung lips, he assumed he could trust her to replicate his mentor Professor Andreyeev's technique for bringing new staff up to speed. It was a predictably Soviet way of handling people, something Bolderova ought to be used to.

"Spend the next six months replicating the miracle. Don't expect me to tell you what to do. You're a PhD. It's all a matter of record, now. While you're learning how to do it, maybe you'll be doing it a little better. Maybe you'll find a way to steal a march on us. In the meantime, I have six years of research to catch up on. Call me if something escapes the lab and starts eating people. Otherwise, see you in October."

He left her, staring after him, no doubt a thousand questions on the tip of her tongue, and retired to a private office Deo had set up for him in the Greenhouses. Far beyond the politics of the Mound, he could read his journals and do his thinking under trees and vines. Knowing how to repair his own chromosomes from low doses already, he paid little attention to radiation, which in that section was much higher. The Greenhouses needed natural light and could not be buried.

He spent the better part of a year there, sometimes sleeping in a little room there while the red sands shifted outside. Occasionally, he awoke to the sound of blasting in the distance, Duplessis' caving teams digging into the Basin cliffs, or Jerry's ice miners sinking new boreholes.

Life, on Mars and on Earth, passed him by.

Anita adjusted to the rough-and-tumble life of a Colonial Cop. It was just as well, she would tell him later, that he was not often there to see her when she came home. The rough-living proles would occasionally bedeck her with black eyes or deep scratches, even one time, a broken hand.

Determined to prove herself as a frontier cop, she shed ten kilos and turned herself into a wiry fighting machine. Her life got better, and she was promoted to Deputy Chief.

Jerry threw himself into his work and became a rich man all over again after patenting a new means of drilling into Mars' deep deposits of primordial subsurface water. Showers went up to ten minutes or two fives a day for the rich, and now the proles could have two minutes every day. The Greenhouses expanded around him, and the variety of fruits and vegetables exploded.

Jerry, however, did not wish to share his life with anyone. There were prostitutes here to meet his manly needs, and as for the rest...he was definite that there was only one Patricia.

How could you stick to your guns about that in an eternal lifetime? He hoped Jerry was wrong.

Captain, now Mr, Leuprecht, endured his exile in the polar wastes without complaint. He was happy, as he said he was.

For those who had thrown in their lots with Duplessis, who arrived on the *John Carter* in May 2042, and did not go back, it seemed that they had made the right choice.

Mars was expanding, a thriving, vital place of enquiry and commerce. In 2043, just one year, fifty of *Forbes'* billionaire's list relocated to Mars. Like Dennis, they'd been drawn by the lure of a Monaco-style entrée investment package, followed up by no income taxes and minimal capital gains levies.

Soon, they were calling the planet "Marsaco" on the stock exchanges. The wealth kept coming. And it began to show on the surface. Emirates Mars City One was a showpiece built on the edge of the Valles Marineris, with Emirati oil cash, Dubai *chutzpah*, and Japanese robots. By 2045, some 10,000 people were living there, a mix of Emiratis and Saudis, and talented foreigners.

Now, the Martians had advanced, in less than a decade, from living in burrows like sightless rats, to pushing thin, soaring towers into the edge of space. Eschewing the simple cover of soil, the Emiratis preferred radiation-reflecting plastisteel and carbon-carbon fibers, all manufactured in low-gee factories.

Soon, the Japanese were making their robots here too. With Duplessis' new heavyweight freighters coming online, finally there was something to send back to Earth on them besides red rocks and burned-out employees. The trade imbalance reversed itself virtually overnight.

Suddenly, Dennis had something to spend his money on again. Remy Martin and Super Tuscans were available in Duplessis' new chain of Duty Frees, something Dennis had been wise enough to invest in.

Duplessis ruled over it all with a light hand, occasionally, as in the case of Leuprecht, switching to heavy. He got away with it for several reasons. First, Boeing's late efforts aside, he controlled 90% of the transportation infrastructure in the Solar System. What he built worked. Grand speeches and flag-waving counted for nothing if you couldn't get to Mars. If Merlin Duplessis didn't like you, he could make that trip very time-consuming and expensive, or prevent it altogether.

Second, Duplessis had studied the 1967 *Outer Space Treaty* very carefully. Written in a time when spaceflight was a game for states, it only precluded national claims on territory beyond Earth. Not private ones. But Duplessis played his hand carefully. He did not explicitly state that he owned Mars, and was careful, at least at this point, not to seem too Napoleonic. He just built structures on anything he found interesting enough to own. Nobody could do anything about it.

Lastly, he used his not-inconsiderable charm to make some very important allies. The Emiratis were solidly in his corner. He cared not a jot that their city was an outpost of Sharia law. That was their business, and he left them to it. Likewise, the Chinese, with their Great Wall 2 City 100 kilometres from EMCO on the Valley rim, appreciated his indifference towards their appalling human rights record and belligerence towards the North American Republic. Chinese money was just as good as anybody else's, and Duplessis was glad to take it.

But he didn't have it all his way. His relocation to Mars as a permanent base of operations had more to do with SCC investigations back home, and a rumoured pending Interpol warrant than it did with any headstrong whim of the CEO's.

Arrest warrants counted for shit on Mars, and when one was finally issued for Dennis, Duplessis offered to have him wipe his ass with it and mount it in a special case in his office.

Dennis declined as politely as he could manage. Under the charm was a bitter man with a big mouth, a man who'd never stopped hating his dickhead father, nor possessed the insight into his own behavior to deal with it clinically. Charming in person, on Twitter he was a terrorist, making Donald Trump seem steady and sober by comparison. He picked fights. He made enemies.

These enemies remembered. They made plans. But for the moment, their plans lacked one essential element:

He was here. They were all the way over there.

And over there had its own problems. Simmering resentment over unequal access to the miracle led to widespread rioting, which many people attributed to a shadowy coalition of anarchist terror groups, and the Practical Socialist Party, an offshoot of the left wing of the Democratic Party.

He watched with Anita as policemen were lynched in front of news cameras, and bankers set on fire. But it worked, for some people. Some people included Rosario Sanchez, the gap-toothed, long-necked Stalinist who became President at the age of 35 as a result.

"You still like her ideas?" He had asked Anita, a tad insensitively, after Rosario had used the image of a lynched policeman in her campaign ads. The answer had been bitter silence. At least they knew they had made the right choice.

As governments in Europe, Asia, and South America hurried to repeat America's rash move, capital fled Earth. 90-100 %

tax rates, confiscation and nationalization, and the stoking of chaos left capitalists with little choice but to put themselves in Duplessis' hands.

In a famous, time-delayed encounter on CNN, Sanchez had excoriated Duplessis as a sweatshop capitalist, and threated to arrest him. His response showed up on t-shirts on three worlds the next day:

COME AND GET ME, BITCH

Thus, did Mars grow rich and powerful. By 2045, it's GDP was number 9 in the Solar System. It was predicted by the UN to rise to number 3 by 2060. New buildings went up everywhere. People could spend their money in Duplessis' shops, which led to some of them returning to Earth with rather less than they'd expected at the start of their contracts. New wealth led to new expectations, and labor unions, despite Duplessis' open antipathy to them, began to appear on Mars.

Much of this history, Dennis only caught second hand from Anita, or others with more free time of greater interest. Because Dennis, having caught up on his homework, teamed up with his new team of *wunderkind* to expand and perfect the miracle.

In Dennis' mind, when he left for Mars, the miracle was only half-perfected. He'd retreated from the increasing chaos and disorder of Earth, expecting others to follow in his place.

His two counterparts in the so-called "Triumvirate?" From what he could see, they'd done little but enrich themselves back home, content to exploit the vast market offered by 150 million vain Indian rich people, not caring about lowering the price point or improving the miracle itself.

From what Dennis could see, there was only one man who cared enough to follow in his path. A young biochemist from California named Henrik Kassabian had been attempting to find the kill switch in cells throughout the body, and to link the miracle to other stem-cell related functions, such as reproduction.

He'd sent for Kassabian after reading his breakthrough article in *Science*. A year later, Kassabian had arrived.

He was an acquired taste, to put it mildly. An Armenian mother's boy with a neck like an ostrich and the social skills of an escaped experimental animal, the first course of business with him was addressing his sub-par hygiene abilities. Like any good manager, Dennis delegated.

"This job is shit; you know. Now, he is thinking I want to make shower with him!" Bolderova exploded. "Don't laugh, or next Nobel Prize be for 'Scientist Whose Insides Explode Best.' Come, I show you my tits…but only in airlock."

But the kid's skills couldn't be matched. While he worked on the linkage between immortality and reproduction, Dennis studied the ways in which cells could be protected or rehabilitated from trauma. Together, they worked on ways to make the process cheaper. Freed of the financial constraints of Earth-based biomedical corporations, who were rarely interested in bringing down the price of treatments (Duplessis had so many other revenue streams, he didn't care), they could work at their own speed and discretion.

It was a scientist's dream. Dennis remembered it bittersweetly, because, just as they were preparing to publish their landmark finding, the world changed irrevocably.

Nobody would be giving speeches in tails and a top hat in Stockholm anytime soon.

2117

Flyover detour

Amtube Emergency Surface Station 203
North of Quay, New Mexico

The train had come to a sudden stop fifteen minutes before, followed by a rushed emergency evacuation.

As so many travellers, Dennis never paid attention to emergency procedures demonstrations. He just went with the flow, keeping a careful grip on Latoya and his briefcase, in that order.

They had piled into massive elevators, with a faint smell of electrical smoke chasing them, then shot to the surface in an ear-popping rush. Most of his fellow passengers, Dennis observed, actually did look scared. Few things could scare people these days.

But of the few remaining ways for final, ultimate, decisive death available to Normies, a fire underground was one to be taken very seriously. Even the most advanced cell regeneration techniques could not handle the results.

They were herded off the elevators by harried crew members, into a crowded but air-conditioned room. Outside, bright sunlight and flat, red desert.

The elevators went down for another load. "Any idea what happened?" Dennis buttonholed an attendant.

The attendant, whose poor teeth and weak chin suggested an Unco on a probationary work permit shrugged his disinterest. "I dunno. Something about a fire south of Albuquerque."

"Jesus, I need some air." Latoya looked nauseous.

"Can we go outside?" Dennis asked.

"Sure, sure. It's all fenced in anyway. Some locals might come and look at you. They don't see too many Normies out here. Don't get into it with them. We'll announce when it's safe to go back on board."

"Thanks." They pushed through an open door to find a scattering of smokers already enjoying the open air. Smoking had made a resurgence since the miracle, much to Dennis' disdain. Well, you couldn't tell people it was going to kill them anymore, could you?

The land was hardpacked red rock and shifting sand. A remarkably well-kept road ran just past their enclosure. Metal caging surrounded their area. A jackrabbit skipped past them.

"Oh, cute." Latoya swigged water and handed him some. "It's an oven out here."

"43 degrees, it says. Must be New Mexico. Used to come here with my family when I was a kid."

"You had family?"

"No, my dad worked for DoE on contract with Battelle Labs. Sometimes he'd do a stint at Los Alamos and we'd go with him."

"Ah, nukes and stuff?"

"Yes indeed. My family has a long history of fucking up the world. I'm just following in dad's footsteps." He looked out to the horizon, thinking of Mars.

"Remind you of Mars?"

"How did you guess? Sky's the wrong colour. And there's no jackrabbits. But otherwise…"

A crowd had begun to form, muttering amongst themselves, comparing theories and rumours. Had the miracle never arrived, most of these people would have had no memory of the chaos of the 2040s. But now, many of the people discussing crackpot theories and worst-case scenarios had lived through that time, and a lot could remember further back, like Dennis. Contested elections, COVID-19, even 9/11.

Of all the things Dennis had expected the miracle to bring, the permanence of trauma was not one of them. The world could no longer forget. Even those who had no memory, like Ronald, had their horrible dreams.

Ronald's dreams. His eating habits. Was he eating a menu of bad dreams?

His attention was drawn to a dust cloud in the distance. He focused in on a convoy of vehicles headed down the blacktop from the direction of Route 40. *What were they doing out here?*

The loudspeakers relayed an announcement. "Folks, that electrical fire down the tunnel was a minor one. We're just ventilating the tunnel to ensure air quality. We should be re-boarding in about twenty minutes' time. Thank you for your patience."

As the announcement was repeated in Spanish, Dennis noticed something about the trucks, which by now had stopped parallel to them on the road. Men dressed in fatigues were clambering around in the bed of the first truck, pulling down a tarpaulin to reveal what looked like a large agricultural blower.

"Latoya! We need to find a way back down!" He grabbed her arm and pulled her towards the elevator kiosk. A new relay had arrived from the tunnel, and the new arrivals jostled for space as Dennis pushed against them, seeking to slip into the cab.

They had almost made it inside when the blower's loud motor started. Dennis smelled raspberries, of all things, before everything went black.

Somewhere in the High Desert
Dusk

One of Dennis Rosso's biological peculiarities, that is, before he invented the rest, was a curious resistance to sedatives of all kinds. For any sort of surgery, he typically required twice the average dose for a man of his height and weight.

So it was that, still smelling fresh raspberries, he awoke, Latoya still sleeping on his lap, to the sights of the High Desert night, and a canopy of stars the likes of which he had not seen since Mars. Drowsy and in need of companionship, he found his old friend, rising just over the horizon, the steady, solid red of his former home.

The near-night was chilly, and he cinched up the collar on his suit jacket. Dennis searched himself for the Glock but could not find it. They had been searched, bound loosely by ropes to the bed of the truck, but not really restrained.

And they shared the truck bed with five others. None of them were conscious. Dennis peered up cautiously, noticing the other truck following closely, other lumpen shapes in its truck bed. The blowers, or whatever they were, were long gone.

Suddenly, a drone moving low and fast whooshed past them, almost even with his height.

In the cab of the truck, there was a commotion.

"*Que es eso?*"

"*Es un dron, idiota.*"

A radio crackled. "Enough driving, idiots, we know where you are."

The middle passenger keyed the mike. "We got the people you wanted."

"Just shup up and pull over, *por favor.*"

The convoy came to a stop. There was Spanish chatter as the convoy pulled to the side of the road. It was the only other language besides English, thanks to the time he'd spent here as a boy, that he could get by in. One of the many things Dennis had meant to do with immortality was learn more languages. So far, passable Swedish had been his only accomplishment.

He did not think that would be of much use out here.

Instantaneously, a large helicopter with silenced rotors blinked into existence over his left shoulder. On the other side, an VSTOL transport flared for landing, it's lights blinding their kidnappers, and silencing the Spanish chatter.

Three seconds after that, every single one of their kidnappers' heads exploded, and they folded lifelessly into the red sand. Dennis pulled Latoya closer to the truck bed and tried to shield her.

English-speaking men now surrounded them. "Kent, get them flamers out and make sure those beaners stay dead dead, got it?"

Dennis recognized the 'ole boy accents and casual, almost friendly racism of the North American Special Forces. "How about these folks?"

"We take 'em back. We's 'rescuing' 'em."

"Sure." Kent considered over a wad of chew. "Coulda sworn I saw somebody move here, though."

"Fair enough." The leader announced into his radio. "Masks on, all units, masks on. Time for a touch-up."

Dennis smelled raspberries again, and his vision dimmed.

2045

The red foam

Rosso Labs Mars
Hellas Base

It was deadline time in Rosso Labs Mars. That meant that very few people left the lab for anything but a hot meal and a shower, and very little sleep was had by anyone.

Dennis and Kassabian were approaching their final submission deadline, detailing their new, linked therapy. The miracle now came with a means of disabling somatogenic reproduction, while enabling cell regeneration. What's more, the updated miracle, Dennis' contribution to the project, could enable cell regeneration proof against not only senescence, genetic disorders, and neoplasms, but against all but the most final accidents and acts of violence.

Finally, immortality would really mean exactly that. Unless one got incinerated, blown up by zero pressure atmosphere, or irradiated till you glowed. Being dissolved or shredded to a pulp wouldn't help, either.

Dennis worked, bleary-eyed, through the night, wondering idly if their breakthrough would create a new golden age of cowardice. Who would want to explore deep space or fight wars while risking eternal life?

But part of him suspected that the economy would find a way to manipulate the poor into doing what was required. So much for making the miracle available to all.

That would have to wait, if it happened at all. Besides, he reasoned, was it really up to Dennis Rosso to solve all of the world's problems?

Duplessis would be happy if he solved just this one. Being able to promise eternal life to the roughnecks needed to build Mars was the ideal recruiting tool. And sponsoring the first Nobel Prize to be won on another planet wouldn't hurt Q-Space's stock price, either. And so, the great man called often to check on progress. Dennis gritted his teeth, swallowed his pride, and delivered his reports like a good underling.

Kassabian was immune to the pressure, so it seemed. Against all odds, he'd managed to solidify a relationship with Bolderova, as soon as he'd started using his shower water allotment. Eastern European women seemed to consider brains more important than big dicks. That would save him some money on his next adjustment.

But as the deadline neared, reports from Earth began to hint at an ominous shape on the horizon.
It started, or seemed to, in Tokyo, Seoul, and Singapore. A fulminant respiratory plague of unknown origin, one which resulted within 48 hours of the onset of symptoms in a red foamy discharge from the respiratory system, then death.

Of course, it was christened "The Red Foam," in short order.

This was no COVID-19. Early reports suggested a disease that preyed on all available bodies, not simply the aged and infirm. And the mortality rate was closer to 75% than a meager 2%.

Worst of all: The miracle, at least not it's early iterations, was no defense.

In the first few nights in the lab, the tone of the news reports went from professional calm to emotional panic. By the end of the first week, it was in Vancouver, Toronto, New York, Seattle, and LA. Also, Rome, Paris, and Barcelona.

Midway through that update, the feed went dead. Dennis was thinking the worst until he decided to call Duplessis. He was summoned for a closed-door meeting the next day. The boss was flying in from Acidalia Base to consult his number one Biology expert, so the press release went.

"Yes, just head straight to the spaceport. No, don't worry, Maxim will get you on. Honey, you're fine. I just want you here, that's all." Dennis waited awkwardly as Duplessis disengaged from his wife. "Goddamnit. She's freaking. Having to get two kids to the port in time all by herself." His hair was unkempt, and he looked on the verge of madness.

"Let your people handle it, Merlin. You've got so many."

He stood suddenly and walked to Deo's picture window. The *Mark Watney* was two days away from launch, and it was being loaded onto the launch gantry in anticipation. Rumor had it that six time-expired workers were refusing to return to Earth until the Red Foam was under control.

"You know they won't go home now? That's why I cut the feed from Earth. I can't have a panic."

"Imagine what people will say then, if you bring your wife and kids here, from LA, in the middle of a pandemic. With the news feed cut? You've already got enough shit with the wildcat strikes and Duty-Free protests. Don't make it worse. Sunshine is the best disinfectant."

"I...I need them here, Dennis."

"Then get them here, but in the meantime, build a quarantine station. The same rules have to apply, to everyone. From what I've seen, if that shit gets in here..."

Duplessis turned to face him. He wiped his eyes. "Yes, you're right, of course."

"Do you want my advice, Merlin?"

"You are my new Red Foam advisor, aren't you?"

"Okay. I'll wear that hat. First, restore the feed from Earth. Two, build a quarantine facility at an isolated location, capable of keeping two shiploads of people alive for thirty days, if need be. The shiploads cannot mingle. Third, get on the air. Be honest. Be Churchillian. You can take control, quell people's fears, stir the war mentality…"

"You do it."

Dennis was ready to weep in frustration. "They only know me as a guy who fucks around with genes. For all they know, it was someone like me who started the whole thing in the first place! You're one of them, a gearhead, a technocrat…"

Duplessis slumped in his chair again. "I can't. I can't think right now. I need someone I can trust to talk to them, Dennis. I'll delegate to you the necessary authority. Just get it done. Dismissed."

Dennis found himself in the hall, where Deo was waiting. "Well?"

"Well, Prithpal, looks like I'm the new Red Foam tsar."

"Lucky you. What do you need from me?"

"All planet video feed at 2100 Zulu. And put the police on standby."

Deo grinned mirthlessly. "That good, eh?"

"He put me in charge. It may not take him long to regret it."

2100 Hours

To avoid any sense of usurping Duplessis' authority, Dennis insisted on giving his broadcast from his lab. It would, Deo suggested, have the added bonus of underlining his authority on all matters biological.

Dennis held his little handwritten note in his hands and tried not to sweat. He saw the red light come on and began to talk.

"My fellow Martians, good evening. This is Dr Dennis Rosso, speaking to you from Rosso Labs Mars at Hellas Base. Greetings."

"I wish my address were concerning something of greater joy. But, unfortunately, I speak to you regarding the emerging crisis on Earth. The crisis of so-called 'Red Foam' disease. We do not know exactly what causes this disease. No one has isolated its causative agent in a lab. But we do know that its danger is great. We cannot, and will not, allow Red Foam to reach the Red Planet. That is out solemn guarantee to you."

"Some of you have no doubt noticed a blackout on the feed from Earth, which began today. We originated this ban, in order to prevent panic, until we could speak to you and reassure you that you will be protected. After this broadcast ends, unrestricted communication with Earth and the Moon will be restored. We firmly believe that continued censorship will only breed rumors and conspiracy theories."

"But this openness requires a commitment from you, the Martian people. We need you to stay calm, to keep working, to squelch rumors and defeatist talk. Inevitably, there will be shortages and hardships. Hardships we must all bear together. This is your role to play. All work stoppages and industrial actions need to stop until the crisis has passed."

"In return, we promise that no ship from any other world will be allowed to land on Mars without first reporting to a remote quarantine station for a lengthy period of observation. We also promise that no Martians will be ordered to return to Earth until the crisis is passed."

"This will mean greatly curtailed travel between Earth and Mars, for the foreseeable future. In addition, the police have been authorized to prevent unauthorized off-base travel, until the crisis has passed."

"Stay calm. Stay positive. Stay alive. Together, we can ensure that the Red Foam never sullies our beautiful world. On a positive note, many of you may know me from my work in immortality research. Tonight, I can report that we are on a breakthrough in broadening the scope of the miracle and enabling access to it from across society. Stay the course on the Red Foam, and I guarantee that the miracle will be made available free, to everyone who demonstrates their loyalty to Mars in this dangerous time. Let us move forward, into immortality, together. Good night, and good luck."

Down the hall, Duplessis dropped his tumbler of scotch. But inside the lab, Deo could only smile. Anita clapped slowly. "Positively Churchillian, baby."

Dennis grinned ironically. "So was Gallipoli. Let's see how it goes."

Two Weeks Later

At first, things went well on Mars. Opening up the channels to Earth, and not sending anyone back, proved popular policies. The nascent labor unions gave up their industrial actions, provisional on fair and equal distribution of hardship during the emergency.

That would be a hard one to manage with the caviar and champagne set in the Mound. But Dennis took the high road and assembled small groups of first-class residents to explain the road ahead. On Anita's advice, he refused to host any meeting of more than a dozen people.

"Demagogues can't function in front of small crowds. You'll be the boss." She kept him calm and focused. It helped that, aside from a few people despondent over the fate of people back home, going wild, there was little for Anita and her fellow cops to do. Most people were just glad to be out of reach of the Red Foam.

The staff members who would've been on their way home on the *Mark Watney* were easily accommodated in the old, grungy housing units which were slated for recycling. This brought some grumbling from old hands, but once Dennis did the math, he was able to offer the retreads no more than two to a pod. Things calmed down after that.

One thing nagged at him, and another pissed him off.

Duplessis, half-crazy with worry over his wife and kids, was self-medicating with booze and weed, best kept out of the public eye. Kassabian was intent on finishing their study, but he saved enough time to talk Duplessis out of one of Dennis' most important measures.

"Dennis." Duplessis greeted him one night, unkempt and stinking of chronic. "Henk tells me this quarantine unit is a waste of money. We don't have the resources right now. So, fuck it. The last ship is on its way. If it breaks out on board, well…three months ought to tell us if that's going to happen. So, fuck it."

Dennis fought to contain himself. *What the fuck was Kassabian playing at?* "What if they lie?"

"What?"

"What, if, they, lie? Wouldn't you, to get off a plague ship?"

"Bah." Duplessis waved an unsteady arm. "They won't. Because they'll all be dead. We can't waste resources right now."

"So, you'll make the announcement then?"

"What announcement?"

"What do you mean, what announcement? I made the big broadcast you couldn't make, and I promised the people a quarantine station. So, now we have to admit that there won't be one, right?"

Duplessis set down his tumbler with a thunk, his face suddenly hard. "Read, and sign."

Dennis read the memo with a furrowed brow.

Q-SPACE MARS
EMERGENCY GOVERNING BODY

POLICY MEMO 45-103
INFORMATION DISSEMINATION
CLASSIFICATION:

EX-3 AND ABOVE ONLY

UNTIL FURTHER NOTICE, ANY AND ALL DISSEMINATION OF NEW POLICY OR EMERGENT EVENTS RELATING TO THE CURRENT EMERGENCY WILL BE CARRIED OUT WITH THE AUTHORIZATION OF THE CEO ONLY.

THIS IS TO PREVENT PANIC SITAUTIONS AND MAINTAIN A COMMON FRONT AMONG THE MEMBERS OF THE GOVERNING BODY. THIS RULE IS ENACTED WITH <u>NO EXCEPTIONS.</u>

FAILURE TO ABIDE BY THIS NOTICE IS AN OFFENCE UNDER Q-SPACE MARS GOVERNING REGULATIONS (EMERGENCY) 51.01.22, PUNISHABLE BY EXILE OR UP TO TEN YEARS IMPRISONMENT.

PLEASE SIGN BELOW TO ACKNOWLEDGE YOUR ACCEPTANCE OF THIS AGREEMENT:

Dennis held the memo with a crushing grip. "So, we're back to total control now? Was that Kassabian's idea too?"

"No. It was mine. I am capable of a few of my own ideas, you know. Look around."

"And what is your plan for the Captain who insists on landing?"

"Marquardt? He won't. I picked him myself."

"Like Leuprecht. Ever seen him handle a ship full of dying passengers?"

"There's always the Planetary Defense System." Duplessis stared at him coldly. The PDS was a sextet of remote lasers in orbit, designed to ward off stray asteroids, or so said Duplessis when the UN had accused him of building a military capability.

"You couldn't."

"Let's hope it doesn't come to that."

"Let me guess. Another decision you'll delegate to me when the time comes."

"If I think it's your job, yes."

"Fuck you."

"You can say that behind closed doors. But if you say it out there, you'll be playing hockey at the Pole with your pal Leuprecht. Sign the fucking form, Dennis."

Knowing Duplessis held all the cards, his head swimming, he signed, dropped the pen on the desk, and walked out.

"We're tied together you know! Sink or swim!" Duplessis called after him as the door closed.

2117

North by northwest

Unknown Location
North American Federal Facility?

Dennis awoke to the faint aroma of raspberries on a very thin pillow. For the briefest moment, he thought he was on Mars again.

Then, he smelled fresh desert air, stood up, and walked over to a narrow, open window. Outside, flat land in every direction, red and flat.

"Good morning, Doctor."

Dennis looked up at the ceiling. "Good morning, assholes."

"How do you know we're assholes?" The voice from the speaker sounded genuinely offended.

"You work for the government, I'm just assuming."

"How do you know that?" It was like matching wits with HAL9000.

"If you were Mexicans, we'd have had our faces burned off to the sound of chainsaws by now."

"And *we're* the assholes?"

"Touché. What's for breakfast?"

"Oh hoho, you'll never believe it. I can keep you here and make you eat so much you'll never get out of the cell. Plus, there's a fucking bar."

"Feds who say 'fuck?' In my age, you were all goddamned Mormons!"

"What's a Mormon?"

"Sometimes I forget how much I like the future."

Thirty Minutes Later

This was not exactly what Dennis had been expecting, it was safe to say.

Yes, he was in a Federal Detention Facility, somewhere in the Los Alamos Reservation. Yes, he had been brought here by a special team of NA Marshals, specially trained to look and act like a Mexican drug cartel.

But he was not handcuffed to anything. There was no bright light in his face. What's more, he was sitting in a bright, spacious, comfortably outfitted dining room, across from Latoya, with one agent sitting at their table, another at the door.

A picture window looked out at the vistas once painted by Georgia O'Keefe. A buzzard flew past the window as a steward poured coffee.

"Sleep well?" Dennis broke the silence.

"Um, yeah." Latoya smiled at the young agent coquettishly. "Turns out raspberry is my thing."

"Jesus. This coffee is good."

"Martian." The agent spoke. He was compact and serious, but evidently capable of charm. "The new Colombia, apparently."

"Well, bloody past...good coffee. It all fits."

"I'm sorry...but how on Earth did we get here?"

The young agent shrugged. "*So* much chatter coming out of Atlanta. Feng, JC Bryan, suicides...Virgil the Holocast Pimp, Gandalf the Death Wizard...I mean, wow, right? Then we got word you were coming back to the Left Coast...I mean, hell, we just had to pinch you and see if you were real."

Dennis smiled. He talked like a Millennial. He just had to know. "How old are you?"

"137 in September."

"And you still didn't know what a Mormon was?"

"What can I say? My generation wasn't very well educated."

Their plates were set in front of them. Eggs, Real bacon and ham. *Lord above.*

"Is that...is that what I think it is?" Latoya was stunned.

The agent smirked. "Eat up. There's real farms on the Lunar Farside. Guests of the government have certain privileges."

The bacon was smoky and salty. The ham was maple sweet. Dennis was transported back to a life beyond Mars, and, momentarily, robbed of the faculty of speech. Finally, he gulped some orange juice. "Why?"

The agent shifted in his seat with discomfort. "Look, we've seen Feng's figures too. It bothers us. But we're quite curtailed in what we can do, especially since the excesses of Sanchez and her clique. We need to be careful. You guys seemed to be on the right path. Then, we got word that Feng and Lontraine were looking around for Uncontrolled gangs who might do the job on you between Oklahoma and Arizona. We decided it was either avenge your deaths or get in on the game, right Mikey?"

The hulking agent in the doorway responded in a flat Boston monotone. "Right."

"So, we swooped in and saved the day, the way G-men do, right?"

"Right."

"Okay, Mikey."

"So, everybody else is okay?" Latoya pushed.

"Oh yeah…well just one asthmatic porter. Sorry about that."

"What do you know about us?" She stayed on him. Dennis was too busy on his ham.

"You're Latoya Summers, like it says on your ID and DNA." The agent shifted to Dennis. "You, on the other hand…"

Dennis wiped his mouth. "Ah."

"Yeah, you're Dennis Rosso. Class "A" War Criminal, according to the UN. The masking DNA was wearing off anyway, You're basically a celebrity lookalike now."

Dennis sipped at his coffee and looked at the picture window again. "So, Agent…"

"Agent Fisk. Lewis Fisk."

"So, Lewis, what do you think of that?"

"Fuck the UN, Dennis. You're a North American, father of the miracle, hero of the Martian Revolution, and you are going to help us fry Feng and Lontraine for whatever bullshit they're playing."

Latoya raised an eyebrow at him. He patted his mouth with a napkin. "I like the sound of that, Lewis. Does this come from on high?"

"The highest it can come from. The President himself. But, there's a catch…"

"Of course, there is."

"Feng and Lontraine will back off if they think you're protected. So, I'm afraid we're going to have to play *North by Northwest* for a while."

"*North by Northwest?*" Latoya was puzzled.

"It seems our friend Agent Fisk does know his 20th Century culture, Latoya. It just means we're going to have to run for a while longer. Which leads me to ask…"

"More bacon?" Fisk smiled.

"More…everything." Latoya closed her eyes.

"You're like Grace Kelly…with an appetite." Dennis jabbed her.

"When I find out what skinny white girl you are referring to, you are dead, Professor."

Six Hours Later

Much later, after night had fallen and Latoya had learned who Grace Kelly was, Agent Fisk escorted his "prisoners" back to their cell, alone.

Mikey had assembled a fortuitous rope out of bedsheets, out of sight of the cameras. The window, also not on camera, was pried open. Friendly locals awaited their arrival with a warm truck only 500 meters away on the road.

Fisk popped a sedative, smiled, and went weak at the knees just as Dennis delivered an ineffectual right uppercut to his pretty face. It seemed a shame to mess up such a nice face.

He pocketed Fisk's gun and badge and crawled over the windowsill into the night.

2045

Mission moon

Mars
Hellas Base

The news from Earth got steadily worse. One month after the first report, Red Foam was everywhere.

Except China. A fact that made Dennis explore a known fact he'd ignored, whether out of liberal sensibilities, or the fact that a genetically tailored bioweapon was too evil a prospect to face.

The Comm Logs for the base was as far as he needed to look. The day of the first announced cases on Earth, China Great Wall Base 2 had shut itself off. The excuse? Security drills.

Now, all the bases on Mars were prohibiting travel in case the incubation period was freakishly long. But Great Wall 2 had seemed quite prescient, hadn't they?

Now, Dennis was determined to get his hands on a sample of the virus and start working. He knew this was not possible on Mars. He didn't want the virus on Mars any more than anyone else did.

That meant Antarctica or the Moon.

On Day 43 of the crisis, three things happened:

The WHO announced a planetary death toll of 1,000,000,000 from the Red Foam.

President Rosario Sanchez was "accidentally" locked out of a secure facility by the NA Military, and infected by the Red Foam. She died two days later, to widespread mockery.

And Dennis Rosso met Merlin Duplessis, after receiving a tip about a quarantined Moon Tug at Shackleton Base on the Moon.

Duplessis sat in his glass and aluminum office, a haunted, skeletonized version of his former self. He toyed with one of those ball bearing executive toys on his desk. "Chinese closed their base down, the day it broke."

"Yes, Merlin, they did."

"And now, there's a moon shuttle at Shackleton. Most of the people dying, but one dude, with an antidote, who says he helped make the whole fucking thing."

"Yeah, Fu Wen Yueh. Nobel Prize winner too."

"Apparently, they're asking for you. They've got nobody of your calibre there, they say."

"I'm asking you to send me."

"Alone? Because I can't spare Kassabian."

Dennis fought the urge to sneer. "Then give me Bolderova."

If the name registered, it didn't penetrate the dope and booze fog. In this instance, Kassabian had not chosen his friends wisely. "Fine, take her. *Mark Watney* leaves two days from now. Extra fuel will cut the travel time in half."

"By that time, *Martin Gibson* should be here. How are things on board?"

Duplessis waved a tumbler, eyes hollow. "Fucking Marquardt. Says his mains power is out. Things are pretty tense. He's got to limit comms."

He's lying. "Right. Well, I'd best be going."

But Duplessis was already looking out the window at nighttime Mars. "Fine. By the way, you're taking the Football to the Moon."

"But…the time delay?"

"Kassabian's worked out the procedures."

"Then let him do it!"

"It has to be you." The answer was final. Dennis did not argue it, because he knew it was also right.

T-Minus 18 Hours

"No!" Anita tossed a memento of Niagara Falls with startling strength, just about beaning him.

"Careful Anita! You'll break the seal!"

"Yeah, I will! I'll break you! Duplessis' trained seal, right! I know there's no quarantine! So, who's in charge? You or Kassabian? Huh? *Din javla idiot!*" Another souvenir, this one from the Grand Canyon, bounced off the bed clock.

"Anita, please! They asked for me! It's the only way I can study it without bringing it here! We cannot bring it here!"

She stood, surrounded by broken souvenirs, and broke down. "But…why you…why you, there, so far away from me, when that fucking maniac is just going to bring it here anyway?"

Slowly, cautiously, he enveloped her in his arms. It was not easy to comfort a muscular, angry, combat-trained woman.

"He's too weak to make the decision he'll have to make." Dennis revealed a small key hidden amongst the dog tags around his neck. "I have the football, as we say. I'm taking it to the Moon."

Anita coughed and gripped his shoulders. "It's almost an hour, round-trip. How can you…"

"The agreement is, Marquart brakes into a wide, non-landing orbit, proves he has no infected and no dead on board, then he lands at Phoenix Station if he does. Phoenix has been reduced to 25% staffing, just in case."

"And if he deviates? You kill Duplessis' wife and kids, right?"

"Yes." Dennis nodded. "At his express delegated authority."

"Oh God. This hardly seems like the right time…but an e-mail came in from your mother. You know her and video messaging."

"Are we going to be okay?" He searched her green eyes, flecked with gold.

She shrugged. "Is anyone? Let me get you a drink, Dennis. You're going to need it."

My dearest Dennis

My favourite Martian

Interplanetary greetings. I'm afraid this message is goodbye from your poor, earthbound mother. Things are looking very "shady" here at Shady Acres, even by Arizona standards.

It's so beautiful outside, if you just close your ears to the noise. The car alarms, the screams, the gunshots. But if you look away from the human world, out into the valley, the natural world looks poised for a comeback. Maybe they figured "Two legs have Mars and the Moon; we can take this one back."

Please get to the bottom of it, if you can. It seems awfully fishy, as your father used to say.

Half of the patients here are dead, and they started keeping the bodies in Wing 2 after the body people stopped coming. The smell is atrocious now, in the desert heat. You had to move me to Arizona?

Most of the staff, even the lovely Filipinas, have stopped coming. Either dead, sick, or looking after others closer to home. I cannot blame them.

I wish I had taken the miracle, but even still I understand that it might not have saved me in the end. I simply didn't want to live without your dad, can you understand that, my little menace? I bet, if anything should happen to Anita, that you would feel the same. I have seen the way you look at that woman.

He looked at "that woman" now as she brought him a scotch rocks, and he did not let her go, burying his face in her chest until he could read another line.

Mr Lim is here. He is the only one who has kept coming to see us. He is the pharmacist, and he has the pills that will do the trick.

Failing that, he has a gun. Mr Lim is from Taiwan. He says not too many Chinese people are getting sick. He says you should look into that.

Honey, I am going to have a big glass of wine and swallow my pills. Mr Lim has put on some seventies rock now, my favourites, Clapton, Zeppelin, Pink Floyd...all the stuff that used to drive you nuts. Ha ha...it's my funeral.

I am very proud of you. If you can, one day, come back to Earth and give me a good burial. I love you.

MOM

Dennis gulped his scotch and buried himself in his wife's arms, the bravado and assurance of the past day forgotten for the fraud it was.

A little boy who had lost his mother, he let himself be tucked in, and drifted off to his last sleep on Mars for many months to come.

2117

Indian land

Bumble Bee
Arizona

The nighttime "escape" from Federal custody was only risky in so far as Latoya landed on Dennis from 3 meters up, resulting in two likely cracked ribs on his part, and a permanent chagrin on hers.

Their *Coyotes*, Rosalinda and Herculio, were delightful, offering first class service in their air-conditioned, antique Rivian van, as well as a complimentary trip to a black-market doctor in Gallup.

Whereas other areas of the former United States had come apart at the seams after the Red Foam and "The Exchange," as it was daintily described, this part of the country had retained some semblance of structure.

Of course, it was hard to remember that in the night, as their van sped past the still-hot near miss craters south of San Luis, where the Chinese had tried, and failed to take out Los Alamos.

Dennis Rosso had seen a nuclear explosion close-up. He shuddered in the chill night when he saw those almost perfect black disks in the red earth, shining back their moonlight to its source.

Latoya had merely stared and held him tighter.

But this was not some barely functioning, post-apocalyptic wasteland like Florida. Thanks to the loose confederation of Hispanic areas (Some flying the US flag, some the Mexican, others something else entirely) and the Native Americans (Almost all flying the Stars and Stripes), law and order, and basic services were assured. They could see a doctor on the Zuni reservation (To their surprise, a Johns' Hopkins graduate doing a WHO placement), check in with Sheriff's offices in Holsbrook and Show Low (To their surprise, staffed with well-fed deputies in modern cars), and be dropped at a functioning bus station in Claypool.

Along the way, Rosalinda and Herculio, a happy, rotund couple in their forties, regaled them with tales of hapless banditos, almost as hapless *Federales*, and the mestizos who really knew the score. They knew Agent Fisk well, as it turned out.

"Yeah, he's okay. He just gotta learn to stop tripping over his meat, you understand?" Herculio laughed as his wife reprimanded.

Both *Coyotes,* as it turned out, were both moonlighting Sheriff's Deputies with a standing brief to turn in anyone dangerous to the *Federales* in Los Alamos. People still came north from Mexico, though.

"If you seen it down there, you wouldn't ask why." Rosalinda shuddered.

Dennis decided, as the *mariachi* played and his second Corona went down smooth, to probe a sensitive subject. "You guys take the miracle yet?"

They looked at each other and paused before Herculio spoke. "Yeah, but not the official version, you dig? Not good enough to get past a Normie scan. There's a guy in Phoenix…"

"Shh!" Rosalinda hushed him.

"Don't worry." Dennis reassured her. We have business in Phoenix anyway. If you give me his address, I can teach him a few things."

Rosalinda looked back at him. "You can do the miracle?"

Latoya interjected. "He dabbles."

So it was that, at 7:30 AM, they found themselves deposited on a suburban street north of Phoenix, desperately hungry, with only the vaguest idea where they were.

The bus driver seemed to sense that. He was a man with a wide Mestizo face, in a starched uniform, a gleaming and ancient .357 on his hip. "I come back here in 45 minutes. Wait on the other side, and I'll get you. *Comprende?*"

"*Si, muchos gracias, senor.*"

It didn't take Dennis long to get his bearings as the sun came up. "Oh, there it is."

The sun's rays flooded the valley from the east, lighting a painter's easel of browns, reds, yellows, and oranges. Georgia O'Keefe's colors. His mother's favorites. Not far over the horizon was the *Jornado del Muerto,* the first place on earth, in 1945, where the sun had risen in the West.

"It's so lovely, Dennis." Latoya kissed him with feeling.

"This is where my mother took her last views, during the Red Foam. I was too far away to help." He looked back across the road. Traces of the old building's foundations were still visible, but now a pre-Columbian vegetable garden was dominant. They wandered across. A lean brown man with a hoe, stripped to the waist, challenged them.

"Hey! This is Salt River Pima land. What's your business?"

"Uh...I'm sorry, but my mother died here. During the Red

Foam. I just came to see where she died, is all."

"That was a long time ago." The man rested on his hoe and considered. His long black hair bounced on the wind. "You came to see her, which means you care about her spirit. But why did you take so long? You immortal, just figured, 'Hey, I'll get around to it?'"

"A little bit. I have been back since 2113."

"From where?"

"Mars."

"Hmm, you've come a long way. My brother went there in the Marines. He ain't never come back, neither. Let's say a prayer for them both, and I'll show you where they dumped the ashes after they burned the home in 2045."

"They burned the home?"

"Full of Red Foam, I guess. Nothing else to do. After that, a lot of the retirees who used to live around here who were still left moved away. We took back our land. Don't worry." The shirtless man indicated a tall, sharp stone with curious inscriptions, situated on a red earth mound. "We remember them for you."

"Thank you."

Dennis lingered a while at the site, while the man, whose name was Stephen, lit sweet grass and chanted gently. When Dennis shook himself free of his trance, the sun was high in the sky and his stomach was rumbling. "Bet you're hungry."

"You could say that." Latoya shielded her eyes against the rising sun.

"Let me make myself presentable and grab the old Q-Truck. I'll treat you to some Huevos Rancheros and give you a lift to the Amtube."

"There's a station out here?"

"Phoenix is a weird case. Kind of part of North America still, kind of not. But this isn't Florida or Michigan. There's nobody running around with a skull on a staff telling people to eat other people."

Dennis and Latoya looked at each other. "Funny you should mention that."

"Yeah, well, we Indians had laws before you did. So, we've got streets, and power, schools, hospitals, and cops. No need to be afraid out here, unless you insist on certain things."

"Such as?" Dennis quizzed. Stephen looked like he was carved from soapstone, only occasionally letting his facial features betray emotion. His eyes were a curious deep gray.

"So-called 'property rights.' If your claim doesn't go back to the time of the Spanish, forget it."

"Glad I didn't buy property here."

"Gimme a second. Gotta get someone else to hoe this row for me."

While they waited for Stephen, they looked at the land, trying to imagine it in decades past. "When your mother was here, it must've been very different." Latoya wiped her brow. "Damn it's hot."

"They cocooned themselves in air-conditioning. They came here to get away from the cold, then took refuge from the heat. Never happy. Subsisting on cabinets full of pills. Long lives, but the last $1/3^{rd}$ a constant battle of aches, pains, expensive surgery, painful treatments."

"Sounds like you thought about it a lot."

Downslope from them, a group of Pima people worked a

beanfield with hoes and rakes. They wore bright white smiles. Women worked with babies on their backs. "See that?" Dennis pointed to them. "That's life, right there. Hard, maybe short, but it's real. Not shielded from the land, but part of it. That's what I thought a long life ought to be. So, I changed my focus from esoteric research, to really changing people's lives. And that's how the miracle came about."

"But those people have children, Dennis." Latoya said quietly.

Dennis sat on a large rock, heavily. "I know, I know. Like anything, the miracle is all about trade-offs. And it's about power, money, all the rest of it. I couldn't control it once it got out of the lab, any more than those bastards who created Red Foam could. Man has become two species, and that's my doing."

Stephen bounded out of the beanfield to meet them, wearing a natty guayabera shirt and a Panama hat. "Let's go, I'm starving."

Old Arizona Café
Phoenix

New Phoenix was a replica of the kitschy charm of Sedona, set down inside a crumbling metropolis. They drove through blocks of tidy, yet utterly deserted streets. Block-by-block, heavy machinery was demolishing buildings, after salvage crews had picked them clean of everything useful. In the end, the plots were used as urban gardens.

"This is remarkable, Stephen." Dennis craned his neck to watch three Mexicans load air conditioning units on the back of a flatbed. "Real recycling in action."
Stephen shrugged. "Nobody wants to live in houses where the Red Foam killed everyone, or where fallout came in from Los Alamos. We can rebuild it the way we want it, a human city on a human scale."

"You sound like an expert, Stephen." Latoya complimented him. "I get the sense you're not just a farmer."

"You're right. The University still runs courses, free for anyone who wants them. I got my Masters in Community Planning in '12. We're cannibalizing the old, inefficient city, and building a solar powered, earth-cooled new city on it's grave. Of course, some things, like the stadiums, can't be replaced. Demolishing them would be inefficient. So, they stay there as reminders. Here we are."

As Stephen parked the truck, Dennis peered down the street at the bulk of State Farm Stadium. He remembered a report from Fox News during the height of Red Foam, when it was being used as a massive field hospital. Did fans still think about that when they cheered on their teams?

The café was a curious construct, reminding Dennis immediately of Mars. Surrounded by a lot full of crops they were sure to be tasting on their plates, it was a long cylinder of corrugated steel, buried 2/3rds up in red soil, then topped with solar panels. They stepped down a long ramp to get inside.

"We got the idea from Mars, actually. Looks familiar?" Stephen queried him.

"Yeah, it does. Keeps it cool in summer, warm in winter, right?"

"Yup. And not a dollar spent on the meter. Hey Donna." Stephen greeted a buxom blonde waitress. "These are my guests, Dennis and Latoya."

"Welcome to Phoenix." Donna spoke in a southwest white drawl. Dennis looked around. The noisy, close, brightly painted place hosted a diverse crowd, speaking English, Spanish, and native tongues.

"Not what you expected, huh? The media always makes it seem like we pushed out all the white people." Stephen swept the room with a long arm. "We didn't. We just took advantage of a historical moment to end the bullshit. If you accept the way things are now, then howdy, neighbor. Hey, we got a table."

Dennis quickly realized that the meat on the menu was real. "How do you get away with that?"

Stephen smiled and poured coffee. "Nothing to get away with. We're autonomous. We accept that this is still 'America.' It couldn't be anything else. So, the Feds can work here, provided they don't throw their weight around too much. We contribute tax revenues to the common defence, which is cheaper than having our own army. Our people can live and work on the other side, under certain conditions, and you folks can do the same. Babies get made, not eaten. Very few people get turned away. But everyone works, and there's no damned caste system like there is on your side."

"Caste system?" Latoya raised an eyebrow.

Stephen laughed ironically. "Oh, come on! Normies and the Uncontrolled? Might as well say Brahmin and Untouchables, or Whites and Coloreds."

Dennis nodded. "It has the same effect. Is the miracle available here?" He knew the answer, but didn't want to endanger Herculio and Rosalinda's contact. Stephen seemed a little...doctrinaire.

Stephen shrugged. "Sure you can. But it won't pass muster over there. Most people here don't want it, and if they do, they don't want to get sterilized. What's life without kids?"

Dennis nodded. "And most people feel this way?"

"Not my brother." Stephen looked away for a moment. "Not Randy. He wanted to live long enough to see the galaxy." He flagged down the waitress. "He got Mars, anyway."

The food, when it arrived, was spectacular. Chicken with mole sauce. Huevos rancheros with succulent tomatoes, running with juice, and spicy habanero sauce. Tacos al pastor.

"Judging from the look on your face, I'd say you're considering moving here."

"Jesus. Real meat."

"Remind me to give you my contact's name in LA. He runs a *carniceria*. Mexicans don't do cloned meat. Should we try the margaritas?"

The rest of the afternoon was lost in laughter, fast friends, and strong tequila.

2045

Mission moon

SS Mark Watney
Halfway to Earth-Moon System

"You're here." Bolderova floated in her foot restraints as Dennis propelled himself through the hatch. "Thought I'd check the bar first."

"Considering there's no bartender on this flight, I think I'm being commendably sober. Well, let's have the bad news."

Bolderova hit the play button on the remote, and the face of a harried British scientist appeared on screen.

"Good Evening, or whatever it is there, from Porton Down. This is Dr Hugh Pinchcliffe with the NATO daily report on Red Foam, synthesizing the work of scientists all around the world. As always, let us remember who have died to bring us so much of this information, so that others may live."

"Amen." They both muttered.

"First up today is a new report on morbidity and mortality from the CDC in the United States. If you will look at the figures on screen, you will see a clarification of infectivity and mortality patterns from around the world. This information once again points to ethnicity as the most important variable."

Infectivity: R0: 2.3 (Symptomatic), 3.1 (Asymptomatic)

Susceptibility to Infection (Global): 72.6%

By Ethnicity (Selected):

Sub-Saharan African: 90.8%

Arab: 84.8%

Amerindian: 64.1%

Subcontinental Aryan: 80.7%

Caucasian: 88.3%

Han Chinese: 9.2%

Other Asian: 44.2%

Australoid: 45.6%

Other/Mixed: 66.5%

Mortality Rates:

Global: 66.5%

Sub-Saharan African: 70.4%

Arab: 68.9%

Amerindian: 52.2%

Subcontinental Aryan: 52.3%

Caucasian: 49.8%

Han Chinese: 3.2%

Other Asian: 33.7%

Australoid: 40.2%

Other/Mixed: 40.6%

Pinchcliffe cleared his throat, in the way English seemingly always did when about to deliver horrible news with no upside. "The ethnic variability in susceptibility to infection and mortality rates appear to point to only one conclusion, when combined with the other information at our disposal. It is Porton Down's considered opinion that this information must be accepted, no matter what the incendiary implications."

Bolderova looked at Dennis with a pained expression. The answer could only mean war.

"Porton Down concludes, with 95% probability, that Red Foam is a genetically engineered bioweapon, incorporating ethnic DNA tailoring for maximum kill ratio in selected groups, and minimal in the origin group. That origin group being Han Chinese, we therefore conclude that this bioweapon is a product of the People's Republic of China, and that this nation has committed an act of war on numerous UN member states by releasing this murderous weapon on the world."

"This conclusion, it should be noted, is not merely the result of statistical analysis. Outlined on the table below is the multiplicity of intelligence analyses contributing to the G-2 assessment, in conjunction with Four Eyes:"

NATO 45-233: ARRIVAL OF ASYMPTOMATIC PRC AGENT "SUPERSPREADERS AT NA PORTS OF ENTRY

NATO 45-240: PRC DEFECTOR FROM BIOWEAPONS PROGRAM DEBRIEFED IN TAIWAN

NATO 45-241: PREMATURE CLOSING OF PRC BASE ON MARS REPORTED BY Q-SPACE

NATO-45-447: ARRIVAL OF TUG "SANTA MARIA" WITH HIGH-RANKING PRC DEFECTOR AT SHACKLETON BASE, MOON; ACTIVE RF DISEASE ON BOARD

NATO 45-449: GENETIC ANALYSIS OF SAMPLES FROM 32 LOCATIONS BY CDC AND PORTON DOWN SHOWS "SPLICING" INDICATIVE OF BIOWEAPON

NATO 45-456: INTERCEPT OF PRC NATIONAL COMMAND SIGNALS REVEALS PREPERATIONS FOR TAIWAN STRAITS CROSSING

NATO 45-457: DEFINITIVE ACCOUNT OF CHENGDU BIOWEAPONS CONTAINMENT FAILURE: ACCIDENTAL RF RELEASE TWO WEEKS BEFORE FIRST REPORTED CASES

NATO 45-459: XINYANG OUTBREAK KILLS MANY UIGHURS, FEW HAN CHINESE

"For our scientific audience, please communicate, as calmly and factually as possible to your political and military commands, the importance of this conclusion. As always, we encourage spirited and fact-based objection and dissent. For our political and military audience, we suggest consideration of immediate retaliatory options, and a unified demand for an unadulterated vaccine that be made available immediately."

"God bless you all. As always, this briefing is considered:"

MOST SECRET

"If only they knew that a commie was listening in." Bolderova sighed.

"They're sharing this with the Russians, or they will if NATO drags it's feet." Dennis shook his head. "Jesus, this is bad."

"Navalny won't hesitate to hit. He won't wait for commissions of inquiry or such bullshit."

"NATO's secret weapon. The Russians."

"Why would they do this, Dennis?"

Dennis floated to the window and spotted the tiny blue spot they were headed to. A tiny blue spot wreathed in pain. "Like so many historical milestones, somebody left a fucking door open. It walked out of that lab in Chengdu on someone's shoe."

"That simple? What about all the evidence of intentional spreading?"

"I don't deny it was designed for mayhem. But was it intended to get out? I doubt it." Dennis chewed a nail. "Sure, the world was passing them by. Twenty-five years of suspicion after COVID-19 had never really cleared up. Their strident manner of communicating with the world was out of fashion, to put it mildly. Duplessis was conquering space, with the PRC along for the ride. None of it amounts to a *casus belli*."

"But once it got out, and they lied about it, then tried to profit from it…"

"It fits the pattern of COVID-19. Get the rest of the world on their backs, then get yourself in the best possible position to take advantage of the chaos. That's NATO's pretext for war."

"It sounds like a good one to me." Bolderova's square jaw was set. "Motherfuckers."

An intercom tone sounded. Dennis answered. "Dr Rosso."

"Doctor, it's Captain Kesuke. Priority communication from Space Force. Our eyes only. See me in my cabin."

"Yessir." He locked eyes with Bolderova. "Something tells me twice the maximum speed is not fast enough."

"Fuck this waiting. We can get there tomorrow, I am up for it. Go, talk to the Americans. Let's get there."

Captain Kesuke's Cabin

Kesuke admitted him to the VIP cabin, now empty on this funereal cruise, and converted to his needs. His crew were all enjoying hitherto unknown privileges. A small price to pay, Dennis considered, for what they were flying into.

Kesuke was freakishly tall for a Japanese, a ridiculously fit Jiu-Jitsu enthusiast who wasn't shy about exploiting his looks and his captain's wings for recreational purposes. "Dennis, welcome. We're waiting for General Lopez. He's a flat-topped hardhead with no taste for scientists. FYI."
"Thanks Yuki. Does this call for some Hokkaido Homeopathy?"

"If by that, you mean, this?" He held up a cold-sweating bottle of fine Sapporo sake.

"Um...if you insist."

Kesuke poured the syrupy, cloudy liquid into two bulbs. "*Kanpai*. I believe my ancestors used to drink this before crashing into your ancestors' battleships."

"How appropriate, considering the mission parameters are probably similar. My Uncle Ed curses your Uncle, by the way. Eight thousand feet down off of Okinawa is a real drag."

"My Uncle is honored. Oh, that's good. Here is bigshot, now."

Lopez appeared, scowling. "I assume you've heard the Porton Down briefing, Rosso?"

Now, the game of waiting began. Each response involved an eight-minute delay. Which they filled with surreptitious sake shots.

"Yes General." Kesuke had a hopelessly lost expression on his face. "May I brief Captain Kesuke?"

"No need. Kesuke, the PRC designed Red Foam as a bioweapon, tailored to wipe out other ethnic groups. Once it's done its work, they're going on a military offensive, starting with Taiwan next week."

"Bastards."

"Exactly. We intend to make them pay. But, there's on problem. Since Comrade Sugar Tits got herself locked out of Iron Mountain, the Acting President, Senator Russell, is in charge. But Senator Russell wants one more piece of evidence before being the first President in one hundred years to let the big ones fly. He wants it to be you, in a room with Yueh, getting him on record as saying they designed it, they lost control of it, and they took advantage of it. We can't wait three weeks for that, though."

Kesuke stammered out a defence. "But my ship is already at maximum Delta-V, General. We can't get there any faster."

"You've never seen the *NAS Buzz Aldrin* in action, son. She's already en-route to your location. Once there, she'll match speed and velocity, secure a docking collar to the *Watney*, and decrease your transit time to three days with one mother of a burn. We're sending your instructions, Kesuke, on secure telemetry. Make it work."

The screen went blank. "What an asshole." Dennis concluded.

Kesuke seemed haunted. "For a Japanese, what he is asking is… it is very difficult. To accomplish your mission is a worthwhile goal, Dr Rosso. But to do it so we can unleash the *Pikadon* on the world again…I am troubled."

"Yuki." Dennis floated next to him and put his arm around the Captain. Kesuke was clearly uncomfortable but did not shift. "What they have done will guarantee them control of all the worlds, maybe for all time. Nuking them is the only way. I'm sorry, but it's true."

"Bad things for good reasons. Again. We never change, Doctor. You may have made us live forever, but you cannot make us better people."

One negative aspect of a long life is that one never forgets the most barbed and perceptive criticism. And so, Dennis forever retained this one.

2117

MIRACLES ON THE CHEAP

Phoenix
Salt River Pina Hostel

Dennis awoke in a solid beam of strong, pure sunlight, the taste of hot vomit on his tongue.

Latoya groaned on a bunk beneath him. Stephen snored opposite him.

Dennis extricated himself as silently as he could, slipped into some moccasins, and went for a walk.

Soon, he found himself on a sun-baked street. A street-sweeper crawled by,
while large cats drowsily appraised him from their perches. It was the only way to appraise a neighborhood. Dennis recalled a teenaged trip to France, sneaking around in a suburban Paris neighborhood. Fat cats, brewing coffee, pain raisin.

He stopped in the middle of the street as it occurred to him.

This is not a foreign country. This is, or used to be, America.

He dug in his pockets and retrieved the note Rosalinda had given him:

Lim Pharmaceuticals
Advanced and Confidential
Genetic Medicine

According to the address, it was right around the corner. Dennis was so impressed by the size of it, more like a supermarket than the storefront he was expecting, that he almost bowled over the Asian man sweeping the sidewalk out front.

"Sorry."

"Why don't you watch where you go, hah? You need a genetic treatment for blindness! I can help!"

Dennis stared at the man. Stocky, younger than he ought to be, but wasn't everyone? Exactly the way he'd have expected the "Mr Lim" from his mother's e-mail to look.

"I look like movie star, eh? Like Jackie Chan, still making films! I could do it, too!" Lim made an impressive bicep for him.

"Tell about the home down the street." Dennis decided to go for broke. "During the Red Foam. You were a pharmacist here, weren't you?"

Lim looked aghast. "So long…so long ago. I try to forget…but…but…" His eyes welled with tears.

"It's okay." Dennis put an arm around him. "You can tell me. My mother was there. She mentioned you in her last e-mail."

Lim's eyes went wide. "You…you want revenge? It is fair. Maybe what I do is against God's wish? It's so hard to know these days. So hard."

"No, no revenge. Just…understanding. I would've wanted someone like you there if it was me. The Red Foam was…well, it was hell, wasn't it?"

"So bad. Seeing everyone die, except us. Everyone began to look at us, like we were responsible. I have to show a lot of people where Taiwan is on map! Were you here?"

"No. I was on Mars. I saw the exchange from the Moon."

"Whoa. I want to hear about this. Come inside for tea. I still have time before we open. Come in!"

Lim Pharmaceuticals

The building was a much larger version of the café from the day before. It was squat, mostly underground, and mounded with soil on two sides. A massive solar farm capped the roof. Gray water percolated out of rooftop taps in the early morning, to irrigate the crops in the soil.

"It's impressive…what should I call you?"

"Roger. My dad, he like James Bond, so he name me after Roger Moore. Mr suave, ha ha."

"Great." They entered a cool, spacious floor of examination rooms and diagnostic equipment.

"Biggest unlicensed miracle facility in North America! 50,000 patients a year! I have forty doctors and 300 other people on staff! Upstairs is the lab floor; we do better work there than most licensed places!"

"Have you ever looked into getting a license?"

"Ha ha, of course! They say, fuck you, not very nice people! They don't want anyone outside Normie areas to have the miracle. Even though we promise to do it the approved DCC way, right? With sterilization, okay? All about control, right?"

Dennis nodded. His carefully tended creation had become the anchor of what Stephen called "The Caste System."

They sat in Lim's office. He served green tea. An old clock ticked in the corner. A monitor showed early arrivals clocking in. "My people are the best! Everybody thinks Mexicans and Indians just good for farming, but they work so hard! Harder than Chinese!"

"I've heard good things about you. But I need to know about my mom."

Lim stiffened and looked out the tinted picture window to the mountains beyond. "I do the prescriptions for your mother's home. Which one was she?"

"Adeline Rosso."

"Rosso? You...Oh, wow, she never stop talking about her boy. I can't believe I am bragging about my unlicensed work, and you...you win the Nobel Prize? But you don't look anything like him..."

"Don't worry about it. My miracle has become...perverted. Used to separate people. I don't object to what you're doing here, Roger. Not one bit. As for the looks...well, some weird shit happened on Mars. About my mom..."

He cleared his throat and looked out the window again. "Towards the end, it was very bad. Everybody on staff die or go home to families. Only me coming, with my daughter... because we couldn't get sick. Your mom, very nice lady, very strong. She ask me to do it."

"I knew she would."

"She said she didn't want to live in this world anymore. 'Too fucked up, Roger.' She say, 'A real bummer.' She funny, too. So, one day, I go alone with sedatives and my gun. Make sure. Only six people left alive anyway. I waited to see if pills do the job... oh my God. I waited too long."

Lim dissolved in tears now. Dennis refilled his cup and waited. He had to hear the end. "What happened next, Roger?"

"Pills all worked. I know my job. I set home on fire and put big signs out, 'Danger: Infected.' Then, I go home. Only to find... only to find...another fire."

"What?"

"They come to set fire to my business, and my home, with my family inside. My girls. I could not protect them. They all die, because China start the virus. I did not show map of Taiwan enough, I guess. My girls…oh my God."

They sat in silence for a long while. Lim's messenger chimed, going unanswered. His secretary knocked on the door, giving Dennis a suspicious look through the glass. Lim waved her off.

"I start from nothing again, selling smuggled Mexican pills. I build this place on the grounds where my family was murdered. I show them. And I keep showing them."

Dennis pulled out a memory stick. "See this? Give this to your designers." He set it on Lim's desk.

"What is it?"

"A gift from Rosso Labs Mars. The ultimate iteration of the miracle. Better than the real thing, and indistinguishable in testing. Take it, it's yours. The only condition is, you see somebody doing things with the same attention to safety and quality, you let them have it for free, too."

"Why are you doing this?"

"Because it's time to rattle some cages."

Amtube Shuttle Station
Phoenix South

Stephen bade them goodbye at the curb. He shook Dennis' hand. "Glad you met up with Dr Lim. He does good things. Even if you don't want to live forever."

"Why don't you want to live forever, Stephen?" Latoya quizzed him.

Stephen rubbed his chin. "Life is a river that runs in a circle. Living forever is building a dam. Breaking the stream that runs from us to our children, and all the way back in time. It might be your way. It's not my way. Good luck." He hugged Latoya and disappeared into the crowd.

"I never thought anyone could make me have doubts about the wisdom of living forever. But that guy makes the case." Latoya looked into the crowd."

"You could always stay here and be a bean farmer."

"Shut up. Let's make that train."

The station was heavily secured, and their passports attracted an instant red flag. An unsmiling rail cop directed them to a small interview room, then locked the door behind herself. When the door opened a minute later, to their surprise, it was Fisk. "You're late."

"For what?" Dennis shrugged. "We were learning about the South West. Interesting people here."

"You've got a date in LA." He handed Dennis a holocard. "Lontraine's stem-cell supplier has a warehouse there. Started getting rich with a new nutrient medium in '96." He leaned in to whisper to Dennis. "You can keep the gun. Just in case."

Dennis tapped the card, and all sorts of manufactured protein danced in circles around it. Steaks, lobster, hamburgers, chicken...transplant organs.

Transplant organs? "Wait a second, does this supplier do medical tissues too?"

Fisk shrugged. "Why not? It's all just protein. Come on, let's get you on that train."

As the train shunted out of the station, the holocard nagged at Dennis. Latoya grabbed his hand.

"Something bothering you?"

"Everything's bothering me." *It's all just protein.* "We need to be careful in LA."

2045

Kamikaze rendezvous

SS Mark Watney
Approaching Earth-Moon System

The time leading up to the rendezvous had been frenetic, with precious little sleep. Given the skeleton crew on board, Kesuke could not afford to let anyone sit this one out.

And so, as the minutes ticked down to zero, Bolderova was sitting on the flight deck in an Engineer's chair, while Dennis, wearing an ill-fitting spacesuit, waited in the docking airlock with Krenz, the other engineer.

Krenz, a humourless German with a buzzcut and arms the size of tree trunks, briefed him on his role for the 30th time. "This is highest speed rendezvous in history between two manned ships. Can afford, no mistakes. The docking collar is supposed to affix automatically. But it is not rated for this speed. If *Aldrin* cannot make the grab, we open airlock, with you securing my harness and guiding me. I grab docking collar with big arms and pull it to the airlock. You've got it?"

"Yes."

"No questions?"

"No."

"Ha. We'll see."

A continuous feed from the bridge heightened the drama. "Aldrin at 22,500 K and closing at 177,300 KP/H. Capture phase two on Z-Bar trajectory." Collins was the other engineer, even less lighthearted than Krenz.

Soon, Dennis could see what had once been a tiny blip resolve itself into a spaceship on the airlock monitor. And what a strange ship it was. The *Buzz Aldrin*, named after the Apollo astronauts' "Dr Rendezvous," was mostly fuel tanks and engines, clustered around a tiny crew compartment.

Kesuke had explained it thusly: "It's only job is to make things that need to go faster get there faster. If you didn't bring enough Delta-V, *Aldrin* is like your mom. She brings your lunch to school, so you don't pass out."

What the *Aldrin* had been doing in deep space in the four years since she'd been commissioned, no one would say. But rumor had it, she'd just returned from Jupiter.

Jupiter? What the hell was going on out there?

"Prepare for airlock depress." Krenz announced in a basso profundo. "Three, two, one…"

Dennis was hanging on to a handrail and hooked to a three-point zero-gee harness. But he still flew almost halfway out into deep space with the rapidly sublimating atmosphere. Krenz almost drifted out of reach, and impulsively, Dennis reached for his boot.

"It's okay, Dennis. Look."

In the distance, *Aldrin* was braking. Six massive thrusters, designed to slow and match velocities at unimaginable speeds, formed a halo around her. Soon, she had gone from a rapidly moving interceptor, to a massive companion he felt like he could reach out and touch.

Ahead of them, the Sun, God of the Worlds, shone in blinding, auroral light. Dennis swallowed profound, unspeakable emotion. *What horrors had to transpire, for me to witness such beauty?*

Not for the first time since that cold day in Detroit, he gave thanks to Providence for the miracle. For its possibility, and for allowing him to be the one to find it. Now, he could see such a wonder in anyone of a million systems, should forcefields hold and suns refrain from exploding. But this was the first.

Comms from the bridge brought him back to business. "*Watney*, this is *Aldrin*." A pinched Southern accent announced. "We're matched on course and velocity. Permission to slave your helm to our control?"

Kesuke responded. "Permission granted." There was a noticeable lurch, then a smooth transition.

"*Watney*, we have you. Prepare for docking collar deploy."

"Send the collar, we're ready." Krenz announced.

"Copy that, *Aldrin*?"

"That's affirm. Deploying." On the side of the *Aldrin's* pencil-thin crew compartment, a hatch opened, spilling orange light into the ether. Slowly, the light was blotted out by an inflating shape, which soon resolved itself into a long, obscene proboscis, headed towards them.

"We see your docking collar." Krenz announced. "On course, looks good."

Dennis looked at the two ships, now flying formation. The *Buzz Aldrin*, product of the no-nonsense North American military, designed purely for function, and named after a real space hero.

The *Mark Watney*, underneath her, as functional in her form as a 1950s car, all swoops and streamlining, designed by a fantasist and named after a fictional space hero. Sunlight glinted off her burnished hull, and Dennis shaded his visor.

"Damnit, *Watney*, we got a jam. We can't free her. We're gonna need you to come to us."

Krenz looked down at Dennis. "I'll go up. Just make sure my lines don't get snagged. When I give you the word, reel in the cable, okay?"

"You've got it." Over Krenz' head, the narrow docking collar had stalled, and now drifted like a flaccid cock. Krenz, encircled by a yellow and black grappling tool, rooted to *Watney* by firm, carbon-carbon cables, gave a thumbs up.

"Reeling him out now." Dennis announced. He positioned himself next to an open control unit outside the airlock, and suddenly, Krenz moved quickly towards the American ship.

"Slow your rate. By half." Krenz cautioned him, and Dennis adjusted his controls. "It's good now. Steady."

Krenz' tiny figure was quickly lost in the glare of the sun, a mote between two giants. "Talk to me, I can't see you now."

"One hundred meters. Aldrin, can you see me?"

"Turn on your beacon."

Suddenly, a strobe came on, its pulse imprinting his optic nerve even against the background of the sun. "You've got me now?"

"Yes, you are clear. Fifty meters. Slow your rate."

"Got it." Dennis reduced the rate of approach by half. The bridge was silent. Looking down into the airlock, he could see the approach from Krenz' suitcam, the long docking collar filling out as it inflated, the rigid collar popping up like an aroused member. Krenz rotated, the probes on his harness now outstretched, lining up with the blinking lights, green and red, on *Aldrin's* docking port.

"Dennis, I have control now." Krenz' voice was taut with concentration.

"You have control." From only having practiced this in VR, Dennis thought he was doing well. But now, it was all in the hands of the taciturn German.

"Five, four, three, two…one…capture. Stand by Dennis, I am bringing the collar in."

"Copy that." Dennis looked down to the markers the docking collar was supposed to hook into, then pressed a button on his wrist to lower the platform he stood on back into the airlock. Krenz was closing fast, the strobe becoming disorienting. "Cut the strobe, Aldrin."

The strobe blinked out. "Cut. We show fifty meters your end. Thruster adjust needed."

"Do it."

The monotony of the strobe was replaced by thrilling, pounding jets of orange fire overhead. Now, only Dennis's head was out of the airlock. He reached his arms up as Krenz' boots came into view.

The German landed on him like a rugby tackle, knocking him on his back. Somehow, he held on. "Cut the drive!" He yelled.

"All drives, cut, we've got it from here!" Together, they reached for the metal skeleton of the grappler, pulling it down and lining it up with *Watney's* airlock. One-by-one, the green and red lights extinguished. Free space disappeared from view, and the starfield was replaced with bright white, artificial light again.

Krenz checked an indicator on the wall, Dennis catching a glimpse of his tumbling, spacesuited figure on the monitor.

"Bridge, repress now."

Kesuke responded. "That's a hard dock, guys! Great job!"

Krenz patted him on the shoulder, surprising him. "Good job, spaceman!"

The two men looked up, as the air from *Watney* and *Aldrin* gushed in from both sides, and filled the long, Kevlar tunnel.

Two Days Later
Approaching Lunar Orbit

NA Buzz Aldrin did not land on spherical worlds. Therefore, all it could contribute to *Watney's* arrival at the Moon was a long and powerful burn to bleed off the insane Delta-V that Kesuke had concluded could only have been the result of a gravity assist from the Outer Solar System.

"They've been out there. Way out there, Dennis. No wonder they look like they've seen the Starchild."

"Seen the Starchild," an allusion to the plot of *2001: A Space Odyssey,* was already space traveller's slang for voyaging out beyond the Asteroid Belt. Dennis's curiosity was piqued. What the hell was going on out there? Had the powers that be seen the Red Foam, and decided a starship full of immortals was Earth's only hope? Where better to build it than out there, far beyond prying eyes and killing viruses?

They could only speculate. The tunnel between *Aldrin* and *Watney* was one-way only. "Civilians not allowed."

But Dennis had other mysteries waiting for him. As the *Watney* approached the vertical solar panels ringing Shackleton Base, he wondered if he could solve them. And, at what cost?

Earth hung low and engorged on the horizon, as it always did at this latitude. Dennis looked at his home world close-up for the first time in five years and wondered if he could save it.

2117

California normal

Amtube Intercontinental
Pacific Terminus Cesar Chavez

The train had completed its run from Phoenix in less than 45 minutes. Soon, they were emerging from the tunnel, passing through South-Central LA under wired metal caging and elevated crosswalks.

"Nice to see some things don't change." Dennis muttered.

Latoya awoke and gripped his hand, eyes blinking awake. "What's that, honey?"

"LA is still a dump." A man across the aisle harrumphed at him and hid behind an old-fashioned hard copy of *The LA Times*.

"Oh my." Latoya looked out the windows in shock. South-Central had burned in the 2045 riots, shaken to pieces in the 2057 9.1 quake, and then been slowly reclaimed by nature. Though it was nominally part of North America, the city and county seemed to have lost their grip on its governance.

As the train continued to decelerate, they could see that much of old LA was in this condition. Rubble garden, the original residents long since fled, only makeshift buildings arising in place of the old houses and strip malls that had once defined the broad and endless city of cities.

The train announced the first stop in a soulless voice. "Gardena." Dennis took the card Fisk had given him back in Phoenix out of his breast pocket. Latoya looked at the hologram.

"Where that warehouse is?"

"We could get lucky."

"That'd be a first."

Dennis saw a Chinese man budging past the departing passengers to find a seat. He found on, across the aisle from them, and sat staring out the window, with that look that only comes from ownership. "Excuse me?"

The man was broad, and solid, a glinting TAG on his wrist the only concession to wealth display. He flinched at the enquiry. "Do I know you?"

"No, but I'm guessing you're from here. I've been gone a long time. Wondering what happened."

"It's all online."

"I've been a little busy." Dennis leaned forward and whispered. "Besides, they don't always tell you what you want to know."

Outside, the wasteland had been replaced with low, functional apartment blocks. Hovering LAPD airships were the first sign someone actually cared about what happened here.

The man sighed. "Okay. I've been gone all month. Coast-to-coast trip, sales, you know? Buy me lunch and you get a story."

"What's for lunch?" Latoya asked.

"Best noodles in town. And in this town, that's saying something." Finally, the man smiled.

Noodletown
Wilshire

Fortunately, Alex Zhang's favorite noodle place was impossible to miss, and two blocks from Cesar Chavez Station. Noodletown was the ultimate progression of the Hawker Centres Dennis had seen in Singapore. Every food obsession you could have, under one roof.

Only in this case, with typical California excess, it was one single food obsession, obsessed on over seven floors with a combined floor space of five football fields. All painted bright yellow.

This had *definitely* not been here the last time he was…in 2037? He knew it was on a speaking tour. He had been talking advanced biochemistry and bioethics to audiences interested only in the spiritual and economic implications. At the time, he'd wanted to give up and go home.

Now, he was thinking that the Californians had been on to something. Dennis had settled on a Tokyo Ramen, which smelled delicious, chased by a cold Sapporo. As Alex had hinted that perhaps attitudes towards real meat were "flexible" here, he was hoping Stephen's fabled *carniceria* was a supplier here. One bite into his pork slices, and he was certain.

Latoya had selected some sort of Thai concoction, whose aromas almost made him regret his choice. There were always seconds, of course.

Even at 1130, the place was jam-packed and maximum-loud. Asian eating factories always were. He'd regretted never seeing Great Wall 2's effort, which was, by all accounts, legendary. Even on Mars, they'd had a full selection of live fish.

Latoya's voice revived him to the present. "Why this guy, Dennis?"

"Well…this is going to sound crazy. But the way he looked out that window…well, it was like he knew the place. And we need somebody who knows the place. I mean, do you know LA?"

"Well, no..." Pensively, she broke out her chopsticks.

"Neither do I. I mean, it's been eighty fucking years since I've been here. It's a big, mean place, where a lot of stuff has happened. This ain't Atlanta."

"You don't need to tell me. I mean...where are all the black people?" She whispered the last part.

"From the way South-Central looked, they sure as hell don't live there anymore."

"Found it." Alex sat at the table with a self-satisfied smile. "*Char Kway Teow.*" He sniffed at the plate in satisfaction. Golden noodles writhed in dark brown sauce. "Best this side of Singapore." He clinked Dennis's Sapporo with a Tiger and drank greedily. "Won't get anything else done today. Ah, fuck it."

"You don't seem very Chinese." Latoya said it with a smile, and like so many attractive women, Dennis noticed, got away with it.

"I'm a banana, for sure. My family got us here after the Exchange."

Dennis glared. "You mean, after the Red Foam?"

Alex shrugged. "My story, my words. After the Exchange, like so many people, my family fled south. But Singapore could only take us temporarily. Peru agreed to take us, and we lived in Lima till I was ten, then snuck up to Cali in '54. The place was still smouldering, and we had to fight for everything. My dad tried to build a corner store, but some crazy black people chased him out. But after '57, the Big One...most of those people left or died. Now, it's all Chinese refugees and Central Americans."

"What's it like there?" Dennis was like a tourist on his own planet, starved for knowledge and context.

"You saw it." Alex shrugged again. "Even the LAPD doesn't give a shit. They haven't even tried to rebuild south of the I-10. If you want to get out, you've got to get noticed."

"How'd you get noticed?"

His mouth full, Alex held up a hand. "Not me, my dad. He was a biochemist in China. He came up with a way to make Agar mediums faster so you could make nutrients fast, so you could clone faster. He sold it to Nutriworld in '61. Before long, we were living in the West Valley. I could finally go to university; we could all get the miracle. It was a good time."

Dennis shook his head. "Your dad is a biochemist?"

"Yeah, so am I. So what?"

He looked at Latoya, whose eyes were full of caution. "I'm a biochemist, too. I won the 2035 Nobel Prize. Do you know who I am?"

Alex dropped his chopsticks. "Yes…I mean, I know who won the prize that year, everybody does, but you don't…I mean you don't look like him, man. You look more like the other guy, frankly…wait…are you?"

Dennis held out his hand. "Dennis Rosso, at your service. Now, I really do need to meet the esteemed Dr Zhang. Can you set it up for me?"

"Well, Dr Rosso…I would love to, but my dad is retired. He's very particular about who he talks to…"

"Too particular for the father of the science?"

Now, Alex Zhang was acting Chinese. He bowed his head, subtly, and hurried not to give further offence. "Never! No, I will set it up! Come to our home, tomorrow, for lunch!" He handed over a holocard with a map programmed in. "I am sure my father will be honored."

"As will I." Dennis slurped his broth. "Damn, these noodles are *Oishi.*" He turned the card Alex had given him over. Meats danced in a circle. He took out the card Fisk had given him in Phoenix. *Identical.* Latoya' eyes went wide.

Alex Zhang smiled nervously and hit his beer hard.

**Chateau Marmont
Hollywood**

There were certainly many more practical places Dennis Rosso could have stayed in LA. But as a boy, his imagination had always been captured by the tales of dissolution and debauchery associated with this ancient castle in the Hollywood Hills. And so, he pulled the rental Rivian Roadmaster to the private driveway entrance, barely scraping the modern behemoth inside.

"And now? How do we get out?" Latoya giggled.

"Sheer force of horniness." He replied.

Like so many natural forces, Dennis reflected, these things worked better when they were not questioned. Soon, they were making vigorous love where perhaps, once, Warren Beatty had plowed his way through the ingenue population, or Jim Morrison had slept off a drug binge. You could *feel* the ghosts. They leaked out of the still visible cracks from '57 and followed you everywhere.

As he stood in the private garden nursing a Tequila Sunrise, Dennis reflected on ghosts. Once, there were so many, in a world where the dead outnumbered the living. Even now, thanks to the Red Foam and the Exchange, there were still so many.

But one day, perhaps, thanks to him, there would be no more. Only a few, like him, would remember the dead, and if those rememberers were spread throughout the galaxy, who would be there to care about Morrison, or John Belushi, or Helmut Newton?

Latoya appeared beside him, a tranquil look on her face. She stole a sip from his drink.

"You like it? I could make you one?"

She laughed. "I can't day drink like you soused scientists."

"What's the matter, Latoya? The old you would've been all over me with questions about that thing back there, with Alex Zhang. Now…nothing."

"The old me? You haven't even known me two weeks, Doctor Rosso! And as for getting to know you, you aren't even wearing your own face!"

He sat heavily on a bench. "You wouldn't like my own face."

She sat beside him and took a much larger sip. "You don't know what I like. Anyway, maybe I am just learning to trust your instincts. You sure did find Alex Zhang right off the bat. I have a feeling you are on a journey, maybe one like a circle, like Stephen was talking about? Part now, part then. You know the answers now. I was just there to get you started and help you along the way. Maybe this whole thing is for you to find out what the point of your life has been. Maybe, what the point of everyone's life is going to be now. Shit."

"What?"

"Thass a good fucking drink. Listen to me carry on." She began to giggle.

He made two more Tequila Sunrises. Then they made love again.

Hollywood Arco 7
Burbank

Burbank was an old studio city north of the Hollywood Sign. Now, it was peppered with massive, ziggurat-like arcologies. In one of those arcologies were the offices of Samuel Benzleman, Doctor of Psychiatry.

As Latoya had slept off, loudly, her second Tequila Sunrise, it had occurred to Dennis that, if Ronald's account of his horrific dreams was in anyway representative, then many others must have had them. Many others having such dreams would give rise to a "syndrome" of some sort, and eventually, an ambitious head shrinker would specialize in this "syndrome" for all he was worth.

And where else to look but Los Angeles? New York was a radioactive crater, so that left LA.

And so, Dennis had secured an appointment with Dr Samuel Benzleman, "Specialist in Acute Immortality Somnolence Maladjustment Disorder (AISMD)."

His office commanded a view of the two LAs, side-by-side. Painted orange by low sun, ruin jungle against modern glass and plastisteel. Like two Berlins, when he was born, or two Koreas, now one single ruin.

"Dr Kassabian?" At least Benzleman was not one of those pricks who kept you waiting. He reminded Dennis of the actor Paul Giamatti, a slouching, bald-headed man, famous for never changing himself, miracle or not.

People made many choices with the miracle. Some, more interesting than others. "Hello, Dr Benzleman. So good of you to see me on such short notice." He extended a hand and Benzleman took it. The shrink looked like he'd come from the tennis court. "Good game?"

Benzleman waved a hand in mild disgust. "Never. I'm always dumb enough to play my girlfriend. She refuses to tell me what work she's had done that made her that good."

"Maybe she's just that good?"

Benzleman gave him a sideways glance. "Natural talent? A quaint notion."

"After what I've seen, I like quaint notions."

"Hmm. Okay. We'll I've blocked off the rest of the afternoon to talk to you. Put a few noses out of joint, but frankly, I don't care. How many times will I get to talk to a Nobel Prize winner?"

Ah, yes. THAT Nobel Prize. The one they should've shared. The one that left Kassabian with two, and him with one. Decades later, he still had to will himself into calmness.

It was a very strange thing, he realized, going to see a psychiatrist as someone else. But explaining the whole thing took up too damned much time. He realized Benzleman was looking at him, expecting interplay. "Doctor? I can get changed, or we can just get started..."

"Let's get into it." Dennis plopped down on the sectional, a ridiculously comfortable thing. There was only one thing missing...

"Drink?"

"Ah..." One more Tequila Sunrise and he'd be taking out every star on the Walk of Fame. And a few of their owners. "Water is fine."

They passed those few moments of discomfort common to all

first encounters with a psychiatrist. "You've been to LA before, Doctor?"

"Call me Henrik, please." He tried to recall the biography, then realized that Kassabian was from here, and lying to Benzleman was going to be more trouble than explaining himself. "Actually, call me Dennis. I'm his arch-rival, Dennis Rosso."

Benzleman looked at him skeptically. "Or, is it possible you are delusional?"

Dennis sighed. "Last act of the Martian War. 2113. He was on one side; I was on the other."

Benzleman's eyes went wide. "And then what happened?"

"Actually, Doctor, I came here to ask you some questions."

"About what?"

Two Hours Later

Dennis had read somewhere once that psychiatrists had terrible rates of suicide themselves. One hour of listening to Benzleman, who had clearly needed to unburden himself to someone, anyone, had convinced him that this was the case.

It had to be. The stacks of patient files on the coffee tables made Latoya's collection look trifling by comparison. These were the tales of the living, mostly.

And they were all the fucking same.

Ronald's dream of crawling bi-chromatic corpses was repeated, with only minor variations, in almost all of the under-eighty patients.

The over-eighties, instead, developed a calm, peaceful certainty that they had seen it all, and were moving somewhere better. The intensity of this feeling, Benzleman had deduced on his own, increased with both age, and number of restorative or cosmetic tissue additions received.

Dave and Tammy Phillips. So sure of themselves. He'd put it down to religion, but he just hadn't asked the right questions.

Benzleman was standing at the window now, looking out at the bisected city at dusk, herbal tea abandoned in favour of single malt. "You can't see it when you look out there. And if you had to guess, you'd guess wrong, Dennis."

Dennis looked up from the file of a man who had fed himself to Great White Sharks. He figured Virgil would've been jealous of that one. "What's that, Sam?"

"Well, if you had to guess which side of the city was more miserable, you'd guess the south side, right? It looks like hell. But the real misery is over here, where people are rich, and they live forever."

"How can you be so sure of that, Sam?"

"I spend four days a month running a clinic in Inglewood. I hear the stories shrinks were hearing a hundred years ago. I drink too much, I think I'm gay, my wife doesn't love me anymore. Not horrors like these. I hate to say it, Dennis, but I think you might have to give that Nobel Prize back."

Dennis smiled grimly. "Only if Kassabian gives his back first."

"What do you think? What should we do?"

"You can send a questionnaire to your patients. To the under-eighties, ask about diet. Now there's a lot of black-market meat in this town, so focus on people who eat the legal stuff. For the over-eighties, you're already on the right track. Just get as much info as you can on clonal tissue treatments received by that group. And set up a control for both groups."

"So, it's not inherent to the miracle, then? It's something that came after?"

"It has to be. If it was inherent, this would've cropped up sooner. Everything you've seen, and everything my colleague has seen, has come up since 2110. Something changed then. And the change is accelerating. But only among people who open themselves to it."

"A mutation? An additive?"

"My moneys on an additive, Sam." He stood to leave. "You talk to the DCC about this yet?"

"No…I mean, should I?"

"Hell, no. They're into it, whatever it is. And it's in both the food supply and the organ chain."

"God almighty."

"Here's my card. Talk only to me. Got it?"

Benzleman nodded. "Yes. Okay. We'll send out the questionnaires today. What about you?"

"I have a lunch date tomorrow. With a blast from the past."

When he drove out of the Arcology, Virgil's jetpack suicides were playing on massive billboards to staring crowds. Some people were cheering.

The change is accelerating.

2045

The infinite horrors of dr yueh

Shackleton Base
The Moon

In his thirty years as a scientist, Dennis Rosso had learned to play power games. Few professions were more hierarchical than science.

It had only been natural for the third and fourth-tier scientists at Shackleton to treat a Nobel Laureate like Fu Wen Yueh like a superstar on his arrival. As much as you could treat someone in isolation like that. For weeks, people had been hanging on his every word.

Now, Dennis let him sit. Oh, he watched Yueh out of the corner of his eye, of course. One monitor was always focused on the too-tall Chinese with the stooped shoulders and thin, narrow face.

At first, Yueh was composed. However, as the waiting game entered its third day, he began to pace. For a Chinese, it was the equivalent of a psychotic break.

The waiting was not all a game, however. Dennis had arrived on the Moon scarcely wiser than he had been when he'd left Hellas. That was because most of the briefing materials, containing a *casus belli* with China, were considered too sensitive for transmission.

On the day of his arrival, he had received two critical data sticks: One was a summary of earthbound knowledge and observations about Red Foam. The other was a summary of the unfortunate fate of the crew and passengers of the *SS Santa Maria*.

Neither made for a good sleep aid. For 72 hours, with only staggered breaks for fitful sleep percolated with horrific nightmares, Dennis and his staff had watched a synopsis of the dissolution of the Planet Earth.

Red Foam incubated slowly, one critical factor in its spread. But once symptoms arrived, the disease was a horror show in fast-motion. Exhalations came out as bloody red foam, hence the name. Facial muscles became slack and stupefied, like Ebola, leaving the dying and the dead with hollow expressions of horror witnessing on their faces. And, worst of all, in some cases, there was a sudden, animalistic aggression like Rabies, contributing still further to the spread.

Dennis watched one video from a train station in the UK. Seventy years later, he would still see it when he closed his eyes.

Shot from above, an obviously unwell woman shambles into range of the security scanners, heading for a ticket desk. Others in the lineup spot her face, seeing the telltale signs, and begin to part. Some run.

This triggers an atavistic response in the woman. She begins to grab, bite, flail. She corners a little girl, separating her from her mother, then savaging her. A policeman beats on her with a baton, to no avail, then produces a taser. She nearly chews through his right arm.

This is not a zombie movie. The bitten souls do not immediately spring into action and attack others. Instead, assured of their fate, they fall to the floor and weep. There is nothing that can be done.

Sacrificing their lives, the other passengers pick the woman up, and toss her in front of a speeding Eurostar.

Curiously, though survival is possible for other, less violently acquired cases of Red Foam, for the Rabies-style, it is virtually impossible. A mutation, perhaps? Or, an intentional, souped-up version, deliberately designed to maximize fear? Dennis made yet another note.

Bolderova, on the other hand, had seen enough. "I did not come to watch movies. I came to fight this thing. Time to get started."

Bolderova was a virologist, a natural addition to his team, Red Foam or not. Viruses were ideal in gene therapy due to their natural tendency to highjack cells and inject foreign genetic material. She knew her stuff and was too damned headstrong to control anyway. "Fine. But for fuck's sake, be careful."

"As careful as I can." He didn't like that answer, but he let it go.

The *SS Santa Maria* arrived two hours before a directive forbidding all arrivals at Lunar and orbital bases from Earth went into effect. It would serve as a *prima facie* rationale for such a travel ban from then on.

Santa Maria had brought a routine crew replenishment, as well as visiting researchers from Sweden, Taiwan, and Argentina. Of these, the Taiwanese researcher was immediately considered suspect, due to discrepancies between his documents and the manifest submitted by the Republic of China.

The reason for this soon became apparent when the real Taiwanese researcher was found locked in a closet at the Star Portal orbital transfer base. At this point, Dr Yueh revealed his identity, and was separated from the other passengers.

He had now outlived his Taiwanese counterpart, who, like 90% of the people on Star Portal, was dead of Red Foam.

The passengers and crew were sequestered in giant, pressurized maintenance bays dating back to the construction of the radio telescopes. Three bays could hold the people from three shuttles in isolation, with rudimentary facilities. What's more, adjacent workshop and living quarters allowed separation between researchers and subjects.

Most reassuring for the people at Shackleton Base: it was all over a hill, separate from and out of sight of them. If the Red Foam got out, nobody was coming to help them.

By the time Dennis and Larissa had arrived, one tug had already cleared quarantine, and another had four days left. The people inside Bay 2, denizens of the *SS Far Hope,* paced like caged animals, for though despite the fact that the situations in other Bays were supposed to be kept quiet, it was clear they knew that Bay 1 was a place of horror.

For indeed, it was. One of the crew, a steward, it turned out, had visited Hong Kong days before departure, and not disclosed this fact. On the fifth day of isolation, he came down with a fever and body aches.

Within the next ten days, fifteen of the 22 passengers and crew sickened and died, leaving the rest helpless, either stoic, catatonic, or raging. Seven, including Dr Yueh, kept isolated from the rest, still lived. Three had the Red Foam, and four would most likely not get it now.

Of those infected, two showed signs of recovery, and the other, as Dr Poole, the volunteer from Shackleton supervising Bay 1 put it in her uniquely insensitive way, was "circling the drain."

Luckily, there had been no Rabies-type patients. Bolderova would now focus on the recovered patients and the antibodies in their blood, and the unique factors in the blood of the immune. Two of the immune were not Asian, which made them of particular interest.

As far as interests went, for Dennis Rosso, there was only one.

He intended to talk to Yueh one-on-one, and break down the entire genesis of Red Foam, how and why it was made, how it was released, and what exactly it would take to stop it.

Would Yueh realize that his admissions, once made in front of a recognized global scientific authority, would likely sign the death warrants of hundreds of millions of his countrymen?

If he was anything like the scientists Dennis Rosso had known throughout his career, then he couldn't resist a little bragging.

He turned away from his restless quarry and looked out at the glowering Earth that depended upon it all. Never in his life had he felt such pressure.

Thirty-six Hours Later

Dennis had finished with videos of the Red Foam. For much of the intervening time, he had watched skilled policemen, interrogating elusive and intelligent killers.

There was little storm and drama to their approach. They formed a rapport, demonstrated an intimidating command of the facts, then put their case to the quarry as a *fait accompli*. Yes or no. Zero or one?

As he entered the observation room opposite Yueh's cell, he knew he would never be more ready. He only hoped he was ready enough.

After all, Yueh was willing to talk. He had brought himself here. He had already admitted that Red Foam was a bioweapon, not deliberately released, but negligently so, and that China had acted on this accident belligerently, not humanely.

But there could always be something left out. Some self-serving tidbit that could let off the guilty or provide an unwarranted alibi. Some missing piece that could make the difference between billions saved, or a thin patina of survivors clinging to the ruins.

And they had put it all on him. Twelve years ago, he'd been the biochemistry world's Willy Loman, an also-ran hacking out a living in a wasteland city.

But now, he was a Nobel Laureate, as was the man he would interrogate. And nobody would ignore what they said.

Yueh looked up from what he was reading. "Took you long enough." He spoke primly accented Cambridge English.

Dennis smiled and sat down. The thick glass between them gave Yueh's face an orange tinge. "A Cambridge man, yes."

"It does take you a long time to read a dossier, doesn't it?" Yueh folded his long legs in annoyance.

"Say, neighbour." Dennis smiled again. "Let's pretend that we've both got the brains the Nobel Committee gave us the credit for, eh?"

"I haven't given you any reason to think I don't."

"Oh really? You seem to have forgotten how many airlocks there are around here. Such a confusing array of switches."

Yueh smiled condescendingly. "Physical threats? Really? I thought they were sending me an intellectual, not an Irish policeman."

Dennis opened the file in front of him. "Never underestimate the Irish, Dr Yueh. Now, here's the deal. The world is depending on us for the definitive version of events. Nothing held back, no 'nice version' to save face. Something your part of the world is notorious for, I'm afraid. If we don't give them that, and a vaccine, in short order, I'm afraid we could be going out the airlock together."

"I doubt you'd have anything to worry about."

"Well, at least we've established that you do. And don't be so sure about me. Plagues where men of science are of little help are historically bad for men of science."

"It was an accident."

"What was?"

"The release. The virus was designed by me along with a six-man team. A chimera, with elements from Influenza, Ebola, and Rabies. The worst of all possible nightmares. But the real trick, the real coup, was tailoring it for reduced virulence among Han Chinese. Other Asians benefitted somewhat, of course."

"When did you do this?"

"The initial research began in 2037. By 2040, we had perfected it, and were ready to install if on DF-9 ICBMs as a last-ditch weapon."

"Who authorized the development?"

"The Politburo. They were afraid that the West, following your development, was on the verge of producing a race of super soldiers, unkillable, fearing nothing."

Dennis laughed, causing Yueh to frown. "They sure got that wrong. The only people they can recruit for the armed forces these days are the ones who can't afford the miracle any other way. Looks like you misjudged our intent."

"I agree. We did. I had lived in the West, unlike the members of the Politburo. I argued that, given time, immortality would simply produce a race of lotus eaters. You would destroy yourselves."

"Did your argument work?"

"Yes. The warheads were shelved. The virus was confined to a single facility, in Chengdu. The only thing that I had recommended be done that was not was the production of a vaccine. The Politburo considered any further handling of the virus too risky, for any purpose."

"Tell me about the accident."

"This I only know second-hand. My colleague, Dr Shen, has communicated what is probably a more accurate version to the rebels in Taiwan. Apparently, during an inventory of BSL-4 substances in the lab, a vial was put in the wrong place, then removed for research without the proper precautions. During an airflow inventory, the agent was discovered at large. By then, it was too late. A foreign teacher in Chengdu was the first victim. We isolated him and arrested several hospital staff with loose tongues. The city was cut-off. It was then that I was summoned to the Politburo to give expert advice at a special, closed-door session."

Dennis looked down at his notes. The other defector, Shen, had corroborated his account. He knew what was coming next. On this, everything depended.

"What was discussed at this meeting?"

"I knew things had gone seriously wrong when I heard the Chairman's remarks. 'Now, comrades, we are presented with an opportunity in the guise of a setback. Many of us were in decision-making roles the last time this happened, with COVID-19. Then, we acted only half-heartedly to defend our interests. And what was the result? The world suspected and hated us anyway! We lost a major share of world trade. Nations armed against us, becoming more suspicious of our influence. This time, I suggest, as distasteful as it may be to our Socialist values, we take advantage of this accident, and seize the mantle of the world's only superpower, decisively!' At that, the applause was furious. I was horrified. Old man Le, the conscience of the Politburo, 88 years old, was the only one to stand and denounce the Chairman. I can still hear the words of this brave, dignified survivor of so much history. 'Silence, silence you gangsters! You have become the enemies of the world! They will turn on us and destroy everything we have built! Stop, before it is too late! Go back to your lab, young man, and bring us a vaccine in atonement!' He disappeared after that speech."

"What were your specific orders?" Dennis realized he was talking about his mother's death. That, and so many others.

"Early on, we had optimized the role of asymptomatic spreaders as an alternative, 'stealth' delivery mode. This allowed me to follow the Chairman's orders to the letter. We infected 230 agents of State Security, of whom only 24 became ill. Of the remainder, 56 showed signs of powerful abilities to spread with an R-Nought of 4 plus. These we dispatched to North America. We had declared war on the rest of the world."

There it was. The smoking gun. "Will you help us? My colleagues will need your advice, on everything from splicing, to percentages, to ethnic susceptibilities…"

Yueh held up the book he'd been reading. "Will they need a vaccine?"

"Wha…what? You have one? I thought you said you didn't…"

"We haven't made one. But after I sent the super spreaders out, I had some time on my hands." Yueh peeled the pages of the book apart to reveal long lists of equations and formulae. "Decontaminate this and get started. It should save you a few months."

"But why didn't you show us sooner?"

"You said so yourself. Two Nobel's are better than one." Yueh smiled sadly. "I can be the disease, and the cure, too."

Dennis stared at the scribblings and the man who had made them. *I can say the same thing.*

Ninety Minutes Later

Dennis sent the interview to General Lopez and Dr Pinchcliffe by encrypted telemetry. Lopez responded immediately. "This is dynamite. And he's done work on a vaccine?"

"Yes, so he says. The book is still being decontaminated, so once we've had a chance to check it out, I'll have Dr Pinchcliffe check it out."

"Sorry, Dennis. Dr Pinchcliffe died yesterday. Suicide. Lot of that going around."

"Jesus."

"You look after yourself now. Get that vaccine up. Do it for all of us."

"You make it sound like…"

"Houston's a write-off, Dennis. Look." Lopez steadied the camera and focused on the window of his office. Flames rose in the horizon. "Better to burn out, than fade away? Guess we'll see if Neil was right. Goodnight, Dennis."

"Goodnight General." With leaden feet, even in the pixie-light gravity of the Moon, he walked down to Bolderova's lab, expecting to find her hard at work.

Instead, he found her in her lab, minus safety hood, drinking vodka. Her face was red and her eyes bloodshot. A body, one of the shuttle passengers, lay on a gurney behind her. "Larissa! Why aren't you wearing your hood? Larissa!" He shouted into the intercom until he was hoarse.

She smiled bitterly, took another gulp of vodka, and held her thumb up to the window. There was a small cut at the end, oozing blood.

2117

Of templates and vengeance

Malibu

The original cliffs of Malibu had fallen into the sea long ago in the 2057 earthquake. Dennis remembered watching it live from Hellas, when he lived inside a cliff.

True to form, instead of moving a few kilometres north or south, the Angelino urge compelled the rich survivors to rebuild the cliffs, grain by grain, where they had once been. Dennis did not need to ask why. He was certain the answer would be something like, "It's Malibu, dude."

He pulled the Rivian into Zhang Peifu's driveway and looked at Latoya. "Only in America can someone like this guy get rebranded and make a mint off of us."

"What do you mean? You don't even know him."

Dennis opened the door with a grim look on his face. "I know his work."

Alex Zhang opened the door with a nervous smile. A tiny, white decorative dog flounced about at his feet. For a moment, Dennis thought of Kassabian and his damned dog. "Good morning, come in, please! Summer, down please!"

The place was breathtaking even by LA standards. A long, slim house that descended to the cliff with graceful increments, a massive living room dominated by a Steinway, a panorama of the angry Pacific, waiting to devour more houses.

"It's beautiful." Latoya was smitten. "The air…wow."

"My father says it keeps him young. I remind him, we are all young, forever." Alex smiled.

"Do you ever have nightmares, Alex?" Dennis came out of the blue with it.

"What? Oh no…not more than usual."

"I guess you don't eat that cloned crap, do you? No need, in LA." He saw a slightly older looking Asian man dressed all in white cotton, wearing a Panama hat, seated on the lawn. "That must be your father."

Alex Zhang coughed. "Yes. Allow me to introduce you."

As they got closer, Dennis could see that the man had chosen to keep the white hair, and the signature mole, of the Chinese patriarch. One of the curious social outcomes of the miracle, before it had been legally bound to sterilization, had been the debate amongst first-generation recipients who had children: How young do I go?

Given that the miracle could, if maintained properly, effectively freeze a person at a certain age, was it wrong for parents to want to look younger than their children? The net was full of freakshow sites of people who had chosen to do just that. It seemed that Zhang Peifu had made the graceful choice. He was youngish, but obviously senior. People would know who got the first cut of BBQ pork at family gatherings; whose glass was always filled first.

The elder Zhang gave a small bow. The rounded lawn would've allowed a rambunctious child to roll into the sea. Dennis guessed there were none. "Dr Rosso, the father of the miracle. How nice to meet you."

Dennis shook the finely manicured hand. He looked back at the house, where Latoya had chosen to stay behind and keep Alex talking. "Quite an impressive reward, for a lifetime of work."

They sat on the bench, watching the whitecaps pick up in the gathering wind. Clouds scudded in overhead, threatening the kind of weather that once cost Malibu an address or two. "I owe it all to America, you know. After everything, the land of opportunity."

Dennis nodded. "And forgiveness."

The elder Zhang looked confused. "Pardon? I don't follow. Perhaps my English is not so good."

"As good as your virology and biochemistry? Oh no, of course not." Dennis reached into his pocket and retrieved two bamboo nubbins in a sealed plastic bag.

"What's this?" The elder Zhang peered at the bag.

"The chopsticks your son used at lunch yesterday. Or, the business end of them anyway. You see, when I heard his name, saw his face…heard the story…"

A shadow fell over the elder Zhang's face. "Oh yes. Of course. It was bound to happen, someday. Are you with the authorities?"

"No." He figured leaving out the link to Fisk was a good idea at this point. "I'm a private actor, if you will. A rogue scientist, on the hunt for what's spoiling my legacy. And I think you might know something about that."

The elder Zhang examined the chopsticks more closely. "May I?"

"Of course."

"I am curious, how you would have found my DNA? You are the first, in 72 years of looking! And I am sure, people would still be looking, if they could find my sample. But nothing escaped The Exchange."

The EMP pulses generated in The Exchange had destroyed many databases, including those kept by government bodies, of DNA. Physical samples, and their holders, had often been vaporized, too. "Nothing escaped The Exchange...on Earth. That was neither where I received this sample, nor where I kept it."

"Ah, yes. It must have been you. Who else would they have sent to interrogate the traitor Yueh?"

"God rest his soul. He gave me your name. And your DNA. You couldn't change one, why didn't you change the other?"

The foolish little dog bounded up to the elder Zhang at that moment, and he scooped the thing up in his arms. Something about Hannah Arendt came to mind. *The banality of evil.*

But how was Zhang Peifu any eviler than Fu Yueh? One was the subordinate, the other the master. Perhaps his memory of Yueh was sepia-toned by time, by rapport, by dramatic endings.

"In China, there are so many people. Only so many names. And, at first, I used genetic masking, much like I assume you have done, sir. But soon, it became apparent. No one was looking. The world wanted to forget, as did I. I saw my country burn. That, I felt, was my punishment. I owed it to my children to build them a better life with my skills."

"And if only you'd left it there, I'd have never come looking for you."

The elder Zhang let the dog go to bark at a seagull. In the distance, the desalinisation plants at Point Mugu glowered over nature, slaking the giant city's thirst. "What do you mean?"

Dennis sighed in exasperation. "Doctor, I didn't come here for revenge. Your plague killed a lot of people I cared about. And Yueh told me it was all because you were scared of my invention. How do you think it is to live with that for seven decades, to live with that knowledge? But I'm not here for revenge, not for me."

"Then why are you here?"

Dennis withdrew another sealed bag from his pocket. This one contained a sticky green paste; one Fisk had couriered to him the night before. "I'm here to ask why you still want revenge. And why you're using this to get it."

2045

Ship of the damned

Shackleton Base
The Moon

It is not an easy thing to watch a friend die, slowly, and in agony.

But Larissa Bolderova would have it no other way. "Observe… observe the clinical symptoms with minimal intervention, Dennis." She insisted through chattering teeth on the third night. Apparently, blood-to-blood transmission eliminated the lengthy incubation period. "You have the eyes…to see what others don't."

"But Henrik…" Kassabian had been calling the base frantically since Dennis had alerted Duplessis to the accident. But Bolderova would not take his calls.

"I can't…if I talked to him…would be, too hard."

And so, she progressed, rapidly downhill. The antidote conveyed by Yueh was administered, with the faint hope that it would work on a Caucasian. On the fourth day, it produced a brief glimmer of hope. One that lasted only twelve hours… then, catastrophe.

The Red Foam spewed out of her mouth and nose, killing her in hours on the fifth day. Every second of the obscenity was scanned and filmed, at Bolderova's express command. Now, as suited technicians bagged her lethally hot body, Dennis watched from the window. An intercom chimed.

"Yes...yes, this is Rosso."

"Sorry about Doctor Bolderova." It was young Dr Poole. "But there may be some good news, about the vaccine. Doctor Yueh thought you ought to see this."

He bounded down in the light gravity to the command center. Yueh, now out of quarantine, was supervising the vaccine team. Dennis had to fight for that one, but his logic was unbeatable.

"He designed it. We're using his formula. It's either that, or we throw both of them out the airlock."

Since nobody volunteered to replace Yueh, especially after news of Bolderova's accident, Dennis got what he wanted. Yueh pointed to a monitor where a single rabbit munched contentedly on greenhouse carrots. "First vaccine trial of 57-N."
"Any others?"

"She was the only one that got it."

"We still have rabbits?"

"Only a dozen. This time we do six and six. Then...I take it."

"You're Asian. That won't prove a thing." Dennis swallowed. "I'll do it."

That night, twelve rabbits were infected. Three nights later, six of them were dead. And on that night, Dennis Rosso sat in the same little cell Yueh had stayed in, waiting for his shot. Yueh and Poole arrived, wearing protective clothing. Yueh carried a syringe. Poole carried a larger needle, and three vacutainers.

He closed his eyes, visualizing Bolderova's last hours. If he was infected, he was getting his ass blown out of the nearest airlock, that much he'd already made clear. He looked up at Yueh and laughed.

"What is so funny, Doctor Rosso?" Yueh asked in his clipped Cambridge accent. "I admire your *sang froid*."

"Courtesy of 20-year Macallan." He raised his glass.

"An excellent choice."

"I just thought it was funny, that's all. The man who beat death, and the man who brought it back with a vengeance, in the same room. And now, one is much likelier to die than the other. God's little joke."

Yueh's face was sad. "How I wish the roles were reversed. Here we go."

"Ouch. I always was a pussy with needles." Poole's blood sample was even worse. Six hours later, they were back.

He'd been reading Pepys' *Journal of the Plague Year.* How people never changed. One single cut from Poole's scalpel, and he was infected.

Curiously, he was too tired to care now. He went to sleep and snored for seven hours. When he awoke, it wasn't his choice.

"Dr Rosso? Dr Rosso!"

He sat up straight. "What?" He rubbed his sore arm. "What?"

"Message for you. Mr Duplessis."
"Put it through." *He might only have 48 hours to live, and this was the way he was spending it? Well, there was still that half-bottle of scotch.*

Duplessis looked crazed. His eyes were wild, and he wore a stained singlet. "Dennis, Dennis is that you? Oh man, it's gone to shit here. So far fucking gone! Kassabian's gone nuts and taken off for Phoenix base. He's got the other key for PDS, so even if you keyed yours, it won't work now! He's saying you and I killed Larissa, and he's going to get revenge...fuck, man! Why did I ever trust him!

Duplessis lit a joint, then sat swathed in smoke. Dennis stared at him coldly. This madman now had the lives of 30,000 people in his hands. And another madman had just opened the door for the Red Foam.

"That ship is coming in, man! It's landing in thirty minutes! My wife...my kids...I don't know what's going on with them, Dennis, help me! Help me out, man!"

The message dissolved in sobbing. Dennis waited and poured a glass of scotch before replying. "Prepare reply."

The computer acknowledged. "Pending."

"Begin." Dennis looked at the camera sternly. "Merlin, listen to me. I am sitting here in an isolation room, because I am the first human to take Yueh's vaccine. That's right man. And if it works, we'll make enough doses to cover Mars by the end of the month. All you've got to do is keep your fucking shit together. You hear me? You're a disgrace. This planet was your dream. I bought into it, we all bought into it, because of you. Now, what are you going to do, huh? Get stoned and have me make all the decisions? Fuck that. Here's what you're going to do until I get back."

He realized that he was doing exactly what Duplessis wanted. Taking the reins, because the man-child couldn't function. Well, what else could he do? Mars was his home, now. The woman he loved lived there.

"The first thing you are going to do is restore my untapped, priority one link to Anita. I need her advice. Do not fuck with this, Merlin!"

He took a deep breath, then continued. "You will seal off every base on Mars, including Phoenix. You can't trust Kassabian not to fuck that up. Put out an arrest warrant for him and blame it all on him. All of it, got it?"

He took another breath. "You cannot allow anyone to get off of *Martin Gibson* alive. Tell the police there to fry them. All of them."

He paused for a long time. "Send message?" The computer asked quietly, as if aware of the import of what had been said.

"Send."

A half-hour later, he awoke out of a doze to hear a simple reply. "Message acknowledged. Another message waiting, from Deputy Chief Anita Bergstrom. Open?"

"Yes."

Anita looked only slightly less ragged than Duplessis had. She sat in their tiny living room, still in uniform, black reading glasses at the end of her nose. "Damn you Dennis! I don't talk to you for a week and this is what happens? Have you gone barking mad?"

She ran a hand through her hair, a gesture that always made him crazy. He could taste her skin, smell her, feel her smoothness and her roughness, all together. "Still, you are very brave. I am so proud of you." She wiped away a tear. "Damnit, it's bad here. Duplessis has gone nuts, leaving Deo to try and run the show. The proles have been rioting over shortages...bad, Dennis. Lots of bad things happening. Two of our people missing... rumor is they were put out of an airlock, naked. Oh, Christ. And now, that fucking lunatic Kassabian wants to unleash Red Foam...fucking incredible. Deo wants us to go to Phoenix, find him, and kill him Dennis. Tell me what to do. For the first time in my life, I don't have any answers..."

"Reply?"

"Yes." Dennis stared into the camera. "Do not go to Phoenix.

THE STALE MIRACLE

Nobody goes to Phoenix, until I come back with a vaccine, you hear me? Nobody!"

Three days later, Dennis Rosso was still alive. And most of Phoenix base was infected with the Red Foam. The only survivor of the *Martin Gibson* was reputed to be Duplessis' eldest daughter.

Deo and the police chiefs had acted, placing Duplessis under house arrest, waiting for Dennis to return.

And the vaccine, man's only hope, went into full speed production. Suddenly, egg farmers on Earth were cautiously lowering their quarantine barricades to agents promising first jabs of vaccine in return for eggs. Someone, somewhere, was designing an egg-crate that could survive a rocket launch.

Those eggs went to the bays that had once housed the quarantined and the damned of the three shuttles. And in a massively irregular orbit, the *NA Buzz Aldrin* performed a series of gravity assist maneuvers to bring it's Delta-V up to emergency speed for the return to Mars. The maneuvers involved would have to be precise, catching *Mark Watney* at maximum thrust on its outbound journey.

Both ships would carry classified cargo, cargo only Kesuke and Dennis were briefed on.

Watney would carry 25,000 doses of vaccine. "But aren't there 30,000 people on Mars?" Kesuke had asked.
That question would be answered by *Buzz Aldrin's* manifest. Two 50 kiloton nuclear missiles. "Five thousand of those people live on Great Wall 2. They won't be needing any vaccine." Dennis whispered to him. Lopez, still alive in Houston despite his glum predictions, had merely nodded.

"I'd better get to my shelter now. Get yourself a good view of Earth. You'll have a front-row seat."

"Jesus." Kesuke spat. "Like it's a football game. I can just see that guy at the controls of the *Enola Gay*."

But Dennis was already headed for the locker room. "Where are you going?"

"Suiting up. I'm taking the elevator to the crater rim and I'm going to watch."

"You ghoul."

"I started this war. Now, I'm going to watch it end."

To his surprise, Kesuke followed him. They suited up, wordlessly, and boarded the airlock elevator for Solar Tower Three. When they emerged into the Lunar vacuum, they found a small crowd gathered.

"Too bad there's no popcorn." Kesuke muttered bitterly.

"Hey, anybody figure they've got some aimed at us?" Someone in the crowd asked.

"Course they do." A tall Texan in a Space Force suit answered. He pointed towards the horizon. "Betcha not a one gets past there."

"Why there?" Dennis probed.

"You'll see."

Their view of the Earth was almost perfect. The clouds over Northeast Asia had parted, as if on cue. All of Tibet, and everything south of Mongolia and east of Korea was on display. Dennis felt a cool whistling in his ears from his suit's ventilation system. He wondered what Neil and Buzz would make of this.

A warning tone sounded in their ears. "This is the Base Commander. An attack advisory is in effect. A nuclear exchange has begun on Earth. All personnel, seek shelter."

"Does he know we're up here?"

"Who gives a shit? Those ABMs don't do their job, it won't matter where we are." The Texan explained. "Look!"

The first tentative tendrils of rocket exhaust became visible, coming from the east. The North American strike. More tendrils from Europe and Russia. Then, just as the first searing blasts painted the clouds orange in Western China, a scattered retaliatory strike.

More and more hot white and orange fireballs consumed the great conurbations of Eastern China. Cities of twenty, thirty, forty million seared and died in front of them.

The wages of sin is death. The biblical pronouncement occurred to him, just as a sudden, much more local flash caused his helmet visor to go black for a moment. Right where the Texan had said, an ABM had detonated an incoming missile.

"Shit man! Check your dosimeters!" The Texan shouted. "Should be it for a lifetime. I got me forty Rems!"

Dennis checked his dosimeter. *Forty-seven.* He edged behind the cover of a support pillar for the giant solar panel. "You idiots up top! Get back inside!" This time, it was the less formal side of the Base Commander showing. "Get the fuck inside, or I send you back to Earth, without a vaccine!"

Dennis looked at the Earth one last time. Flashes now showed on the eastern horizon. Somewhere or someone he knew was getting hit. "Hell of a day, hey?"

He turned, startled, to see Yueh standing against the crater's rim. "What are you doing out here?"

"Beholding what I hath wrought. Like you. Also, fulfilling a boy's dream. To stand on the Moon. Quite a way to go."

It dawned on Dennis what was about to happen. "Hey…wait…"

"I'm so very sorry." Yueh turned to face the crater, then ripped the oxygen hoses from their fixings. Shooting sublimating gases, the suited body went limp and tumbled over the rim to the crater floor below.

2117

Such a simple thing

Malibu

The bag of paste sat on the bench between them. Such a simple thing, yet both men knew it was not, not really.

Both Dennis Rosso and Zhang Peifu knew it was the key to everything.

Finally, the elder Zhang sighed. "You are a scientist. You know what this is."

"I know what it is *supposed* be. A nutrient medium for feeding the growth of large cell colonies. I've been using it my whole career, as have you. But this is not really all there is to it."

"No. My original success is exactly as it appears. Supplying the highest quality paste to the cellular factories of the West Coast at the lowest possible price per kilo. For decades, that has been the foundation of our business."

"Until 2110. Am I right?"

"You are as good a detective as you are a scientist. I am curious, though, as to how you arrived at this deduction."

"Consumption of naturally obtained animal tissue was prohibited in North America in 2110. Your business experienced 257% growth in Fiscal Year 2110-2111 alone. But that is not the only reason." Dennis paused for deliberate effect. "It is also the year that suicides in North America began a sudden, unexplained increase. An increase which continues to this day."

The elder Zhang looked out to sea, as if knowing he would soon have far less grandiose vistas to contemplate. "Yes. The template was introduced at this time. I am certain you are familiar with the concept."

"Yes. A template introduced through simple organic chemical coding in a feed medium can skew cellular growth in a particular direction. More productive, more nutritious, for example. As we used to say in the lab, 'You are what you eat.'" Dennis shivered again at the implications.

"Yet, even in all those decades, working alone on your final iteration on Mars, never once did you use a nutritive template?"

"Too many unanswered questions. Too many ghosts, in too many corners. I don't like to use what I don't understand. You've followed me closely, I see."

"Over the course of several decades, there was not a month when your name did not appear in the big journals. I was surprised that you were not nominated for another Nobel."

"I killed 5000 people. That might have had something to do with it."

The elder Zhang nodded. "Next to me, you are blameless."

"Tell me about your template. I can see a strong boost in production, but also…"

"Instabilities. I could not obtain a 200% increase in production by weight without them. But by lab experimentation, I discovered the problem. My lab rats went crazy, and tried to kill themselves, after years of consuming the end product. Those who'd received transplants, by comparison, simply went lethargic, and stopped eating."

"And yet, you went ahead and did it anyway."

"I watched my country burn. For years, I hated you, among many others. Killing your miracle bit-by-bit, while taking myself from millionaire to billionaire, seemed like a good idea at the time. And nobody asked any questions. Demand never decreased, and if anyone ever reached the same conclusions you did, they kept it to themselves."

"Why tell me now?"

"Because my body may not feel old, but my soul does. Over the years, I would spend my spare time inquiring into what was happening to people's brains because of my template. The hatred I once felt was drained away. Replaced by pity, then, by guilt. I saw the holos. People killing themselves for spectacle. How horrible."

Dennis looked at the old man, whose gaze remained firmly fixed on the sea, perhaps on the land of his birth, now a shadow of its former self. He was one of the fathers of the greatest plague in human history, and the proximate cause of the subsequent costliest war in history.

But even he could see that Virgil's videos were in poor taste.

Listening to the man's tale of having the hatred slowly drained out of him resonated with Dennis. This man, along with Yueh and others, had killed his mother, his childhood friends, his sister. But in the end, hadn't Dennis killed them, too? If not through deliberate murder, then, perhaps negligent manslaughter? He'd presented a paranoid bunch of old men in Beijing with the ultimate demographic weapon and dared them to act.

"Did you pay anyone to look the other way?"

"I only needed to pay a few; a pittance compared to what I was making. I made a list, already, in exchange for one promise."

"Which is? You realize I am not a Federal Agent? I can't make you any binding promises…"

The elder Zhang patted his hand, leaving him feeling a curious mixture of fascination and revulsion. "They will listen to you. They always do."

"Your family?"

"Yes. Believe me when I say, they did not know. I kept Alex in the dark, certainly about my desires for revenge. They should be looked after."

"I'll talk to the Agent in charge." A sudden question occurred to him. "You didn't invent the template yourself, did you?"

Zhang nodded. "You may have the qualifications of a scientist. But you have the instincts of a detective. I received the sample in 2096. By agreement with my partners, I withheld it from all but experimental use until 2110."

"Why?"

"When people still had the option to eat real meat instead, they would react more severely to any hint of a safety issue with the product. When they lost that option," the elder Zhang folded his hands in his lap primly, "we felt it was safe to proceed. After all, years of warnings about heart disease and cancer risk did not stop them from eating the real thing."

"You said you 'received the sample.' Received it from whom?"

"It was my understanding that this product was developed by your colleague, Dr Henrik Kassabian. Who, if I may say so, you resemble quite closely."

"Jesus." Dennis let the implication sink in. Even now, he was still fighting Kassabian. Was this what eternal life meant? Eternal grudges, rivalries outlasting the stars? "How did the sample get here?"

Zhang tittered and covered his mouth delicately. "If you will forgive the unseemly anecdote, it is my understanding that the sample was transported inside the rectal cavity of a dog in stasis."

That fucking dog.

"Enjoy the view, Doctor. Pelican Bay is nice too, but they don't let you out that often."

"Perhaps now, we will see what a life sentence really means."

2045

The wages of sin

Mars

Hellas Base

As soon as the *Mark Watney* landed, Dennis marched on wobbly legs to Duplessis' office. Anita had embraced him quickly. She was wearing full body armor, a carbine slung over her back.

"Welcome home, honey."

"They're offloading the vaccines now. Get yourself and everyone else who's coming to Phoenix jabbed first, then get Medical Section going on a routine for the rest of the base. There's 200 doses to a case, so leave one on board the shuttle for any survivors at the base."

"Will there be any?"

"As long as Emilie Duplessis keeps her door locked, I can think of one."

"What about you?"

"I have to see him. He has to be involved in what happens next."

"Why?" She grabbed his arm and whispered intently. "Ever since they took him off of sedation, he's been rampaging around his office like a bull. I've got a nurse the size of a refrigerator standing by with a syringe full of knockout juice.

Please, Dennis!"

"No. He's no leader in a crisis, that's for sure. But we wouldn't be on Mars, or even the Moon, nobody would; without him. Without him, Mars will become just another basket case run by career UN wankers. We need him to rebuild. And for that…" He lowered his voice. "He has to turn that key with me. It's the only thing that will save his reputation, after Phoenix."

"Don't do it, Dennis! They didn't bring the Red Foam here. He did!"

"That's not the way the proles will see it, and you know that. This war isn't over until Great Wall 2 is."

He stormed up to Duplessis' office, leaving Anita's bitter protests ringing in his ears. Deo met him in the hallway, with a phalanx of Anita's troops, and the aforementioned giant nurse, who somehow managed to be scarier than anything else.

"I wouldn't." Deo waved a finger.

"I have to." Dennis held up the "football."

Deo sighed and punched in his override code. As soon as the door opened, Dennis was headed straight for Duplessis. A Shakespeare *Complete Works* flew past his head, a book he was sure Duplessis had never read. His intellect did not come from books. The weighty volume bounced off the doors with a thud. Dennis swung the football hard as he could manage in the suddenly oppressive gravity, catching Duplessis under the chin and knocking him down.

"You asshole!" He spat at Dennis from the floor. Duplessis reeked of BO and weed. "I'll put all of you assholes out of the airlock! You, Deo, your fucking slut wife!"

He reared back and kicked Duplessis hard. "Shut the fuck up. The only reason you're not tied to a gurney and drooling right now is me. So, you are going to shut the fuck up and listen to me, if you want to go down in history as anything other than the giant, prolapsed asshole we both know you are. So, shut, the, fuck, up!"

Duplessis stared at him for a minute, then began to weep. "Oh man, it's over. It's all over. I should've kept you here. I should've never trusted that fucking geek! Goddamnit, my little girl is out there all alone, Dennis! All alone! Please, please bring her back for me, I promise you whatever you want…I promise!"

"Merlin, stand up, and fucking pull yourself together." He poured a belt of scotch for both of them. "Drink this." Then, he set the football on the table, and opened it.

"What…what is this?" Duplessis gulped the last of his scotch.

"Dual key arrangement. Strictly symbolic. Only one key turn is required from our end, as General Lopez of Space Force has already armed the warheads, released from *Buzz Aldrin* three days ago. In six minutes' time, those warheads will be within sight of the target."

"Target?"

"Great Wall Station 2. Has there been any response to our attempts at communication?"

Duplessis rubbed his bearded chin. "No. Silence. But the sats say there's life in there."

"Soon, there will not be. Under the circumstances, we must take their refusal to communicate as a sign of hostile intent."

Duplessis' eyes went wide. "Can't we give them an ultimatum?" Dennis was final. In this moment, he was the real President of Mars, and he knew it. "And force them into a launch on warning situation, if they have Red Foam, or a nuke? No. There are 30,000 people living on Mars. We must kill 5000, to save the other 25,000."

"What about the Emiratis? They are so close, Dennis."

"We will give them a one-minute warning." Dennis looked at the football. "Window opens in thirty seconds."

"You do it."

"You don't understand, Merlin. After you let Kassabian bring the Red Foam here, nuking the Chinese is the only thing that will save your ass, politically and literally." Dennis took one key from around his neck and handed it to Duplessis. Outside, a crowd watched. He could see Anita, her stare stony. "Fifteen seconds. Insert keys."

Duplessis aped his movements mechanically. "Key inserted."

"Launch window open. Turn keys to launch on my mark. Three, two, one...launch."

"Launch key to launch." Duplessis slumped in his chair.

"Call the Emiratis. Tell them to duck and cover."

"What are you doing?"

"I have a shuttle to catch. I'm going to bring her home, Merlin."

Dennis stepped into the hallway as Duplessis called the Emiratis. "Mr Deo, please announce the attack on Great Wall 2, as a decision of the collective leadership, ratified by Mr Duplessis."

"Count me out." Anita stared at him.

"Duly noted. Rescue team, follow me."

Halfway around the planet, the 5000 souls of Great Wall Station 2, had, at most thirty seconds to recognize that today was going to be a very bad day. The first missile was an airburst, at 2000 metres, vaporizing surface structures and rendering communications impossible. Anyone who did not survive the first missile was killed by the second, a ground burst which scoured out the subsurface tunnels and dumped what was left of the structure into the billion-year chasm of *Valles Marineris*. A massive cloud of red and black fallout rose higher than the shield volcanoes of Tharsis and encircled the planet.

Of course, the use of nuclear weapons off of the Earth was a complete and flagrant violation of a number of treaties. But China's representative on the UN Security Council had been unceremoniously ejected two weeks ago and replaced by Taiwan's Ambassador. Nobody even mentioned the ugly end of Great Wall Station 2 on the floor of the Assembly. China had no friends, on the Earth or any other world, anymore.

That did not, of course, make most of the people incinerated that day any more culpable.

Over Phoenix Base

The North Pole was in deep summer now, the permanent cap having retreated to the edges of the base. Phoenix now sat on a solitary tongue of ice, surrounded by shifting red dunes.

Dennis stood behind the flight crew as they approached at a cautious hover. "Put some drones out, please."

The Captain was a very tall Canadian who'd flown in every extreme environment, on and off of Earth. "Drones out. Getting a picture. Shit."

The feed from the drones was a low close-up, tracking from the landing pad to the main base and back. "Are those bodies?"

"Looks like." The First Officer held the ship on a steady hover while the Captain maneuvered the drones. On the screen shot floating in front of them, at least a dozen bodies were piled in an airlock entrance, most not wearing pressure suits. Their heads were red with blood, whether from Red Foam or traumatic depressurization, Dennis couldn't tell. Anita came up beside him.

"My God." Closer to the *Martin Gibson*, which appeared to have crash landed and was skewed over on its starboard side, emergency escape lines extended from the ship's main hatch. Two space-suited forms lay in the sand.

"Tracks heading South-south-east. Fresh." The Captain announced.

"Send one drone to follow that track."

"You got it."

"Fifteen percent hover fuel." The First Officer announced. She was a compact Hispanic woman with unnerving focus. "Five percent till manual touchdown or abort."

"Yeah, yeah." The Captain rolled his eyes at Dennis. "I like that spot right over there, about two hundred metres in front of *Gibson*. Nice and smooth. Get seated for landing, folks."

Dennis and Anita went back to their seats. "Thoughts?" She probed him.

"Exactly the shit show we expected. If there's Rabids in there…"

"I know, I know. Shoot to kill." She squeezed his hand. "I haven't gone totally soft, you know. I just have my limits."

"Good thing I'm fresh out of nukes, then."

Phoenix Base
North-East Entrance

Anita led her security detachment in a ragged "V" towards the airlock, which was at the end of a remote corridor. According to the briefing, given by one of Ohan's deputies en route, it was typically only used by Geologists on day hikes into the ice fields. A small rover sat beside it, covered in a red film.

Dennis followed behind with the medical technicians and the videographers. Another group of Anita's cops followed, with more left behind to guard the shuttle and its crew. He suspected this was all overkill, that they would find at most a couple of shattered survivors, and a large number of corpses.

But the video from the UK, the one with the Rabid woman... that wouldn't stop nagging him.

They stopped in front of the airlock. Anita shone a powerful light inside. Ordinarily, they'd have overridden the base's systems from Hellas, getting control of all internal and external cameras and microphones. But someone, most likely Kassabian, had disabled all that before the *Gibson* landed. Now, Hellas' only link to events had been a single, terrified child inside the Solar Flare Shelter of the *Gibson*.

"Emergency channel coms from *Martin Gibson*, can you take the call?" The First Officer announced.

Anita looked back at him and nodded. "Send."

"Hello? Hello, this is Emilie. Are you here? Is that you on the monitors?"

"Yes, Emilie, this is Doctor Rosso. Stay where you are, we are coming for you. We have to sweep the base first."

"Okay...but please, hurry."

He could only imagine what it was like for her. Ten, alone for two weeks now, terrified and surrounded by the dead. The temptation to just open a hatch must've been enormous. "Emilie, this is very important. Did you see anyone in a vehicle leaving the base?"

"No. Just a crazy guy in a little rover racing around. But I don't think he ever left. He was yelling stuff at me, and trying to get in. But the Captain showed me how to lock him out before he…

well, he couldn't get in. He's been quiet for two or three days now."

Kassabian. "Hey, Doc, the drone following those tracks shows a lot of sand and dust in them. Last big gusts around here were last week." The Captain announced. "Whoever it was probably beat tracks before the *Gibson* arrived."

"I sure hope so. Okay, Emilie, sit tight, we're going in."

"Please be careful."

"See you soon." Dennis nodded at Anita, who slapped one of her men on the shoulder. He recognized the big trucker, Terry. Obviously policing paid better. Terry inserted what looked like a wind-up key for a mechanical toy into the airlock controls, forcing the outer doors open.

"Team two, go around the West side and clear there. Meet us at Main 1." Anita deployed the remainder of the force, who hurried into the shifting, sand covered ice.

Inside, it was dark. Terry waited until they were all inside to manually shut the airlock doors. Then, he opened an environmental panel and slowly, with the turn of a valve, repressurized the compartment. "Where the hell…oh, okay. Let there be light!"

The lights came on, forcing their eyes to adjust. "Okay, anybody see anything in there?"

Inside the inner door, a knocked over chair and spilled paper were the only concessions to chaos. "Bad housekeeping." Dennis announced.

Anita nodded to Terry. "Do it."

The doors opened, smoothly and electrically this time. Dennis imagined an odour of decay and death, but he knew this was fantasy. Slowly, they plodded through the hallway, coming around the corner to the first of the geologist's offices. "Oh my."

Anita stepped back from the door. Dennis looked in. Two desiccated corpses sat at a table, their last meal of vodka and tranquilizers spread out before them.

"Smart way to do it." Terry peered in the window.

"Let's move." Around the next corner, the first signs of serious trouble. Dried, brown blood spattered both walls, ceiling, and floor. A desiccated finger sat on the floor. "Jesus, Dennis, look at this."

"Rabids. They had at least one." Terry edged past them both, rifle held ready.

"Officer, what are you doing?"

"I'm expendable, ma'am. Neither of you are." Anita nodded silently as Terry beckoned a young female officer to follow him. Slowly, they followed in formation. "Hold up there, ma'am. It's worse up here. Let us check it out."

"You're on a two-minute timer."

"Roger that."

Dennis' curiosity was killing him, but he knew Anita was in charge. And nobody was going anywhere until she declared it safe. "Chief Bergstrom?"

"Go."

"All dead here. We count ten. Looks like a Rabid went through them like a blender on puree. It ain't pretty." Terry was breathing heavily now. When they rounded the corner, they saw why.

A mound of people, faces twisted in agony, corpses shrivelled and taut with dried blood, lay spilled as if from a soup tureen in front of the cafeteria. The videographers inched forward and recorded the scene. "Fucking hell." Dennis exclaimed. "There's no way out."

"Except here." The young female cop pointed to the airlock. "Guess we know what those people were running from now."

"Team 2 from 1?" Anita got on the radio, frustrated.

"Go ahead."

"All dead in here so far. We've got an obstruction, so you'll have to go in at Main 1 and start clearing yourself. We'll come out Main 2 and work around to where you are."

"Copy. One dead body in a suit out here. Nothing else. We're going in."

They waited for Terry and two other men to go around and clear the dead from the outside door. Then, once the airlock was repressurized, they stepped over bodies with agonized faces. Dennis locked eyes with the big man who'd wanted booze on his last trip. If he'd been coming in from the other side, he might have wondered what could make people flee into asphyxiation.

But he had seen the Rabid. He did not wonder.

Once outside, the party rounded past lazily turning windmills, stepping over cables, avoiding hastily abandoned equipment. On the other side of the complex, a cop from the other team opened the airlock for them. An elevator took Anita, Dennis, and Terry to Ohan's office.

Dread rumbled in Dennis's guts. But when the elevator doors opened, there were two cops standing in front of Ohan's office. "No sign of the Chief." One of them announced. "Just this weirdo."

The cops parted to show a grinning Kassabian, stinking and disheveled, eyes rimmed red, sitting behind Ohan's desk with his feet up. An almost-empty bottle of the Chief's *chicha* sat at his elbow. "Hi, Doctor Rosso. Like what I've done with the place?"

Dennis gritted his teeth. "Hey, asshole! That's not your desk!"

Anita drew her taser and fired two barbs into Kassabian's chest. Kassabian pitched over and rolled in agony on the floor. "Arrest this piece of shit, now." Terry pushed past the cops in the doorway and slapped a set of cuffs on Kassabian, before dragging him to his feet.

"How? How the fuck was I supposed to know I was immune? How?"

Dennis stepped forward with a syringe. "You need your shots, you rabid motherfucker." He jabbed into Kassabian's arm without gentleness or ceremony. "Where's Ohan? Where's Leuprecht?"

Terry pressed down painfully on Kassabian's collarbone. "Ahhh...fuck! Ohan...outside medical wing. Died being a hero! Ha ha...a hero! Leuprecht? Who's Leuprecht?"

Dennis was rushing down the stairs to the medical wing before Anita could stop him. Terry chased after him. They came to a stop in the hallway. Ohan's body lay slumped in front of the door to an isolation room, a pistol in his hand, scratches and bites from a Rabid on his arms. But Ohan had checked out on his own, as the hole in the back of his head attested. The Rabid, her teeth clogged with flesh, lay on her back. She wore the uniform of a Q-Space flight steward. Four of Ohan's bullets had stopped her in her tracks.

Inside the isolation room, two terrified women, faces drawn with malnutrition, stared out at them. Dennis put a space-suited hand to the window glass, and Terry followed suit. The women reached out and touched the glass in response, crying with relief.

2117

Flowers by irene

Malibu

Dennis walked out of the Zhang house, the sun in his eyes. Alex Zhang exchanged pleasantries with Latoya, truly unaware of the weight about to fall on him.

There were a few things that had not changed in the century of upheaval lived by Dennis Rosso. One of those things was; when you pissed off Uncle Sam, his retribution was biblical. There was no way in hell he could keep the family out of it. This time next week, they'd be lucky to be, as Chris Farley used to say, 'Livin' in a van, down by the river." It was just the way it was.

Speak of the Devil. Dennis squinted at the obvious surveillance van parked 50 metres from their Roadster. "Flowers By Irene."

Latoya put on her massive sunglasses. "What did you say?"

"Look." He nudged her in the direction of the van. "FBI. Still as obvious as shit when it comes to surveillance. Remind me to introduce you to *The Simpsons* someday." Dennis started out across the street with a purpose.

"Who are the Simpsons?" Latoya called out behind him.

Soon, Dennis was at the back door of the van, rapping on the metal like a Jehovah's Witness. Another thing that had never changed. The door swung open, and he found himself staring down the barrel of a pistol.

A silenced pistol.

"Excuse me, Agents. I just thought Agent Fisk might like the summary of my conversation with Dr Zhang." He reached carefully into his pocket and retrieved the micro-recorder. The three men inside visibly relaxed and replaced their firearms. "That is, unless you've already recorded it from here."

"Come on now." The athletic senior man, with a dusting of salt on his temples chuckled. "We don't have a warrant, do we?"

"Ha ha, sure." Dennis lowered his voice. "Should be enough for arrest warrants on there. Anyway, if Fisk wants to meet us for lunch, we're headed back to the Marmont. Be sure to let him know."

The senior agent smiled earnestly. "Gee, thanks a lot, Doctor Rosso. Special Agent Fisk is going to be pleased as punch."

"I bet."

"Have a nice lunch."

"You too."

Dennis walked stiffly to the Roadster, Latoya trailing, obviously bursting with questions. "Save it." He hissed. "Follow me."

She looked back nervously one last time and got in the car. They were a kilometer away before Dennis pulled into a vacant lot and jumped out, urging her to follow.

He was 100 metres from the car before he opened his mouth to speak. But she beat him to it. "What the hell was all that? Why are you acting like you just got stung by a cobra?"

"Because *we* just did. Fisk. Fisk is the fucking cobra! Those agents in that van had silencers. Silencers, Latoya. They aren't there for surveillance, they're there to pull a hit. First the

Zhangs, then us. Fisk isn't looking to prove charges against Feng and Lontraine; he's looking to kill the witnesses."

"Jesus! We've got to warn them!"

"How? Why? If we do, we're dead. And old man Zhang deserves it anyway."

"Why do you say that?"

"Because he was one of the architects of the Red Foam. And the template that created the mess we're in today."

She looked shocked. "I assume you had proof?"

"I gave it to the FBI. Anyway, as far as Alex Zhang goes, he'd be collateral damage."

"You cannot be so cold."

"Believe me, Latoya, once, I was a lot colder. When we get a head start on these assholes, I'll tell you a story that'll make your hair straight."

"Jesus, well what do we do now?"

"You got any 'facilitators' on that list of yours in the LA area?"

"You're in luck. And he's close. You thinking of killing yourself?"

"No, but if my guess is right, he's into fake IDs and a whole bunch of other shit."

"They all are, honey. Stolen cars, too."

"Just what we need."

"But then what? Go to who, with what?"

"Latoya, there are still some reporters in this country that give a shit. And if you think I let the FBI have all my proof..." He reached into his pants pocket, retrieving his back-up micro-recorder and Zhang's handwritten list. "Then you've got the wrong Dennis Rosso."

Stearns Wharf
Santa Barbara

"That *has* to be him." Dennis stared at the obvious surfer bum standing next to the obvious last legs Generation 2 electric car. The lot was empty, and even the surf was populated by a scattering of diehards.

"Yeah, that's Leggy." Latoya waved at the man, who did a double-take before waving back. "Give me a second. He's wary around strangers."

Latoya ran over to the tall, lanky, spiky-haired California stereotype, his extended legs making the reason for his nickname obvious. Dennis opened the sunroof and looked up, praying that Fisk and his crew were too busy buying their story and eliminating the Zhangs to have scrambled choppers and drones.

If they checked, they'd have already deduced that the Rivian was nowhere near Chateau Marmont. But why would a self-assured fool like Fisk check in the first place?

He felt a sudden, ridiculous pang of guilt over Alex Zhang. How could meeting a random stranger on the train, then going to lunch with him, end your life? He felt like a serial killer.

But Dennis reminded himself, if he'd wanted an education on being a serial killer, he should've asked his dad.

Latoya waved him up. He checked the car for any remaining personal effects and stepped out.

What he'd left at the Marmont would be a treasure trove of DNA. But pretty soon, that DNA would be someone else's DNA. All they needed from 'Leggy' was a clean car and a fake ID. The rest would follow.

"Whoa man! The father of the miracle, wow! That's like… wow!" Leggy greeted him with the usual incoherent California welcome. They shook hands, limply.

"Get us to Seattle. No complications, understand, Leggy?" He produced a roll of cash.

"Um, yeah, man, yeah." Leggy licked his lips. "Can I keep the car?"

"Leggy, did you not pay any fucking attention? This car is hotter than a Beijing boulevard the day after The Exchange. Push it over a fucking cliff. There's enough money here to buy ten of them."

"Umkay, yeah. Let's do it!"

Dennis looked back at Latoya, who merely shrugged in response.

You are what you eat, and you get what you pay for.

2045

The golden age (2)

Mars
Hellas Base

One of Dennis' favourite classes at MIT was an elective in his first year.

Professor Iannone was an itchy, hairy, neurotic Calabrian with reactionary tendencies. His History 101 class influenced the way Dennis looked at the subject ever after.

Which is most likely why the BLM mobs drove him to suicide the next year. But in one semester, Dennis learned a lot from Iannone Uncensored.

"All nations have founding legends. This is as necessary as a flag, and an anthem."

These words were ringing in his ears as he delivered Emilie Duplessis, the Heroine of Phoenix Station, to her father, the first President of the Republic of Mars. The videographers who had documented the horrors of the Polar base were there too, consciously forming the history of the new country.

And there he was, the President's right-hand-man, formative hero and stalwart ally. When the new nation inaugurated its own awards system, he duly received the highest honour the nation could receive: The Order of Ares, an honour he insisted on sharing with Bolderova and Ohan.

Anita resigned to start an opposition political party, Mars Dawn. Terry became her deputy. Kassabian was convicted of 38 counts of terroristic murder, and sentenced to fifty years in prison, with conditioning. After the drone tracking them ran out of fuel and crashed, the official whereabouts of Joshua and Paula Leuprecht and the ten other unaccounted-for occupants of Phoenix Base were officially classed as "unknown."

Unofficially, his whereabouts were suspected to be 120 kilometres SSE of the Polar Base, at an experimental drilling station codenamed "Homer." It was collectively decided to leave the long-suffering Captain alone for political reasons.

Dennis made it clear to Merlin Duplessis that he was not interested in politics. His experiences in the Red Foam War had convinced him that science was the cure, and politics was the disease.

Duplessis, much more lucid now that he had someone to love in his life again, gently reminded Dennis that many people would draw the opposite conclusion from the events of the last nine months. But he acceded to the demands of the Republic's hero, expensive as they were.
It really was a no-brainer. Dennis was asking to perfect the miracle, on Martian soil, and insisting on leaving politics, where he would've been a serious threat to Duplessis, even with his charismatic and courageous daughter by his side.

And so, Dennis got Rosso Labs Mars relocated to a private facility in the Hellas Shelf, twenty levels with a self-sustained water and power supply. With immigration authorized again in 2047, he could command the best of Earth's universities, and soon his staff grew to over a thousand.

Dennis spent his nights overlooking the growing Lake of Hellas from his balcony, drinking the finest cognac and whiskey, and pondering which mystery he would tackle next.

He spent his days pondering how next to improve man next. Render him less susceptible to pathogens? Or to injury? Make him more self-sufficient, without repairs, like he would need to be on a long space journey, or more perfect at home, to suit consumer demand?

His mind danced with telomeres and oxygenation schemes. And he dreamed of a tiny cove in far southern Chile.

And, as he stared out of that balcony and drank his cognac, he lost the love of his life.

But he had his seasons, and his luxuries. And soon, as the decades passed, he had open air again, as the oxygen welled up from the Hellas Basin to swath the whole planet in its protective girdle.

Soon, the madman who had helped turn the key that destroyed Great Wall Station 2 began to coat the surface of Mars in breathable air. Merlin Duplessis, once again, could do no wrong.

In 2047, the gates re-opened, and the survivors of the Red Foam lined up to take their chances on a new world. They were a different breed from the first wave, scarred by experience, suspicious of politics and grandiose promises.

But, to the children of the miracle, decades were what weeks were, once. Quarrels and feuds simmered down, but never died, as long as their standard bearers lived. And now, since the politics of the new century would be dominated by the figures of the last, a renewed struggle for the future of Mars was in the offing.

In the sub-polar wastes, Captain Leuprecht's commune was growing. And in a little prison cell in Acidalia, Henrik Kassabian kept his head down, worked on his experiments, and counted the days.

2117

Can I help you?

**Highway 101
North of Salinas**

They had pushed the ancient little hatchback all day, hoping to skate past San Francisco by nightfall. But beyond that, Dennis truly had no idea what to do next. Though "Dennis Rosso" had been a fugitive since the end of the Martian Wars, a convenient scapegoat for historical revisionists appalled by the destruction of Great Wall Station 2, he had always had two very great advantages in this respect.

First, most people believed Dennis Rosso was dead. There was no telling who had perished in the destruction of the Hellas Tokamaks. A few people believed it was Henrik Kassabian, but Dennis had overcome this suspicion with one astute maneuver.

He had become, physically at least, his arch-nemesis. This was easily accomplished with the facilities he had available, but it was traumatic for weeks afterward, looking into the mirror and seeing not oneself, but one's *bête noir*.

Yet nobody had ever discovered a better way of proving you were not a wanted man, than adopting the identity of his supposed victim. Henrik Kassabian was hardly a blameless historical figure, but his legions of sympathizers on Earth had restored his scientific reputation and wealth.

As for the rest, he'd done his time, hadn't he? And a popular holodrama which cast Dennis in the role of cowardly manipulator, Bolderova as saintly victim, and Kassabian as maddened avenger, had, as much as it enraged Dennis, made life ironically easier for the outside man.

In short, the classic fugitive life, one of being afraid of discovery at every turn, was not one he was familiar with. They had a, so Leggy promised, "sanitized" car, and two passable false passports.

They also had Dennis's rough-and-ready "road kits." The road kit was an injection of programmed DNA virus which generated a new signature, sufficient to confuse testing. Certain facial features, such as eye-colour and definition of cheekbones, chins, and eyebrows, were altered for up to two weeks.

They could not change their height, race, or other basics, but they could at least fool facial recognition scanners (which were everywhere) and DNA swabs at police checkpoints.

Now, as LA receded in the background, they began looking for a cash-only motel to hide out in.

Latoya kept looking at herself in the mirror. "I look like I've been stung by a bee."

"I didn't say it would make us look more attractive. Just muddy the waters a bit."

"And make us sick as a dog for two hours. Oh God. Never again."

"Well, I for one have my appetite back."

"I could eat. I wonder how long it will take Fisk to figure out what we've done."

"I'd say not long. But that's a damn sight harder than figuring out where we are."

"Unless he gets Leggy." Latoya shook her head. "I don't like the way he was looking at that Roadster."

"Not the brightest, is he?" They passed a lit up holoboard by the roadside. Their pictures stared out at them. There was a picture of the Roadster, too.

WANTED FOR MURDER: ARMED AND DANGEROUS

"Great. Looks like you were right. Poor Alex."

Dennis nodded. "Poor Alex."

"Dennis? What now? I mean, we're set for now, but we can't run forever. We can't go back to your apartment in Seattle. What can we do?"

"I know a guy. Right now, that's all I can say."

Latoya frowned. "So far, Dennis, the guys I know have proven a bit more useful than the guys you know. I mean, you don't even live under your own identity. Do you ever wake up and wonder who you are?"

Dennis nodded as the traffic began to slow. Another thing that never changed in California. "Sometimes, Latoya. But I know who I am. And I know I have a story that would win an obscure reporter all the fame and fortune he could ever want."

"Enough to risk his life going up against Fisk?"

"*She* is not possessed with such concerns. As long as her cats are taken care of, she'll take on anything."

"Why'd you call her a 'guy?'"

"Because...er, well, she bounces back and forth. She's been both, a couple of times over. Sometimes it's hard to keep track."

"I see. How do you know her?"

"I go to the same coffee shop as Lynn. She recognized me as

Kassabian and wanted to write my story. I promised her, if she waited, I'd give her something even better."

"Lynn? Seriously?"

"Ah, I think she's decided to be gender-nonconforming. Her insurance won't cover all the switcheroos anymore. Small paper, you know."

"Our lives are dependent on a cat lady named Lynn?"

"Correction: A cat gender-nonconforming person named Lynn. Yes, basically. She's very good at what she does." Ahead of them, the reason for the slow down had become apparent. In the red-tinged dusk, police lights strobed, and reflective vested-officers directed traffic. "Shit. A checkpoint. Be cool."

"Oh, I'm cool, Dennis. Whew. I'm cool."

The Highway Patrol officer was the height of a small redwood. Aside from some new-fangled gadgets on his vest and belt, his look was the eternal California cop, moustache and mirrored shades to boot. "Good afternoon folks. This is a routine fugitive apprehension checkpoint. Identifications please."

Dennis handed over their passports. The cop scanned them. A green light flickered on his scanner. He heard Latoya exhale audibly.

Dennis knew this could mean nothing. Some of the scanners did that to give the fugitive a false sense of security, while the display told the cop something else. Anita had told him that.

"Open wide for a swab, please."

He swabbed both of their mouths. Now, they depended on his mostly experimental Field Kit for their freedom. They waited, mouths dry. Suddenly, the cop was handing them back their passports. "Appreciate your time, folks."

They drove slowly away. "Shh." He cautioned Latoya.

Regal Palace Inn
Prunedale

Prunedale was one of those little places that had bounced back from the cataclysm of 2045 and become greater. Dennis vaguely remembered it from a family road trip in the 2000's as nothing more than a freeway junction and a Starbucks.

Now, pleasant, energy-efficient homes encircled the junction, and a large, glassy, modern hotel dominated the center. It looked approachable enough, and when he and Latoya feigned the embarrassment of illicit sex, the matronly desk clerk agreed to take cash.

The room was spacious and clean, and there was a decent-looking restaurant attached. The only drawback was the service staff. They were robots.

Dennis had avoided robots most of his life. The technology was in its infancy before he emigrated, and after the war, Duplessis' inherent mistrust of AI had severely limited robots on Mars. He had no problem letting the Japanese build them on Mars. As long as they exported most of them.

Only the Emiratis felt differently. With lots to do in a limited lifetime, they had to. Robots were essential in Emirates Mars City.

Now, on Earth, few people would waste money on robots. Life was now measured in millennia, or perhaps eons, so what was the need? Money was spent on travel, food, drink…luxury. Robots toiled mostly out of the public eye, in jobs too dirty or dangerous even for the Uncontrolled.

And, they changed beds and cleaned toilets at the Regal Inn.

He was making his way down to dinner when he bumped into one. By common convention, robots that interacted with humans were only mildly anthromorphic. This one was squat and broad, with a bullet shaped head and a glowing, permanent smile. It rolled around on force repellers and carried a sign affixed to it in English and Spanish:

CAN I HELP YOU? PUEDO AYUDARTE?

Before he could brush past it, the bot was upon him. "How is your stay so far, sir?" For some reason, bots always had a weirdly distorted, high-pitched voice, perhaps to prevent them from posing as humans. "Everything tip top? Clean as a whistle? Ship-shape?" They also came programmed with loads of annoying mid-Twentieth Century slang.

"We just got here." Dennis sighed. A living creature would take the hint that he was trying to get past. But the glowing-mouthed idiobot would not be deterred.

"Anything I can do? Anything the rest of the Regal Inn team can do? Refrigerator temperatures a-ok? Air conditioning super-duper? Holo picture bright and lifelike?"

Finally, Dennis pushed the bot against the wall with one hand. Though he knew the bot was ten times his strength, he was taking underhanded advantage of Asimov's Laws to express his displeasure. "Listen, you metal imbecile. Everything is a-ok, tip-top, pip-pip, and shipshape. If it isn't, I will call the desk, understand? So stop acting like a silicon Jehovah's Witness, and get the fuck out of my way. I'm hungry."

"Sure thing, Mr Kessler! Happy to help! Can I tell you about the specials in the Ponderosa Lounge? First off, there's a 10-ounce Prime Rib with all the trimmings…"

"Jesus Christ."

"Nearby houses of worship include, but are not limited to…"

The Ponderosa Lounge

"I was wondering where you were." Latoya scrutinized the menu. "I mean, it all looks good, but after all this talk of clonal horrors…"

"I slipped the desk clerk something extra. Ours will be real. This is cattle country, baby."

"Poor little cows."

"The Garden Salad looks great."

"I'll have mine medium rare."

Dennis took a small blue cube out of his backpack and activated it with a thumbprint. He registered Latoya's quizzical look. "Insurance. I own it, and I barely ever use it. But it could be the only way out of a jam if I need it."

"Do I want to know?"

"Might be more fun if you don't, actually."

"You're worried, aren't you?"

"Of course I am. There's so many things that can catch you up these days. One reason actual serious crime in Normie areas is so low. There's too many ways to get caught."

"We ditched our computers, our phones, our car, everything. Now, we look like versions of ourselves in anaphylactic shock, and we can fool a DNA test. What more can there be, Dennis?"

"There's always something. Always."

Regal Inn
Basement

Unit 102-R was due for a charge, and so, forty minutes after it's unfortunate interplay with the guest in 505, the robot slid into a rack next to three others of its kind, beginning to hum and warm.

During this time, in accordance with Federal law, 102-R uploaded it's record of human and DNA interactions to MAXIMUM, the fugitive prevention database. There was no special reason for this, and 102-R was no more a crime-fighting robot than it was a gardening expert.

It was just a routine duty expected of such capable machines. As offworld data banks powered by massive solar panels allowed systems like MAXIMUM to process quadrillions of encounters on eight worlds simultaneously, lawmakers and cops alike agreed; why not?

As it uploaded its interactions with humans and the traces they left behind, 102-R beamed a brief record of a man with a bad temper and a very confusing helix to a Lagrange point in the Earth/Moon system. Before long, this encounter had been flagged for review.

Soon, with everything tip-top and shipshape, 102-R resumed its duties, with a full battery and a glowing smile.

2096

Prodigal sons, prodigal daughters

Approaching Emirates Mars City
Valles Marineris

It is possible, Dennis Rosso reflected, to put one's head down to a task, then wake up, and find fifty years have vanished.

As he reflected on this, a phenomenon well known to parents, his 'copter approached Emirates Mars City on a low and dizzying path, the great valley of the Solar System below. Soon, the black scar that was Great Wall Station 2 imposed itself. Slumped into the canyon, part jagged breakage, part sensual melting, the scene of Dennis Rosso's crime was a reminder that the passage of time had not erased everything.

A new, nationalist government in Taipei had begun to call his actions a war crime.

For much of the intervening time, if you'd have asked Dennis to expound on even local events, like the steady rise of Emilie Duplessis, or that of her political rival, Anita Bergstrom, he'd have drawn a blank. All he knew of the Duplessis' dynasty was, they left him alone to do what he did best and did not interfere. As for his ex-wife, he knew even less.

The pilot was circling around Great Wall 2. Forty years ago, the radiation levels here would've made that foolhardy. But now, all things except humans died down. The vista made him think of more than his reputation.

When he turned that key to destroy this place, he'd destroyed his marriage, too. She just couldn't get past it. Within two years, it was over.

He'd been content to sit at his lab bench, while the busy bees of Rosso Labs Mars perfected his miracle. Now, he could not only stop your own body from killing you over time, but he could inure you against all but the most catastrophic ends.

By 2075, he was certain he could've saved 90% of the victims of the Red Foam. All but the Rabid. Stretching and strengthening telomeres, oxygenating cells, encouraging reproduction, where once death was final...he could make humans almost indestructible.

Like the original iteration of the miracle, this came with consequences. The Red Foam had delayed one of these, namely, overpopulation. But, as Earth's population quickly rebounded, aided by practically limitless fusion power and the desalinization it made possible, Kassabian's solution of linking sterilization to immortality became the only acceptable option.

One particularly useful feature of his invention, namely an override key to allow sterilization reversal, gave nations the confidence to regulate fertility.

Kassabian gave his first Nobel acceptance speech, in 2052, from prison. That one, Dennis did not begrudge him. The second, in 2060, was a very different story.

By this time, Kassabian had used a network of celebrity friends on Earth to support his image makeover. From scientific madman and Typhoid Mary to political prisoner of conscience, in one easy leap. When he, and his dead girlfriend Bolderova were given the credit for the Red Foam vaccine, he was not the only one who was enraged.

But Kassabian, shamelessly and boldly thanked "The Eighteen," whom Dennis assumed were his Davos and Cannes pals, and lapped up the attention. For some reason, he'd been allowed to keep a scraggly-looking dog now. Rumour had it, he'd already cloned it once.

But the Republic of Mars was a powerful country now. Duplessis ruled as head-of-state, a transitional position until a two-party democracy, one of whose parties was run by his daughter, could take over the government. When that might be, was anyone's guess. Anita pushed for things to move faster, but when she lost a referendum in 2080, her cause lost momentum.

Dennis Rosso had saved Merlin Duplessis' ass. At the cost of having himself branded a war criminal. But one benefit of Duplessis' continued power: There was no way in hell Kassabian was getting out one day earlier than the scheduled end of his sentence, no matter what Drake, LeBron James, or Greta Thunberg thought. And once he was finished, his ass would be thrown off of Mars, never to return.

But now, in 2096, the year of Kassabian's freedom, Dennis received a surprise summons to Emirates Mars City. For him, and only him, by the Martian Emir.

As they neared the graceful, carbon-colored spires of the great city, now home to 100,000 people, Dennis Rosso could not help but wonder if the old Emirati was not calling in his favor. Perhaps it was time to repay his salvation on the *John Carter*.

Emirati Mars City
Palace of the Emir

Dennis looked around at his sumptuous surroundings, thinking back to his first few years on Mars. Short showers, bland food, shortages of everything. Now, he sat in a teak chair, facing the big, gruff old Emir, his face lined and hardened, but otherwise unchanged, behind his massive desk. A room the size of a shuttle hangar overlooked not Mars, but the grand interior of the city, waterfalls built into the canyon walls, wild greenery scaling the cliffs, fountains and terraced apartments everywhere.

"How come you have never visited us?"

"I've been busy, Your Excellency."

The Emir laughed loudly. "Oh my, and you are immortal! Imagine me, a poor Muslim with one life to live."

For that reason, Dennis reflected, the city looked different from anywhere on Mars now. There were kids...everywhere. Women in long black abayas pushed strollers, tailed by more kids. Twenty-somethings bounded excitedly from one shopping temptation, arcade, or restaurant to the next. "It's a vital place you've built here."

The Emir held up a finger. "Vital, because it has real life. And it's counterpart, death."

"My miracle is not mandatory, Your Excellency. We are all free to choose."

"Sorry if I preach. I am starting to sound like a Saudi, yes? How is your tea?"

"Delicious. Very hard to get good tea here."

"Not here it isn't! Hell, you can even get whisky in the shops and restaurants, if you aren't Muslim, that is. Like I said, we aren't the Saudis. I just..." He withdrew worry beads from his road and began to fiddle with them. "I just worry about my fellow Martians, that's all. You know, after we travelled here on *John Carter*, I got off and joined twenty Emiratis and twenty Pakistanis...and here we built this place, us and the robots!

Now look at it!"

"It's quite an accomplishment."

"But, Dennis, I worry. I worry about the stresses Merlin is under. I worry about the politics. I worry about you. And what happened last week…"

Dennis sat on the edge of his chair. "Is this why you called me…"

The Emir sipped at his tea. "He shows up with 32 people. A caravan, towing RTGs so hot we had to bury them in marscrete. A crazy looking bunch, like…like a cult. He came to me because he remembered me, and he does not trust Duplessis. He called for you, because you tried to help him, once."

"Leuprecht. Captain Leuprecht."

"Yes, Dennis." The Emir raised a finger again. "But it has been a very long time since he was the 'Captain' of anything. Except this bunch. Believe me when I tell you, I admire what they have done, if the stories they tell are true. But he has gone…gone bamboo, they would've said once."

55 years in the Martian wilderness? How could he not be crazy? "What does he want?"

"Somewhere to live."

"But they had that."

"Yes, and something went terribly wrong. An explosion and fire. They had no comms links with the outside world to begin with, so all they could do was drive for the nearest place. Not all of them made it. Listen, Dennis, it's not giving them the facilities to live on their own that bothers me. It's…"

"Yes?"

"It's whether or not they should be left alone at all. He's gone crazy out there...they have pictures of Kassabian, Dennis. They say he is their saviour. He freed them from bondage, like Moses, and set them on their journey. *Allah yaghfir lisani!*"

"Have they been inoculated?"

"Yes." The Emir was emphatic. "That was non-negotiable, although there was really no argument. It seems the Captain has not completely forgotten he was a man of science, once."

"And what is he now?"

"You heard the Abrahamic references, my friend. If I keep him here too long, some of my more literal-minded brothers will be itching to slit his throat in his sleep."

"They'd better cut it all the way off. He has the miracle."

"And yet he will not entertain sharing this with anyone else. His thoughts, at least on this particular, are curiously Islamic."

"Can I see him?"

"Of course. Come with me." They exited the Emir's offices and quarters, a spotless space dominated by white stone and endless fountains, decorated with the geometric patterns and calligraphic art of the Muslims. Outside, two unobtrusive bodyguards joined them as they entered the stunning Great Atrium.

"You need security, Your Excellency?"

The Emir looked cranky on the subject. "Can you believe this? Yes, unfortunately, in recent years a separatist movement has emerged, agitating for us to break away from the Republic and declare ourselves an independent Islamic State. So far, though they are loud, the adherents of this movement are not numerically significant. But politics in Islam is rarely peaceful. Cutting back on the Saudis we admit has lessened our difficulties. These Wahhabists are nothing but trouble, I tell you!"

Dennis waited while the Emir engaged in pleasantries with

some well-rounded admirers. Then they boarded a massive, transparent elevator, and began descending. One of the bodyguards, whom Dennis now noticed was Caucasian, sealed off the elevator with a palm print. The other, a stolid Nepali, stared out at the levels of the Great Atrium with binoculars.

"You notice that my men are not Arabs?"

"You follow the Janissary model?"

"Very good, you know some history."

"I also make it."

"So I have seen. Yes, I strictly hire non-Muslims, mostly veterans of the British or Indian armies for my security. This way, nobody gets religious notions, do you see my meaning?"

"Yes, of course. I take it nobody is castrated?"

The Brit manning the elevator controls smiled a little. The Emir roared. "There's nothing they can use them for here anyway! They have to travel to the fleshpots of Hellas and spend their cash!" The elevator's grand vistas were replaced with flat marscrete as they went underground. Soon, the elevator stopped.

The underground level was cold and soulless. Their breath hung in the air. The bodyguards checked in with a colleague behind a sealed door, which opened to reveal a single large room, better warmed than the outside, appointed with Bedouin-style rugs, pillows, and even tents. One of two pictures of Kassabian adorned the walls.

A blonde woman tapped a long-haired man facing away from them on the shoulder. He turned, and Dennis looked into the lined, weather-beaten face of Josh Leuprecht.

Leuprecht got to his feet. His eyes were cloudy and unblinking now. His face bore the certain smile of the fanatic. He was not the same man Dennis remembered from their last meeting; this was already apparent. He bowed to the Emir as children ran circles around them. The Emir waved a hand. "I believe you know each other."

Leuprecht put out a hand. It was missing a baby finger. "Of course, I do. Welcome, Dennis. The Community of the Phoenix welcomes you."

"You've started a cult, Josh?"

Leuprecht frowned. "Clearly, you don't understand. Let me explain it to you, in private." He pointed toward a row of rooms. "And I go by Joshua, now."

"Another biblical allusion." The Emir frowned. "Well, I am sure you two will want to catch up. Tell the guards here when you want to return, Dennis."

They both bowed slightly as the Emir left. "I'm sure you have questions."

Dennis exhaled. "You could say that." Leuprecht ushered him to an unadorned room, containing nothing but a plastic table, two plastic chairs, and a 2094 desk calendar with shots of both Emirates Mars City and Mecca.

Leuprecht closed the door behind him and sat opposite Dennis. "He keeps us nice and contained down here, doesn't he? So far, I'm the only one who's seen the inside of what they've built here. It is impressive, isn't it?"

"Yes, Josh…ua. It is. Makes you wonder what he's afraid of, doesn't it?"

Leuprecht smiled and pointed to the ceiling.

"I just assumed that. Nothing I wouldn't say to his face. Why did you do it? You'd almost finished your sentence, Mars needed pilots, and we weren't getting any new ones from Earth! Instead, you wandered off, God knows where…"

Leuprecht put up his hands in supplication. "Easy, Dennis. You did know where. We saw the drones passing by every so often. You could've come to check."

"We got the distinct impression that you wanted to be left alone."

"That was the correct impression. We did."

"So why here? Why now? Why goddamned fucking Kassabian?"

Leuprecht made a stern face. "Please do not blaspheme."

"Blaspheme? Blaspheme? He went there to bring the Red Foam to Mars!"

"That is simply what Duplessis told you, Dennis. What if I told you I knew something very different?"

"What?"

"He warned us the ship was coming, and that there was a Rabid on board. He told us to take our transports and run. He said he had a vaccine formula, but Duplessis wouldn't let him into the lab. So, he stole a hopper off the pad and came to us, intending to formulate enough to save us."

"He left something out! He had the keys to the Planetary Defence System. We could've shot the *Martin Gibson* out of the sky!"

"I doubt highly that Merlin Duplessis would've allowed that. With his daughter on board? Seriously, Dennis, for a man once so determined to rebel against Duplessis, you've been awfully trusting of him. One more thing he told you, and you believed."
"I could say the same for you, Joshua."

"Except that I was there. I saw the Prophet arrive. I heard his words of warning. I witnessed him stay behind, to work alone, fearlessly. Paula and I took ten other people who followed the word, and we drove to an unused satellite station we knew had water, power, and a habitation section, to wait things out. And we wound up being fruitful and multiplying. The Prophet protected us, by keeping the pestilence away."

"Are you listening to yourself? What's wrong with you? You're an educated man, how can you believe this shit?"

Leuprecht's cloudy eyes had the calm of the certain. "You did not live it. I did. A certain clarity comes to you in the desert. That is the clarity Allah once brought Mohammed, peace be upon him. But now, these people…" He waved a hand at the ceiling. "These people are too swaddled in comfort to have that clarity anymore. Only we, isolated from the carnal world for so long, retain it."

Dennis looked at his long-abandoned friend, then looked out the window at his flock. While he had been trying to perfect man on the cellular level, Leuprecht had been seeking a more ancient solution. "What do you want, Joshua?"

"A place to live, as we did before. The fire destroyed our habitation modules and our hydroponics. Our power sources were generating unhealthy amounts of radioactivity, I'm afraid."

"And what will Duplessis get for this magnanimous gesture?"

"Peace. We will even take in our Prophet, so he does not need to be troubled by a rivalry I am sure would worry him."

Kassabian? Even the most space-happy Martian wouldn't vote for him. "You'll go right back out there? None of this even tempts you?"

Leuprecht stared at Dennis with his now disconcerting eyes. He had a fleeting vision of the man leading an army of followers out of the desert, like Mohammed, to take the world for his tribe. But how could 32 people conquer the world?

"All I need, is out there. In that room, my people. And above, the space to wander, and gain clarity."

"Surely you must need medical attention. The miracle?"

"The miracle distracts those of us who have it from attaining clarity. There is always another day in which to learn; therefore, what is the urgency? The man who has no time to waste, is the man who truly learns."

"You have the miracle. So does Kassabian. How can you teach, if you cannot learn?"

"Look at my face. You look no different than the last time I saw you, Dennis. Can you say the same for me? I will give you a blood sample before you leave. You will see that, in a sufficiently harsh environment, the miracle is finite."

"But that's what I've been working on for the last fifty years! Making it effectively infinite! Ask Paula what she thinks, I mean, really thinks…a woman wouldn't see it the same way"

Leuprecht put a hand on his arm. "Paula died of Acute Radiation Syndrome on the journey. The miracle cannot remake dissolved chromosomes. That, is the power of God."

"I'm…I'm sorry. But the offer still stands."

"No. Those of us with the miracle will eventually age and die. Mars wills it. Those of us without, will be fruitful as God intended, and will learn the immortality of the soul. That is our way."

"And all those people out there agree?"

Leuprecht folded his hands in his lap. "Ask them, if you do not believe."

All that Dennis Rosso knew of cults he knew from the strange movements of the late 20th century, Jonestown, Waco, the Reebok Suicides. He did not intend to wade into the midst of their politics. Perhaps cut off in the wilderness was the safest place for this bedraggled band. "I'll talk to Duplessis. Make sure that Kassabian knows about your offer."

"Oh, he knows." The smile was strangely certain. That left only one of them feeling anything like certain. On the way out, a young girl of about four pressed a paper flower in his hand. He kept it, and when his misgivings were realized many years later, he still had it.

Acidalia Maximum Security Correctional Facility

Along with hundreds of thousands of other Martians, and not a few people back on Earth, Dennis Rosso was watching the live feed a few months later, as Henrik Kassabian was released at the end of his fifty-year sentence.

Despite the efforts of a cavalcade of celebrities to bring him back to Earth, Kassabian had proved his mercurial nature by rejecting their petitions, as had Duplessis. Clearly, the Head of State had decided that a visible and vocal enemy on Earth was more of a threat than one closer to hand, with a small, vulnerable, and cut-off following.

Dennis had briefly emerged from isolation to advocate for Leuprecht's little community, to the public disgust of both political parties, but Duplessis Senior would not be swayed from his decision. He and the Emir granted the Claritians a tract of land in an otherwise unremarkable sector of Margarifter Sinus, built them a facility with room for growth and a single emergency antenna, and deposited 33 members there two weeks before Kassabian's parole. A new arrival at Emirates Mars City had boosted their numbers.

Kassabian only added one rider to the contract: his current terrier, Nobel Warrior 3 (get it?) was dying of cancer, so badly metastasized that only freezing and return to Earth could possibly help him. Since a junior executive in the JC Bryan corporation was heading back home and offered to take Nobel Warrior 3 as special baggage, he got his wish. He also got the means to clone more little friends, which should've rung alarm bells at the time, but did not.

Kassabian explained his reasoning in a curt e-mail to Dennis, just before his release.

You may not understand what I am doing, or why. But the world of all those Hollywood phonies holds no interest for me. Like you, I am a scientist, and the idea of doing my work in isolation, with no distractions, appeals to me greatly.

I have hated you, but that is no more. I forgive you. Perhaps you should forgive me, as now you realize there is more to the story of Phoenix base than Duplessis told you.

I have a quiet place to work, a unique community of specimens to work on, and, if I produce something the world wants, I can always bring them back to my door.

How's your work going?

Dennis had kicked the monitor off his desk when he read that. "I forgive you?" *Fuck you!* The thought of Kassabian gradually going blind and insane in a UV-scoured, only partially terraformed desert made him smile in secret. And what was that about a "Unique community of specimens?" Did Leuprecht have any idea what they were getting into at the hands of their "Prophet?"

He couldn't muster up enough outrage to return to public life. Besides, he had his lab bench to return to, and a vial of blood from Leuprecht that raised more questions than it answered.

What did happen to the miracle, untended? And why hadn't he looked into that more?

As if to underscore his decision to retreat from the world once again, as Kassabian walked past the news reporters, he held up two fingers to the cameras. Clearly written on his palm was the phrase:

Count Them

Dennis kicked over another monitor. Paying attention to the outside world was getting expensive.

2117

Obligatory chase scene!

Regal Inn
Prunedale

Dennis awoke when a word repeated itself in his dreams.

Clarity.

He stirred and crept to the window. Pulling back the curtains, he saw men standing around a van. He checked his watch: 03:05.

Flowers By Irene.

Dennis let the curtain fall back into place and padded back to the drawers. He found his pants and retrieved the blue cube. He hit the button marked "Summon." Soon, the little display flashed back to him:

Acknowledged. ETA 03:00.

"Latoya, get dressed now. Grab only what you need." He whispered to her.

"What? Hey, what's…"

"They're outside in the parking lot. Looks like they're having coffee and talking plans so far. But we don't have long. Get dressed. No lights!"

Hurriedly, they prepared themselves in the dark. When Dennis peeled back the curtain again, the men were dispersing. "Come on, let's go!"

Latoya struggled to put her last shoe on. "Wait! Jesus Christ, Dennis, where?"

He held up the blue cube. "You'll see in one minute, come on!"

Dennis pulled open the door, his heart in his throat, and calmed only slightly when he saw no G-Men. He took Latoya by the hand and led her to the stairway, opening the door gently. From the lower floors came echoing footsteps. "Come on!" He hissed to her.

But, in the echo chamber of the stairwell, their steps could not go unnoticed. Soon, the steps below hurried, and a man's voice sounded out. "Cut them off! I think they're at eleven now!" "Fuck this quiet shit!" Latoya pounded up the steps ahead of him with an impressive burst of speed. "High...school... track...star!"

When they came to the roof exit, she kicked it open, filling the stairwell with a shrieking alarm. They staggered out onto the gravel roof, looking up at a ghostly quiet contraption which blinded them with a searchlight.

"Oh no! They've got us!" Latoya cried.

Dennis tossed a couple of cinderblocks against the door and took out the blue cube. "No! We've got us!"

"Huh?" The chopper emerged from its own light, hovering with four rotors on stilted arms just above them. A wispy ladder descended from its open belly. Dennis pushed Latoya to move. She scrambled up the ladder, Dennis close behind, as the door began to buck and slam.

"Airwolf, go!"

"You are not secure." The machine replied sternly.

"Override! Go!"

"Departing now." The machine moved with a lurch, and Dennis feared for a moment he would fall. But Latoya now grasped his wrists, and his feet found purchase on the ladder again. As he heaved up into the belly of the chopper, the first men pushed their way through the stairwell beneath them, and shots came in their direction.

"Doors closing. Doors closed. Force shields activated." Now, as the chopper sealed itself, they were protected. But Dennis felt a searing pain in his foot.

He lifted his leg and saw blood dripping from his shoe. "Shit." Gingerly, he removed it to find a hole through the middle of his arch. "Fuck, that hurts!"

The chopper chimed in. "First aid kit located under forward bench."

"Lucky this flight comes with a paramedic." Latoya retrieved the kit as they flew in darkness. "Aren't we a little low?"

"Ouch. No, Airwolf is programmed to fly like that in a threat situation, to avoid detection."

"Airwolf?"

Dennis shrugged. "Show I used to like as a kid. What do you think of him?"

She stopped working on his wound for a minute to look around. "Nice. Like the inside of a limo. You've even got a bar! But why on Earth…"

Dennis shrugged and tightened his jaw as Latoya applied a stinging antiseptic to his wound. "When I got back from Mars I was in a low place. I bought toys like this to keep myself amused. Haven't seen him in…how long has it been, Airwolf?"

"Two years, twenty-three days, one hour, and sixteen minutes.

Dr Kassabian, your attention: Two unidentified aircraft on an intercept course, seven kilometres out. Please secure belts for evasive maneuvers."

"Here we go. No adventure is complete without a chase scene." Dennis secured his straps and helped Latoya with hers.

"Oh man. I hope I don't throw up." Latoya moaned.

"Sick bags are located in the dispensers to your left, ma'am."

"Thank you, Airwolf, I don't usually…"

"Evasive port!" The chopper stood on its side; the black form of a redwood forest perilously close. Two shapes with spinning rotors hurtled past. Then, the chopper went into a sickening spin, coming out the other side with a low-level burst of speed that left Dennis glad it was still dark.

"Mmmph….arggggh." Latoya vomited into her sick bag.

"Evasive starboard!" Now, the chopper hurled itself in the opposite direction, skimming over top of one of the pursuing shapes. Dennis looked out his window to see the shape in clear view as it changed course and stuck with them.

"This is the Federal Bureau of Investigation! Land your vehicle and surrender, or you will be downed!" The hailing came in over their speakers.

Dennis raised his voice. "Broadcast! Fuck you, Fisk! You killed the Zhangs, and we're not going to be next!"

There was a pause. "How do you know we killed them?"

"You usually bring silencers to a surveillance?"

"Fuck!"

Now, they flew sinuous courses through giant, ancient forests, Airwolf projecting their course in night vision displays. The FBI choppers were close behind them, but if they were armed, they were holding off.

"Airwolf, how do we lose them?"

"Crazy Ivan is the recommended course of action."

"Crazy Ivan?" It was a term he remembered from old Tom Clancy novels; a ball-breaking head-on attack meant to throw the other guy off his nerve. "But these are Federal agents."

"Doubtful. These choppers are non-Federal standard. Their registration numbers return a private business owner."

"What? Who?"

"JC Bryan, Incorporated, of Atlanta, Georgia."

"Fuck it! Crazy Ivan!"

"Hang on, please. Maneuver in fifteen seconds."

"Oh God!" Latoya rolled her eyes and puked again.

Dennis had a front-row seat for what happened next. Airwolf headed straight for a tree-studded bluff, then entered a tight orbit around it. Rather than splitting up, as experienced Federal machines would likely do, the corporate choppers stuck together. Now, Airwolf reversed his turn in blurring speed, causing Dennis to retch and lose focus.

When he regained it, Airwolf was flying full-speed between two choppers.

When he looked back, there was a single fireball, and another set of spinning rotors hurtling towards a bouncing, brutal landing on a valley floor.

"You okay?" He touched Latoya's arm. She demurely folded up her sick bag.

"Hmmm...okay, okay. I didn't watch that last part. Are we okay?"

"Yes, I think. For now."

"Destination: Seattle. ETA three hours and fifteen minutes. Please relax. Both adversaries disabled. There are no signs of other pursuers."

"Thank you, Airwolf. That was nice work."

"I watched your TV show, as instructed."

He turned to Latoya. "You want a drink?"

"Oh God yes."

They drank in silence as the redwoods of California gave way the flatter, more desolate emptiness of northern Nevada and eastern Oregon. "What's on your mind, Dennis?"

"Fisk is a phoney. He's no G-Man, or at least, he isn't anymore. This whole thing is JC Bryan, and one crooked Fed in the right place."

"Well, maybe he's burned up back there anyway? And isn't that a good thing? I mean, isn't it better to be going up against one company and few crooked executives than the whole government?"

Dennis nodded. "I suppose so. But there's one thing that really bothers me."

"What's that, honey?" She put a hand on his knee.

"They used us. They used us all along, to get rid of the Zhangs. I mean, do you think Alex getting on that train was a coincidence? In a city of how many million people? We walked right into it."

Latoya smiled. "And now, we're going to walk right out of it."

2112

deserter

Hellas City
Mars

Dennis Rosso was now 122 years old.

He had the dreams of an old man, in which, he was always such, as in life, he was not. The body had changed, yet the mind had not. But in this dream, he had been dreadfully concerned with time, something he rarely was anymore. He had no idea why. He awoke, to a strange noise coming from the windows.

One of the curious effects of living too long was that friends became enemies, enemies became friends, and the unthinkable happened too often to be thought so anymore.

Take for instance, Anita. Dennis moved her arm gently to allow himself to slip out of bed, unnoticed. In 2098, after she had won election to the office of Prime Minister for the very first time, he had been sleeping in this very room after a victory party held by Mars Dawn.

The whisper open of a door, a gust of outside breeze, and she was there, more than fifty years after she had left.

"I needed you." She had said, simply.

"You divorced me." He had replied.

"I'm undivorcing you."

"You can't do that."

"Yes, I can, I am Swedish. For us, all things are permitted."

And that was that. They did not bother to get married again or explain to anyone what had happened. They simply lived as if fifty years was a brief pause, acknowledging, perhaps, that now it would be, for people whose lifespans could be measured in eons.

He stirred from bed, hearing rattling on the windows growing ever louder. He walked to the giant picture window overlooking Lake Hellas and saw the red pebbles and sand grains blasting the outside of their balcony.

Down below, whitecaps formed on the usually quiescent waters of the great lake. Dennis cursed under his breath. He had meant to go out on his boat tomorrow. Now, the waters would be murky and clouded red. They'd stay that way for weeks, unless he got Jerry involved.

He *would* get Jerry involved. The ever-striving, apolitical entrepreneur, now almost as rich as the Emir of Mars, still nowhere close to Duplessis though, was always happy to help in return for a genuine Earth BBQ and a chance to meet some of Dennis' cute lab technicians.

There was a steady supply of lab technicians. BBQ was more of a problem, most countries on Earth having banned actual animal flesh two years before. But Dennis had a guy in LA. By the time the meat arrived at Hellas, shipping costs alone made a chuck roast cost more than the finest Kobe.

But he just couldn't eat the JC Bryan garbage. He couldn't do it. The only time Dennis ever came out of hiding anymore was to encourage Duplessis to veto any bill advocating extending the meat ban to Mars. That was tricky, because both his daughter and Anita, who agreed on few things, agreed on the meat ban.

One good thing about Merlin Duplessis, though: South Carolina whole hog could activate his Presidential veto. It made for some interesting parties.

The ties between them all, and perhaps their maturity, hidden behind 30-year-old faces and bodies, kept Mars peaceful and prosperous. Emilie Duplessis was the baby of the group, but her respect for her father, and Dennis and Anita for having rescued her from the nightmare of Phoenix Base, kept her civil and engaged.

The economy responded, as economies do, to peace and prosperity. Mars was, once again, a desirable investment location. The growing bodies of water on the surface, and breathable oxygen in the atmosphere in measurable amounts for the first time in recorded history, didn't hurt. Though much closer and easier to get to, the Moon could never compete with that. It would never be more than an industrial and scientific outpost. Mars was where you emigrated to stay.

Plus, if you wanted to, you could still have kids here. Mars needed babies.

"Are we going to have that balcony window polished again?" Anita came up behind him. "It's so expensive."

Dennis shrugged. "I'll just get Jerry to do it. I was going to call him to filter out the lake anyway."

"I assume you have the meat of some poor, murdered, very expensive animal coming from Earth?"

He laughed. "That, and good bourbon, are his only weaknesses."

"That, and girls who look like they ran away from convent school." Anita made a face. "It's disgusting."

Dennis laughed again. "How do you know? Everyone these

days looks like they'd need ID to get into a bar, thanks to me. And those 'little girls' could be a hundred, for all you know."

"Hmm, I guess it's true. Well, come back to bed!"

"Why?"

"I'm going to show you what a hundred-year-old woman can do!"

**Three Months Later
Ohan's Lookout
Lake Hellas**

Dennis recalled his first steps on Mars, all those years ago, and shook his head in amazement.

Somewhere underneath them were the ruins of the old Hellas Base. Humans now lived on the shores of the massive lake or in the steep cliffs above. Hellas, due to its geological peculiarity of being far below datum point on Mars, was still the only place on the planet where humans could reliably count on being able to do what they were doing today, at least in summer.

Dennis' boat bobbed against its pier. Kids took running jumps off that pier into cold glacier water, still bubbling up from inside the planet, decades after the first wells had been drilled. On a grass-studded, red sand beach, guests sat on picnic blankets and tended hibachis.

Dennis adjusted his sunglasses and looked down at himself in amazement. He was wearing shorts. Shorts and flip-flops.

On fucking Mars.

Anita bounded up to him, wearing a just-too-small bikini that was just right. "Here he is." She pointed to a speck, shadowy against the crater rim. "Sounded like he was too busy to make it."

"Guess he was craving a real hotdog." He held a Bavarian smokie up to her and wiggled it obscenely.

"Gross. Let me cover up for a meeting with the First Citizen."

"You might get more concessions if you didn't." He called after her.

"Don't give me any ideas!" She yelled back. Dennis looked back at the chopper, which flared for landing in the midday sun and set down gently. As the rotors slowed, Duplessis emerged with his youthful paramour, Juliana, his daughter and her new husband, and their combined brood of five children, who ran ahead, shrieking with excitement at the sight of the other kids already swimming.

"Is that who I think it is?" His lab administrator, Sandro, looked astonished. Sandro was wearing a too-small golf shirt and socks with sandals.

You couldn't blame people on Mars for not knowing how to dress for the heat, could you? "Yes, Sandro, that is the man himself. We go way back. Way back."

"Wow."

Duplessis made straight for him. Lately, he'd had some touches of gray added, something that was more in vogue among men than women. Looking distinguished was no handicap to men of Merlin Duplessis' stature. "Dr Rosso, I presume?" His old, worn joke.

"The Boss himself." They shook, firmly. "Smokie?"

"They do look good. But we need to talk, first."

He gestured to Sandro. "Sandro, can I trust you not to burn the Boss' smokie?"

Sandro reacted like he'd been asked to charge a machine-gun

nest. "Yessir!"

They walked back up the gentle hill to Duplessis' chopper. Dennis noticed another vehicle parked far away. "Keeping your security close, I see."

"Not too close."

"When was the last time you needed security to come down to the Lake, Merlin?"

"Come inside and let me bring you up to speed. Then you'll see."

Feeling another crisis coming on, Dennis suddenly felt older. "Great."

Duplessis closed the doors behind him. Dennis admired the interior. "Nice vehicle."

"Japanese make them, along with that line of robots they've been pumping out. I can get you on the list."

"Sure. What else can I spend my money on? Besides thirty-dollar hotdogs, that is?"

Duplessis stared at him. Now Dennis saw the worry, recognizing that face from 2045. Was he going to have to take over again? "Dennis, it's far worse than many people realize."

"What, the UN? This sanctions bullshit? Let them, Merlin. We don't need them. I can do without the hotdogs. So what if some celebrity wankers want our heads on platters? We don't have to give them."

Duplessis shook his head. "Two weeks ago, that's what I thought, too. Then, this guy showed up at the airlock in Acidalia City and knocked politely. Listen."

Duplessis brought up a holo and darkened the windows. A tall, robust young man in a bodysuit sat across the table from two investigators. A transcript ran at the bottom of the holo.

INV1: PLEASE STATE YOUR FULL NAME AND DATE OF BIRTH.

SUB: MATTHEW JACOB LEUPRECHT, JUNE 20, 2097.

INV1: WHERE WERE YOU BORN?

SUB: CLARITIAN COLONY, MARGARIFTER SINUS, MARS.

INV2: PLEASE STATE WHY YOU HAVE COME TO ACIDALIA.

SUB: I AM DEFECTING FROM THE CLARITIAN COLONY. THE LEADER, HENRIK KASSABIAN, IS A MADMAN. HE HAS GONE AGAINST THE HOLY TEACHINGS OF MY FATHER. HE HAS ALTERED THE MEMBERS OF THE COLONY, PARTICULARLY THE CHILDREN, WITHOUT THE COLONY'S CONSENT. AND LASTLY…

INV1: WHAT, SON?

SUB: HE MURDERED MY FATHER, JOSHUA LEUPRECHT.

"Jesus Christ." Dennis could see Leuprecht's keen alertness in the boy, his restless nature and questioning intellect. Why had his father forgotten who he was?

INV2: HOW DID YOU GET HERE? MARGARIFTER IS ON THE OTHER SIDE OF THE PLANET.

SUB: I FLEW HERE, ON THOSE WINGS I SHOWED YOU.

INV1: THESE ONES?

The investigator brought up a holo showing a light, flimsy looking wing covered in photo-voltaic cells. They unhooked it from a dummy, wearing a skinsuit like Matthew's, to reveal a more robust looking jetpack, with what appeared to be pulse cannons attached.

"What the hell?"

"We tested it, Dennis." Duplessis shook his head. "It all works."

SUB: YES. I GLIDED HERE, POWERING UP IN THE DAY, TRAVELLING ON BATTERY AT NIGHT. THESE WINGS CAN TAKE ME ANYWHERE ON THE PLANET. WHEN WE REACH OUR TARGETS, WE DISCARD THE SOLAR WING, AND SWITCH TO THE JETPACKS, ATTACKING WITH OUR CANNON AND PERSONAL WEAPONS.

INV2: ATTACKING WHOM?

SUB: THE REPUBLIC OF MARS. KASSABIAN HAS BEEN CO-ORDINATING AN ATTACK WITH THE UN FOR YEARS NOW. ONCE HE SCORES SOME SUCCESSES, HE'S SURE THEY'LL COME IN.

INV1: WHY IS HE SURE?

SUB: HE'S GOING TO GIVE THEM THE WAR CRIMINALS THEY WANT. DUPLESSIS AND ROSSO. HE'S GOING TO ACEDE TO THEIR TREATY AND ECONOMIC DEMANDS TOO.

INV2: WHY?

SUB: YOU KNOW WHAT HAPPENED DURING THE RED FOAM, RIGHT?

INV2: HE BLAMES DUPLESSIS AND ROSSO, RIGHT?

SUB: YES. HE IS OBSESSED WITH KILLING THEM BOTH, WHICH IS ACTUALLY HIS INTENTION.

INV1: WHY DID HE KILL YOUR FATHER?

SUB: HE GOT INTOXICATED ONE NIGHT, KASSABIAN DID, AND TALKED TO MY DAD. MY DAD WAS SUSPCIOUS OF HIM ALREADY AND RECORDED HIM. HE CONFESSED TO LETTING THE RABID CREW MEMBER INTO PHOENIX BASE. HE IS GUILTY OF WHAT HE WAS CONVICTED OF. WHEN HE REALIZED MY DAD KNEW, THE NEXT DAY, HE KILLED HIM.

INV2: HOW DO YOU KNOW WHAT THEY TALKED ABOUT?

SUB: I WAS THERE WHEN IT HAPPENED. I WAS TEN.

INV2: DO YOU KNOW WHERE THIS RECORDING IS?

SUB: NO.

INV1: SON, ACCORDING TO MY MATH, YOU'RE ONLY FIFTEEN YEARS OLD. BUT YOU LOOK TWENTY-FIVE, AND, IF YOU DON'T MIND, NOTHING LIKE YOUR FATHER. WHY SHOULD WE BELIEVE YOU?

SUB: MY BODY HAS BEEN SUBJECT TO GENETIC ALTERATION AND STRENGTH BOOSTING SINCE I WAS TWELVE. AND I AM NOT SUPPOSED TO LOOK LIKE MY FATHER. I AM SUPPOSED TO LOOK LIKE CAPTAIN ALBA OF THE PLANETARY DEFENCE FORCES, SO I CAN INFILTRATE HIS BASE AND TAKE OVER HIS COMMAND. MY HONOR IS LOYALTY.

A picture of the real Alba flashed across the holo. They were identical.

INV1: HOW CAN YOU PROVE ANY OF THIS?

SUB: I CANNOT. BUT I BET DR ROSSO CAN. PLEASE TAKE ME TO HIM.

Dennis sat staring at the now blank holo, stunned.

"I should warn you," Duplessis spoke up, "Deo thinks this is all an elaborate plot to get this boy wonder to assassinate you. All he'd have to do is get close. I mean, how many of them could there be? Fifty? One-hundred?"

"We let him take a cloning package to clone that dumb fucking dog. Did we inspect it?"

Duplessis sat heavily on his couch. "No. Too happy to be rid of him. With your recommendation, I might add."

"I know, I know. How long do we have?"

"He won't say, until he sees you. Maybe he figures we're going to kill him. Clearly he thinks you can verify what he is."

Dennis nodded. "I can. Take me to him."

"Now?"

Dennis smiled. "The hotdogs will still be there."

Martian Planetary Defence
Special Investigations Division
Hellas City

The military base on the edge of the Hellas Basin was a recent creation, a child of drum banging in the UN and celebrity sabre-rattling. Everyone hated Mars these days, and if there was one thing Duplessis and his rival political parties could agree on, it was sharpening Mars' big stick.

Don't like us? Fuck you.

For this reason, Mars had attracted many immigrants from Earth's last fashionable pariah state, Israel, a place hated by many of the same people who now railed against Mars. For that reason, a great many of Mars' new defenders were short, robust, hard fuckers who wore yarmulkes on Saturdays and answered every question with a question.

Duplessis introduced him to two such men as he got off the chopper at the base security pad. The air was noticeably thinner here, and the sky only a little less pink than it had been fifty years before. "Doctor Rosso, this is Colonel Shamir and Major Ne'vman. They're in charge of analyzing Matthew and his information."

"Bullshit." Shamir had more hair on his arms than Dennis would've thought possible. His only concession to youth was slick, full, black hair. He wore his beret in the epaulette, Israeli-style. "He just wants to get close to you."

"I disagree." Ne'vman was tall, skinny, and bespectacled, and seemed more like an American Jew than an Israeli. "Besides, why don't we let Dr Rosso decide if he wants to take that risk? This all reminds me too much of Yom Kippur. Look how we paid for ignoring the signs then."

"Shmuel, that's total crap. Yom Kippur is ancient history. Tanks with diesel engines and jet fighters. Might as well study sticks and stones."

"So is Cannae. We still study it, don't we?"

"*Schmegegge!*"

Dennis felt himself going faint. "Uh, do you mind? I live at the bottom of the basin, I'm not used to this without a spacesuit."

"Oh, sorry, man. Come on in." They entered a small, informal base, in which more Hebrew was spoken than English, and wide-hipped, ravishing girls with dark eyes and tight fatigues ran around.

"I should've joined the Israeli Army." Dennis observed.

"You a Red Sea Pedestrian?" Ne'vman questioned him.

"According to my dad, I'm Jew...ish."

"Yeah, like me. I just like to fight, basically."

"You've come to the right place."

Much sooner than he'd expected, after a short elevator ride, he was staring at his friend's son. It was perhaps, easier, in that one-way glass separated them, and that Matthew looked nothing like his father.

But it was still not easy. Matthew looked up and met his eyes, startling him. "Dr Rosso."

"What? Hello, Matthew." The others whispered amongst themselves.

"I am sorry, but my eyes are much more capable than yours. One of Dr Kassabian's inventions."

Dennis looked at Duplessis, who raised an eyebrow. "I was wondering if we might talk."

"I would like that." The boy smiled.

"I would like to talk to you, too." Duplessis offered.

Shamir put up a firm hand. "Only one. Not two of you at a time." He looked at Dennis. "*If* war is coming, this country will need leaders. Just you."

So, Dennis found himself sitting, as calmly as he could feign, across a table from a child who had possibly been sent to kill him. "I am no interrogator, Matthew. The answers I need cannot be found in a cell. Only in a lab."

"I know about you." Matthew looked at him intently. He smelled of the ancient sands of Mars, of smells Dennis had not smelled in so many years. "You got Dr Yueh to confess to starting the Red Foam. My dad told us stories about you."

Dennis choked back a tear. "Dr Yueh wanted to confess. He had a conscience. He was a good man, asked to do bad things. Like you."

Matthew nodded. "Yes. Yes, I am glad you can see that."

"I promise you, son, that I will seek the evidence that will prove what you say. But that evidence may take days to gather. Those people outside the window need two questions answered, right now: When, and Where?"

Matthew squinted hard, as if concentrating. "Bring me a scribe pad, and a pen, please."

2117

Lynn's big scoop

Seattle
Wallingford

As a boy, Dennis had read a book written by a bank robber. His advice on being a fugitive?

Hide in plain sight.

So, that's exactly what they did. Airwolf dropped them, replete with a survival kit he'd stashed in the chopper for just such an eventuality, in the forests of Discovery Park. They hiked out, merging with the other day-trippers enjoying a glorious Seattle summer day. The shot Latoya had given him dulled, but did not eliminate, the pain of a bullet hole.

"Why come back here?" Latoya pressed him.

A gaggle of pre-school children, a rare sight, passed them, chatting excitedly. Everyone stared. "Here is in plain sight. Here is where Lynn lives."

"She…is she a she right now?" A hundred years of enforced orthodoxy could not make most people comfortable around the Lynn's of the world.

"Yes. She seems happy these days. But she still prefers non-binary language."

"So, you said you met…uh…them…having coffee?"

"Yes. Seattle's gift to the world."

"If you mean the overpriced, snooty variety then sure."

"Next thing, you'll be knocking Nirvana."

"Who?"

Dennis laughed. Coming from Seattle meant having to defend it every five minutes in conversation. You either got it, or you didn't.

When he'd gotten back from Mars, wearing a servo-powered exoskeleton and the face of another man, he'd holed up in an arcology apartment arranged by Earth adherents of the Claritians. They were humorless, credulous pogues, and he got rid of them at the first opportunity, by giving a curt and baffling speech at their annual congress.

"God has given you free will. Take your free will and find another prophet. I'll be the guy feeding the ducks. Do not disturb me."

They mostly obeyed that injunction. All but one, who tried to kill him on the street outside the Blue Star Café one afternoon. The stab wound healed easily, but the next day he pulled all the strings he could and got himself an increasingly hard-to-find pistol permit.

The next dickhead who brought a knife to a gunfight with his prophet (peace be upon me) would regret it.

He was tired, his tall frame sagging under the weight of Earth gravity and recent tragedy. He could not change his appearance too overtly now, as his return as Kassabian, and the story that went with it had drawn too much attention. So, he did what he figured Kassabian would do in his shoes.

He grew his beard to biblical length, wore dark glasses, and went out rarely. He experienced the outside world vicariously and did not engage. When he had to go out, he made it brief. A coffee and a croissant. An hour spent reading Cormac McCarthy or Emily St John Mandel by the lake.

Luckily for him, North Americans in the 22nd Century had attention spans not much longer than those of the 21st. Quickly, even his neighbors stopped giving a shit that one of the pole stars of an interplanetary war was living in their midst.

He began to relax. He bought expensive toys, like Airwolf, packing a picnic lunch and flying the Grand Canyon. He began to go out for coffee.

He was at his favourite java hole, *Complications*, a typically pretentiously named Seattle joint, serving hot brown liquid costing far more than it ought to. Dennis was halfway through *Bomber* by Len Deighton, engrossed in the lives and tortured dreams of RAF aircrew in a war nobody remembered now. Perhaps the lives of those he had lost in a very recent war made it more meaningful.

But then, a very gender-non-specific person with broad shoulders and a squinting, lopsided face tapped him on the shoulder. "Good book?" The voice was husky, but not too husky to be female.

One needed to be careful these days. "Excellent. You know him?"

Unbidden, the person sat at his table. "More of a fan of *Goodbye Mickey Mouse*. *Bomber* is just a bit too…clinical. Like an account of cervical cancer written by a gynaecologist." The person studied his face. "I know you."

Oh shit. "I am sure you don't."

"I am sure you've been offered billions for your life story. Why haven't you taken it?"

Dennis decided not to fight it. "I don't need the money. And I don't want to talk."

"My name is Lynn. I am a man, right now, if you were wondering. But I prefer neutral pronouns. I change my mind too often. I have no money to offer you. But I am loyal, and honest. If you ever want someone you can trust to tell your story, then call me." Lynn slipped a card under his book and walked away.

LYNN FOGARTY
PEOPLE REPORTER
SEATTLE REVOLUTION

He'd looked at the card then, thinking little of it, and filed it away. But over the next three years, Lynn was there, a more-or-less constant presence in his life. He found himself talking to them, not about what Lynn really wanted to hear, but about other things, Seattle politics, the Mariners, cats versus dogs (Lynn got quite heated about that last one).

One night, when coffee had switched to beer, he dared her to switch back to a woman.

"Why, tough guy, you gonna fuck me?"

"If that's what it takes."

So, she did, and he did too. But they seemed to agree, mutually, that the sex, however satisfying, was standing in the way of a good story. Now, he and Latoya were boarding a streetcar and heading straight for that story.

On the viewscreens in the car, the Most Wanted poster featuring them played every five or so minutes. But it had not been updated. There was no mention of Airwolf. The emergency kits must've been working. Nobody on the train played them the slightest mind.

The cars were sparsely populated. Few people commuted to work anymore, most either working from home, or not at all. There were no children, here. "I killed the world." Dennis announced, to nobody in particular.

"You had help." Latoya's head slumped against his shoulder.

Soon, Dennis's eyes were blinking open again as a voice announced: "Wallingford."

They alighted across the street from an eternal institution. The Wallingford Sign had once been attached to a gasoline filling station and sub-par coffee shop. Now, neither existed, but the sign remained. Dennis recalled its witticisms as once being a little more…on-target, but still, it was sacred ground. Today, the sign read, in 20th century magnetic letters:

MY ROBOT HAS A MEMORY DEFECT

I SAY SHIT, HE REMEMBERS IT

He recognized her, standing in the bushes behind the sign. She turned and let them follow.

They followed her, past non-descript, here today, gone tomorrow boutiques and take-outs, past the place where boyhood Dennis had once filled three bags full of shlock toys before shipping out for Los Alamos (Archie MacPhee's, now long gone), around the corner to the gracefully decrepit Blue Star café.

"What's so special about this place?" Latoya demanded.

"Got stabbed here once. Also, the bacon grilled cheese is damned good."

2112

ATTACK OF THE SPIDERMEN

Hellas City

Matthew spent his days at Hellas alternating between the military interrogators and sessions at Rosso Labs. His existence was kept a complete secret, but it could not be kept a secret from the one man who mattered.

Dennis and Duplessis were hanging out on his balcony one afternoon, three days after Matthew's surprise appearance, trying to fathom the unfathomable. "He has to know Matthew's come over to us. The timeline he's giving us is garbage now." Duplessis stared down into the great lake, which was scintillating in the midday sunshine. The pressure of impending crisis was clearly wearing on him now, but Dennis was hopeful that his daughter's presence would stabilize him.

"Not necessarily." Dennis countered. "For all he knows, Matthew got lost and crashed somewhere. He said he was careful to disable his tracking devices."

"All the more reason for Kassabian to be suspicious. It's not like there's a lot of places he could go, is there? He has to assume the plan is compromised."

Dennis found the logic hard to refute. "So, if not two weeks from now, when?"

"If I were him, I'd hit us as soon as I could."

"Maybe we should just go arrest him. We know where he lives."

"Pre-empt? No way. Deo is convinced, and Shamir is too, that the whole damned thing is a ruse. Kassabian trying to get us to violate his rights, something all his Hollywood and Davos pals would shit themselves over. He's already got them whipped into a lather. Plus, there's a UN vote next week. The EU is seriously proposing to land a UN force to protect the Claritians."

"As if they give a shit. It's the rare earths they're after." A recent discovery of rare earths 200 kilometers from the Claritian Colony had renewed fervour in Martian mining stocks. Few materials were valuable enough to justify mining them and shipping them to Earth, but rare earths were the exception.

"Of course, I know that." Duplessis slumped his worryingly skinny frame into a recliner. "But the idiots on Earth who believe everything the BBC says don't. That's our political problem, in a nutshell."

"How's the mobilization going?"

"We have 16,700 men and women against what? Matthew says 80 'Flyers?' Another reason to suspect the offensive will be political instead of military. How does Kassabian, even a fucking whack job like Kassabian, expect to conquer Mars with eighty fighters?"

Dennis sat in the couch beside Duplessis. "Except it's not that simple, Merlin. These are not eighty ordinary people we are talking about here. I've been studying Matthew for three days now, and it seems like Kassabian has militarized some crucial elements of our work over the years."

"Oh, I know, they're all Immortal. Most of us are, too."

Dennis shook his head. "No, it's not just that. He's accessed, somehow, my work after the war on protecting immortals against trauma. Quick cell regeneration, I mean, really, really quick. Incredible reflexes and phenomenal conversion of food energy into muscle and brain mass. I mean, does Matthew look fifteen?"

"No, he doesn't."

"His growth, and the growth of all the others was accelerated to produce an army in record time. Some of Matthew's fellow soldiers are as young as five."

"No. Five?"

"Yes. But they look like sixteen-year olds on steroids. And their mental abilities are combined with a childlike vulnerability to suggestion and command."

"Jesus. But still, there's only eighty of them."

"Yes, but every one of those eighty can change their appearance with a simple injection of templated DNA."

"Templated?"

"Grown in a specially designed nutrient solution that shapes the outcome. So, if they want a fighter who looks like you, they don't necessarily need your DNA. They can simply approximate, using features from the genome. Like a make-your-own bear sort of thing."

Duplessis shook his head. "Fuck. We put him in one place with fifty years to think this shit up, and zero distractions. We should've just whacked him at Phoenix Base. Christ."

"And the suits? Proof positive against even heavy lasers and projectile weapons. You've got to get a lucky hit on a head, or an engine nacelle. Their physical conditioning allows them to walk on walls and exist in much lower atmospheric pressures than we can tolerate. They can subsist off of water distillers and nutrient packs in their suits for weeks at a time, and their solar power cells recharge their weapons. Worst of all, their training is based on the last bunch of nasty children to almost take over a planet."

"Come again?"

Dennis had remembered Matthew's statement to the investigators. *My honor is loyalty.* It had given him an opening he needed. "Kassabian studied and applied the training and organization of the SS Hitler Youth Division in the Second World War. Ruthless to prisoners and civilians. Complete obedience to the *Fuhrer*, in this case, Kassabian. Fight to the death mentality. We'd better pray that it's a political ploy."

"In that case, how come we have one of these perfect, loyal warriors in our guest suite?" Duplessis raised the obvious question.

"Too much of his father in him, I guess."

"Are you certain of that?"

"Unless he can manipulate the helix in bone marrow, yes. That boy is Matthew Leuprecht."

The communicator chime in Duplessis' watch went off. "Yes?"

"News from Emirates Mars City." Deo reported. "The Emir is dead. You've been invited to the funeral, along with Dr Rosso, and Misses Duplessis and Bergstrom."

"When?"

"In accordance with Islamic tradition, it must be tomorrow."

"Fine. RSVP for all of us."

"Sir, in the present situation..." Deo was expressing a doubt Dennis shared, full-blast.

"I know, Prithpal. I know. But we cannot insult the new Emir. Emir Muftab must have our full support and understanding."

"But that's just it sir. It's not Muftab succeeding his father. Muftab is also dead. They were inspecting a new communications array when their chopper suffered a rotor failure. They died together."

"Convenient." Dennis sneered. "It's Suleiman, isn't it?"

"Yes." Deo answered.

"Don't go." Dennis leaned over and looked at Duplessis closely. "You wanted to know when the attack is coming? Here's my answer: tomorrow, at Emirates City. Suleiman is a snake. Muftab was committed to continuing his father's path. Suleiman is a narrow-minded, greedy bastard with his pockets full of Davos gold. And we're going to go over there, all of us, together?"

Deo chimed in. "I agree with Dr Rosso 100%."

Duplessis stood suddenly and yelled in frustration. "You're right! You're both right, I know! But goddamnit, what the hell are we supposed to do? We need allies right now, not enemies! I can't afford to piss off the largest, and richest colony on this planet right now! A third of our security force and half of our transport? We have to go, Dennis. We have no choice. To refuse would be a mortal insult, one Suleiman would never forgive."

Dennis looked at Duplessis in resignation. He and Deo were right, he knew that in his guts. But Duplessis was right, too.

In one moment, they had lost the initiative. The Battle for Mars might have been lost before it had begun.

Emirates Mars City

Mackenzie, the big Canadian who'd flown them into Phoenix Base all those years before, cruised around Emirates City cautiously before landing. Since bringing Duplessis' daughter back, he'd become the boss' preferred personal pilot. His countryman Terry was in charge of their tiny security detail, and hung over Mac's shoulder as they slowly hovered the transport in.

"Big troop presence boss." Terry announced, "But you'd expect that."

The perimeter of the city, with fingers of enclosed greenery and satellite factories extending for kilometers, was ringed by clusters of pressure-suited men and squat tanks and personnel carriers. Dennis looked out his window and saw holoscreens on the main body of the city, a manmade iceberg with 4/5ths of its bulk below the rim of the great valley, flashing images of the Old Emir in happier times. He seemed to greet them personally to his own departure.

In these days, the rituals of death were unfamiliar. Dennis simply hoped this ritual of death was not a prelude to more death. Anita touched him on the hand. "Whatever happens, stick close to me."

He turned to her and smiled. "Public displays of affection are frowned on in Islam." He kissed her softly. "One for the road."

What could be done, except hope for the best? Deo, Shamir, and Ne'vman had been left at Hellas with a detailed war plan should the shit hit the fan. They would hit Margarifter Sinus and Emirates City hard, with everything they had, then dig in and wait for the UN. Hopefully, public opinion would go into backlash mode, and Mars would be saved by unpleasant images of blue helmets being marched into captivity and scooped into body bags. A populace too sensitive to eat meat would likely have no stomach for a drawn-out war.

"Looks clear, boss." Terry nodded to Anita.

Anita turned to Duplessis. "These heels are killing me. Let's get this over with."

Emilie Duplessis held her father's hand and laughed. "Good words for posterity, Anita."

"Honesty makes a nice tombstone, my grandpa always said."

"Take us in, Mac." Duplessis commanded.

Emirates Mars City
Great Atrium

The funeral had been a brief, almost peremptory affair, conducted under a temporary pressurized barrier. The Emir and his eldest son had been consecrated to the red soil of his adopted world, with their wives watching silently, under the frowning gaze of Suleiman.

Inside the city, monitors showed giant crowds, the city's women, not restrained from weeping, wailing and tearing at their hair. "I feel like I'm in the tenth century." Anita whispered to him.

"You are." Dennis whispered back.

Now, they sat arrayed around a massive table, on the ground floor of the atrium which dominated the city. On the numberless levels above them, the lesser inhabitants of the city watched. A slight bluish shimmer was the only hint that a forcefield protected them from purposeful or inadvertent intrusion.

Suleiman sat close to the Republic's party, a recognition of their importance. The UN Ambassador to Mars, Tolyakov, a plump, rotund career diplomat, strained to hear their conversations.

As servants poured tea, Dennis noticed an empty chair between Tolyakov and Suleiman's. He nudged Anita. "Somebody couldn't make it."

Anita shifted uncomfortably. "Don't be so sure about that. Maybe somebody's preparing a grand entrance."

Duplessis and Suleiman were now engaged in political talk. Emilie looked on, fascinated.

"As you know, Mr Chief Executive, my father was always interested in the best relations with you, ever since he first travelled here on one of your magnificent spaceships. With Dr Rosso and Ms Bergstrom, as I recall."

Duplessis sipped his tea. Terry stood over his should, unobtrusively waving a molecular scanner over any food or drink delivered. "A tragic flight, I'm afraid. Your father saved Dr Rosso's life, I believe."

Dennis nodded. "He did. A very courageous and strong man, he was."

Suleiman looked at him coldly. "And yet, there are many here who say he should not have saved you, Dr Rosso. Your science is hardly Islamic."

Dennis was damned if he was going to take any shit from a regicidal bastard like Suleiman. "Not much modern science would pass a religious test, I'm afraid. Surely that cannot stop us from admiring each other's accomplishments. Like this fantastic city, for example?"

"Built by robots. A home for lazy, greedy, acquisitive people. Frankly, a better home for Jews, if you ask me." Suleiman sneered.

"Is it on the market?" Dennis teased him. "My Rabbi said I should get into real estate."

"A witty man." Suleiman raised his tea glass. "Like the tiger, an endangered species."

Dennis smiled falsely. "Haven't you heard, Your Excellency?

I'm going to live forever."

"Are you sure about that, old sport?" Henrik Kassabian emerged from the phalanx of security people and sat beside Suleiman. The guests stared in shock. "Because you never know what may happen next."

Suleiman smiled indulgently. "Please, welcome my special guest, the *two-time* Nobel Laureate Dr Kassabian." A pointed shot fired at Dennis.

Anita gripped his hand tightly. Kassabian wore a phenomenal suit of what appeared to be weaved metal, which changed colour depending on the light. He looked decades younger than he had on release, trimmer, clear-eyed, muscular. "Welcome back, Henrik. Adapting to the straight life, are we?"

Kassabian stared back at him. "If by this you mean shepherding a small, religious minority through the shoals of oppression and prejudice, quite well, actually. You see, Dennis, I know all about your little scheme to catch us out. Oh, don't look so surprised, Merlin! You see, the United Nations here has graciously offered to protect my people."

Duplessis grimaced. "Your people, or the trillion dollars of rare earths under their feet?"

Kassabian smiled. "Can't it be both? At any rate, it won't fall into your hands. Not once your poorly prepared and concealed plans for a pre-emptive strike are made public." He made a dramatic show of looking at his watch. "Which should be, right about now."

"We've been had." Anita whispered urgently, pressing a button on her wrist to alert Mac to fire up his engines.

"Now, you hold on one damned minute!" Duplessis pounded the table. "We were only protecting ourselves!" He gave Dennis a desperate look and plowed on. "We've been interrogating a defector, Matthew, who tells us..."

It was the new Emir's turn to be enraged. "How dare you, you dog? Weapons pointed, not only at Dr Kassabian's little colony, but at my city! My city, while you come here under a false flag of truce? Well, I tell you this! You and your Zionist mercenaries will not succeed! Because you will never leave here alive!"

Kassabian smiled sickly at Dennis. "Look up! Look way up!"

Just then, a hush came over the atrium, the last silence of peace. The blue forcefield over their heads flickered out. Halfway up the window side of the atrium, at least two dozen dark figures moved quickly down towards them, scuttling like spiders.

Kassabian laughed. "Lookie what I made!" He spoke into his watch. "Attack!"

Behind the Republic's delegation, the security men were already pulling their charges to their feet and getting them moving. Dennis was bodily lifted from his chair, his last view of Kassabian being as he stood next to the UN Ambassador, laughing like a maniac.

Above, the spidermen alighted from the windows, and began dropping to the floor under rocket power. Dennis looked frantically around for Anita as Duplessis shouted into his watch "Focus! Focus!"

Suddenly, a wall of the Emir's mercenary security appeared in front of them. Dennis recognized the sandy-haired Englishman from a prior visit. "Step aside!" Terry commanded.

The Englishman opened his mouth to speak. At that moment, ten of the spidermen landed between the Emir's men and theirs. The Englishman yelled "Get going! Bay 7! We'll hold them!"

Anita surged to the front, waving a pistol! "Move it! Now!"

Now surrounded, Kassabian's troops were forced to turn and defend their backs, as the Emir's men opened fire on them. Pushed along, Dennis glimpsed the nightmare troopers of the enemy, matt black armored, both arms turned into extended weapons, powerful jetpacks on their backs.

As the beleaguered party reached the Bay 7 elevator, with his last glimpse over his shoulder, Dennis witnessed the end of the heroic Englishman and his men, in a flurry of red and blue energy bolts. Stepping over the charred husks of the mercenaries, Kassabian's troops turned towards the Bay 7 elevator.

Now, all of their security people and Anita were firing at once as the doors closed in painful slow-motion. Bullets pinged impotently off the armor of the stormtroopers, one of their number only going down when Terry hit him in the thigh with a round from a compact grenade launcher. Dennis flinched as one of their number took an energy bolt directly to the chest and dropped, sizzling and smoking.

"Jesus! Oh my God!" Emilie Duplessis was hyperventilating as the elevator accelerated towards the landing bays.

Anita grabbed her firmly. "You survived Phoenix! You can survive this!"

Wordlessly, Emilie nodded, wiped her eyes, and bent over to pick up the fallen officer's weapon.

The stench in the confined space was about to overwhelm Dennis when the doors started to open. "Here." Terry handed him a pistol. "Depleted Uranium rounds. Should do the trick. Know how to use it?"

"I've seen it on TV."

He smiled crookedly. "Good enough, I guess. Let's go."

They spilled onto the red concrete loading docks, a hunched, terrified band, not daring to stop. Four men in civilian clothes ran in front of them, holding their weapons up in supplication. "Go that way, the bastards have cut off Bay 7 already!" A wiry little Nepali man announced. He held a compact grenade launcher like Terry's. "Go!"

"Looks like the Emir's army has had a change of heart!" Duplessis yelled.

"Let's hope it's enough to hold them off." Anita spoke into her watch. "Mac, can you move to Bay 6? Bay 7 is blocked off!" They moved rapidly, following signs for Bay 6.

"No can do. Surrounded by hostiles. Field's holding, but just for now."

"Spidermen?"

"Huh? No, looks like Emir's Army."

"Guess not all of them had a change of heart." Dennis knelt to catch his breath.

"Fuck, we need to get out of here." Terry pointed out the obvious. The sounds of battle from around the corner advertised the Nepalis were making a stand.

"Mac, can you move your ship at all?" Anita yelled into her watch.

"No, the fuckers have a force clamp on me. It's on ground power though, I can see the cables."

Dennis looked across the bay and saw a power box. He got up and ran to it.

"Dennis! Get your ass back here!" Anita screamed at him. But he kept going. The sounds of battle reached a high pitch down the hall as his blood hammered in his ears. He reached the box, finding it code locked. So, he put Terry's pistol up to it, and squeezed the trigger.

The lights went out immediately. "I'm free!" He heard Mac yell over the din. Dennis turned to the source of the sound, then turned to see red-visored eyes staring at him.

The man, or thing, was massive, easily 3 meters tall in full battle armor. Smoke poured from a damaged leg joint. It put its cannon-hand up to his chest to fire.

Dennis pointed the pistol at the enemy thing at put a DU round through its right eye. The enemy dropped like a sack. Just then, the bay was flooded with pink light, and the air rushed out of the decompressing space. Dennis choked and staggered, finding himself on his knees, vision fading.

But then, Anita was there, fitting a little rebreather mask over his face, and helping him up. Together, they stumbled and fumbled outside, to find Mac holding the shuttle in a perfect hover. They scrambled up the ladder, the door closing behind them.

The shuttle swung crazily as energy bolts overwhelmed the shields, sending it flying into the side of a fuel bowser. "They're behind us, folks." Mac announced calmly. "Hang on now."

Dennis and Anita slumped into their chairs, looking up in time to see four of their enemies, all armoured behemoths with jets and wings, standing on the dock, firing at the shuttle. Suddenly, the glow of a rocket engine overwhelmed their powers, and the four enemies sizzled and vaporized as Mac fired away from Emirates City on overdrive.

"Fuck fucking fuck." Duplessis spoke for all of them.

Ninety seconds later, as the last of the Old Emir's loyal soldiers battled his son's treacherous allies to the death, dozens of kinetic missiles fired from the Republic shredded the Pearl of the Solar System.

The Battle for Mars had begun.

2117

Let me tell you a story

The Blue Star Café
Wallingford

The Blue Star Café had been in a genteel state of decay when Dennis came here as a boy in the 1990s. Now, it seemed frozen in time, like so many of its customers, a place of thick and smooth woodwork, and overgenerous portions.

The crowd was thin today, as everywhere. Dennis and Latoya followed Lynn, who was dressed in outrageous, rainbow-striped gumboots, blue jeans, and a green anorak, defying the heat. Latoya opened her mouth to ask, but Dennis beat her to it. "She always dresses like that. She says her hormones are so fucked up now she's given up on regulating temperature."

As they slid into the booth, Lynn sat, poker faced, regarding them owlishly from behind little classes. A holocorder sat on the table in front of her. Finally, she smiled. "I don't know you. I'm Lynn. She and her, please." Her hand shot out. Latoya shook it.

"She and her?"

"My preferred pronouns. I've bounced around a bit, but until Henrik's big scoop pays for me to be a unicorn, I'm settled."

Dennis smiled. "Always surprising, you are. Last time you were a them and their."

Lynn shrugged. "A foolish consistency is the hobgoblin of small minds."

Latoya caught on. "Mark Twain, right?"

"She's well read, Henrik. I'm impressed. No more cult cookies for you, I see. The ones with brains are hard to handle." Lynn winked at Latoya, who smiled sheepishly.

"I've never had any cult cookies, Lynn. That's because I am not Henrik Kassabian."

"Holy hell, you could at least wait until I turn this thing on! Who the hell are you then?"

"His archrival and enemy of more than fifty years, Dennis Rosso. Nobel Laureate in Biochemistry 2035, and inventor of everlasting life. At your service."

"You're shitting me."

"Lynn, I can give you all the proof you need later. For now, I need you to listen." He squeezed Latoya's hand. "Isn't that all any of us need?"

"Fine, Henr...Dennis. Fine. I could also use a 20-ounce beer and a grilled cheese sandwich."

"Let's do that."

Once their drinks had arrived, and nerves were settled, Lynn resumed prying. "Please state your full name for the record. And date of birth."

"Dennis Arnold Rosso, June 2, 1990." His foot had finally stopped hurting.

"If you are Dennis Arnold Rosso, why do you look like Henrik Artem Kassabian?"

"Because I killed him. Or, more accurately, ordered him killed, and then assumed his identity."

"When and where did this happen?"

Dennis stopped, the whole scene flooding back to him. He took a deep drink and closed his eyes. "That episode is…difficult. I'm going to need to build up to that."

Lynn sighed. "Dennis…the deal is full disclosure."

"Don't push him." Latoya was suddenly fierce. "You don't know what he went through."

Lynn held up her hands. "Honey, the final confrontation between your man and Kassabian is legendary."

"Legendary bullshit." Dennis chuckled. "Let me start at the beginning. Well, maybe not at the beginning…let me start with the last day of the old world. November 9, 2033."

"Jeez Louise." Lynn rolled her eyes. Even Latoya giggled, but Dennis was undeterred.

"You've heard of Schrodinger's Cat, I suppose?"

"Of course." Lynn paused while the food arrived. "Ugh, too many fries. Yes, of course. Cat could be dead, could be alive, and he's both until you look inside his little box."

"That's the whole point, Lynn." He waved a fry at her. "Until I opened that door, I was one me. And then, I was another. When I drove up to Bio-Frontiers that morning, I was a stoop-shouldered, balding 43-year-old with a weak chin, a dead kid, and one divorce behind me. I had two mortgages on my home, a ten-year-old-car, and I was seriously considering a mail-order wife. But that sequence I'd suppressed the night before changed everything. If I hadn't found the kill switch, maybe I'd have given up. And then what would've happened?"

Lynn waved a hand. "Somebody else would've found it. Or maybe not. Maybe we'd still be dying of old age. So what?"

Dennis closed his eyes. "Yueh told me the Chinese designed Red Foam because they were threatened by the miracle. The miracle inspired Kassabian to pursue his dream; an army of supermen. Now, people are killing themselves in numbers not seen for a century. People with the miracle. Now, we're building starships, knowing that the people who start the journey will actually get to finish it. 'So what?'"

Lynn nodded reluctantly. "Okay, okay. So, you're kind of a big deal. What happened then, when you turned on that light?"

Three hours later, and Dennis was still talking. He had not told his story in so long, if ever, because he had been busy living it. Not only was he still talking, but now a crowd had assembled.

Customers, staff, passersby drawn by the crowd. Lynn tolerated them, as long as they understood: *This is my scoop.* She ordered another round for them all, as the Battle of Mars' opening salvo came to a close.

"I don't get it." Ralph was a barkeep with a limited attention span. "Why'd Kassabian hate you and Duplessis so much?"

"He blamed me, and Duplessis, for the death of his girlfriend. Being a two-time Nobel Laureate, his revenge had to be grandiose."

"That really burns you, doesn't it?" Neole was a massive ebony man, a resident of a nearby radical commune.

"Yeah. He stole our work on the Red Foam. We risked our lives for that."

"Okay, okay…drink your beers, proles." Lynn waved her arms. "Is there nothing good in the holos tonight?"

"Not since they took Virgil's *Suicide Scans* off of Holoscene." Etienne was a scrawny skateboarder, far too young to be in the Blue Star. "That shit was nuclear."

"No shit?" Dennis asked. "Virgil's off the air?"

"Yeah." Neole nodded and sucked his teeth. "Nigga was arrested. Supposed to be tight with you two."

Latoya and Dennis exchanged glances. "Guess you'd better keep going, then."

"I never understood how eighty guys, even with wings and armor and shit, beat all of you." Ralph ventured.

"Well, that's not exactly how it happened." Dennis explained. "Let me tell you a story."

2113

The tightening circle

Hellas City
Underground Command Center

Dennis sat at the conference table, chin in slumping hand, watching Duplessis work his daily miracles of command.

This time, for whatever reason, the man had repaid Dennis's gesture of confidence in him one-hundred-fold and had risen to the challenge of wartime command. Last time, he was a mewling baby on the edge of stability. This time, he directed, issued orders with confidence, bolstered by belief in final victory.

It didn't fucking matter, though, he thought bitterly. They were still losing the war.

Kassabian's supermen/spidermen were everywhere and nowhere at once. Very few seemed to have been killed outright. They could arrive in the single digits at an outpost surmised to be unconquerable and turn it within hours.

In the last months of 2112, and the first weeks of 2113, Kassabian's *ubermensch* had conquered every major settlement on Mars save Hellas. Only the impregnable rock of the Hellas fortress had preserved them, that, and the tireless courage of the Israelis.

Matthew had agitated ceaselessly to be put into action. "You cannot win a war on the defense." He had appeared, dressed as a simple soldier, Israeli-style, a month ago. "We must beat them at their own game."

"Them? Goddamnit, them?" Shamir had challenged him angrily. "You're one of *them!*"

Matthew had leaned over and looked the Colonel in the eyes. "No. I am a human being, like you. That, is why I am here."

Matthew's proposal had been a simple one. Reverse engineer as many supersuits as possible, and he would train handpicked men and women to fly them. They would pick a point of weakness in the enemy advance, and, with maximum media coverage, they would livestream the defeat of Kassabian's forces.

With a UN landing force en route, nobody could argue: A serious reverse at this point for Kassabian was their only hope of blunting his momentum and widening cracks in the always fragile UN façade.
Kassabian's warriors might be able to beat the Martian Republic. But they could not occupy it. The UN would have to do that. They were ordinary soldiers. Soldiers who could be killed.

When Matthew announced he was ready, requiring only a few days for finishing touches, Dennis was surprised to hear that those touches included the addition of four new personnel to his force:

Terry, Anita, Major Ne'vman, and himself. "What? The last three I get, but I'm an egghead! I can't fight!"

Matthew had placed a steadying hand on his shoulder, reminding him so much of his father, and explained slowly. "I heard about you at Emirates City. You made the right choices, at the right times, without hesitation. So will they. That is all the being a combat leader is about. There is nothing else. Do not ask your men to do anything you will not. And if you must do it yourself, do it decisively, and effectively."

"Is that what the Hitler Youth taught you?"

"Yes." He replied simply. "In historical context, they were monsters in the service of an evil regime. But on the battlefield, they were second to none. Simply ask the British and Canadians who fought them in Normandy in 1944."

"So I've heard."

"They engendered hate. Hate that made the British and Canadians better soldiers, fully invested in their cause, and determined to destroy the Third Reich. That is what Kassabian has done for us. Now, we will show him what we've learned."

And so, between UN satellite passes, under the watchful eyes of Israeli fighters, they practiced war in three dimensions, with graceful loops and whirls over the great lake, dives and sudden stops, pulverising attacks from the hover.

When their training days would finish, instead of collapsing in exhaustion, he and Anita would take each other in passion, and then he would realize that, in war, he had found his true home. As had she.

Never again would he feel so alive. Now, like a Kamikaze pilot seeking death, he waited to be told where he would die. He looked across the room as Duplessis spoke and saw his old friend Kesuke, likewise awaiting paradise. Kesuke winked at him. In battle, they would stay close.

How many lives had he already lived, thanks to his own miracle? Now, as he stood ready to surrender the gift of eternal life for freedom, he realized that the true gift of the miracle was not eternity. No, it was being freed of the threat of a trivial death, in return for the chance to give your life for something that *mattered*.

Death rested on his shoulders, but it did not feel heavy. No, as the Japanese would maintain, it was as light as a feather.

"Target for tonight." Dennis sat up at Duplessis' announcement, smiling to himself. He'd been reading Deighton, too. "Kassabian has set up a major staging base in Sabaea to support the UN landing, which we believe will take place in two weeks' time. We'll attack at 0100, Matthew's spidermen going in first, followed by fighters and hovertanks from the main force. Everything will be livestreamed on Holocast. Our chance to show those bastards we can still fight. See Colonel Shamir for passwords, frequencies, and start times. Dismissed."

Dennis stood, dizzy for a moment. Here he was, going willingly into battle for the first time, something he'd thought about often, with a Vietnam veteran for a father. And yet, he was 123 years old. His father had been 19. What a lot of life to lose.

Kesuke slapped him on the shoulder. "You weren't meant to life forever. Neither was I. Let's do this and enjoy our sake in heaven!"

"You're a real bummer, Kesuke, you know that."

"Hahaha...banzai!"

He looked sadly at Anita, then turned to go to his locker room, and prepare for death.

Over Sabaea

Dennis Rosso had lived on Mars for decades, but never had he seen his home like this before.

The stars were out in their multitudes, the still-thin atmosphere unable to dim their light, which reflected off the rims of the myriad craters. They carried light rebreathers, their faces exposed to the chilling air, until finally it was too much for him. When he put down his visor, the whoosh of air in his ears was replaced by a deadening silence.

They were observing radio silence now, flying at 50 meters on automatic inertial guidance. Matthew had been confident that their surprise, just this once, would be absolutely total. Sensors would be scanning higher up, for big, metal objects, not acting on the supposition that the attack would come from their own kind.

They were not spidermen in the true sense, Matthew had warned. Just the closest facsimile Martian society could produce on short notice. They could not repeat the feats of acrobatics demonstrated at Emirates Mars City, but they could match the incredible mobility of their enemy.

And hadn't the man said that war was all about getting there first with the most? That was why they were on the back foot now. Perhaps that would change this morning.

An alert flashed in his helmet.

INITIAL POINT IN 50 KM
2 MINUTES TO TURN ON HEADING 240

There was nothing he needed to do. It was a curious thing, being flown to your death by a machine. In the quiet, nothing to do but meditate; nothing to occupy you but fears, reminiscences, and regrets.

Dennis looked to his left. Someone was waving at him. He realized it was Anita when she grabbed her tits. He laughed out loud. She, at least, was one thing he did not regret. He had lost fifty years with her. But then, they had rejoined as if nothing had happened. The nature of their relationship allowed for this. And the nature of her personality demanded she be here with him. She was better suited to it then him, anyway.

They turned sharply. Now, the alert readout flashed the final few steps.

PITCH UP TO ATTACK ALTITUDE IN 1 MINUTE-GLIDE WING JETT

ARM WEAPONS
SELECT "GROUND ATTACK" ON WRIST CONTROLLER
GOD BE WITH YOU

He waved to Anita, then flipped a toggle switch, clearly marked in dayglo orange, to arm his weapons for ground attack. They were about to gain height quickly in a dizzying maneuver which allowed wave upon wave of them to heft the massive bombs they were carrying with increased momentum. Lightened, they would attack from above with increased agility.

Now, in the final seconds before shedding his glide wings, he weighed 1200 kilos. Ahead of him, he saw gossamer shapes falling and spinning in the starlight, as Matthew and his wingmen shed their glide wings. Next, the flare of rocket motors signalled the first attackers' steep climb onto their targets.

He felt a shudder in the center of his back as his glide wings gave way.

CAUTION
EXTREME ACCELERATION
PRACTICE G-EXERCISES
3...2...1...
ZERO

Once, when he was a boy, his father had taken him to New York. They had ridden the express elevator to the top of the World Trade Center, back before the terrorists destroyed it. That was the closest thing he could compare this to. It was far more personal than the launch of the *John Carter*, as it was you yourself that was the rocket. He could only yell out in joy, as he'd yelled at the age of eight, as he turned into a rocket ship, a boy's ultimate fantasy.

He grunted out his breaths like they'd been trained, straining against the G-forces. Then, at the peak, a moment of weightlessness as the bombs fell away. He pitched over onto his nose, seeing the first bombs explode, getting his first look at the enemy camp in the light of fire and blast.

Kassabian, I hope you're down there. Special delivery for you, asshole.

ASSUME MANUAL CONTROL NOW
MINIMUM ALTITUDE 200 M
BEWARE BOMB FRAGMENTS

He took control of his suit now, an instinctive form of flying using body movements instead of a controller. By squinting and moving his eyes, he could control his target sights and tactical array. He zoomed away from the center of the battle, hoping to attack from the crater's rim.

On the ground, Dennis could see frantic, running young men and women in bodysuits, scrambling to get into their armor, which sat propped on stands, out in the open. Others gave up the task, and instead manned cannon and pulse weapons on the perimeter, bringing their fire skyward.

A diving spiderman was hit in the engines, turned into a flaming meteor, and crashed straight into a row of empty armor suits, tossing in them in the air like pebbles.

Bolts flew past him; one so close he could hear it sizzling. Over the scream of his own engines, he heard Matthew announce on the radio. "First wave landing. Watch for friendlies on the ground."

In an instant, his target reticle flashed red, signifying an identified enemy. He saw a spiderman on the ground, about to fire on the descending first wave. With a clench of his right fist, he fired a hypersonic rocket, which cut the man in half in a shower of sparks and gore. Dennis shouted in triumph, resulting in a scolding from an unknown trooper. "Quit yelling on the radio."

Chastened, he forgot how low he was.

PULL UP PULL UP
DANGER
PULL UP PULL UP

He managed the briefest of retro fires from the reaction jets in his boots, before ignominiously crashing into a bluff and rolling down the crater rim.

When he came to, four spidermen outlined in red target boxes were almost on top of him. One was gesticulating to the others. *A leader. Kassabian?*

Dennis rolled and tried to bring his weapons to bear, but the crash had fucked his systems up. His right arm could barely move its servos, let alone fire. His left still had a working pulse rifle, though. He took shaking aim at his pursuers at the same time as they let loose a flurry of energy bolts and rockets over his head. Dennis was pelted by dirt and rocks from the collapsing bluff behind him, and now the enemy, sensing triumph, began to sprint towards him.

Curiously, though in mortal danger now, Dennis felt no real apprehension. He was where he belonged, doing what he ought to be doing. If he was to die, so be it.
For this, you invented immortality? So you could get yourself killed?

He heard his father's voice in his head and began to laugh. He was still laughing when Anita and Kesuke landed behind the enemy troopers and blasted them at close range. He stood, slowly and carefully.

"You okay?" Kesuke came over to him.

"Flying is for the birds. Thank you." Anita joined them.

"I think it's over."

"Already?" Dennis looked around, seeing the devastation of the enemy camp as a whole for the first time. Dead enemy, within and without their armored suits, lay strewn around the crater. Flames, quickly dying in the weak air, licked at makeshift buildings and vehicles. "We kicked their asses."

"Alright, all units, consolidate. Let's set up a perimeter, second wave, while first and third look for survivors and prisoners. Move it out."

Anita took charge. "No time to celebrate, you heard the man, get your asses moving! You too, Rosso!"

"Yes ma'am!" He decided very quickly that he liked that side of Anita very much. He fired his boot jets and ascended the crater rim in time to see a photo negative flash as an Israeli jet destroyed two low-level, fleeing spidermen with a single missile from high altitude. "Jesus! Scratch two more bogeys, looks like a jet got them. 10 klicks north-north-east."

"Copy." Anita replied. "Your weapons back online?"

"Yeah. I turned it on and turned it off, like IT always said."

Anita laughed. "One from two, we've got a perimeter. Looks like our friends caught two runaways."

Matthew replied. "Good work. Losses?"

"Zero. Dennis is a little banged up, but he's okay."

"We lost three. Third wave lost one. Since you can spare the bodies, send a couple out to see if one of those low flyers is Kassabian."

Dennis put up a hand. "I'll take Dennis. Blum, you take this sector."

"Roger that." Blum was a taciturn Israeli. His English was not the best, so you could only make him laugh with fart jokes. Dennis followed Anita at low speed out to the smudge of black smoke marking the grave of the two runners. For extra insurance, she broadcast their status to the top cover fighters. "Tophat, Tophat, this is Ground 2. Examining your kill site, over."

"Copy. We get anyone important?"

"We'll let you know." They set down on the burn line of the now-extinguished fire. Armor and body parts were strewn all over, bubbling fat melting out of the inside of one torso piece and another helmet. "My God. Modern war is not pretty." Anita muttered.

"When has it ever been?"

"One from two."

"Go."

"We'll need to take DNA to know anything here."

"Not surprising. Take your samples and get back. Sounds like something's up on the comm nets."

Dennis took out two DNA field samplers, his own design, built to process and preserve DNA in the ugly conditions it would often be found in in war. Matthew had endured enough needle jabs. He handed one to Anita, who delicately scooped some of the bubbling fat from the torso and sealed it up. He could see her mouthing a prayer as she placed the container back in her pocket. Dennis got his sample from the helmet, part of an earlier model suit, in which a still intact skull grinned at him. "Let a smile be your umbrella." He whispered.

"What?"

"Nothing ma'am."

"Let's get back. We're vulnerable out here." They had just reached the crater's rim when Matthew came on the air again.

"All units assemble. Refuel in groups from the captured

bowser, and follow me back to Hellas City, top speed."

"What's the situation?" Anita asked.

"Kassabian put out a distraction, and we fell for it. Now he's hitting us hard. And 500 UN troops just landed on the north slope. We're in trouble."

2117

This is your life

The Blue Star Café
Wallingford

Dennis paused in telling his story, motioning for Lynn to pause the recording. Latoya put an arm around him. "I need another beer."

Neole put nudged Ralph with a massive arm. "This man's dry. What's wrong witchu?"

"Hey, lost in the story, like everyone else. Another round?"

"Come on kids, drink up." Dennis smiled. "It's all on the villain's card anyway."

In just over three hours, he had told so much, hopping from past to present, that he had nearly told it all. *Nearly.* But soon, he was going to tell his audience to get lost.

He could tell Lynn, and he could tell Latoya, what had happened at Hellas City just before the fall. But these people were still strangers. Perhaps it was time he asked them some questions?

"Are you okay, pal?" Lynn put a hand out to him.

"Yes. But the last part…it's hard to say."

"Anita, you mean?"

"Not just her. Kesuke...Terry...Matthew...the Israelis...hell, even Duplessis. I loved the crazy son of a bitch, you know that?" He began to weep, holding the tears behind his fist. "Oh Christ."

"Hey man." Neole put a massive hand on his shoulder. "We getting you down? We can go, it's cool. It's just been a while since I've heard a real story like that. One that had death in it...real people, fighting for something real. It draws you in, know what I'm saying?"

"Speaking of real people...what if I asked you a few questions. Or maybe, just one?"

"Fair enough." Nicole was a skinny blonde, a stripper, for the fun, not the money. "We owe you, right?"

Etienne wiped a mop of hair off of his face. "Sure. Ask anything."

"Back when my dad was a kid, they used to have a show on TV called *This is Your Life.* They'd bring some famous person out, and then people would come on and tell stories about how that person had affected their lives. Or so my dad tells me. I never saw it myself." Dennis paused. "I've heard a lot of bad things about my invention lately. In fact, I've been hearing them for eighty years. But never once have I just asked a group of ordinary people, not scientists, or politicians, just ordinary people, what the miracle has done for them. I just...well, I really want to know, is all." He stared into the foam in his beer.

Neole spoke first. "I'm the first man in my family to live past forty. Ain't that some shit? My dad died when I was 12. I never knew my Pops. Heart stuff, killed us like clockwork, you know? I always used to think about things I wanted to do in my life, you know, normal shit like 'See the Grand Canyon,' but then I'd shut it down. 'Won't live that long.' Well, when the miracle came along, I started saving up for it. Worked all kinds of shit jobs. Did some things I ain't proud of. But, after I somehow survived the Red Foam, bang, all my relatives left me their money. June 1, 2048, I became a new man."

"You see the Grand Canyon?" Dennis smiled.

"Hell yeah. Been to all the continents, and the Moon too. I been a miner, a soldier, a pirate, hell I was even a cop for a while. Life is like being a kid forever now. 'Impossible' doesn't exist. Pick the hat you wanna wear, and that's you."

Dennis nodded. In a lot of ways, his life had been like Neole's. *Pick the hat you wanna wear.* "Ralph, what's your story? You tending bar to meet people, or what?"

Ralph shrugged bashfully. "I'm still paying mine off. But it was worth it. It's worth it every day. I'm from Jersey, an Uncontrolled Zone by the New York impacts."

"Sorry, man."

"Meh, I wasn't alive when it happened. I grew up there, looking across the river, seeing those big black craters shine in the sun. My mom used to tell me they were God's footprints. Which they kinda were, I guess. We grew up where there was lots of radioactivity, so my mom got sick. I crossed over to work, not exactly legal you know, so maybe I could get her a black market miracle..."

"Hey, I know a guy. As good as the real thing..." Dennis offered.

Ralph sighed. "Nah, too late. She died. Her last message was 'Spend it on yourself, son. See the world, and I'll be with you.' That was twenty years ago. In the meantime, I got Legal in the '14 Amnesty, and three years ago I got the miracle. I ain't never been nowhere like Neole here, but hearing his stories, I know I will soon. It's the...the potential to do it...or whatever. That's what makes me happy. And yeah, I like tending bar. I'd do it for free."

"Kinda like me and stripping." Nicole added. Etienne sat up straight and paid attention.

"Should you be listening to this young man?" Latoya grilled him.

"Hey, I'm fifteen. Way old." The rest laughed, and he blushed.

"Basic Income only pays so much." Nicole continued. "I'm an exhibitionist anyway, and it's a great way to pay for all my mod cons." She hefted her oversized tits. "Plus, I've performed all over the world. I'm man crazy, I guess, so those are my souvenirs. The lovers, plus the places. Before you, Dennis, a hundred-year-old chick couldn't have had that much fun without breaking a hip or something. I like to think of it as my reward. I buried a husband and two kids in the Red Foam. I was nurse, and…well, forget that. Maybe that's the one problem with your miracle, hon."

"What's that?" Dennis was feeling woozy now. The beers, the emotion…the hole in his foot.

"You can live forever. But how do you forget? Will any of us live that long?"

The rest of them were silent for a while, considering. Ralph hurried down the bar to tend to a new arrival.

Etienne spoke, finally. "What a crazy-assed world to be born in."

"Your parents won the lottery?" Lynn asked.

"Yeah." He sipped at a purloined beer. "And they got me. Guess they've never gotten over the disappointment, since they keep putting in for another. I go to school with ten other kids. The same ten kids since kindergarten, except for one who moved away. You don't know what it's like to be a kid today. Nobody to hang out with, nobody gets your problems, 'cause when you talk, they're all like 'The Red Foam, blah blah blah.' You guys are all like parents from the old days, who spent all their money on themselves, and left their kids at home with a pot of mac and cheese."

"Huh." Neole shook his head. "Didn't know you had that in you."

"You have the miracle, Etienne?" Dennis asked.

"Of course. My parents got it done when I was two. Afraid of losing me. Ha, I wonder if they'd still do it now."

Dennis suppressed a smile. The miracle may have killed many things, but it hadn't killed teenaged angst. "We'd better get going."

"Hey, do we get to see how it ends?" Ralph asked.

"I wind up pissed and mopey at the Blue Star Café, Ralph." Dennis laughed. "Goodnight, friends."

The three of them walked quickly to Dennis' arcology. "Aren't you afraid they'll be watching?"

"53,000 people live here. There are 26 different entrances. If I thought I was still up against the FBI, Lynn, I would be worried. But I'm not. Fisk doesn't have the resources to cover this place, let alone the whole city."

"You're suddenly forgetting our murder warrants out of California?" Latoya added. "The local cops might have the manpower to cover 26 entrances."

"Ah, but this is Seattle. It's a fugitive haven for a reason. If the Chief of Police here wanted 26 entrances covered," Lynn explained, "The killing would've had to take place in downtown Seattle in broad daylight, yesterday. A California warrant is old news, even if it is for murder. Take Neole, for instance. He's wanted in Illinois. Nobody bothers him."

"Aw, I liked Neole." Latoya sighed.

"You can still like him. He just shot the wrong gangster, that's all. One the Mayor of Chicago found useful. No loss." Lynn stopped and looked up at the bulk of Arco 5, it's navigation lights dotting the pyramidical structure all the way to the top. "Jesus, what an eyesore."

"I like it. Come on." Dennis led them on a jog through a lightly wooded area, down a rolling grassy hill, to a maintenance entrance. He'd acquired a keycode for an employee-only entrance a year ago, thinking he might need it if anyone ever remembered who Henrik Kassabian was. It had only cost him a case of Martian whisky, swill he was well rid of.

He noticed that Lynn was dragging behind, fumbling with something, panting heavily. "Lynn, come on, don't dawdle!"

Rising over the grassy hill, engines a barely detectable whisper...a drone. "Lynn, move your ass!" Latoya yelled. Dennis had opened the maintenance entrance, but now he let it close, resigned. "What are you doing?" Latoya demanded as Lynn ran heavily towards them.

"Too late to get in that way. We might as well go to a public entrance. Let them try something where it's lit and there's witnesses."

Latoya nodded. "Okay! Come on, Lynn, damnit girl!" They jogged around the corner on the sidewalk, the lights getting brighter, the drone running parallel to them now, lazily escorting them.

When he turned the corner, Fisk was holding open the door for a woman and her three dogs. Dennis counted four more suits, at least, lurking in the shadows behind pillars and trees. "Hi asshole."

"Well, well. Here I was arguing with the guys that you *would* do something as dumb as come back to your home base. 'No way!' They said, 'He's a brilliant scientist!' But of course, they don't know what I know, from long experience." Fisk had swaggered his way over to Dennis now, a bantam rooster full of threat and self-satisfaction.

"What's that? How to suck six cocks at once?"

"Really? Such language in front of the ladies? I mean, dude, we're the old guard here! Children of the nineties! Historical relics who kept the torch alight." Fisk was warming to his subject as his men emerged from the shadows.

"What the fuck are you talking about, Fisk? You're a corrupt, former FBI agent who got fired for running interference for people smugglers. After you spent five years in prison, that is. Probably where you learned to suck cock, am I right? After that, you went to work for Lontraine at JC Bryan, where he let you in on the secret of the century."

"Wow, for a scientist you're a pretty shitty detective." Fisk laughed. "What fucking 'secret of the century?'"

A couple, laughing and grabby, went silent as they walked through the middle of the tense scene. Dennis hoped against hope that someone would find it suspicious enough to call the cops, before Fisk got finished monologuing. "Good old Nobel Warrior 3. Kassabian's favourite mutt. Lontraine brought him back in '96. But that's not all he brought back, is it?"

The drone, as if a human rubbernecker, now hovered directly above him.

Fisk licked his lips. "Okay, dude. You're not gonna live long enough to finish that thought. Get your ass to the van." The gun was out now, pointed at his stomach. If someone happened by...

"Oh sure. Like I'll go with you to a fucking van. You got a puppy,

Fisk? How about some candy? How do you usually pickup dates?"

Fisk smiled. "I got a high-tech update. I love this century."

Suddenly, Dennis' body went rigid with an agonizing electric pulse. He dropped to the ground, twitching and spasming. He heard Latoya scream, saw Fisk over him, levelling his gun at her. He wanted so desperately to go for his gun…but…his hands could not stop twitching.

Then, a flash erupted behind him, followed by four more in quick succession. Fisk did a little puppet dance, the gun flew out of his hand, bouncing painfully off of Dennis' cranium. The drone that had just tasered him dropped in front of him and smashed to pieces on the pavement.

There were shouts, indistinguishable at first, then recognizable as deliverance. Now, he was sitting up, Latoya looking in his eyes, applying pain stimuli to his nerve endings.

He still could not speak. *Stop it. I feel it. I fucking hurt enough.*

Then, like a broken stereo, his sound came on again. "Dennis! Dennis!" She embraced him.
"I'm okay, I'm okay!" He looked around as large, flat-topped men in trench coats swarmed and disarmed Fisk's men. One stood over him and roughly wrenched the pistol off of his belt. "Thanks, I didn't need that anymore." He saw Lynn standing over him, snapping pics. "Hey, Lynn…what the hell were you doing anyway?"

She put down her holocorder and shrugged. "Calling the police, dummy."

2113

Masada

Hellas City

In modern warfare, 20 minutes was an eternity.

Dennis considered that aphorism as he crested the butte that ringed the Hellas Basin. 20 minutes ago, they had been on the offensive. Now, victory's scent was in Kassabian's nostrils.

They flew in a loose formation, jinking and weaving to avoid the UN laser lances they now knew were overhead. How they had gotten there, two weeks ahead of schedule, was a question for later. But all Dennis knew, as he watched one fighter after another plummet to the ground in flames, was that Mars was doomed.

He had heard the Israelis muttering amongst themselves about Masada, the apocalyptic last stand of the Jewish rebels against Herod, 2100 years ago. How much Hellas looked like the sacred place of the doomed fanatics. How there was no real hope except a good death.

He'd been optimistic at the time and had considered such talk nonsense. But now, as he looked over the rim of the butte to see Hellas in flames, surrounded by burning landing craft and trundling tanks, he had to give it to the Jews. Theirs was a pessimism founded squarely on prior experience.

Mars was doomed. The aircraft which had been providing top

cover to them 20 minutes before were now flaming wrecks on the cliffs, or in the basin below. There was no sign of Kassabian and his spidermen; however, hundreds of UN troops and their armor support had encircled the base on the top of the cliffs.

Matthew had zoomed out ahead of the main body, then circled back to where the others orbited. "Kassabian is in the city. He and his force bluffed their way past the guards using false faces, now they're shooting up the basement levels."

"Why?" Anita floated next to Dennis, holding his arm.

Dennis recalled the construction of the city; how the lower levels had massive gates and sluiceways, to allow overflow from the lake to run into the city's water supply. It was one of Jerry's genius touches. "The sluiceway doors. They can let the UN troops into the city then. It'll all be over if they do."

"We've got to get in there while there's still time." Ne'vman's armor was battle blasted, and he sounded pained. "We've got fuel and ammo for one last pass, I read."

"Yes." Matthew nodded. "We back up the rearguard with a strafing pass, everything we've got. Then we land right on the elevator shafts and drop down using our boot retros."

"They grounded the elevators?" Terry questioned.

"Wouldn't you?" Dennis answered. Suddenly, the space beside him sizzled, and Terry, hit and sparking, plummeted to the ground in a blaze of blue light.

"They've got us on sensors!" Matthew yelled. "Strafing pass, then land on my mark, go now!"

Quickly, they fanned out to deprive the UN ships in orbit of decent targets, then accelerated to attack speed, dropping as low as possible. On the ground, the Israelis held their fire as they passed overhead.

He could see, at most, 40 or so men and women left in action. Half, likely wounded.

Masada it is, you motherfuckers. He looked to his right and saw Anita zooming ever lower, her arms straight out now, ready to fire. Dennis looked back at his own sensors, seeing a group of UN infantry leapfrogging courageously forward, a tank supporting them, both targets outlined in red.

He fired, sending a flechette pulse round towards the infantry, and a kinetic missile at the tank. Dennis had no time to see the result, as he quickly reversed course, skidding over the heads of the astonished Israelis and landing on the steel cover of the elevator hatch.

In the distance, explosions bloomed as his comrades either found their marks, or crashed to their deaths. Dennis quickly realized the cost when only six of them landed on the elevator hatch. Ne'vman hadn't made it either, and Kesuke was grievously wounded, smoke pouring from his right arm joint.

Dennis extinguished the fire and wrenched his friend's mask open. One of Kesuke's eyes was hanging out. The pilot collapsed in his arms.

"Captain! Wake up, damnit! The mission's not over..."

Kesuke smiled deliriously. "No, you're right." He gasped. "But at least we know who's going to blow the entrance."

Shamir staggered up to them, his battered plastisteel vest cinched against his guts, which appeared to be leaking out. "Mazel'tov Dr Rosso. Nice shooting out there."

Matthew and Anita conferred quickly and stepped forward. "We've got the UN on the defensive for a moment, but it won't last. Kesuke has volunteered to blow the entrance after we've descended. At that time, Colonel, you and your troops can surrender with honor."

"No. There will be no surrender." The old war dog leaned against Dennis, then, with a supreme effort of breath, stood like a soldier. "No surrender."

"Please, Yakov." Anita pleaded. "The UN troops aren't barbarians like Kassabian's creatures. No offence."

Matthew gave a rare look of amusement. "None taken."

"They'll take your surrender, Yakov, you don't have to do this."

"I'm afraid it's been agreed. To the last." Several of Shamir's young soldiers, not a one unwounded, came up behind him. "Nations are founded on myths. Myths like us. Whether they treat us well or not, we need to die."

"Yes." Kesuke agreed weakly. "But hurry it up."

"Okay." Matthew had clearly agreed. "I take Paul, Yitzhak, and Ariel to the sluicegates, and blow the locks. Anita and Dennis, you go to the command center and get the Duplessis' the hell out of here. Paul, open the hatch!"

"What?" Dennis was blindsided. "What about you?"

Anita put a steadying hand on his shoulder. "My love, there's no time. Whatever happens, we'll be together."

"Yes." He nodded. "Yes."

The hatch he'd landed on raised to reveal a black void descending over 2300 meters. The spidermen gathered on the edge. In the background, the Israelis were singing in Hebrew as they organized their lines for a last stand. Dennis peered into the darkness below, hearing the echoes of fighting, explosions, screams. He felt dizzy and disconnected from it all.

I am 123 years old. Today, long after my time, I shall die. I invented immortality. But it was not for me.

"Sluicegates first on five. Dennis and Anita, twenty seconds later. Go now!" With that, Matthew stepped over the edge into the long, wide void, freefalling at first, the others following at intervals.

Dennis looked at Anita. She blew him a kiss, then walked over the edge. He swallowed hard, then followed.

Were it not for his sensors, he would not have known what to do next. But, still at their post in his little, battered ship, his computer helpers told him what to do.

Dennis looked down, seeing the blue flares of retros at the very bottom of the shaft, hearing echoing slams as troopers hit the floor of the shaft. A blinding orange light, joined by three more, announced that torches were cutting through the shaft door.

RETRO TO HOVER IN 3...2...1
HOVER

With a sickening shudder, he came to a stop. The retros moved him up slowly to float beside Anita, whose altimeter was in slightly better shape. Dennis felt even sicker when he realized that, if he'd been assigned to Matthew's team, he'd have hit the floor at terminal velocity.

A vault-like door greeted them.

LEVEL 42
COMMAND AND ADMINISTRATION
THE ANSWER TO LIFE, THE UNIVERSE, AND EVERYTHING

Dennis snickered, being sure Duplessis had ordered that Command and Administration be located on Level 42. And that a Douglas Adams quote be added.

"What on Mars does that mean?" Anita lit her torch.

"Duplessis was always a big Douglas Adams fan."

"A who? Just get cutting." Dennis joined in, and soon, they were retroing back as the one-ton door fell 1500 meters to the floor. The tunnel got noticeably lighter, then darker again as a slam came from the top. Someone had closed the top hatch.

"Anita from Kesuke. We saw your torches. Are you clear?" The voice was pained and quiet.

They were both inside a corridor, with flickering blue lights and the smell of electrical fire greeting them. Ahead, the starlight glow of Hellas Lake beckoned. "Yes, my friend." Anita replied. "Holding on?"

There was a pause. The mike opened, to the sounds of close-range battle, oaths and imprecations, last prayers. "They're everywhere, guys. Time for me to blow. *Hanasaku!*"

The shaft shook and rattled, suction almost pulling Anita out into it, before Dennis wrapped arms around her and pulled her back. They checked their suits.

"I'm at zero." Anita announced. "You?"

"Fuck it. I've got one percent. Let's strip down, baby."
They stepped out of their damaged, stinking suits, drawing personal weapons from a hatch on the back, a rebreather, and a set of sighting goggles. "Let's go see Duplessis." Anita announced.

Dennis stopped her momentarily and kissed her deeply. "Sorry. I don't know when…"

She touched his face, reminding him of that time in Stockholm, when she had rescued him, the first of many times. "Shut up, soldier. Let's go."

He followed her through darkened corridors with no signs of life. Screams were coming from somewhere, but not from here. "Anita, turn right."

"Got it." Dennis was following a schematic on his wrist display.

"Here?"

"Yes, here." There was a set of double doors. As he touched the comm pad, the lights came on.

A screen blinked to life. Deo squinted at them. "Holy shit! You are alive!"

"Let us in. Matthew sent us to get you."

The inside of the command center was a patina of disarray over a structure of panic. Emilie Duplessis, holding her baby, embraced Anita. Her husband was nowhere to be seen. Deo and Merlin Duplessis rushed from comms console to comms console, giving multiple orders, many conflicting.

Outside the windows, an unwelcome surprise: The rocket flares of twenty UN transports, unmolested by defensive fire. They were landing on the shores of Hellas Lake.

Dennis took another look at the scene of headless confusion in front of him, spat on the ground, and spun Duplessis around with one hand.

The great man looked at him in astonishment. "Er...Dennis... how are you?"

Dennis looked back at him, feeling something hot simmering in his chest. "How am I? How the fuck am I? Don't you want a sitrep, glorious leader, or are you content to move around phoney panzer divisions on an imaginary map? How am I!"

The rest of them stared in silence. The baby began to wail. "Dennis, you've upset the baby."

"Upset the baby? Upset the baby? Oh, goddamn it, if there's one thing an apocalypse can't have, it's an upset fucking baby! Here's your fucking sitrep, whether you want it or not: You are ten minutes away from losing this war. Yes, we destroyed their base at Sabaea. But then, they landed here with most of their spidermen, and a UN force that somehow skipped two weeks of space travel to show up in Martian orbit, ahead of schedule. Now, your Israelis are all gone, and all but six of your spidermen, including us are too. The other four are on a suicide mission on the basement levels, to kill Kassabian and seal the sluicegates, before the UN can waltz in here and bring about your downfall. And right now, Merlin, just right now, I am wondering why I ever gave a shit!"

"It's...it's over?" Duplessis looked like someone had only now informed him the battle wasn't going well. He slumped into a chair. Dennis knelt next to him.

"I'm sorry, my old friend. But we've got to get you out of here. You're going to have to go guerilla for a while, okay?"

Duplessis wrapped his arms around Dennis and sobbed quietly. "They're...they're all dead?"

"Most of them, yes. Matthew and few others are fighting in the basement. But we have to think of the civilians. The UN will treat them humanely. We have to get out, call Hellas City open. Spare as many as we can."

"They...oh God, Dennis, I fucked up bad, again. Lopez warned me, two weeks ago. He warned me that two smaller signals had calved off the UN fleet, taking refuge behind an asteroid crossing our orbit. But I said nothing."

Dennis shook Duplessis like an abusive parent shakes a crying baby. "You what? You fucking idiot! You fucking stooge...how could you? How could you?"

Anita pulled him away. "Dennis, enough. What's done is done." She pushed him towards the windows overlooking Hellas Lake. Now, the UN troops had deployed ground-effect craft on the lake, craft which were speeding towards the cliff edge.

"I'm sorry, Dennis. I thought it was misinformation! Lopez

was...well, he was compromised, they were talking about indicting him too for Great Wall 2...I thought they wanted us to reveal our batteries and satellites..."

But Dennis was not listening to Duplessis' excuses. He was looking at the surging UN attack wave on Hellas Lake. And then, focusing in, he saw a lone man on a slow boat, weaving his way between the UN attack craft, which seemed to ignore him as elephants ignored flies.

There was something familiar about that man...tall and skinny, ten-gallon hat....

"Jerry! Jesus Christ, it's Jerry!"

Anita came up next to him and scanned the lake. "Holy shit, it's Jerry! Do you have his comms channel?"

"Hang on." Dennis scrolled through his wrist comms until he found the channel he wanted.

Cornell Subsurface Inc.

"Jerry, Jerry is that you? It's Dennis!"
The channel crackled to life. "Holy dogshit, it is you, you old pirate!"

"What the hell are you doing out there, you Texan lunatic? Can't you tell there's a war on?"

"Well, ah certainly don't recall asking any of these folks over for breakfast, do you?"

Dennis smiled. "No sir, I do not."

"So, ah figured I'd just head on over to my pump controls in the center of the lake, and, er...open things up a bit."

Dennis stared out at the lone hero, his mouth agape. "Dennis, what's he going to do?" Anita pressed him.

"All that water in Hellas Lake comes from a subsurface aquifer, that Jerry built the controls to. Now, he'd going to open them."

Duplessis, re-energized, walked over to the window. "What's going to happen?"

Dennis nodded as it suddenly made sense to him. "He's going to flood the basin, unload a Mediterranean's worth of water right now. And if the sluicegates are closed…"

Anita caught on. "All those boats will just rise, like they're in a bathtub."

Dennis grabbed Anita. "Get a hold of Matthew. Tell him to keep the gates *open.*"

"What?" Duplessis was aghast. "Open?"

Dennis nodded. "Yes, open. Jerry's about to flush 500 Blue Helmets and a billion dollars of hardware down the proverbial shitter."

Duplessis smiled. "Yes."

Matthew's voice came over the comms. "You want what, Anita?"

"Hold back and get out! Come up here! We're about to flood the lake!" Anita shouted. "The UN force will flood into the aquifers and drown, with the spidermen! Get up here now!"

"Roger that!"

Dennis looked out one more time, in time to see Jerry cranking open a manual wheel to open the lake levels. Mission accomplished, he stopped, turned towards them, and gave a snappy salute, before a wave overcame him and he disappeared.

"Jerry." Dennis mouthed his friend's name. "Jerry."
Now, a gentle rising, unnoticed, most likely, by the passing armada, increased in intensity and force. Little waves lit by starlight became huge breakers, which became a tsunami.

Everyone in the command center was looking out the windows as the first UN boats foundered and flipped over. Soon, a brewing foam of upended boats and flailing men descended the sluices and poured into the bowels of the city, with a deafening roar that reached up even to their level, drowning out conversation or even thought.

Dennis watched the spectacle with tearing eyes, tearing not for the dying men below, but for the Israelis who had fought so hard, hoping at least a few of them were still alive to see this. How they would appreciate the Old Testament wrath, this time wrought not by God, but by Jerry.

Suddenly, he looked up to see Matthew hovering in front of the window. "You're still here?"

"Events have overtaken us." Dennis replied.

"I called Mac." Matthew answered. "He'll be at the landing dock by the Tokamaks in five minutes."

"Great." Dennis kicked at a trashcan. "How do we get there?"

"Grab on. We can take you all." Beside Matthew, Yitzhak hovered into view.

Dennis nodded and went to look for Duplessis and Deo, while Anita and Emilie clambered onto Matthew's legs. Deo intercepted him. Duplessis was sitting, vacantly staring at a situation map which was now all red and no blue.

"We're staying here." Deo said simply.

Dennis brushed past him. "Like hell." He knelt beside Duplessis. "You built this world. If this is the final curtain, you'd damned well better be there for it."

"There. Here. What's the difference?"

"The difference is, you're responsible. And if Kassabian comes after us up there, which I'm sure he will, you have a chance to end him. And then, your version is the only one that counts."

Duplessis nodded slowly, then stood up, and followed him to the window.

2117

House arrest

Seattle Arcology 5
"Henrik Kassabian's" Apartment

Dennis looked around his suddenly unfamiliar apartment, feeling like a man who had fallen from a great height and miraculously survived. He rubbed his neck, feeling the subdermal patch which now allowed the Seattle Peace Force to track his every move. It would stay in there, he'd been assured, until the FBI arrested him, or concluded definitively he hadn't killed the Zhangs. Latoya had to get one too. His whole body still felt the weird, dissociative effects of the tasering.

Latoya brought him a scotch. "Medicine, tough guy. Doctor's orders."

"Yes ma'am." He took it gratefully. When he sat up to drink, he saw the lights across Lake Union, and sighed to himself.

Lynn sat at his dining room table, perusing decades of documents. She looked up. "Penny for your thoughts?"

"What's a penny?" Latoya asked.

Dennis laughed. "Once upon a time, money was worth so much that you could actually buy something with its decimal fractions."

She snuggled up next to him. "That implies your thoughts are not worth so much. I reject the thesis."

"Well?" Lynn pressed him. "I mean, you've convinced me. The FBI is probably working on a warrant for your bone marrow, and looking at your data from the Zhangs before they buy in. But the case isn't closed yet."

"Why not?"

"Because." She smiled. "We haven't heard the sad ending yet, Dennis Rosso. It's a great story, but it needs an ending."

Dennis looked out at Lake Union again. Suborbital transports dropped steeply on approach to SeaTac, replacing the 767s and Airbuses of his youth as a plane watcher. "I was just thinking of how, if it's dark and you really convince yourself, this view almost looks like the one from Hellas City."
"Hellas City is gone, Dennis." Latoya whispered.

"Yes, of course. The most beautiful thing we ever built on another world, and I helped destroy it. Like Great Wall 2." He sighed. "Kassabian or Rosso, I am a war criminal, I suppose."

"The jury can't decide that," Lynn interjected, "without the evidence. And you're still on the stand."

Dennis nodded. He blinked, hard, and he was there again.

2113

Gotterdammerung

Hellas City
Level 42

Matthew and Yitzhak rose slowly on their boot jets, ponderously rising over the shattered glass front of Hellas City. They fired flares from their backs, flipped forward, and headed for the bluff overlooking the city, where the twin fusion reactors that powered the city stood, still untouched.

Dennis was frankly terrified. It was one thing to ride *inside* one of these things, another thing entirely to hang off the outside like a baby monkey. The wind whipped at him, and he gasped for air at the very top of Hellas' thin envelope of breathable atmosphere. Below him, Lake Hellas, swollen to twice it's normal size, frothed and bucked with surging waves like a waterpark.

Opposite him, Duplessis clung to Yitzhak's boot with closed eyes. Deo crouched at the feet, yelling something nobody could hear. Dennis looked over to where he was looking. The twin Tokamaks loomed ever closed, massive, squat domes with huge exhaust hoods streaming hot blue gases.

Over them, a singular dot, circling. *Was that Mac?*

If Dennis hadn't concluded from the start that Kassabian would meet them here, he'd have been more worried about the plan. After here, where would they go? Hide out and wage guerilla war?

He was tired. Guerilla war was never in his plans.

But killing Kassabian was. Beyond that, he had no plan.

As they flared for landing, Dennis could see the smoking hole where the Israelis had made their Masada. Now, the plain swarmed with UN troops, and long, meandering lines of prisoners being marched out of the city. There was no sign of the spidermen.

They set down, gently, on the rocky surface next to the Tokamaks. Dennis and Anita set out to inspect the reactors while the rest waited for Mac to land.

Anita went ahead of him, rifle pointed in her direction of travel. She rounded the corner of the first Tokamak, Dennis moving fast to keep up. Then, he stopped in his tracks.

Anita stood in the center of a group of spiderman. Her hands were up. Dennis spotted Kassabian, his visor up. "Yes, come on over, Dennis." At his feet, one of his interminable, stupid dogs, this time wearing a rebreather.

"Dennis, they'll kill you!" Anita's face was anguished. "Run! Run and tell the others!"

Frozen, he could not decide. Then, Kassabian reached out with a mechanical arm and picked up Anita by the head. Her feet kicked as she lifted off the ground, a bloodcurdling scream coming from deep in her lungs.

Kassabian calmly reached under Anita, grabbed her pelvis with his other mechanical arm, and ripped her in two in a shower of gore. Then he tossed her head and chest over the Tokamak and into its hot exhaust. The woman Dennis loved evaporated before his eyes.

"No! Fucking die!" Dennis began shooting at Kassabian, who merely blocked his bolts with the force shields on his arms, laughing maniacally. The dog at his feet ran around excitedly, yapping.

The other spidermen, five of them, stood watching, like children told to stay out of a playground fight. Dennis stopped 50 meters from them. Kassabian lowered his arms, still laughing. "Come on Dennis, now you're a single guy! I did you a favor!" His voice lowered, and his smile disappeared. "Now, you know how I felt, when you killed Larissa."

Dennis snapped up his rifle suddenly and fired at the dog, which sizzled and exploded in a spray of hot guts. "And your little dog, too!"

"Kill him! Kill him!" Kassabian screamed in anguish as Dennis ran, unarmed, hoping to get as far as the others before he died. But now, from the corner of the building, Deo and Duplessis emerged, firing grenade launchers into the throng of spidermen.

He dived behind cover just as Deo blasted a spiderman in the groin. The return fire set Deo alight, making him writhe in agony, then go fatally still. Duplessis kept blasting and reloading. "Go, Dennis! They need you! This is my final act, and it's a good one! Take that you fuckers!"

Dennis reached out for Deo's grenade launcher, just as a blue bolt of energy hit Duplessis in the torso. He looked down, surprised, as his insides boiled away. "Ah, shit." Then, he flared into flame, his last looked fixed on Dennis in a strange lightshow, his eyes burning orange as they melted.

Dennis stumbled forward, hearing the clanking spidermen behind him, unable to process but a single thought: *live*.

Whereas this morning, he'd been ready to die, now, in the cold light of dawn, life mattered again, even if he had lost everything that made it worthwhile.

He ran around the corner to see Mac hovering above the sand, Emilie and her baby scrambling on board by a side ramp, with Matthew and Yitzhak blasting into the sky on full power. He keyed his comms. "Kassabian is right there! Deo and Duplessis and...Anita...they're all dead."

"We know." Matthew replied calmly. "Get on that ship. I'll handle Kassabian."

Dennis staggered towards the hovering transport. Mac's co-pilot reached out for him and pulled him aboard, closing the hatch as he came.

Inside the little transport, Kaitlyn Duplessis filled the cabin with her baby screams. Her mother sat with tears running down her face. Dennis reached out to her. "He died bravely."

"I know." She nodded.

Mac came on the intercom. "Where to, boss?"

Dennis pressed the respond button. "He killed my wife. One way or another, Kassabian dies, Mac."

"Copy that. We're unarmed, but I sure do have one big fucking rocket engine."

"Let's circle back."

Now, out of the cockpit windows, Dennis could see a running battle taking place over and around the Tokamaks. Two of Kassbian's spidermen were now smoking craters. Yitzhak rose high over Reactor 2, firing bolts which set another spiderman careening into the side of Reactor 1. Return fire from Kassabian turned him into a meteor, and he vanished in the exhaust plume.

"Matthew's on his own now." Mac observed. "I'm going in low."

They reversed course, as low as they could go. Now, in thirty seconds, Matthew had killed Kassabian's sole bodyguard. Out of energy, the two supermen grappled like robots, trying to kill each other manually. But Kassabian side-stepped an attack, waited for Matthew to pass, and punched him with servo-assist in the back of his head.

Matthew dropped like dead weight onto his side. Kassabian stood over him, screaming in triumph, then advanced on grinding motors to crush his opponent.

"You see this, Mac?"

"Let me...just get the angle..."

"Let me try something." Dennis found Kassabian's frequency. "Hey asshole."

Kassabian stopped and looked in their direction.

"Made you look. Now!"

Mac swung the transport in a sickening lurch and fixed his rocket motor on Kassabian. Knowing he was dead; the madman had enough time for a retort. "I won it twice, Rosso! Remember that!"

"Light him up." Dennis ordered.

Mac punched the motor into maximum thrust, and as they zoomed away from the battle, Dennis saw his enemy fly apart into his constituent molecules in the plasma. Then, unrestrained, Dennis flew against a bulkhead and blacked out.

In the minute he was out, the grievously damaged Reactor 1 went out of control, and flared with the force of twenty megatons, destroying what was left of friend and foe alike, and much of Hellas City.

When he came to, Dennis stood, rubbing his neck. He looked out the window. A mushroom cloud rose over Hellas City, working its way skyward. "Wow." Mac shook his head. "Just wow."

Dennis collapsed into a seat, weeping. Emilie Duplessis sat next to him. "You did everything you could, Dennis. For all of us."

He shook his head. "No. No, I couldn't save Anita. He destroyed her like a sick kid kills a bug. Oh God."

Emilie waited until he had finished blubbering, then handed him a thin package. "Matthew wanted you to have this."

"What...what is it?"

"Recordings...records of what Kassabian did. How he altered the children and trained them. His speeches about how he would create a "master race." That should be enough to finish him with his Hollywood friends. If not..."

He looked at her. She had her father's eyes. "If not?"

"Then a complete set of Kassabian's DNA. You can be him, until it's safe to be you again. And then we can have our planet back."

"Your father was right about you." Dennis touched her cheek. "You're a real leader."

He looked at the package. In thin, concise, cursive, Matthew had written:

When the world tires of lies;
here lives the truth.
For we who carry its banner
Shall never die.

One Week Later
UN Headquarters
Tyrrhena Terra

The transport flared and landed in front of the assembled UN troops and the Ambassador, Tolyakov, who rubbed his hands with glee, huffing giant clouds from his rebreather.

When the hatch opened, a tall man ducked low under the top to emerge, waving triumphantly. The Ambassador and the UN Commander, General Lapriese, walked quickly to meet him.

Henrik Kassabian shook hands with his allies. "Nice to meet you, General. Ambassador, I trust you are well?"

"Yes, yes." Tolyakov huffed. "The Emir sends his regards."

"Certainly. Now, gentlemen, you understood the terms we discussed? No harm is to come to any of these people. Most certainly not the young Duplessis and her daughter. It will be a great olive branch to those who have fought against us."

"You have proven yourself a great soldier, Doctor Kassabian. Now, you show yourself to be a diplomat." General Lapriese flattered him.

"Oh." Henrik Kassabian smiled enigmatically. "I am a great many things."

2117

Man, reborn

Arco 5
Wallingford

For a long time after Dennis finished his story, they sat and drank in silence. Dennis handed Lynn the package from Matthew after an interval. "It's all there. Your story brings down more than just JC Bryan and Dr Feng. The myth of Kassabian the Great can bite it, too."

"I thought he didn't have the recording of Kassabian's confession?" Lynn raised an eyebrow as she inspected the package.

"Oh yes, he did. He just didn't trust anyone but me with it."

Lynn smiled wearily. "Pulitzer, here we come." She looked at her watch in alarm. "Jesus, Dennis, it's eleven o'clock, and I'm shitfaced, on an empty stomach. I'm dropping this stuff off at my publisher and heading right back to the Blue Star. You guys coming? They do some awesome Mexican breakfasts."

Dennis and Latoya looked at each other. They wanted something else, right now.

"Haha, okay you kids. I can tell when I'm the third wheel. I'll see you later. Oh, by the way, Dennis?"

"Yes?"

"You never asked me to tell my story. About how the miracle

changed my life."

"I would like to hear that."

"I've never been sure of who I was. At the most basic level, you know? Not just gender, but other things, too. Journalist or novelist? Revolutionary, or reactionary? With the miracle, I've had the time to find out, without worrying about regretting my choice. For that, Dennis, I thank you."

The door closed behind her. Then, Dennis and Latoya stripped and stepped into the shower.

Hours later, they lay in each other's arms. The only noises, engines over SeaTac, birds over Lake Union. "You want to hear my story?" She asked, finally.

"The one I wanted to hear the most, yes."

"I grew up in a neighborhood where life was short. I lost two friends in shootings by the time I was twelve, Dennis." Her chest heaved at the memory, eyes welling up. "It used to make my mother so mad. 'We lived through all this,' she used to say, 'so you all could kill each other?' Till the day she died, she couldn't understand it. We were saving up for her, but she insisted I go first. I had to watch her die, knowing I couldn't follow."

"That's what the miracle did for you? Jesus."

"Let me finish. After she died, I found a whole bunch of notes I wrote to her when I was a kid, stuff like, 'I'm going to be a doctor, and make you feel better,' and 'I'm gonna be an astronaut, and name a planet after you.' She was my sun, moon, and stars, Dennis. So I decided, I was going to do it for her. Everywhere I go, she's there. And now, unlike her, I have the time."

"The time to run around the country with a war criminal and get shot at by phoney G-men?"

Latoya sighed. "She would've loved that."

"Thanks for telling me that, by the way."

"You're welcome. It's better than a Nobel Prize?"

"Hearing about how people's lives have changed, for the better? Sure, it is. I don't even know where that prize is anymore. Maybe a trophy on some UN General's shelf. The thing is, when I found the miracle, and I don't mean 'invented' it, I was a burned-out, bitter guy, a failure desperately trying to live up to my father had done. But my father specialized in destruction. I wanted to specialize in creation. Up till now, I wasn't sure which side I'd come down on. Now, maybe I do. That doesn't mean people haven't used the miracle to divide, that they haven't abused it, like Kassabian, or that they haven't corrupted it, like Feng and Lontraine. But my work, *my work*, that was for the good. And now that I'm going to be me again, maybe I can take my work back."

"Assuming you don't get sentenced to thirty years at the Hague, that is."

Dennis shrugged. "I'll learn some hobbies. A language or two. The Universe will still be here. Will you?"

"Maybe after a couple of trips around the world, or something like that."

"Fair enough."

In the hot, still afternoon, the windows were open. The sounds of an argument began to drift in. "Fiona don't do it! Please, Fiona!"

"Carl, please! Don't try and stop me! I can't take the nightmares anymore!"

They both sat bolt upright in bed. Five minutes later, they were on the bedroom balcony, looking up the solar windows, which glinted painfully in the bright sunshine, to Dennis' upstairs neighbor.

Fiona was a slim and pale girl, with red curls down to her ass, and cartoonishly outsized breasts, clad only in her underwear. Her boyfriend Carl was a big, broad-shouldered man with a limited vocabulary. "Hey, Fiona, this isn't a good thing, you know? Death from way up here is just kind of like...uh...final, you know?"

"Listen to Carl!" Dennis yelled up the sloping side of the pyramid. "He's very...uh...smart!"

Fiona began to laugh hysterically. "Now I know it's time to die, when Carl is considered smart!"

"Hey, honey, he just loves you. You seem like a sweet young girl. Why would you try and kill yourself?" Latoya could pour on the syrup when required. Dennis was impressed.

"Sweet young girl? Hell lady, I'm 72! I haven't been a sweet young girl since Sanchez got locked out of Iron Mountain. Oh man, I laughed at that...ow! Fuck!" Fiona's feet retreated from the scorching solar windows. "That shit is hot!"

"Hey, Fiona?" Dennis decided to try another tack. "You said you had nightmares, right?"

"Yes, Professor. Dudes all crawling over each other and shit. Creepy! And it never stops, no matter how high I get!"

"Now, you need to listen to us, Fiona. Latoya and I just finished investigating your problem. It turns out, it was a problem with cloned cells. Do you eat a lot of cloned meat, or have you gotten a lot of transplanted tissue?"

Fiona self-consciously grabbed her tits. "Maybe. What's that got to do with anything?"

Latoya whispered in his ear. "She's an easy 38DD. It's a wonder she can even stand up."

"It's just that we know what's wrong! It was a problem in the cloned tissue supply. Go to your doctor, get yourself on some heavy tranquilizers, and within a month or two there'll be a treatment for it! I'll work on it myself!"

Fiona bit her lip. "So, you're like, an actual scientist?"

Latoya whispered again. "*This* is who survives the Red Foam?"

"As actual as they come. If you just wait for the police…" Just then, a harried-looking police sergeant appeared behind them on their balcony. "Oh, hello officer."

The cop was a broad-faced Pole with a look of anxiety. "Shit, third jumper this month, man. I'm not exactly batting a thousand. She talking nightmares and shit?"

"Yes, Sergeant…"

"Sergeant Proscobski. You're Doctor Rosso, right?"

"So they tell me. How'd you know that?"

"You're under house arrest, how do you think I got in here? Listen, can you do me a favor?"

"Sure."

"Talk her down for me? I am in serious shit if I lose another, man."

Latoya rolled her eyes at him. "Uh, happy to help. Fiona?"

"Yes, doctor?"

"Would you come in if I guaranteed you that you could stay at home, on tranquilizers, no psych ward?" The cop shrugged and nodded. "The police agree, Fiona."

"Fiona!" Carl whined. "Please?"

Fiona blew bangs away from her face. "Ah, shit, okay." Her heel touched the solar windows below the balcony. "Ow! Ow, fuck!" Now a flailing arm was burned. "Ah…shit!!!!" Suddenly, Fiona began to slide down the pyramid. "Ah! Help me! I don't wanna die!"

Latoya yelled, "You coulda fooled me!" The flailing, screaming girl almost slid past Dennis, but he reached and grabbed an ankle. Soon, Latoya and the cop had joined him, and they pulled the screaming, swearing girl up onto their balcony. Once the cop had reluctantly taken her down to the lobby to meet the paramedics, Latoya embraced him.

Dennis was unexpectedly emotional. "Wow. That felt good."

Latoya smiled at him. "Feels good to save one for a change, doesn't it?"

"Yes. Yes, it does."

She raised an eyebrow. "You just about got away with it."

"Got away with what?" Dennis was genuinely puzzled.

"Not telling me. Not telling me why you wouldn't say you 'invented' the miracle anymore. You didn't tell Lynn the whole story, did you?"

Dennis stopped and stared out the window. That way was due south. Where the miracle lived.

"Dennis?"

He turned to Latoya. "No, I didn't tell the whole story. I left out the part that might hurt people."

"People? What people, Dennis?"

"The Yaghan. People think they're extinct. And they want it that way."

"Why do they want it that way?"

"So nobody will ever know that they live essentially forever. That they are the source of the miracle."

2028

Fountain of youth

Puerto Williams
Chile

Dennis Rosso was 38 years old. This was when age still meant something.

In his mind, it meant encroaching scientific irrelevance. Einstein, all scientists remembered, had published his first papers of importance right after he'd started shaving. Personally, he was already walking away from a disastrous marriage and a dead child. Three thumbs up, said the specialist in mutations.

This was how he found himself at the very southern tip of the Americas. Having been fired from American Biometrics for wild speculation about immortality, he'd taken his mother's suggestion perhaps too literally.

"Looking for a fountain of youth? Isn't that in South America somewhere?"

"I thought it was Florida, ma."

"Bah, you seen those old mummies? More wrinkles than Liberace's ass. Go south, young man!"

And so, with a backpack and a rapidly diminishing savings account to his name, Dennis Rosso wandered the streets of a Patagonian one-horse town. For in Puerto Williams, there was, literally, one of everything. One school, one bank, one post office...etc.

At least he'd had the good sense to come here in December. The weather was placid, if the wind wasn't blowing from the Southern Ocean. Then, it was chilling.

He'd done minimal internet research before coming, and so he knew very little of what to ask. But he had the Spanish he'd picked up in Los Alamos (which, as it turned out, was an archaic, colonial dialect), a *Lonely Planet Guide*, and a rough, working theory.

15,000 years before, man had crossed the land bridge between Siberia and Alaska. Then, in overlapping waves, they'd filled up the whole massive landmass in less than 10,000 years.

If he were to find the most truly evolved and experienced biological specimens, the hardiest travelers, then the southern tip of the continent was the place to look, right? These were the people who had come the farthest, who the most had to have happened to.

When he'd woken up in Puerto Williams' only hotel worthy of the name (of course), he'd rubbed his eyes that morning and admitted to himself: *You're a fool with a quarter-baked theory. Go back to smoking dope, idiot.*

But he'd come so far...

Puerto Williams was a blustery, green, luscious place that looked and felt like it was on a precipice. The people had all been washed up here by circumstance. All except the people he was looking for.

The Yaghan, or Yamana, depending on who you asked, no longer existed in their pure form. When he asked at a local watering hole over a pisco sour, he was told by the bartender that the last purebred, *Abuela* Cristina, had died five years before. But, he added, "There's some half-breeds up the road."

On his third day in town, sick of doing nothing but asking locals who pretended to know nothing, then getting drunk and waking up the next day praying for death, Dennis drove his rental jeep up to a collection of ramshackle huts and dilapidated outbuildings that reminded him of an Indian reservation back home. He knocked on a few doors, but nobody answered. As he was about to drive away, he saw a curious-looking wicker basket made of green reeds, sitting on someone's porch.

Dennis made to touch it, but became uncomfortable, feeling he was being watched. He took a picture instead and drove back to town for lunch. In the restaurant, he overheard two men talking.

Dennis was conscious that his Spanish was rough, but he trusted what he heard.

"I tell you; I saw them out there. I was fifteen."

"Probably just looking because they were naked, right?"

"I said I was fifteen."

"Okay, okay. What did you see?"

"Back behind where the half-breeds live, there's a bay."

"By the Caleta Pentalon?"

"Yeah, that one."

"I've been there a million times and never seen a thing. Have another beer." Clearly, this was a liquid lunch. The two men, who looked like fishermen, had giant hands and sunburned faces.

"Are you listening?"
"Fine, fine. Go ahead."

"Okay, I walked around the houses. Into the reeds they make

their baskets from, right? I got right down, almost to the beach, before I saw them." The storyteller genuflected. "Mother Maria, right out there in the freezing waters, at least one hundred of them. Men, women, and children. All naked, fishing and diving for clams."

"Naked? All of them? I've never seen a half-breed do that." The listener scoffed.

"I'm telling you; these were no half-breeds! The Yamana live!"

Dennis quickly finished his lunch and drove back to the reservation. He was careful this time to park far back, out of sight of the road. Then, he loaded a sample kit into his backpack, hoping against hope, along with his camera. Then, he set out through the tall reeds for the bay.

After an hour of muddy trudging, with the reeds a meter over his head, he heard children's laughter. Cautiously, he emerged to find a pebbly beach, covered in driftwood and seaweed.

At the water's edge, the wind was chilling. He could only imagine how cold the water was. Across the strait, giant peaks rose up on the Argentinian side.

Still a little upslope of the frolicking children, he lay on his back, hoping not to be observed. He took out his sighting scope and zeroed in on the source of the noise.

In a shallow tidal pool, two dozen Yaghan between the ages of four and twelve splashed each other and played games of chase. They were completely naked, save for a shiny substance, most likely some sort of animal fat, which had been smeared on their bodies.

The Yamana live!

Scanning the beach, Dennis quickly figured out where the adults were. In the lee of a pair of smashed ship's boats, fifty or so Yaghan, completely naked, their skin showing the same glinting sheen as the children's, huddled around a giant fire. Just down the beach, more gathered in the mouth of a cave.

Dennis remembered how the *Tierra del Fuego* had gotten its name. The Land of Fire, from these fires, these people.

He considered the theory, sketchy as it was, that had propelled him here. A people that had arrived at the end of the world, having surpassed every challenge and absorbed every bit of knowledge possible. It seemed that they had, at least, conquered hypothermia.

Dennis heard the snap of a twig behind him and rolled to pinpoint the noise. A large spear with a modern steel tip was thrust at his neck. Behind it, a naked man with a greased-up body and straight black hair. His head was long and thin, a characteristic of the Yaghan. An older man looked over his shoulder. The two men conversed briefly.
Dennis began to sweat on the cold beach. Were they considering killing him? Was this a secret worth protecting? Finally, to his astonishment, the young man addressed him in lightly accented English.

"What are you doing creeping around here?"

"I...I'm a scientist."

The old man said something in the young man's ear. The young man laughed. "So, not just here to look at naked girls?"

"No! No...er...I was interested in the stories about the Yaghan. For instance, how can you tolerate this weather, totally naked? What other special abilities do you have?"

The two Yaghan exchanged a meaningful look. "Maybe we should kill you."

"No! No...listen...I just want to take some blood samples. See what makes you different. If you let me do that, I won't tell anyone. I'll respect your secret."

The old man and the young man conversed again. "The scientists from Santiago used to do that all the time to Abuela Cristina. That's why we hid. Like the Spanish, always wanting more life."

Dennis' eyes widened. "You mean…you're…"

"Come with us to the group. You may speak. Then we'll decide." The young man put out a hand. "I am Horatio. This is my father, Fuegio. Come."

Dennis walked unsteadily along the pebbles, the two Yaghan, despite their bare feet, proceeding in a more surefooted way. "I am Dennis." He almost tripped over a root. "I am a biochemist."

"What does that mean? You make medicines?"

"Sort of. I am looking at ways to change the body by changing the genes. I bet your genes are very interesting." He looked behind him to see the children following at a distance.

Fuegio said something to Horatio. The younger man laughed. "Yes, exactly like the Spanish!"

"I'm not here to steal anything." Dennis protested.

"Only our blood!" Horatio replied. "Here, sit here."

Behind the ruined boats, half the community stared at him. The other half converged from the cave and the children's pond. Dennis considered the faces staring at him. There was a mixture of ages, yes, but two things surprised him: One, there were no obviously infirm people. Perhaps the environment quickly disposed of them. Two: though there were children, there were not nearly as many as he would've expected. And zero infants.

His rough theory was being built up, having meat added to its raw bones. Then, the Yaghan started to yell questions at him. Horatio struggled to translate them into English.

Did you bring needles?

Can you bring Abuela back, scientist?

Are you a reporter? Did you bring a camera?

Are you going to tell everyone about us?

"No." Dennis answered the last question sincerely. "I want you to be left alone in peace."

"Hah. Spaniard." Horatio strode up to him. "After you make a great discovery? I speak English and Spanish. Unlike many of our people, I have worn the Spanish clothes, and travelled in their world. I can read books and use a computer. I know how this usually goes."

"Yes." Dennis nodded. "The white man lies, and the people suffer. You are right, Horatio. That is how it usually goes."

Fuegio mumbled something to his son. Horatio laughed. "My father is a peacemaker. He says I am too quick to start a war with people who have machine guns and jets. He asks, what would it take to keep you away?"

Dennis swallowed hard, hoping his limited time as a teacher had equipped him to explain biochemistry to Neolithic people. "My job is to learn things from DNA. DNA is what makes all of us who we are. I think, just from watching you, that you are special. You can tolerate temperatures that would make me sick. And, from looking at your group, I believe there is something even more special about you. You can live for a very, very long time."

Horatio did not bother to translate. "Spanish, I have been watching you. My cousin from the village told me about you. He works in the hotel. I think there is something special about you, too."

Now, Horatio and Fuegio addressed the assembled tribe. One of the older women present handed him a steaming glass of tea. After two sips, he was feeling addled. *Probably hallucinogenic. Careful.*

The sun was still high, late into the evening, but the waves were almost on them when the group reached its decision. Horatio spoke for them. "If we give you the blood from our bodies, will you lie to the other Spanish about us? Will you pretend you know us not?"

"Yes. I promise. But if I get what I want, people will have no reason to bother you."

"How do you know that?"

"Because they will have the miracle that lives inside you. That is what I want."

Horatio frowned. Fuegio watched him with sad eyes. "Be careful, Spanish. In a long life, like the ones we live, there is room for much sorrow."

By the time the sun finally set, Dennis was staggering through the reeds, carrying forty blood samples in his backpack, and fifteen in a woven reed basket.

It would take him five years to figure it all out. But when he finally did, the words of Horatio would begin to make sense.

2117

The world's biggest liar

Arco 5
Wallingford

89 years later, Dennis Rosso finished telling his story. He looked at Abuela Cristina's wicker basket on his dresser and smiled.

Latoya nudged him. "How many people have you told that story to?"

"Three. All women I trusted with my life. My mother, Anita, and now, you."

"I'm flattered." She kissed him deeply. He responded with ardor. "Hang on, hang on. First of all, I'm hungry. Second of all, how the hell did you keep the Yag…Yaga…"

"Yaghan people."

"The Yaghan people. How did you keep them out of it?"

"I lied and faked like a sonofabitch. I covered my tracks, made the key organic solvent seem like a synthetic. Did it so well, the results were actually replicable. I'd promised them I wouldn't let their secret go."

Latoya smiled wryly. "With the added bonus that it made you seem smarter."

Dennis shrugged. "I'm a second-rate biochemist at best. My

only real talent is instinct."

"What was it, really? What really let them live forever?"

"Well, for starters, they didn't live forever. For instance, there was nobody there still alive who'd made the actual crossing of the Bering Strait. They didn't start living longer until they came to the place that made them. Tierra del Fuego. So, I figured it had to be something in the local environment. On a hunch, now there's that instinct again, I grabbed a handful of reeds on my way out with the samples. Turns out, that was the key."

"The reeds? Like in the basket?"

"The very same."

"But I thought all they did with those was make baskets and hats?"

"Yes, that's true. But one day, after I'd found the anomaly in their cells, and traced it back to the matrilineal line, thinking it was in the mitochondrial DNA, I saw a video on YouTube. It was from an old Canadian travel show, and Abuela Cristina was making a basket."

"It got in through the skin..." Latoya's eyes went wide. "Or... she licked her fingers to make the weave!"

"Precisely. Thus, inviting a powerful mutagen into her system. One nobody had ever investigated, because, well, it's a humble reed, right? Meanwhile, the females passed it on to their offspring, male and female, because basket weaving is a woman's job, right? Meanwhile, the 'Half-breeds', most of whose mothers didn't weave baskets, or did it only rarely, stopped passing the mutagen along. I mean, you had to be ingesting it every day for years in its natural form. So, I synthesized the mutagen from the reeds, and diluted a solvent from it, and *eh voila*."

"No wonder you had to keep it a secret. Imagine all the backpackers and new agers harvesting reeds the day after you made the announcement?" Latoya laughed. "Of course, now you're in the clear. You can tell the world!"

"And lose my only Nobel? Fuck that! I may be a hero, but I'm no dummy. They can pry it from my cold dead hand."

"If you ever find it, that is."

"Yeah." Dennis sighed and thought about pizza. But before he could put on his pants, there was an insistent knock at the door.

"FBI! Henrik Kassabian, open the door, FBI!"

"Henrik Kassabian is dead, don't you read the news?"

"Okay, Dennis Rosso, whatever. Open up! FBI!"

"Oh, I'm so fucking sick of those guys." Latoya sighed.

NEWS RELEASE:

FOR IMMEDIATE DISSEMINATION

FROM: FEDERAL PROSECUTION SERVICE, WASHINGTON STATE DISTRICT

FOUR-YEAR-OLD MYSTERY SOLVED AFTER ARRESTS OF BOGUS FBI AGENTS; PRODUCT ADULTERATION AND BRIBERY CHARGES LAID

A SHOOTOUT IN THE WALLINGFORD NEIGHBORHOOD OF CENTRAL SEATTLE BETWEEN OFFICERS OF THE SEATTLE PEACE FORCE AND MEN POSING AS FBI AGENTS HAS RESULTED IN THE ARREST OF FIVE MEN, AND CHARGES AGAINST TWO MORE MEN IN THE ATLANTA, GA AREA, INCLUDING THE ACTING DIRECTOR OF THE DISEASE CONTROL COUNCIL.

ON SATURDAY NIGHT, THE FBI SEATTLE FIELD OFFICE WAS NOTIFIED OF THE ARREST OF FIVE MEN FOR IMPERSONATING FEDERAL AGENTS, AS WELL AS WEAPONS AND ASSAULT CHARGES. THE FOLLOWING MEN WERE DETAINED:

FISK, LEWIS, AGE 137
CROMWELL, STEVE SQUARED, AGE 110
MITSIUK, ANDREI, AGE 92
BEVELTON, D'FONTAINE, AGE 45
GO, CHAR TSE, AGE 30

FISK, A FORMER FBI AGENT DISCHARGED IN 2105 FOR CORRUPTION, HAD TO BE RECONSTITUTED AFTER SUFFERING OTHERWISE FATAL INJURIES.

ALSO DETAINED AT THE SCENE WERE THE SUBJECTS OF A MURDER WARRANT OUT OF CALIFORNIA:

KASSABIAN, HENRIK, AGE 108
SUMMERS, LATOYA, AGE 45

THESE INDIVIDUALS WERE, BASED ON EXCULPATORY EVIDENCE FOUND AT THE TIME, RELEASED WITH BIOMETRIC MONITORING.

INTERVIEWS CONDUCTED TODAY AT THE FBI FIELD OFFICE RESULTED IN THE FILING OF MURDER, ASSAULT, KIDNAPPING, FILING A FALSE POLICE REPORT, AND POSSESSION OF A PROHIBITED WEAPON CHARGES AGAINST FISK AND HIS COHORTS.

THE ATLANTA FIELD OFFICE TODAY ARRESTED THE FOLLOWING MEN AS A RESULT OF INFORMATION OBTAINED IN THE INVESTIGATION:

FENG, CRAIG LO AGED 70
LONTRAINE, TYRELL AGED 92

FENG, ACTING DIRECTOR OF THE DCC, WAS INDICTED ON CHARGES OF BRIBERY, MALFESEANCE BY A FEDERAL OFFI-

CER, AND ACCESSORY TO PRODUCT ADULTERATION. FURTHER CHARGES OF MURDER MAY BE FORTHCOMING. LONTRAINE, COO OF JC BRYAN INC IN ATLANTA, WAS INDICTED ON CHARGES OF BRIBERY AND PRODUCT ADULTERATION. FURTHER CHARGES OF MURDER MAY BE FORTHCOMING. FOR MORE ON THIS CASE, SEE THE RELEASE FROM THE FOOD AND DRUG ADMINISTRATION:

URGENT: PRODUCT RECALL ZHANG INDUSTRIES NUTRIFORMS 25-001 THROUGH 66-017, POTENTIAL SUICIDAL EFFECTS IN HUMAN CONSUMERS
THE SUBJECTS "KASSABIAN" AND SUMMERS WERE RELEASED WITHOUT CHARGE. EVIDENCE WAS PRESENTED UNDERMINING THE MURDER CHARGES AGAINST THEM. FURTHERMORE, A BONE MARROW SAMPLE PROVED THAT "KASSABIAN" IS ACTUALLY THE FOLLOWING INDIVIDUAL:

ROSSO, DENNIS AGE 127

FOR MORE INFORMATION ON THIS CASE, SEE THE DEPARTMENT OF JUSTICE RELEASE:

NEW EVIDENCE LEADS TO SHELVING OF WAR CRIMES CHARGES AGAINST FAMED NOBEL LAUREATE; CANCELLATION OF INTERPOL RED NOTICE

FOR MORE INFORMATION, OR TO SCHEDULE INTERIEWS, PLEASE CONTACT LAUREN WILKINSON AT WWW.FBISEATTLE.GOV

EPILOGUE

SCHRODINGER'S CAT

Phoenix, Arizona
Lim Pharmaceuticals

Dennis Rosso lolled on Roger Lim's couch while the anesthetic wore off. He woke up with a start to see his mother's angel of death smiling at him. Next to the real Roger Lim was a cut-out photo of him dressed as a mincing James Bond, holding a scalpel like a pistol.

"Hey, man, you okay?" Lim smiled. "Jeez, I think it work! You look like yourself again! That Kassabian was one ugly mother! I don't know how girl like Latoya fall in love with mutt like that! Now, you good looking, see?" Lim rolled a full-length mirror over to him.

His head clearing, Dennis got to his feet. He'd been living in his enemy's body for four years. The man who'd pulled Anita apart in front of him. "Thank you, Roger. Thank you so much." He embraced Lim in tears.

"Okay, okay, now you go all interior decorator on me, holy shit. Here, have a Corona. Too hot outside for this."

Dennis sat back on the couch and drank two beers in quick succession. Lim held a paper up in front of him. "Your friend, hey? Funny looking lady, but okay. You really live through all this?"

He took the day-old copy of *The Star*. On it, Lynn stood, arms folded, in front of a mountain of files. *His files.* The headline was breathless:

THE ROSSO FILES, PART FOUR: HOW THE UN GAMBLED ON A FASCIST MANIAC AND DESTROYED A DEMOCRATIC STATE. AND HOW DENNIS ROSSO GOT THE LAST LAUGH. PART OF A SIX-PART SERIES ON THE FATHER OF THE MIRACLE. FROM THE SEATTLE REVOLUTION.

Dennis scratched his head. He'd come to Lim because he could count on Roger for discretion. Every step he took now, there were demands for interviews, speaking gigs, endorsements, even marriage proposals. Switching back to his original appearance ought to give him a head start and some peace and quiet. For a couple of days.

In the long run, he needed something more permanent.

Latoya walked in. She gasped. "Wow. Did you really look like that once?"

Dennis touched his face. "Is it...is it okay?"

She smiled. "Way better than before. Way better. But, er... Roger?"

"Oh hey, no problem, he keep Kassabian's enormous junk."

Latoya laughed. "You said you picked him because he was discreet?" She kissed Lim on the cheek. "Thank you, Roger."

"You kids come by anytime you in Phoenix. Now get out, before reporters get here! I'm still not technically legal, okay?"

On the street, the sun hit them like a face punch. "Jesus." Dennis looked up. "I need a hat."

Latoya tapped her nails on his arm expectantly. "So? Where now?"

"Well, lunch with Stephen at the Old Arizona, then I'm laying flowers on Mom's grave…"

"No, Dennis, seriously. What now? I quit my job for you. You've got me now, 100%. But we better get away from this shitshow. Earth is just not an option right now."

Dennis took a deep breath. I had, or have reservations on the SS Olympic, under Kassabian's name. A twenty-year trip to Epsilon Eridani. I'm sure they'll be understanding."

"Twenty years on a ship?"

"We can go under for a while or enjoy the amenities. Trust me, there are one hell of a lot of amenities."

"And how do we know there aren't bugs there that'll eat us from the inside out?"

"We know. Robots have been there for twenty years already, making it nice for us. Of course, there's always Mars. The UN has finally agreed to elections, and Emilie Duplessis is a shoo-in to win. They're already fixing up my apartment. *Our* apartment."

"You lived there with Anita…wouldn't it be hard?"

"Well, I could always have them build me a palace. After all, my name has been suggested as a possible next President."

"Mars. Wow. How to decide?"

He took an old coin from his pocket. "The way people always used to decide these things. Before Schrodinger came along."

"Heads, or tails? My momma taught me this one. I call it, and until it shows, the cat is alive or dead." She licked her lips and looked up at him. "But whatever happens, we're going together."

"Damned straight."

"Heads, it's Mars, tails, it's the stars." Latoya announced. He flicked the coin into the air. It landed on his hand, and they both caught their breath.

Around them, the people of Phoenix passed by, unaware that the future of a very small universe was being decided in their midst. Unaware, too, that the man who'd given them an endless future was about to find out his.

OTHER BOOKS BY THE AUTHOR

Non-Fiction:

A Life on the Line (2020)

Acts and Offences: Opinion, 2017-2020 (2020)

Fiction:

The Will Bryant Thrillers:

Southern Cross (2016)

Back in Slowly (2017)

The Wolf of Penha (2019)

Only the Dead (2020)

Spectrum (2020)

Other:

Goodtime Charlie (2018)

When Yer Number's Up (2019)

Bomber's Moon (2019)

Slowly, the World Burns, While I Help to Fan the Flames (2020)

The Troika of Osip Teitelbaum (2020)

Expo City: A Police Story

Coming Soon:

An Unearthly Glow: Critical Man and Other Nuclear Lullabies

Made in the USA
Columbia, SC
27 October 2023